You Don't Have to Live Like This

Benjamin Markovits grew up in Texas, London and Berlin. He is the author of six previous novels: *The Syme Papers*, *Either Side of Winter*, *Imposture*, *A Quiet Adjustment*, *Playing Days* and *Childish Loves*. He has published essays, stories, poetry and reviews on subjects ranging from the Romantics to American sports in the *Guardian*, *Granta*, *the Paris Review* and *the New York Times*, among other publications. In 2013 *Granta* selected him as one of their Best of Young British Novelists and in 2015 he won the Eccles British Library Writer in Residence Award. He lives in London and teaches creative writing at Royal Holloway, University of London.

Further praise for *You Don't Have to Live Like This*:

'What pins you to the page is Markovits's patience with the complexity of the subject. He is especially nuanced – and brave – when writing about race.' *TLS* Books of the Year

'Astute observation on race, politics, love and human nature.' Arifa Akbar, *Independent* Books of the Year

'An occasionally satirical, frequently discomforting and consistently impressive novel: a strikingly current portrait of tinderbox race relations that also raises enduring questions about the good life and the nature of truth . . . Highly recommended.' *Daily Mail*

'Bold and brilliant . . . For Markovits – as for Dickens, Joyce and

Woolf before him – the city is a constantly evolving organism against which the best stories can be told.' *Prospect*

'Intense and very funny . . . It is about money, race and urban acedia and features a cameo from Barack Obama every bit as brilliant as Hollinghurst's Thatcher in *The Line of Beauty*.' *Guardian* Best Novels of 2015

'With the national media roiling with articles about race, justice and class, particularly in that struggling Michigan city, this story could not be more timely . . . Markovits is a master at describing the devastated and deserted streets of Detroit.' *Washington Post*

'As up-to-the-minute as a cable network's "Breaking News" bulletin, though far more thoughtful and better examined . . . So few fiction writers deal directly with street-level economic and cultural conflict in the present day that you're grateful *You Don't Have to Live Like This* exists at all.' *USA Today*

'Impressive . . . Markovits builds this novel out of straight-plank prose, its lines and structures as pleasingly solid and clean as those of a shaker chair . . . Masterfully executed.' *Guardian*

'[A] subtle and finely poised novel . . . Markovits uses Detroit as a rebuke to certain forms of American idealism, and does so with nuance . . . Marny is an unwitting archetype for his generation, a childish man who does not understand his own desires and motivations, who wants connection but cannot articulate why.' *Spectator*

'A very smart book, with vividly drawn characters and densely woven themes.' *Daily Telegraph*

'Markovits articulates this irretrievably messy subject with exhilarating clarity and a good deal of bravery . . . The prose delivers spare, fast-paced social realism (think Jonathan Franzen on Slim-fast) and the plot is multi-stranded and gripping.' *Sunday Times*

'Entertaining, insightful, humorous yet of serious purpose. This is a very good novel.' *Herald*

'Brilliantly plotted, wonderfully nuanced and masterfully controlled.' *Irish News*

'Markovits's seventh book captures a peculiar creature of this time: the young liberal entrepreneur who wants to create a model for urban renewal and make a buck or two doing it . . . Markovits's prose is clean and restrained, and his ear for the way his characters speak is rarely off . . . *You Don't Have to Live Like This* is very much a novel of Obama's first term, when the idea of a post-racial America still had some dream-like currency, written early in his second, when racial conflict became one of the central stories of his presidency.' *vulture.com*

FABER & FABER

YOU DON'T HAVE TO LIVE LIKE THIS

a novel

BENJAMIN MARKOVITS

First published in the USA in 2015
by Harper Collins Publishers,
195 Broadway, New York, NY 10007

First published in the UK in 2015
by Faber & Faber Limited
Bloomsbury House, 74–77 Great Russell Street
London WC1B 3DA
This paperback edition published in 2016

Printed in the UK by CPI Group (UK) Ltd, Croydon, CR0 4YY

A portion of this novel appeared, in slightly different form, in
the spring 2013 issue of *Granta*.

This book is a work of fiction. References to real people, events, establishments,
organisations, or locales are intended only to provide a sense of authenticity, and are used
fictitiously. All other characters, and all incidents and dialogue, are drawn from the
author's imagination and are not to be construed as real.

A CIP record for this book
is available from the British Library

ISBN 978–0–571–31342–6

FSC
www.fsc.org
MIX
Paper from
responsible sources
FSC® C101712

2 4 6 8 10 9 7 5 3 1

FOR GWEN AND HENRY

1

When I was younger I was never much good at telling stories. If I scored a goal at Pee Wee soccer, which didn't happen often, I used to try and describe it for my brother over lunch, over the hot dogs and potato chips. Then he kicked it there and I ran here and he passed it to me there. My brother called these my "this and then this and then this" stories. I don't know that I've gotten any better at it.

We shared a bedroom for years, but in sixth grade I moved into the backyard extension, built out of the old garage. It had its own door to the garden and on Saturday mornings kids used to leave their bikes outside and walk straight into my room. By that point I'd given up on soccer; my friends and I played a lot of Dungeons & Dragons. There would be six or seven boys sitting on my bed, on the floor, on the chair by my desk, with dice, pieces of paper, pencils and home-made maps. We kept the curtains closed and the lights on.

My parents began to worry about me, my mother especially. "You seem like a reasonable human being," she liked to say. "You don't look violent."

I was kind of scrawny, blue-eyed and fair in the face but black-haired. My brother, who is three years older, belongs to a completely different physical type. Brad played tight end on his Pop Warner football team and might have started in high school, too, except my mother wouldn't let him. When we were kids he used to sit on my chest with his knees on my puny biceps, trying to make me say stuff I didn't want to say. "Dungeons & Dragons is gay. Say it." If I refused, he'd kneel up on his weight until I squealed.

Most of my friends graduated to more strategically sophisticated games like BattleTech and Risk, but when I was fourteen or fifteen I realized that the real thing (war, I mean) was much more interesting than any fantasy. I started reading Churchill's memoirs and Sandburg's life of Lincoln. Probably my favorite battle of all time is the second El Alamein. Tank strategy in the Sahara turns out to be highly complex, and I checked out from the public library all the biographies of Lumsden and Montgomery I could lay my hands on. But I also had a soft spot for Nelson at Trafalgar and Meade at Gettysburg.

I didn't wear fatigues around school or sign up for ROTC or anything like that. In most ways I was a pretty average nerd. Military history was just my nerd specialty. I got good grades. I played the trumpet in band. The only weird thing I did, apart from read books about war, was collect lead soldiers. My bedroom was full of these guys, arranged in actual troop formations on the windowsills and in my closet and on top of the chest of drawers. They freaked my mother out. She couldn't understand why I spent so much time on what she called tiny metal dolls.

The truth is, I didn't really understand it myself. My childhood was happy and suburban. I used to ride my bike to elementary school and when my brother and I were small we sometimes set up a lemonade stand in the front yard. When I was older, over the summer, I made six bucks an hour mowing lawns. My parents paid for everything else, but I had to pay for my "war shit" myself, my father said. Yard work in the heat of a Louisiana day was the only kind of suffering I put myself through as a kid. I probably dreamed about war because I wanted to know what I was made of—under the gun.

My mother hoped I'd grow out of it, and I guess I did. Two weeks before the start of freshman year, I wrapped the soldiers in cotton wool and packed them in shoe boxes. I didn't particularly want to go to college, but my parents made me.

What do you want to do with yourself then, my dad asked.

"Don't know," I said. "In your day I might have got drafted."

"Not if you went to college, you wouldn't."

He was a journalist and union organizer (from Montreal, originally); a tolerant, social, easygoing guy. Even as a kid I could tell that women liked him. But he didn't know what to do with my obsessions.

"What's going on here?" he said. "You want to enlist?"

"Mom would never let me. Besides, I'm too chickenshit. Guys from my high school have enlisted. Not my type. Anyway, it doesn't have to be war. I'd be just as happy gold-rushing or homesteading or something."

"I think you missed that train." Later, he said, "I don't understand what the hard work was for. All those grades."

"You tell me, Dad. Getting grades is basically the only thing I know how to do."

"So go to college," he said.

My mom helped me pack and they put me on a plane to New York. It was my first time flying into JFK, but I didn't go into the city. Instead I caught the Limo to New Haven, which sounds grand but was really just a regional bus service. You always had to wait for the bus to fill up—sometimes it took an hour, a bunch of kids sitting on their duffels. Six or eight times a year, for four years, I made that journey: in August and December, in the second week of January, after Thanksgiving or Spring Break, in June. Every time you go back home you feel a little older, every time you leave you feel younger again.

When I showed up at Yale I wasn't ready for the chances that came my way. I didn't even know what they were. Something in my personality had to change to make room for girlfriends, that much was obvious. But I didn't realize until later that my classmates were checking out more than the opposite sex. They were looking for the kids who might cut a figure in the world one day: future senators, millionaires, newspaper editors, hotshot lawyers. It helps to know important, influential people. Some of them even hoped to become such people themselves.

Not me. I majored in history. I got more grades. I went through the usual transitions, involving girls and alcohol. In high school my friends and friendships were very innocent—my college friendships were less innocent. But I had a pretty good time. Even if the feeling didn't go away, that there should be a better test of who I am than middle-class American life.

MAYBE THIS IS WHY, TWO days after graduation, two days after throwing my hat in the air, I flew to England. My brother was winding up a Rhodes Scholarship at Oxford before going to law school in Chicago. I lived with him for a couple of weeks, then took over the lease on his flat. It was one of these psychologically complicated family financial arrangements. I didn't win any scholarships but my dad offered to pay my way. And what started out as an MSt in US history turned into a doctoral thesis and took up five years of my life. I liked Oxford. The big idea behind English postgraduate education is to leave you alone; this suited me fine.

For a while it seemed that all of that stupid homework was paying off. A suburban kid from Baton Rouge, going to Yale and Oxford, moving up in the world.

But after grad school nothing turned out quite right. It's hard to get a job in America with a British PhD. I shifted to London and supported myself with adjunct teaching, while working my dissertation into a book. At least, that was the plan. In fact, all I did was teach. Since I was paid by the hour I had to put together a lot of hours. Eventually I landed a nine-month maternity cover in Aberystwyth, five hours by train from London—a midsize Welsh town, the kind of place you might go to for a weekend break. Good hiking territory. Wet suit surfing in the bay. I wanted a permanent job, but the department just kept renewing my short-term contract. They had me teaching heavy loads, running admissions, sitting on committees, doing the stuff that nobody else wanted to do.

Geographical distance is a powerful thing. The kid who used to sit around with his buddies fighting dragons had come a long way—almost five thousand miles. The evidence was just outside my door. Row houses and cheap bakeries, charity shops and pharmacies on the high street. The annual rainfall. A lot of reasonable decisions had brought me here, and not just decisions but a fair amount of effort and even some good luck. My college friends, with a few exceptions, seemed to be in the same boat. Working harder than they wanted to, making less money, living somewhere they didn't want to live.

2

Robert James was one of the exceptions. I ran into him at our ten-year reunion—outside Zapatas, a Mexican dive bar we used to go to for the cheap sangria. His friends were leaving while mine were going in, but they had to wait for a girl to come out of a bathroom, and I stood around with Robert for a while, catching up.

We'd been drinking since four in the afternoon, and the street lamp light gave me a headache. My jet lag was pretty intense, it left me open to strong impressions. All these people I hadn't seen in years, these people who knew me, or knew what I used to be like. And here I was again, seeing them again. It was like a big chemical experiment, where you took these known quantities, these guys you used to live with and eat with and sit in class with, and poured them out into the world, to see what they turned into. Of course at the same time you were trying to work out what the chemical reaction had done to you.

"I hear you made a lot of money," I said to Robert.

You wouldn't know it by the way he dressed: North Face jersey, loafers, a pair of clean blue jeans belted high. But it didn't matter anyway, with his looks. In college we called him the Greek God— he had the face of one of those statues. There was something impersonal about it. You could never tell what he was thinking, not that this meant he was particularly smart.

"I did okay."

"So what do you do with yourself all day? Kick back?"

He began to explain himself very carefully. Lately he'd been working on a couple of political campaigns, mostly fund-raising—fund-giving, too, he said. There was a guy we both knew in college, a law student at the time, who lived in the dorms and used to play squash with us occasionally in the steam-tunnel squash courts. A big barrel-chested black guy named Braylon Carr, with a football background and postgraduate degrees from Cambridge and Stanford. Anyway, Robert had helped him run for mayor of Buffalo. These Rust Belt towns were having a hard time—American cities all over the place were dying out. But if Braylon could make a difference in Buffalo, it would turn him into a major Democratic player.

"I'll let you in on something. He's going to be the first black president of the United States." For some reason this mattered a lot to Robert. "Wouldn't that be a hell of a thing to be a part of?"

"It doesn't sound like a full-time job."

But he'd started a hedge fund, too—a hedge of hedges. Basically, he went around the world picking funds to invest in.

"Does that keep you busy?" I said.

"I just got back from two weeks in China." He had to repeat himself, because of the noise inside, and leaned towards me with his hand on my elbow. "You get to a point," he said, "after a few days, when you know the routine. You've got two pairs of shorts and socks, a spare shirt, another pair of pants. The hotel takes care of the washing—they fold it up nicely and hang it outside your door in the morning. You've got passport and tickets. And you think, I could just keep going. I could go on like this as long as I wanted to."

"Somebody said you got married."

But he didn't seem to hear me; he was drunker than he looked. "I take two percent of the capital and twenty percent of the profit. Even if we lose money, I make money. It's not very hard to make money. You just need to be able to work out what two percent is."

"Is that right."

We stood there in the street while people went out and in. Everybody we saw was thirty-one, thirty-two, thirty-three years old. There were bald guys with guts and desk-chair asses, wearing suits and looking like your parents' friends when you were a kid. I recognized some of them, too—like those Escher pictures, where the real image hovers under the surface. If you screwed your eyes up right, you could see the guy you knew. At least I still had my hair, I weighed what I weighed in high school. But I also thought, something has happened to them that hasn't happened to me.

"Maybe I should move to Buffalo," I said.

"Tell me why."

"Or Detroit or Cleveland. It doesn't matter. Somewhere you can buy a house on eBay for a few hundred bucks." He looked at me and I said, "We could all buy houses. You could probably buy up a neighborhood. I still have roommates."

"I thought you were teaching somewhere."

"That's right. At some Podunk college in Wales. I don't know how much you know about the academic rat race. There's a window of time to get on the ladder, but if the window closes, they don't kick you out, they keep you on. They make you teach so much you have no time to write, and unless you publish you can't get a permanent job. So this two-tier system develops. I'm on the wrong tier."

"Why don't you come home?"

"I'd love to, but there aren't any jobs. And I don't have health insurance. That's the trouble with Europe—the welfare state sucks you in. I tell you, this is not how I figured things would pan out. I don't mean to embarrass you, but my plane ticket out here cost me more than I can afford. I didn't come over to put up a front. I wanted to have some real conversation."

"You haven't changed much, Marny," he said.

Marnier's my last name, pronounced in the French fashion, which my college friends refused to do. So I got called Marny. Greg is my Christian name, but at Yale only my professors used it.

"That's not how it seems to me. Or maybe I should have changed more. I don't know."

The girl came out of the bathroom and waved—I recognized her, short hard curly hair, freckles, she used to be a gymnast. Robert and I once drove out to the beach together. He borrowed his roommate's car, there were four or five of us and she sat in the backseat. This was freshman year. She wanted to be a vet, I remembered trying to talk to her, and she stood in the street now calling, "Come on, Robert, I'm hungry." The rest of their friends started drifting away, but one thing I always liked about Robert is that he never hurried anywhere for the sake of girls.

"Where are you staying?" he asked.

"One of the dorm rooms. I think I'm sharing with somebody."

"Listen," he said, "you're drunk, you're tired. Get some sleep."

"I'm embarrassing you."

"You're not, but they're playing my song. I'll see you later."

Robert likes to joke that this is where it all started, because of some half-drunk conversation. But that's just one of his stories. In college he was the kind of guy who would ask you about some writer, some class assignment, *okay, so what's his deal, what's his line, what do I need to know.* As if you could break a book down into two or three usable ideas. He was famous for walking out of a three-hour philosophy exam after sixty minutes. He strolled to the front of the class, he laid down his paper, and he looked up at the rest of us. "Good luck, folks," he said. I think he did fine, not great but fine. What I mean is, he made quick decisions, but he was very deliberate, too. And when I saw him that day he was already getting restless, he had backseat political ambitions, he had money to spend, he was looking for something new.

3

When I woke up the next morning, I had ten or twenty seconds of real confusion. Partly because of jet lag. It didn't feel like waking up, it felt like being hit on the head and slowly coming back to consciousness. I was lying on the bottom half of a bunk bed and looking out, through an arched window, at a sycamore tree full of campus sunshine. It took me a while to get my bearings, to realize where I was. But even after I did, for ten or twenty seconds, I couldn't remember what I was doing there—how old I was, or if I had to make a class. Then I remembered and the hangover kicked in, but that didn't matter because the years were gone anyway.

After breakfast in dining hall, I caught a train to New York. This gave me two hours to screw my head on straight. It's not a bad journey. I liked looking at the waterside mansions, the poky harbors, the bays, and later on, the big industrial views of Bridgeport and the row houses of Queens. Some of my classmates rode that train to work; some of them had summerhouses on the water. At Grand Central, I transferred to Penn Station and bought a Greyhound ticket to Baton Rouge.

I wasn't going back to Europe, that much was clear. Something had shifted in me over the last twenty-four hours, like back pain.

You get in the habit of living a certain kind of life, you keep going in a certain direction, but most of the pressure on you is just momentum. As soon as you stop the momentum goes away. It's easier than people think to walk out on things, I mean things like cities, leases, relationships and jobs. I guess I might have stayed with friends in New York, but I was tired of imposing myself. If you're going to be a bum, I thought, you might as well bum around at home.

The Greyhound ticket cost two hundred bucks and the whole journey took under three days. We stopped in Philadelphia, Baltimore, DC, Richmond, Raleigh, Charlotte, Atlanta, Montgomery. Staring out the window hour after hour kind of concentrates and expands the mind at the same time; but it's also somehow liberating, it eases the heart, to realize that you don't need anything but a few hundred dollars and a backpack to move home.

I kept thinking about what Robert said to me, about the two sets of clothes and the laundry routine. Every time the bus pulled over, I stepped out to stretch my legs and thought, this looks like a good place to live, maybe I should live here. Then I got back on the bus. From a gas station phone box I called my mom, who promised to clear the stationary bike from my old bedroom.

A colleague took care of my affairs in Wales—packing my room up (I didn't have much) and selling or throwing away what I didn't want shipped. It amazed me how little effort was required to dismantle ten years of my life. Nobody cared if I came back or not. There was still some grading left to do for the summer term, but the department secretary as a personal favor sent my exam papers to Baton Rouge. Basically, I felt grateful for the work; it kept me occupied. My dad had retired and I spent too much time that summer playing golf with him in the morning and watching the afternoon baseball game on TV.

Sometimes I went out with high school buddies. One of them took me duck hunting in his boat, out at Pointe-aux-Chenes. This was later in the year, early November. He worked in real estate but had recently lost his job; both of us found the days and weeks hard to fill. I held a gun in my hands for the first time but there wasn't much to shoot at. Which didn't bother me, I had fun anyway. "This is really a long way from Aberystwyth," I said, kneeling down in the boat, on wet knees. There were little hummocks of what looked like floating grass all over the bayou. The air on my neck felt as cold as a used towel. It was pretty early in the morning and the light grew up around us like something spilling over the rim of a bowl.

The fact is, I don't know where I felt more at home. Nowhere. And once we finished catching up we ran out of things to say. I called him a couple of times but was relieved when he didn't call back. Similar things happened with other people.

I didn't have much luck finding a job. I started out applying for university gigs all over the country. My mother was reluctant to let me go. She said, "I've just got you back"—a coded way of saying she didn't trust my state of mind. But it didn't matter, nobody wanted an unpublished historian five years out of grad school anyway. So I lowered my sights and sent out letters to every private high school in commuting distance from Baton Rouge. No dice.

In January, after a New Year's resolution, I moved to New Orleans for a couple of months. My dad put me in touch with some friends of his who had a big house on one of those gated roads out by Audubon Park. Their daughters were all grown up. I rented one of the empty bedrooms and slept in a cast-iron bed, with these old film postcards Blu Tacked to the wall beside it: Hedy Lamarr, Lana Turner, Gloria Grahame. The girl whose room it used to be was now a resident oncologist at the Tulane Medical Center.

Every day I took the streetcar into the Quarter, where I cleaned tables at CC's Coffee House. But it became clear to me that I wasn't coping very well, and I moved back home.

What saved me is the election. My dad is a Clinton man and I volunteered for Hillary in the primaries, which put me in touch with a lot of interesting people and gave me something to do. My parents didn't mind that it wasn't paid. Probably I put too much of my time and energy into the nomination, I cared too much, and needed to set my own life in order. When she came to Louisiana, some of the volunteers got credentialed to hear her speak at a grim corporate event at the downtown Omni. But afterwards she said to one of the organizers, "I know you can have a better time than this in New Orleans," and somehow I ended up in one of the cabs taking people over to the Acme, which was surrounded by Secret Service and fully booked. I managed to station myself by the door when she made her getaway.

"You from around here?" she said, shaking my hand.

"Baton Rouge."

"Go Tigers," she said. "And what are you doing with yourself these days?"

"Biding my time."

Whenever I couldn't sleep, I replayed this conversation in my head. It took me about a month to forgive Obama—for beating her. But then some friends of mine from the campaign persuaded me to volunteer at MoveOn. There were people who thought they could use the Katrina disaster to turn Louisiana blue. Well, we got within twenty points. But when the votes started tightening in New Hampshire and Pennsylvania, I decided to fly out one week-end to New Haven. MoveOn was sending everyone from Yale up to Claremont for a couple of days, and it seemed like a good excuse for seeing old friends.

I knew that Robert James grew up in Claremont, or near enough, in the countryside around it. His dad had a law office in town—he represented a lot of farmers. Robert mentioned once that he went to Claremont High, which surprised me, because I figured him for a private school kid. But that's probably just the kind of place it is, I thought. A rich man's village. In fact, it looked tougher than that. There was a bookshop and a coffee shop on the main square, but the rest of the commercial units were either boarded up or fronting pizza chains or dime stores or pharmacies with the cigarettes prominent in the window.

Our job was to rustle up votes in the first neighborhood you drove into coming north off the highway. Mountains surrounded us; it all looked pretty picturesque above the roofline. But the houses were cheap and run down, and we had to negotiate some ugly angry dogs before knocking on doors. The kind of people who lived there were the kind of people who wouldn't vote for a black guy, even a half-black guy. I heard a lot of talk in the media about Obama's slick grassroots operation, but the main thing we accomplished was to piss people off. A carful of Yalies going around saying, What are the issues for you in this election? Is there anything I can help you understand?

That was the line we'd been told to spin by the heavily bearded and buttoned dude at Obama HQ. HQ makes it sound too grand, it was a defunct Honey Dew Donuts in downtown Claremont. The place was full of Yalies, wearing overpriced pseudo-workingman's clothes: leather boots, tough khakis and plaid shirts. After each run we reported back; they wanted a house-by-house account of the swing-vote situation. At one point I bumped into Robert James.

He said, "Marny, there's something I want to talk to you about." So he turned to the bearded guy and told him, "Phil, I'm taking off," and led me to his car, which was parked in the square, and we drove out to his parents' house in the woods.

I'd heard about this place in college. Robert sometimes invited a few friends back when his folks were out of town, though I wasn't one of them. Sometimes he just came with Beatrice, his college girlfriend. She was a friend of mine, too, she was my friend first, and maybe that's why I didn't make the cut. Anyway, I never got invited. It was a two-hundred-year-old farmhouse set back off a dirt road, with a one-step stoop and brightly painted shutters beside the windows. Rosebushes lined the path to the front door, and I could see around the side of the house an apple orchard falling away to a pond at the bottom of the garden. The rest of the land was covered in trees.

Robert's mom was as handsome as her son. Steely-haired and unmade-up, she limped around the house in a boot cast. But a broken foot didn't stop her from bringing us coffee and slices of Bundt cake to the screened-in back porch.

"Where'd you get that?" I said, and she smiled at me. There was still something left of the way a good-looking woman looks at a man.

"That's sweet. I made it."

"No, I mean the foot."

"Oh, it was stupid. We were hiking out by Ripley Falls and I slipped on some gravel. Five years ago I would have finished the hike, but I've got old-lady bones. One of them broke. A very small one, but it hurt."

When she banged her way out again, he said, "I've been meaning to get in touch with you. What are you doing with yourself these days?"

"Not much."

"Because I've been thinking of taking you up on that Detroit idea."

Obama's success, though he wouldn't say so, had wrong-footed him. He was late to get on the bandwagon and didn't have the right Chicago connections anyway—he didn't know anyone from the inner circle. Braylon Carr, the mayor he backed in Buffalo, had a difficult relationship with Obama. Bill Clinton had campaigned for him, and Carr had put his neck out for Hillary in the New York primaries. Robert knew the Clintons fairly well. He admired Obama and was trying to make up lost ground, but he wanted something to do in the meantime, something high profile, that would get the right kind of attention. Detroit was all over the news. Chrysler, Ford and GM, the Big Three, had just asked for a $50 billion bailout, and Congress was negotiating a package.

Robert wanted to talk me through the idea.

"I can't buy up the city, but I can put some investors together and buy up sections of it. Nobody wants to move there alone, but you can use the Internet, you can use Facebook—what I'm talking about is a kind of Groupon model for gentrification. The question is," he said, "who would go there and what would they do when they got there? These neighborhoods are in bad shape. It's basically a war zone—I mean that, in the middle of America. People are burning down houses, and not just for the insurance. My friend Bill Russo took me around. It's like driving through London after the Blitz. The city has given up on certain blocks; the fire service won't come out to them anymore. But there are still some beautiful big houses standing empty. You could do whatever you want with them, set up any kind of society. There's a guy who talks about plowing the land into farms. But you'd need a critical mass of people to make it work. People like you, but would people like you move to Detroit? I mean, would *you*?"

"Yes," I said.

Afterwards, he drove me back to Claremont and I went out again with another carload of volunteers. The sun set around half past six, the temperature dropped, and the sky between the mountains turned a very bright evening shade of dark blue. I had that feeling you get when you're a kid out playing in the yard and you see the lights turn on at home—outside looking in. The shape and movements of people, closing curtains and sitting down to watch TV. All these private lives. It seemed a shame to make them open their front doors. Then we drove back to HQ and Phil ordered pizza; later a few of us walked out into the cold country night looking for a bar.

4

Roughly six months later I set off. Obama had won, the economy was going down the tubes, it seemed a good time to try something new. My dad loaned me five thousand dollars and I spent three hundred bucks of it on a secondhand car—a '91 Taurus, the last in the series to offer a stick shift. I figured the shittier the better. On my last night at home, after supper, my father went into the yard to smoke a cigarette. He smoked maybe one or two a month, and it always put my mother in a sour mood. She made a pot of decaf and passed me a cup across the kitchen table.

"He's worried about you, that's why he's smoking again," she said. "You're too old to play games like this."

"That's just not true, he always smokes—a little. What I'm too old for is living at home with you guys."

"I don't mind."

"You sound like Granma Dot," I said.

A year before she died, after a bad stroke, my grandmother came to live with us. She didn't want to be a burden, and if you asked her anything like, *what* do you want for lunch, she answered, "I don't mind." My father used to beg her for an answer, something specific, but she never budged; it drove him crazy. At the same time she was highly critical of everything: the heat, the people, the food.

She died from a staph infection after hip-replacement surgery. This was around Easter of my sophomore year in high school. After the funeral, for which my mom held it together pretty well, she waited until we were alone and then broke down. I was helping her write out thank-you cards; a few friends from Puyallup had sent flowers.

"It's okay," I said, feeling embarrassed. "She was really old. I don't think she—"

But my mother shook her head. "It's not that," she said. "I wanted you to like her more. I don't think you liked her very much. But when I was a girl, she was my mother, there was no one else."

Of course, this was true for me, too, and here was *my* mother sitting across the kitchen table. Every year she looked more like Granma. Dot had bad eyes, there was a kind of film over them, like the skin on warm cream, and glasses made her eyes seem bulgy. My mother had started wearing glasses, too, and not just for reading. With her hair cut short she looked like an old little girl.

Then my father clattered in the door, bringing some of the smoke smell with him. "Come on, kid, you've got a long drive tomorrow. Get some sleep."

He put his hand to the side of my face, so I turned my cheek against it.

"Mom says you're worried about me," I said.

"That's our job. It's your job not to mind too much."

After brushing my teeth and changing into pajamas, I came back into the kitchen to kiss her good night. She was still sitting at the table, which was covered in the bright plastic sunflowers of the tablecloth; they glared under the hanging lamp. My mother let me kiss her sitting down.

"Greg," she said, before I turned away. "I know you won't do anything deliberately stupid. That's not your style. But you're the kind of person who could get himself into situations that you won't be very good at getting out of. There will be people there who don't want you there. They don't think like you do—"

"You mean black people?" I said.

"That's not what I said. That's not what I mean. But I've been doing what Brad always tells me not to do, I've been looking things up on the computer. Detroit is the number one most violent city in America."

"No worse than New Orleans."

"New Orleans is bad enough—that's why we moved out. But there are good neighborhoods and bad neighborhoods. From what I understand, you plan on living right in the middle of the worst."

"You're totally out of touch with these things, Mom. All you know is what you read online or see on TV. The news and entertainment industries in this country *sell* fear, it's what they do, because people like you want to buy it. But that doesn't make it true."

"Who is they? I don't know who *they* is. This is starting to make me angry. You said yourself it's a war zone."

"That wasn't me, but it doesn't matter. I don't want to have this conversation now."

Bending down, I kissed her good night again, and then again and again on each cheek, to lighten the mood. But she only sat there, softening into grumpiness. "You're making a joke out of it. It's not a joke."

"Can I say one thing?" I said. "Don't blame Dad for lending me the money."

This conversation left a taste in my mouth, because of what I said or what she said, I don't know. It's unpleasant to see your parents for what they are, limited people. But you get into stupid fights with them anyway, you're all tangled up. And afterwards you have to deal with the fact that you don't always believe your own point of view.

My dreams that night were very near the surface, they were very plausible. I was getting gas and looking through my wallet for dollar bills. It was a full-service station and I never know how much to tip. Later, back on the road, the lanes seemed narrow, there was a problem with my headlights or the windscreen wipers. I kept falling asleep. I should have pulled over but that's how people get killed in this country, sleeping by the side of the highway. So I lowered the window to let some fresh air in. That only helped a little, every few seconds my head jerked up. I could hear my father in the kitchen, making French toast, and then he came into my bedroom singing, *Wake up, you beautiful girl*, which had been playing on the radio.

After breakfast we loaded up the car. My mother kept thinking of something else for me to take and cluttered the trunk with a hundred odd things for setting up house—a flashlight, packs of batteries and toilet paper, her old coffeemaker. But then there was nothing else and I drove off.

She waited in the driveway until she couldn't see me—this is what she always does after our visits home. I watched her in the rearview mirror. When I turned the corner, and a new street slid over to replace the street I grew up on, with other houses and trees and nobody standing in the drive, I felt like you feel when you put the phone down and the room is suddenly different.

Around lunchtime I stopped at the Walmart outside Hattiesburg and bought a gun. The guy behind the counter—a black guy, as it happens, with a dude-like mustache—was low-key, practical and encouraging.

"What do you want it for?" he said.

"Duck hunting. I'm just getting started."

"We got a Ruger Red Label. That's a real classic gun, a nice starter gun. It'll last you, too."

"Last time I went out I used a Remington."

So he suggested a Remington 870 Express with a compact pump and listed other specs, which I didn't understand.

"Will it fit under the seat of my car?"

"What are you driving?" he said and handed me the catalog to look at while the FBI check cleared. There was a form you had to fill out—I gave my parents' address in Baton Rouge. Afterwards, we talked about shells.

"It depends what you want to use it for," he said. "Are we talking home defense or hunting ducks? Because there's different things I'd recommend." He also suggested a couple of accessories, a TacStar SideSaddle, an Elzetta light mount, with a Fenix LD10. "That's a strong light," he said. "If that catch somebody in the eye, give you an extra couple of seconds. Give you a chance to see who it is." He put everything in a doubled-up paper bag.

I picked up some car snacks, too, chips and soda and brown bread and sliced cheese. As I pulled back onto I-59 a crowd of feelings went over me in a wave. Here we go, I thought, here we come. But I still had another fifteen hours of driving, and a night to get through at a Days Inn motel, before reaching Detroit.

5

Part of the point of driving was to see America, but you don't see much of America from the road. My views on each side were confined to billboards, exit signs and gas stations. The tallest building I came across between Nashville and Louisville was an Exxon-Mobil gas tower straddling a patch of juniper grass by the side of the highway. I stopped every few hundred miles to fill the tank, or stock up on caffeine, or take a leak, or eat—mostly at Wendy's and Subway, as close to the exit ramp as I could find them. There are no locals at these places. The people I saw picking hot sandwiches out of Styrofoam had set their car keys and wallets on the table next to cups of takeaway coffee.

I wanted to make it to Louisville but started dreaming about driving instead of actually driving and pulled off about fifty miles short. It was nine o'clock—a coolish spring highway-flavored evening, with cars like crickets making a low continuous noise in the dark. My motel room was part of a row of cabins running in a long line off the parking lot. The bed linen smelled like cigarettes and air-conditioning. Even after a swim in the roadside pool I couldn't sleep. I kept seeing headlights coming at me and moving past. Everything felt like a computer game.

Then around two a.m. someone started banging next door. A drunk man trying to persuade a girl to let him in. "I won't make you do anything you don't want to do," he said. "You took my fucking money pretty willing." This went on an unbelievable length of time—I guess he was drunk enough to be patient. He certainly didn't mind repeating himself. "Don't make me the angry guy outside the door," he said.

I lay in bed, listening, but either the girl let him in or he gave up or I fell asleep, because the next thing I knew a truck was reversing in the parking lot, and my inside elbow lay over my eyes to keep the sun out.

North of Louisville the landscape started to change, and by the time I got lost in Dayton, looking for lunch, I'd crossed the weather line. There was fresh snow on the parked cars and hedges of dirty snow between them. When I set out from Baton Rouge the previous morning, a white blanket of cloud held the heat in. The Taurus had leather seats, which stuck to my T-shirt, which stuck to my back. For most of that first day's drive, through the open window, the air flowed over my face as hot as a Laundromat. Even outside Louisville, the night was mild enough I could walk barefoot from the pool to my motel room after a swim.

But it was cold in Dayton, and wet in the wind from the snow. I parked outside a Popeye's and spent a couple of minutes standing in shorts and digging out a pair of jeans from my duffel in the trunk.

Eating alone makes my thoughts run on sometimes. There wasn't much to look at, just a view outside of occasional cold-weather traffic plowing through slush. I thought about Robert. We'd been communicating by email a couple of times a week, but I hadn't seen him in the flesh since Claremont. His wife had just given birth, prematurely, to a five-pound boy. They spent the first two weeks in hospital. Robert was traveling a lot. He liked to know there was medical expertise on hand, but his wife, he said, just wanted to get home.

I sat there for a while, letting the ice in my soda turn to water. The street sign at the corner said "Gettysburg Avenue." There was some kind of trailer park across the road, some weird metal canisters, a strip of snowy dirt for cars to turn around in. I mean, real fucking nowhere. Two high school girls were finishing lunch at the next table, dropouts maybe or seniors on a lunch break. A fat one and a pretty one, both eating fries; their chicken wrappings were smeared with ketchup. The thin paper kept moving under their fingers as they pushed the fries around. One of them, the pretty girl (she had a small cute acned face, and a nose ring, and straight dyed-black hair), had to lick her knuckles clean.

The fat one said, "Good to the last drop."

For some reason I felt jealous. They weren't talking much but seemed comfortable together. I missed the friendship of girls, not just in a sexual way, though that, too.

Robert had told me I could stay with him for a few weeks. Longer if necessary. He was renting a mansion in Indian Village, which he planned to use as a base of operations. They had a full house but could always put a mattress somewhere. We spoke on the phone the night before I set off.

"It's good times," he said.

This is part of what I liked about him. In his company, I felt close to the center of the action, whereas personality-wise, I'm a periphery guy. My mother sometimes warned me, *You live too much in your head*. But where else are you supposed to live when you're in the car.

A HALF HOUR LATER, I stopped by the side of the road to pick up a hitchhiker. This girl, who looked about twenty years old, was standing by the access ramp, holding up a piece of cardboard box with DETROIT scribbled across it in fat felt-tip. She had messy blond hair and a white face and looked cold. Her nose was reddening in the wind, and she wore cowboy boots and a faded denim jacket.

As soon as I pulled onto the hard shoulder, her boyfriend came out of the trees and joined her with the bags. They were both German, hitching their way from New York, Astrid and Ernst—or *Ernest*, she said, in her jokey-sounding English-and-American accent. She had the slightly scornful look of pretty girls but turned out to be light-headed and much too chatty for a three-hour drive. I was annoyed with her from the beginning, because of the boy. Ernst sat in the back with his earphones on the whole way. Probably he was grateful for the break. Astrid needed a lot of responding to.

She sat in the passenger seat, peeling an orange and sometimes offering me a piece. The scent of the orange soon filled the car. When she was finished with that, she took a ball of yarn from her backpack and began to knit.

All the artists she knew were moving to Detroit—it was the new Berlin, she said. Hip and cheap. New York was dead already, expensive and dead. The only interesting thing you can see in New York is what money does to cities. And so on.

She asked me why I was going to Detroit and I tried to explain myself. That a friend of mine from college, who had made a lot of money, was buying up run-down neighborhoods and renting out the houses to people who had the skills or energy to bring the neighborhoods back to life.

"Artists?" she said at once.

"Not just artists."

But she took out a pen and wrote my email address on the back of her hand. For an hour she fell asleep, but when she woke again, on the outskirts of the city, she fished out a camera from her bag.

"Do you mind if I roll down the window?" she asked and leaned out of it, against the wind.

"Where are the cars?" I said. "Where is everybody?"

"Slow down. I want to take pictures."

There's a kind of momentum to driving on the freeway. After a while, it's hard to come off, everything passes too quickly—the grassy verge, the trees growing up from the streets below, the exit signs and apartment blocks and office blocks and stadiums. But roads are mostly what we saw, around and below and above. I kept driving over the shadows of bridges and said out loud, the way you do for foreigners, "Spaghetti Junction." But really the whole thing reminded me of those sugar-spun cages you get over fancy desserts. I imagined lifting up one of those bridges with my finger, and watching all of the other highways, and not only the highways but also the exits and avenues and boulevards, streets, roads, crescents, lanes and alleys, pulling away from the ground, because they're all connected, and leaving a tan line across America, the color of earth, with a few worms digging around underneath, some pill bugs and dirty wet leaves.

For a few minutes the sunlight flared in the rearview mirror, blinding me against it. Astrid kept snapping away, and then the angle shifted and the road opened up in front of me, concrete-colored. There was so little traffic all the cars had the air of survivors.

Somehow I had drifted off 75 onto Gratiot. There was an intersection, and then a park, or at least an open space, covered in snow, with trees in the distance and a skyline behind them; and next to the road, a low gray industrial unit, built out of cardboard, it seemed, with the words CHICAGO BEEF COMPANY plastered across it in cartoonish letters. For a second I thought I was in the wrong city, I could have been anywhere. Navigating by freeway is like reducing the country to binary code. Every exit you pass is a yes or a no and by the end of the process you hope to end up at the right answer, the right place, which is what the code means. But after a while it all looks like code and I pulled off Gratiot onto Vernor, and then off Vernor onto a side street, to see if there was anything there.

By this point it was six o'clock, a few days before the clocks went forward. A late winter's late afternoon; the streets looked red. After a few blocks I got stuck in some cookie-cutter cul-de-sacs, with cheap executive-style homes. Their gardens backed onto a cemetery, whose front gate made a dead end in the road. I stopped to look at the map and Astrid and Ernst got out.

"What are you doing?" I said. I could see their breath in the air.

"We'll find a bus or something. Don't worry."

"You can't get out here."

"Americans always think America is so dangerous. Look at these houses," she said. "It looks like Bamberg."

When I left she was taking pictures. The snow made everything seem prettier. Ernst had a guidebook in one hand, like a good German schoolboy. The trees of the cemetery looked like the opening of a wood.

But the streets on the far side of it made me worry. I found Vernor again and followed it for a while, past clapboard homes and factories fronted by wire fence. There were churches and barbershops in single-story brick shacks.

Somehow my dad's presence in the car was very strong. This happens to me sometimes; my reactions take the form of a conversation. But I was also remembering something. A few months after Katrina struck, I flew home for Christmas, and one day he persuaded me to go see the Ninth Ward. It's about an hour's drive from Baton Rouge, the last couple of miles through the city itself. Eventually we entered a ramshackle neighborhood, with sagging roofs and broken-paned windows, but there were still a few cars in the driveways and flowerpots on the steps.

"Is this it?" I asked him.

"How bad do you want it to be?" he said.

Then we came upon streets where the houses looked stepped on. Their insides lay spread out over the yards: refrigerators and rocking horses, cable wires, cheap carpeting. It looked like the end of the world.

"Satisfied now?" my dad said, and I heard his voice in my head, asking the same question, as I drove through Detroit. There wasn't any traffic on the road to force me along. Mostly what I saw was empty lots, not falling houses—block after block of grassland. Trees grew out of the roofs of abandoned buildings. There were abandoned cars, too, and tires, shopping carts and heaps of trash sitting where houses used to stand. The effect was rural, not suburban. Snow turned the lots into fields, and the windows of occupied homes glowed like small fires.

But then I came across a street with the lights on—a row of double-deckers, with front porches and big bays, new siding. Trees, at regular intervals, lined the strip of lawn between sidewalk and road, and cars stood parked along the curb. Probably I'd be living somewhere like this. Robert told me he had a place picked out.

If you looked closely you could see boarded windows and broken steps, but there were also satellite dishes and washing lines, trash cans waiting for collection and kids' bikes on the stoops. There weren't any street lamps, though, and when the sun went down behind the trees and telephone poles, I felt about as lonely as I ever have in my life. After pulling to the side of the road, I checked the route to Robert's house by the light of the glove compartment. I didn't want to show myself in a parked car.

IT WAS ONLY FIVE MINUTES away, but east of Van Dyke the neighborhood changed character. The houses got bigger and turned from clapboard to stone; the gardens spread out. I saw a private security vehicle making the rounds. It waited on the other side of the road while I rolled into Robert's drive, which had an electric gate—part of a tall metal fence, topped by spearheads.

I had to step out of the car to announce myself by intercom. This was the first time I'd been out of the driver's seat since lunch. The air smelled good and cold; it smelled of wood-fire smoke. And when the gate swung open, the security vehicle moved on.

Three other cars sat in the drive. I parked behind a Lexus. The house itself was stuccoed and painted yellow, lit up from below by spotlights planted under the hedges, which grew under the windows. The windows were taller than me, and arched, and there were lots of them. I don't know much about American architecture, but the style looked like something from the 1920s and reminded me of what Robert had said over the phone. It suggested "good times." I pushed the bell and heard it jangling—my heart beat faster than it should have.

Robert was changing for dinner when I got inside. The maid let me in, or maybe the cook, since she hurried afterwards back into the kitchen.

The entrance hall had a grand piano in it, covered in photographs and invitations. I looked at the photos for a minute and didn't recognize anyone in them. There were teenage girls and family portraits, pictures of holidays and weddings, but the cards were mostly addressed to Mr. Robert James. From the Rotary Club of Detroit and the Mayor's Office, from the Ford Foundation and the editors of Time Inc. There were also a number of private invitations: "Mr. and Mrs. David Koerning request the pleasure of your company," etc. Nobody else came down.

On one side an opened door led to a living room, and I noticed someone on the couch, reading a newspaper. He stood up when I walked in and shook my hand.

"Tony Carnesecca," he said. "I guess you're one of Robert's college buddies."

"That's right."

"It's like a fucking reunion around here."

There was a fire in the fireplace and a decanter of wine on the side table, with several glasses.

"What do you mean?"

Tony was smiling and showing his teeth, but I think he wanted to offend me, too. He offered me a glass of wine.

"What I really need is to take a leak," I said. He pointed the way, and when I came back in, Tony was still on his feet; he gave me a drink.

"If this is a reunion," I said, "what are you doing here?"

"Because I grew up in the city and actually know what's going on in this place. Even if I didn't go to Yale."

Tony had the forearms of a short man who lifts weights; he wore the kind of T-shirt that would show them off. Maybe he was my age or a few years older. His hair had gel in it and was carefully presented—a working-class white man's haircut. In fact, he was a freelance writer who dropped out of grad school when he got a contract for his memoir about Detroit. His essays had also been published in *Vanity Fair* and *The New York Times*. He told me all this in the first few minutes, while we waited for Robert to come down.

"You're a bunch of assholes, you know that?" Tony said. "And here comes the pick of the lot."

I thought he meant Robert, but an older man walked in, wearing tasseled shoes and a gray silk jacket and tie. This was Clay Greene, one of Robert's business partners. I kept thinking of him as Professor Greene—he taught at Yale, and even after all this time I found it hard to imagine myself on a level with him. Clay poured himself a glass of wine and sat down in an armchair by the fire. Tony went back to his newspaper on the couch, but I had itchy feet after two days in the car and wanted to look around. There was a bookcase against one of the windows so I looked at Robert's books. It touched me to see so many of our college editions: *Democracy in America*, *The Republic*, *Of Mice and Men*.

"Why do you think we're all assholes?" I said to Tony.

"Because you're trying to help and you haven't got a clue. In a place like Detroit that makes you one of the bad guys."

But I didn't answer him because Beatrice had just come in. Her red hair was piled up high on her head, stretching her neck out long—she looked older and more elegant and somehow on display. From the expression on her face I couldn't tell if she was happy to see me.

6

I suppose I should say something about all these people—about how we met. College friendships can take a lot of explaining. The cement is still wet, deep impressions get made, but there are also a lot of casual footprints that leave permanent marks. When I graduated from Yale, I was determined not to be one of those guys who thinks, they were the best four years of my life. And I managed to move pretty far away from that whole scene, as far as Wales. But now I was right back in the middle of it again.

Robert had a room on the same floor as mine freshman year, but I noticed him for the first time in the dining hall lunch line. I was waiting for a plateful of baked ziti when he struck up a conversation with the guy behind the counter—this tall kind of rickety black guy, maybe fifty years old, who wore a dirty white hat and an apron with his name stitched onto it. Robert introduced himself, like a gentleman.

"Willy," he said. "Is that your name? Do you mind if I call you Willy?"

"Go right ahead," Willy told him, and Robert stuck out his hand. "Robert James."

He had to reach over the food counter, and Willy, who clearly felt uncomfortable, wiped his dirty, sweaty palm on his apron for about a minute before taking it. I remember thinking, it doesn't matter if you call him Willy, he'll still call you sir.

The reason we started hanging out is that Robert saw the squash racket sticking out of my backpack. Whenever he couldn't sleep he'd tap on my door—I never turned the lights off till two in the morning.

"Hey, Marny, Marny," he called. "You up, guy? Want a game?"

There were steam tunnels in the college basement that opened out onto squash courts. Nobody could hear us. The temperature, even in winter, topped ninety degrees, and we could play as late as we liked.

"How come you don't sweat?" he asked me once.

"Because I'm not running."

It felt sweet sending this strong, handsome kid all over the court. Robert rowed stroke in high school and sat on the bench for his varsity basketball team, but he wasn't especially quick on his feet.

He didn't mind losing, though, that's another thing I liked about him. Somehow he always looked like the kind of guy who won. There were a few freckles to go with his almost curly hair; he had the complexion of someone who spent time on boats. It seemed like every weekend a different blonde showed up at his door, but he stayed friends with them, too. Sometimes they came in groups, they just wanted to hang out. All of this was new to me.

EACH YEAR THERE WAS A party before Spring Break called Screw Your Roommate, where the girls ask out the guys, but not for themselves, for a roommate or a friend. It was a combination of blind date and practical joke. One day a girl came up to me outside dining hall and said, "You're Greg Marnier, right? Do you want to take Beatrice to the dance?"

"Which Beatrice?" I said, but I knew which one she meant. We had a philosophy seminar where we both talked too much. In class she dressed like a grown-up, in dresses and low heels, and sometimes took her shoes off under the table and sat with her feet on the chair and her chin on her knees.

"Castelli-Frank. She's about as tall as you, she's got red hair. How many Beatrices do you know?"

"Just her."

"Well?"

"Do you think she wants to go with me?"

"I don't know, but she mentions you sometimes. I'm her roommate. You really get on her nerves. I mean that in a good way."

"It doesn't sound good."

"Look, she likes you, okay. Do you want to go or not?"

"Yes," I said. "Okay. I like her, too."

This cost me a lot, saying yes. I was nineteen years old and had never been on a date—I'd never been in a sexual situation. But then a few days later Beatrice herself came up to me after class and said, "Are you doing anything Saturday night? Because there's this stupid dance and I want to set you up with my roommate."

"I think I met her," I said.

"She's prettier than me."

"I don't know," I said.

"She's nicer than I am, too. I'm a big fan of this girl. I like you, too."

"I don't know," I said. "No. I don't know. Let me think about it."

Eventually I called up the roommate and said no, I couldn't go to the dance with Beatrice, and they must have worked it out together because Beatrice didn't ask me again. But I started hanging out with her after that, maybe because she felt like, okay, at least that's clear. She used to read in our college library, and once when I saw her sleeping there I worked until she woke up, then asked her for coffee. When the waiter came around with our drinks, Beatrice said, "Give me your potted history."

"What's that mean?"

"You know, your life story." And we went from there.

Her mother was from Rome, an actress. She came over to LA to make it in the movies and landed a few small parts in unmemorable pictures before marrying one of the industry lawyers and settling down to raise kids. Beatrice spoke decent Italian and identified strongly with the Italian side of her family. "A bunch of old socialists," she called them, but her American childhood was very privileged. It made her generous with money, and I still have a first edition of E. B. White's *Here Is New York*, which she found in the Strand and bought for me because we'd been having an argument about New York. At that time I was still southern enough to believe that New Orleans is the greatest city in America.

It was a shock to me when she started going out with Robert James. Personally, I liked Robert. For the kind of guy he was, he showed an unusual interest in intellectual ideas, even if he tended to boil them down into something he could digest. He had leftish sympathies. In his own controlling way, he tried to deal honestly with people. But Beatrice belonged in a different league. She was a real highbrow; she had appealingly uncomfortable standards. How she put up with some of Robert's richer friends, and some of his poorer opinions, I couldn't figure out.

Even by undergraduate standards, they had an up-and-down relationship. A few months after they got together, they split up. I don't know why. Nothing that happened to Robert made him look or dress or sound any different, but you could tell Beatrice had things on her mind. Always quick to argue, she started getting angry quicker. Once she saw him waiting in line at Claire's, a cake-and-coffee shop on the corner of the New Haven Green. Only students hung out there. It was overpriced and dark and the cake wasn't very good, but it had gotten a reputation as a date hangout for the short winter afternoons.

Maybe Robert had taken a girl there, maybe he really didn't see her, but anyway, when he kept his shoulder turned, she called out loudly, "Don't turn your back on me. You saw me. I didn't blow you so two weeks later you could turn your back on me."

I wasn't there, but I heard about it from Walter Crenna, who was.

"Did she say that?" I said. "God, did she really say that? What did he say?"

"I don't know. I was at the cashier. I had to pay for my cake."

Walter was probably my best friend at Yale, outside of roommates—a heavy-footed, tall, awkward lit-magazine type. He had a sweet tooth and ate like he talked, slowly, with pleasure. His cheeks were pale and blotchy, but childlike, too; I think he hardly shaved.

By Christmas Beatrice and Robert were back together. In the spring she persuaded him to take an art class. There was something genuinely charming about the way he lugged the gear around (oversize paper pad, easel, paints) and set up openly in the middle of the quad. You could see him mixing his paints, taking his time. It struck me as a public declaration of love—he knew perfectly well he was no good. People stopped by to look at his work, which was not only bad but childishly bad. Still, he battled manfully with perspective, the way a father might, assembling a crib for his baby out of duty. A lot of girls stopped by, too. They could see he was being sweet.

Beatrice and Robert spent part of the summer together, sailing the waters around the James family place near York. She came back the next fall a little more in love than she was before—she liked his father.

But it didn't last; they got along better at home than at school.

For some reason we couldn't understand, Robert cared a lot about secret societies. He was determined to get into Skull and Bones and spent time and energy making the right friends. Beatrice had no patience for this kind of thing. I remember sitting with him on "tap" night. Robert just stayed in his room, and eventually Walter and I went out to bring back pizza and a six-pack of beers. Robert had missed dining hall, but he didn't want to leave in case someone from Skull and Bones knocked on his door. But nobody did.

Two days later I got a note from him, an invitation to join a new club, which was going to be everything the secret societies weren't. "Open, inclusive, intellectually serious."

We went to Mory's, which I had never been to before; Robert had just become a member. There was an entrance on York Street that was hard to find, and inside there were lots of little rooms with beat-up wooden tables and paneled walls.

Robert had some idea of getting us to talk seriously about our futures, but in fact all we talked about is where we wanted to live after graduation—LA, New York, Boston, Chicago, New Orleans. Most of us defended our home states, except for Johnny Mkieze and Bill Russo, who both came from Detroit. Johnny was born in Lagos, though, and went to school at Country Day, which (as Bill pointed out) is as much like Detroit as Yale is like New Haven. Bill's father was a real Detroiter. He grew up in Indian Village and bought his first house on Ellery Street; they only moved out when Bill's mom got pregnant. Now half the block was boarded up, burned down or sitting empty. This may have been the first time I heard about what was happening to Detroit.

At the end of the meal, Robert ordered a Cup—a large urn filled with homebrewed punch. Another embarrassing tradition. Nobody was really drunk enough, but we sang anyway, *Put a nickel on the drum*, all that bullshit, passing the Cup around and drinking and singing. One song led to another. *Bright college years, with pleasure rife, the shortest, gladdest years of life. Bulldog Bulldog bow wow wow. For God, for country and for Yale.* Walter had a beautiful voice, a little thin maybe but light for a big man and clear as a bell. For a while he was singing by himself: *We're poor little lambs who have lost our way! Baa baa baa!* I don't think anyone considered the evening a success.

BEATRICE BROKE UP WITH ROBERT "for good" a few weeks before Christmas, senior year. "Because he had never heard of Pinter," she said to me one night, but I'm sure there were other reasons.

She was standing in the courtyard drinking beer when I bumped into her. "Let's get out of here," she said. "Have you ever been to the top of the clock tower? I know someone with a key."

So I followed her into the library and then up the cold stone stairs. There's a seminar room at the top, and next to the stairwell another door I'd never tried to go in.

"I know the guy who cleans up around here," she said. "A student. He always leaves his key behind one of the books. For smokers."

She couldn't find the key, but it turned out when we tried it a few minutes later that the door was unlocked. There was another staircase behind it, colder and narrower than the first and made of wood, with maybe a hundred cigarette butts underfoot. Beatrice went first. She had on boots with heels and moved awkwardly in the dark. The door at the top was also open, and we stepped out onto a narrow balcony, into the outside air.

There was snow on the ground, a long way below, and Beatrice put an arm around me. She wasn't wearing a coat, just a wool scarf bundled up around her neck, and I found it disconcerting how close her face was. In spite of her good looks, or maybe because of them, she had quite a forceful, almost male presence—strong bones and broad shoulders. She used to swim in high school.

"What are you going to do next year?" she said.

"I'm not sure. I've applied for a couple of fellowships to Oxford. My brother got one and had a good time over there."

"Do you always do what your brother did?"

"Look," I said, "if you want to give me a hard time, you can go to someone else for human warmth."

She let go of me then and stood a little apart. There was not much wind, even up in the tower, but zero cloud cover, and the temperature was somewhere in the twenties. All the time we were talking, students carrying various kinds of bags—backpacks and shopping—came and went through the college gates.

"Oh, it's too cold to argue," Beatrice said and lit a cigarette. When she had finished, with cold jittery fingers, she breathed in and out and leaned against me again.

"Why did you really break up with him?" I asked.

"I told you, because he had never heard of Pinter. Do you know what his GPA is? Three point two, three point three, something like that. God, I sound like such a snob—I am a snob. But after two years of dating I finally realized he isn't very bright. Does this make me a bad human being? But you don't believe me."

"No, not really."

"You think he is very bright?"

"I think he has a kind of efficient intelligence. But that's not what I don't believe."

"Yes, he has a kind of intelligence. The trouble is, he thinks it is better than *real* intelligence."

"I'm not sure what that is."

"Yes, you are. It's what you have, it's what I have."

"The way you put it doesn't make it sound very nice."

"It's very important to you to be nice, isn't it? I think this is why you don't have many girlfriends."

"Do girls not like nice boys?"

She let go of me again and eventually she said, "This is a very stupid conversation. This is the kind of stupid conversation I had freshman year." And I could see (I should have seen it before) that she was really quite unhappy, and that her bright sarcastic mood was just the surface of it.

To change the subject, I asked, "And what are you going to do next year?"

"I don't know. For a while, Robert and I talked about moving in together, probably in New York. Finding jobs. Maybe I'll do that anyway."

"What's Robert planning?"

"I think he's stuck, and he knows it. He's not as smart as his father is; he knows that, too."

"Walter is convinced he's going to run the country some day."

"Walter is a little in love with all of us," she said.

Somehow her saying this changed the tone again. It really was very cold, and Beatrice had begun to look pale. Her lips were blue and the cigarette in her hand shook.

"What am I doing, let me give you my coat."

"No, let's go back down," she said but stayed where she was, so I put my arm around her again and rubbed her side. "I don't want to go out in the world," she added, in the mock plaintive voice of the spoilt pretty girl.

I thought, if you were normal, standing here like this, you would kiss her. And it's true, I had been sort of in love with her for almost three years. I say sort of, because what made me unhappy about it was mostly the fact that this feeling of being in love had so little to do with my actual relations with her, with our friendship, which was real enough. My sexual feelings towards her were adolescent, somehow masturbatory, not very nice. While in reality I was a pretty good friend to Beatrice.

She said again, "Let's go back down," and this time we went.

When we reached the landing, where the cigarette butts were, the light of the seminar room showed along the edge of the doorway. And for a second I thought, in a mild panic, that someone might have locked us in. But the door opened easily; the light inside seemed very bright.

It was much warmer, too, and Beatrice said, "God, I was getting fucking cold. I kept thinking you were going to kiss me." Walking through the courtyard afterwards she held my hand.

I DIDN'T SEE MUCH OF Robert that spring, which was our last term at Yale. Everybody was busy applying for whatever it was they wanted to do in the fall. Walter planned to take a year out before applying to theater-studies programs. Maybe live with his parents in Maine and write plays, or teach part-time at the local high if he got bored. Beatrice won a Shorenstein Center scholarship at the Kennedy School in Harvard. Her undergraduate major was comp lit, but she had decided to do a master's in international development.

Nobody knew what Robert had lined up. A few weeks before graduation I got another invitation from him, this time delivered by email. He was organizing an end-of-year dinner with one of his poli sci professors, Clay Greene. The email went out to most of the usual suspects: me and Walter, Bill Russo, Johnny Mkieze. Even Beatrice got an invite. I guess they were on speaking terms again. Robert promised everyone a free meal at the Grand Union Café.

Clay was an important figure for Robert, because of the life he led, which was comfortable, gracious and politically involved; he gave Robert a sense of the possibilities. The Greenes came from an old Virginia family. They still owned land overlooking the Chesapeake and Clay threw weekend parties there for selected friends, associates and former students. For a certain kind of ambitious prep school type, getting invited to Professor Greene's house over the summer was part of the point of going to Yale.

Dinner at the Grand Union was his treat. Clay had booked the private room, which wasn't easy to find—you reached it by a staircase next to the kitchens, and Robert kept doubling back to make sure nobody was lost. The guest list consisted entirely of his personal friends, but Robert presented us all like some kind of cream of the crop.

This was the deal. Clay wanted to recruit a handful of graduating seniors for a new business venture. The original idea came from Robert, which was to sell political information to large companies on a subscription basis. We don't need poli sci majors, he said, just people with a strong grounding in the humanities and an interest in world affairs. There would also be plenty of part-time work to go around, consultancy jobs, office management positions.

Meanwhile the food kept coming. Amuse-bouche. Bottles of champagne to start and then two kinds of wine. Someone had taken care of the ordering; there were no menus, no choices. Waiters just came and went, always with full hands.

Clay sat between Robert and Beatrice, and she did a good job keeping the professor entertained, leaning in to make herself understood. Putting a hand on his elbow. I figured she must have patched things up with Robert. Later it struck me that maybe she wanted to make him jealous, but at the time it seemed she was just helping out. It was an awkward meal. Even when they got drunk, nobody had much to say.

"I mean, for God's sake," Walter said afterwards. "I'm a theater major."

Robert kept trying to draw everyone out, to talk them up. But this was never one of his skills, running a conversation. His manner was dry and economical; he did better at introductions. Then he started bragging to Clay about Beatrice's scholarship to the Kennedy School.

To Beatrice he said, "You could probably earn something like forty thousand dollars a year on top of that, just for putting us in touch with the right people there and spending maybe five hours a week doing research for the company."

For some reason, this set her off.

"Come on, Robert. Give it a rest," she said. "I don't care about money as much as you do."

"That's because you don't need to."

"And I'm not going to the Kennedy School for *connections*."

She sounded calm enough, but Robert, who had been acting nervous and stiff all night, lost his cool. "Stop it. You're embarrassing me. And there's no point to it. You made your point six months ago."

So Beatrice said, "I don't have to sit here," and stood up.

Robert started going after her, but Clay put a hand on his shoulder. "Sit down, Robert, sit down. Have a glass of water."

When she was gone, Robert stopped talking for a few minutes and did what he was told. He had a glass of water. His face was pretty red; he always had a sandy complexion. But he was also a bit drunk and looked like a young Wall Street type after a bad day on the floor. Clay made a little general conversation. Have you enjoyed Yale? Do you think you've changed much since you were a freshman? What do you think you'll remember about your time here?

Walter answered, in his serious way, "I don't think I'll forget this dinner, sir." Clay had the decency to smile.

At the end, Robert tried to salvage something from the evening. He stood up and made a speech. "You all know Professor Greene," he began, "but let me tell you a few things about him maybe you don't know." And so on. Finally he said (a line he had probably prepared): "I don't need to tell you what opportunity looks like. It looks like this."

AS IT HAPPENS, CLAY AND Robert *did* go into business together. They opened their first office in New Haven, since it was convenient for the university. Robert was the only full-time employee; he was also a minority partner in the firm. They set up an office in Manhattan a year later.

I kept hearing updates from Walter, who sometimes crashed at his place when he needed a weekend in the city. Robert had a small one-bedroom apartment in Greenwich Village, with a fire escape balcony overlooking Chumley's bar. By this stage he was paying himself something like a hundred thousand dollars in salary. Their monthly subscription rates went as high as thirty grand.

Walter said he hadn't changed at all, he looked just like he used to in college. Robert bragged that he never wore a tie to work. It was his job to bring in clients, something he turned out to be good at. Just before the dot-com crash, he sold his stake in the company for $17 million.

7

I stayed with Robert in Detroit for a little over two months. It took me that long to build up the nerve to move out, into a 1930s double-decker not ten blocks away, on a street in which about half the buildings had burned down. Also, I was waiting for Walter to come up from Indiana. We had a plan of living together for a while.

For most of that time I had a pretty good time. In the morning, I went over to work on the house, which had broken windows and a leaky roof but looked presentable enough. Squatters had burned garbage and newspapers in the downstairs fireplace, and there were burn scars around the hearthstone. When I picked at the paint job a layer of wallpaper tore away with it. There was another layer underneath, leafy and yellow and rough to the touch, like the wallpaper in my grandmother's house in Puyallup. As a kid, I used to rub my thumb against the grain; it made your elbows shiver.

One summer in high school I volunteered for Habitat for Humanity, and a bunch of us middle-class teenagers stripped walls, sanded floors, and painted a run-down row of old Victorians outside of Denham Springs. Plumbing and roofing were beyond us, but we helped and watched. I kept thinking about that summer and what it meant that fifteen years later I was fixing up one of these down-and-out places for myself.

There was no running water, and the toilets started out bone-dry. But the pipework seemed to be intact, which was lucky—people stole copper. Instead of grass, the garden grew mattresses, tires and broken bricks, but this kind of work I could do myself, with gloves on, and I spent most dry mornings wheelbarrowing junk from the backyard to the front. On wet days, the house felt pretty depressing since the upstairs living room ceiling dripped—not much, but enough to fill a bathtub someone had dragged under the drip. I spent maybe half an hour emptying this out, bucket by bucket, throwing the dirty water down the toilet. The damp smell wouldn't go away, and every sunny day I forced open the crack-paned windows at the front and back to get a breeze going through.

I didn't like hanging around after dark. Also, I wasn't in much hurry to move in. Mrs. Rodriguez, the cook, laid out hot lunch for us every day at Robert's house, around the twenty-seater mahogany table in the dining room. So I came back for lunch. I looked forward to this walk all morning. You could see the neighborhood shifting from street to street. Burned-down houses were replaced by boarded-up houses were replaced by empty houses with FOR SALE signs in the window. By the time I got to Robert's house I had climbed about two-thirds of the way up the class ladder.

ROBERT FLEW HOME REGULARLY TO see his new baby and also traveled around to drum up sponsorship. In his opinion, Detroit could be useful as a model for urban regeneration only if it made money. Somebody had to get rich off it, and it was his job to persuade investors that they would. A certain amount of money he was willing to put up himself, and didn't mind losing it either, for his own sake, but the only clear-cut way of judging this kind of scheme was by the profit it made. So it needed to be profitable.

Beatrice served as his deputy whenever he went out of town. We saw a lot of each other those first few weeks since we both lived in the house. She had become an efficient and organized person who could deal with lawyers and manage a large staff. My second day there I saw her dismiss one of the real estate agents Robert had been using to buy up properties—an unhappy, smiley, middle-aged man.

"I don't want to talk to you," she said. He kept trying to explain himself. "You may be right. You may even be honest, though I doubt it. But I've spent enough time listening to you already. Out, out," she said, gesturing and laughing by this time, the laugh of a pretty woman who gets her way. And he walked out.

She suspected him of turning the all-out landgrab into an excuse to raise prices, and so she set up a complicated system of rival agents to keep the prices down. Some of the land was being bought back from the city, which had started paying people to abandon their homes, and she got a good rate for the buyback, too. The city took it in the purse both ways.

Another one of her jobs was to persuade the holdouts to sell, and I drove along with her on some of these missions. "As protection," she said, though I was more frightened than she was. I told her about my gun and she looked at me, shocked.

"Marny, what do you think this is?" she said. "Kabul? Get rid of it. I don't want to hear about it again."

I thought she didn't have a clue. Wearing her Barneys coat and bright stilettos, she clicked up broken porch steps in the melting snow and banged on warped doors when the bells failed to ring. "Darling," she called people, and "honey," but somehow nobody minded. They invited her in.

Inside she would slowly unwrap herself, talking all the time, asking for coffee. Women, she once explained to me, respect a woman who can wear such shoes, and men have their own reasons for liking them. It didn't matter in the end if most of the holdouts refused to sell—she wanted to spread good relations.

I got to know my neighborhood this way, which had once been prosperous. There was still a kind of washed-up middle class. I remember an elderly retired elementary school teacher, Mrs. Troy, who had lived in her house for fifty years. Maybe two-thirds of her block had burned down—she was surrounded by fields. Shopping took all day. She refused to understand the Internet and couldn't drive safely anymore, though her license was valid. There weren't many buses. Her grandson, who used to come around with a few bags of groceries on a Sunday, was serving fifteen months at the Ryan Correctional Facility. She told us all this herself, with a certain pride: he was doing very well there.

No, she wouldn't think of selling. But she wanted us to stay and talk and brought out Archway oatmeal cookies on a china plate.

Most of the buildings looked in much worse shape. The best way of telling if someone lived in them was by the satellite dishes. Cable companies refused to lay cable because locals spliced into the mainline themselves instead of paying their monthly fee. People also stole cable for its street value. So we looked for dishes.

They weren't hard to find. We saw one as big as a bathtub nailed into the side of a grand old Victorian corner house, with gables and turrets. It was so large it had to be attached by a six-by-six square of plywood. Somehow the dish and turrets went well together—the house a kid would design. There were cars parked on the grass in the front yard. The steps to the porch had caved in, so I climbed up first and gave Beatrice a hand.

"Who lives like this?" I said. The windows were all boarded up.

A young, muscular, well-dressed black man let us in. Two other young men sat behind him on a couch, watching TV. The room looked like a frat house after a party: potato chip bags, pizza boxes, bottles, cartons and napkins lay on the floor. The TV did double duty as a source of light.

No, ma'am, they didn't want to sell. Yes, they got the lawyers' letters. There was nothing they didn't understand or wanted to talk about. If white people want to move in, they can move in. See how they like it.

I noticed that the guys on the couch weren't watching TV but playing some video game. This explains why they hardly looked up. The images they controlled operated knives and guns.

Afterwards, on the way out, I said to Beatrice, "You didn't do the striptease act for them."

This is one of my father's phrases, and I thought she might take offense. Which she did, but I was surprised by what offended her.

"What do you mean, *them*?" she said.

It was a wet April afternoon a few days after a snow. Nobody else was out walking, and I had a strong feeling there was a reason for that. Empty streets make you think that everyone else is in the know. But we made it to the car all right.

Later, on the drive home, we had the other argument, too.

"I don't understand what's going on here," I said.

"What do you mean?"

"I thought you broke up with him and now you run around taking his orders."

"That was ten years ago, Marny."

"I thought you said he wasn't smart enough."

"I was wrong, and anyway, it doesn't matter. You realize after a while that there are certain people who make things possible; he's one of them, that's all. There are more important things going on here than my self-esteem."

"Or maybe you think you're really calling the shots, with those short skirts and high heels."

"Why are we fighting, Marny? Are you trying to pick a fight?"

"I don't know what it is," I said. "When I'm scared for some reason I try to piss people off. Maybe I don't like being told that I'm a racist."

BUT THIS WASN'T THE WHOLE story. I found living in the house with her very painful. Seeing her come down for breakfast, with wet hair, and watching her at night go up to bed carrying the day-old *New York Times* and a mug of Celestial Seasonings tea. (When I went into her bedroom I saw many of these mugs, cold and half full, with the tea bag left in, coloring the water.) We spent afternoons as I have described, driving around Detroit together, sharing car space, and sometimes parking and getting out in what seemed to me medium-risk situations. She had become a tough, competent and admirable woman but part of what pained me is the fact that she also seemed diminished somehow—not quite the girl I knew in college. I didn't like the way she took his money, though I was living off Robert's money, too.

ROBERT HIMSELF PUZZLED ME. I figured I knew him well enough at Yale, yet every time I saw him he struck me as more difficult to get at.

The morning after my arrival, after breakfast, he said to me, "Come for a walk with me, Marny."

I realized for the first time what our new relations were when it occurred to me that I shouldn't refuse him. So I put on my coat and second-best leather shoes, which I had sprayed the night before with waterproof sealant. (I didn't own any northern-winter boots.) Together we edged our way along the icy sidewalks. He wanted to point out houses in the neighborhood, the real beauties.

The place we were staying in was only rented, from a retired midlevel General Motors executive. A good guy, Robert said, who believed in the city and had lived in it his whole working career. But even he had had enough and took early retirement to justify a move to the country. Besides, his girls were already out of college; one was married.

Robert wanted to buy the house from him. He thought if the Detroit plan worked out this kind of high-end real estate would shoot up in price.

"You can't help making money," I said. "Can you?"

"I hope not." This was an example of his humor—not so much funny as hard to read.

Later he delivered one of his prepared speeches. The reason I brought you in on this, he said, is not just because it was your idea in the first place. "I wanted a historian on hand, in case this thing takes off. I want you to write about it."

There were plenty of journalists around, interviewing him and Clay and covering the story for newspapers and magazines. Smart guys, some of them, but they weren't *his* guys; also, it wasn't their job to take the long view. Then he spoke about my academic specialty, American colonial history—he'd been reading up on that, too. It's an obvious point, he said, but what people forget about the early settlers is that they were shipped over by private companies; it was a business venture. A typical Robert James pronouncement, vaguely general and matter-of-fact. He believed that what we were doing in Detroit belonged to the same tradition.

I said, "It means a lot for me to be here. I was going out of my mind in Baton Rouge."

"You're one of those crazy guys who isn't meant to be alone," Robert told me, tapping the code into the front gate.

That afternoon he flew to Boston, and from there he went on to Geneva and then Hong Kong. A few weeks later I got a peek at his Detroit diary, which Beatrice was in charge of. Flipping through the pages I caught sight of my name. "Take a walk with Marny after breakfast," it said, under the date.

But even at the time I felt stage-managed. I had opened up to him, in confidence, and he had taken advantage of my confession to give me his opinion. So now I was stuck with it. You don't often get a sense of what people think of you. And the worst thing about sexual loneliness is that you have no practical and tedious duties and arguments to occupy the hamster wheels in your brain. So this kind of thing goes around and around.

TONY LIKED TO SNARK ABOUT Clay and Robert James and the rest, the whole setup. He showed me around Detroit, starting with the big art deco towers downtown—arched halls, mosaics on the walls and floors, gold leaf. It was like walking around the pyramids, they were monuments, not offices, half dead, except for the tourists, and even the ugly new buildings surrounding them had SPACE FOR RENT signs hanging from the thirtieth-floor windows. You could park downtown, there was plenty of room, and every time a People Mover, one of those funny sky trains, passed overhead, Tony pointed and shouted and tried to see if there was anyone in it.

"This was a fucking great city," he said, "when LA was just a small town. And the only thing left is four lousy ball clubs."

We broke into Michigan Central Station together, which reminded me of Sterling Library at Yale. Gravestone architecture, a tall narrow gray slab. Except instead of books it was full of broken glass, wires, loose stones, graffiti, cigarette butts and beer bottles. Like most abandoned places it showed funny intimate signs of habitation: underpants, a can of shaving foam. I cut my hand on the chain-link fence surrounding it and for weeks afterwards had to resist scratching the scab. We went round the ballparks and the fine arts museum and wandered through the asbestos-lined hallways of an old factory, where the radiators seethed and dripped. Artists had taken over the place and filled it with bad watercolors and large lumpy ceramics. We ate Polish food in Hamtramck.

The house itself was full of journalists, politicians, lawyers, academics and other hangers-on. A documentary crew filmed many of our meetings and sometimes followed us around the city in several cars, recording. Clay Greene was going to present. You couldn't tell how old he was, that was part of his appeal. Clay was one of these smooth-skinned good-looking guys who might be prematurely gray or well preserved. This was his first venture into TV, which accounted for some of his personal vanity. The mirrors around him were multiplying, and when he opened his mouth the tape recorder clicked on.

Sometimes, after dinner, we watched the outtakes in Robert's home cinema. There was Clay on the wall, spread out on a flat white roll of screen, and Clay sitting beside me, and both of them were talking, explaining.

Detroit seemed to him a textbook case of the need for private-public partnerships. Most people assumed that the failure of state and market forces meant that Detroit itself was doomed. Urban studies theorists like Richard Florida suggested abandoning the Rust Belt altogether. But Clay believed that a highly directed combination of the two could solve many of its problems. He was very interested in China. The Chinese had been trying to combine free market capitalism with democratic centralism for several years, and had managed to regenerate a number of cities in much worse shape than Detroit. Of course, the government took on a lot of short-term debt. You needed someone willing to play God, or king.

This, as Clay liked to say, was Robert's job.

He had a dry, cordial host-at-a-cocktail-party TV manner, which wasn't entirely humorless. Let me introduce you to a few ideas, very dear friends of mine.

"This city," he said, posing for the cameras in front of Michigan Central Station, in his tasseled loafers and holding lightly onto his linen tie, to keep the wind from blowing it in his face, "lies at the center of so much of what America is talking about and worrying about today: the death of the middle class and the rise of social inequality, the collapse of the real estate market and the decline of manufacturing, the failure of the American labor movement and the entrenchment, almost fifty years after Martin Luther King led the March on Washington for Jobs and Freedom, of a black underclass. Detroit at its peak had a population of almost two million people—it is now roughly a third of that, which means, let me put it this way, that for every family still living here, their neighbors on either side of them have moved away. And their houses—you can see this for yourself because we're going to show them to you—sit either empty or boarded up, or half burned down, or they've been destroyed altogether, and grass and trees are growing in their place. What we are about to witness is a small experiment in regeneration—an attempt to repopulate these neighborhoods, to rebuild these houses, to revive these communities. It is, by its nature, a very local solution to some of the deeper and broader problems America faces today. But if you can fix it here, you can fix it anywhere."

In practice what all this meant is that Robert and a consortium of investors were buying up a section of the city—about two thousand houses, six hundred acres' worth of empty plots and a handful of derelict industrial sites. A few hundred homeowners refused to sell. Even a landgrab like this was small potatoes compared to the scale of the problem. Part of what's wrong with Detroit is that it's too big. Physically, I mean. Almost 140 square miles big. So five square miles don't add up to much. At best Robert hoped to add ten thousand economically active residents to a city that had lost almost a million in the last forty years. Which is why the business model needed to be profitable, so that it could be reproduced in Cleveland, Buffalo, Erie, Milwaukee, East Baltimore, etc.

The consortium planned to rent out the houses, business units, and land very cheaply, not just to individuals but also to groups of people who would organize themselves over the Internet and put in bids. Starting-from-Scratch-in-America was the name of the site— it showed houses and plots of land like an airline check-in chart. Of course, part of what he was selling was just the organizational tools. People who wanted to start over might hesitate to go it alone. But if they stayed long enough, and the neighborhood went up, they also got a share of the profit. That was the other part of the deal, a right-to-buy scheme.

Robert worried that no one would bite, but in fact Beatrice kept having to add capacity to the server. At its peak, Starting-from-Scratch-in-America received a hundred thousand fresh hits a day, from all around the world. Mayor Bloomberg in New York had just suggested opening up Detroit to international immigration. Robert had his lawyers talking to the ICE as well. A bid was "full" when every house and plot in a particular neighborhood had been spoken for by the members of a group. This is when it came to us in committee.

In other words, we sat around all day looking at Facebook, deciding who would get to join our village. Like a bunch of assholes, as Tony kept reminding us. There were Beatrice and Tony, Clay Greene and me, Robert himself sometimes, Johnny Mkieze and Bill Russo. Johnny was living in Grosse Pointe, three blocks away from his childhood home, having followed his father into a job at GM. Bill was just then running for reelection to the Michigan House of Representatives. His district happened to include the section of east Detroit that his old college buddy had been buying up. Robert gave a lot of money to the campaign. It was all very cozy.

But Robert also brought in a team of consultants, specialists in urban renewal, and the truth is, they called most of the shots. I remember a black woman named Barbara—Barbara Stamford from Stanford, this is how she introduced herself, one of these women who jogs eight miles a day and lives off cottage cheese. She wore cheerful bright-rimmed Prada glasses. I asked her once what got her interested in Detroit, and she said her work at Stanford was on "optimal inefficiencies." Efficient economies need to adapt instantaneously to changes in the market, in technology, but there's a measurable human cost to all this. People don't want to adapt all the time, they want to not adapt. What economists do is put a value on everything; you can calculate the cost of adaptation, too, and what she liked to think about was the optimal rate of change. Not too slow, not too fast. Detroit was like a poster child for getting it wrong. But I could tell she was talking down to me.

Once or twice a week we met up in the big dining room, with printouts and laptops cluttering the table. Sometimes I came straight from the house, with the leathery smell of gardening gloves on my hands and paint scabs spotting my hair and pants. The contrast made a deep impression on me, and maybe explains why from the beginning of this whole business, I felt like an outsider.

8

Meanwhile, the weather improved. Baton Rouge doesn't make much of spring, but over the Detroit sidewalks trees bloomed and lawns, pushing off the snow, broke out in daffodils. On Robert's block gardeners in dirty overalls produced expensive and colorful displays of hydrangea, lilac and rose. But even in the overgrown yards of burned-down houses bindweed and dandelions blossomed.

Robert and I went running sometimes on Belle Isle Park, along the river, where the wind was cold but not bitter. A skyline view of Detroit, as clean as you like, stood up straight-backed on the far shore. There were cold blue days busy with clouds and hot white afternoons and gray mornings where the rain came down as hard as if it fell off a roof. But Robert didn't care what the weather was. He liked to get out of the house and ask me questions about what was going on inside it. Also, he thought I spent too much time with Tony Carnesecca. In his hard-to-read conscientious way, which was partly ironic, he said, "Tony's a bad influence. Has he given you any books to read yet? This is the kind of thing he does."

"Yes."

"What?"

"You know, more than one. *Cultural Amnesia*, by a guy called Clive James. *The Confessions of St. Augustine*."

This was true. Tony wanted to raise his kid a Catholic, like he was raised. He planned to give his son everything he himself had as a boy, including some of the misery. Both my parents are Catholic, though my dad gave it up in college, without a second thought. Like you give up mowing the lawn when you move out of home. And my mom found it hard to persist with after they started going out, which she sometimes reproached him for. Tony took her side and kept bugging me to show my face some Sunday morning at St. Barnabas, one of those bungalow-type churches with a sloped roof and yellow-brick front. He pointed it out to me once, from the car. He promised to pay for my pancake breakfast if I went, at the IHOP in Roseville, which is where he always took his wife and kid. But I'd resisted.

Maybe Robert had some Scot Calvinist beef against all this, or maybe he just felt left out. Tony and I had developed a manner, as boy roommates do in college, which was quick, abusive, satisfying and hard to butt into, for an outsider. When he didn't feel like writing he picked me up in his Buick LeSabre and we drove around. Sometimes we drove back to his house in East-pointe, where I met his wife. She was four or five inches taller than Tony and an unusually beautiful and confident woman. Her dark hair and cheerful healthy color reminded me of the old Irish Spring soap commercials. Tony took a lot of sexual pride in her; he couldn't help showing her off. Her name was Cris, short for Cristina. Her parents on both sides were Italian American, and she regularly visited her grandfather who owned a bakery in Clarkston and spoke almost no English.

Cris herself used to be a lawyer, for one of the Big Three, which she hated. She gave it up to become a yoga instructor, which is how she met Tony—he had a bad neck. Motherhood for her was like an excuse to abandon all previous adult restraint, and even though her son was three years old, she still comfort-fed him when he asked for it. "I want booby milk," he said. Sometimes I had to avert my gaze while she picked up this big talky stir-crazy boy and held him on her lap, pulling back one side of her dress to spill a breast in his mouth. His feet almost reached the floor, and dangled. Her skin was the color of panna cotta. I thought Tony was the kind of guy who would mind if I looked. But I liked Cris—she didn't take him too seriously.

Tony was house-proud, too, and talked up his neighborhood to me, even if he blamed himself for leaving the city. His writer's block was connected in his mind to comfortable living. He didn't feel like himself in the suburbs, he felt like somebody else. The trouble was his natural feelings included a high percentage of racial rage and violent fear. Which were useful for work but less helpful to family life. He knew practically everybody on his block. Once, while preparing an omelet lunch for us, he ran out of eggs, so we knocked on a neighbor's door together—really Tony was just showing off. He couldn't help boasting about his happy-families kind of setup.

This neighbor was a retired cop whose wife had left him to move in with her parents in Florida. Their three daughters were all grown up and living out east. Her mother had diabetes and her father couldn't drive or count out pills or shop or cook or change the bedsheets because of forgetfulness issues. The diabetes was what tipped his wife over the edge, but in fact what this guy realized was that their whole marriage for her was just an interruption of her real life. (He told me all this while working his way through a six-pack of Labatts, which he brought over along with the six-pack of eggs when Tony invited him to lunch.) They married instead of going to college. He joined the force.

"I guess we were too young," he said.

And fifty years later she decided she wanted to spend her last days with these people, her parents, who she preferred to him anyway. He didn't even blame her particularly but he missed the kids. They never wanted to fly home to Detroit; they preferred Florida.

His name was Mel Hauser and Tony said, "Marny here is about to move into a house on Johanna Street. I thought maybe you could give him some advice."

"Does he have a gun?"

Mel wore a fishing vest and camouflage pants; his head was balding and grizzled, and even in this mostly smooth state not particularly clean. There were liver spots on it and scabs of dry skin. But his manner was straightforward and attractive.

I said, yes, I bought a shotgun from Walmart, on the drive up from Baton Rouge.

"Don't let the first time you fire it be the first time you need it. Have you played around with it any?"

"No."

"I tell you what. Sometimes I hang out at the academy on Linwood Street. A lot of retired cops still use the canteen. There's a shooting range there, and if you want, I'll book you in. Where do you keep it? Have you got a license?"

"In my car. No."

"I can help you out with that, too."

Then Cris came in with the kid half asleep in her arms. He'd conked out on the drive back from Clarkston, and she carried him into his room and fussed around noisily in the dark to get him down for his nap. The three of us listened to her singing for a while—her voice had been trained by ten years of Catholic school. I guess she knew we could hear her. Eventually Mel said, "All right, all right," and pushed himself up with his hands on his knees and walked out, taking with him the rest of the six-pack. Afterwards Tony gave me a ride back into the city.

"Mel's okay," Tony said, "and I'll tell you something you don't want to hear. The reason our neighborhood works is that everyone's white. Except for Raymond Chu, who happens to be our family doctor, and Amit Patel. Amit went to Michigan and works at the Chrysler design lab. Both are middle-class professional types. These are the people who are taking over our block. Mel's old-school Eastpointe, but the reason he doesn't mind is because of guys like me, working-class white guys who moved up in the world, and because guys like Amit and Raymond have to fit in with everyone else and not the other way around. You can't be a cop in this city for as long as Mel was and not pick up some racial information. And don't expect me to say that some of my best friends are black. My best friends *aren't* black, and there's a reason for that. I know some brothers, and like a few, too, but there's a point beyond which I don't really understand or trust them, and to be honest, the black guys I respect are the ones who feel the same way about me."

"I don't know why you're telling me all this," I said.

"How many black kids grew up on your street in Baton Rouge?"

"You know the answer to that."

"I want you to realize what you're getting into. Detroit is a black city. They don't want you living there."

I GOT MY FIRST REAL taste of this fact a week later, just a couple of days before moving into Johanna Street. I wanted to spend a night in the house before Walter came down, just to prove that I could. This was around the turning corner of May/June. The weather was cool and sunny, with tall clear skies, good roofing weather, and

I spent that last week in work boots and overalls, supervising the Mexicans I brought in at the last minute to help me finish the job.

The Mexicans probably need some explanation. By this point Robert had signed off on the first group of bidders, a network of Latinos, spanning classes and generations and even nationalities. There were families waiting over in Windsor for their visas to come through and lots of back-and-forth traffic across the water. (Canada was softer on immigration.) Part of the deal Robert struck with these people had to do with the fact that they promised to bring skilled labor to the project—painters, carpenters, contractors, electricians, plumbers, roofers and gardeners, who offered to help out on other sites when they could. Their own neighborhood was about twenty blocks north of Johanna Street, towards Hamtramck, and you could hear the sounds of hammer, mower and drill as far as Gratiot. Anyway, a bunch of these guys showed up to lend me a hand.

I met Hector Cantu, who put their bid together, a short, baby-faced dude with thick black hair cut in a Ken-doll perfect haircut. He was maybe forty years old and had left a pretty good job at J. P. Morgan to set all this up. His people worked hard and gave us time to talk together. There was a Spartan grocery store about five blocks away, run by some Iraqi guy, and we often walked over together to bring back coffee and hot dogs for the men. Hector was a good organizer, planner and fund-raiser, but the kind of work he was good at wasn't the kind that dirtied your hands. So I kept him company some, and we watched his buddies sweat.

They laid roof tiles and bathroom tiles and plumbed the kitchen to fit a dishwasher. They laid down grass. They painted the outside walls, where I couldn't reach, in white and green. They rewired the living room and fixed the connection to the Detroit grid, which involved shutting down the street for several hours while they dug up road. It occurred to me that none of this would have happened if Robert James weren't my particular pal. Sometimes Hector and I stopped at one of the few bars still open on East Vernor and had a beer. He was one of these confessional types, always in a good mood, and I heard a fair chunk of his life story.

What Hector wanted to talk about was New York, where he used to work about ninety, a hundred hours a week just to pay the rent on a one-bedroom apartment in Alphabet City. He ate out every night and got drunk on Saturday so he could sleep in Sunday and start the whole week up again on Monday morning, like some cranky old car.

All this was "about a million miles" from the world he came from. He grew up in Farmers Branch, Dallas County. His mother worked in a grocery, where she also cooked, and his father mowed rich men's yards. His whole life long he was this scared nerdy cat who hung around a bunch of crazy kids, mostly friends of his big sister and cousins and friends of cousins. They were better at having a good time than he was but put up with him anyway. Then he got a scholarship to Rice, where he minored in business studies because he wanted to be the guy "who paid my father to mow his lawn and not the guy on the John Deere." At one point a couple of years ago he realized that the only time he had any interaction with the kind of people he grew up with was when he ordered in and the restaurant sent somebody over with his bag of food.

Was he happy? He wasn't unhappy. He had a good job and money to spend on himself. He sent money home, too, and bought his father for his sixtieth birthday a 1987 Mercedes 190E, with wood-panel trim. His father liked messing around with engines on the weekend. Sometimes when he went to bars tall white girls paid attention to him because of the way he dressed. But there was nobody he thought, you could be a mother to somebody, "a mother like mine." And eventually he realized (this is what he told me), you have been blessed with many talents and gifts, and out of all this blessing and good luck, this is the life you have made. "This stupid life. That's what I felt. I wanted to start from scratch."

He had a disturbing habit of using language from Robert's website. People who talk a lot eventually run out of their own thoughts and phrases and have to borrow materials from other sources. Not that he cared. He was one of those people whose smile says nervously, Life is good. I realized soon enough that none of his Mexican buddies respected him. They liked him okay but thought he had his head up his ass or in the clouds. The jobs they sent us on were the kind we couldn't fuck up, like buying hot dogs.

When Angelo, one of the electricians, had to shut off the electricity on the street, he told me and Hector to explain what was happening to the neighbors. So we walked down the road together, knocking on doors.

Already a few people had started to move in. A guy called Eddie Blyleven who used to work in insurance, an ex-jock, blond-haired, recently divorced, whose daughter came at weekends. There were a couple of single dads, in fact, with weekend kids. Steve Zipp had a six-month-old baby, his first. He looked about forty-five, a nervous, badly dressed, pale, black-haired midwesterner. His shirt collars were too big around his neck, he wore cheap suits, but I'll get to his story later.

There was a house at the end of the block where a family of holdouts lived, a mother and son, and Hector knocked on their door and the son came out.

"Yes?" he said. He had kind of a faggy accent, but he was a big black guy, built like a linebacker, with muddy-looking skin and lots of little pigtails of kinky hair hanging down to his shoulders. Maybe he was thirty-five years old—some of the muscles were turning to fat.

"This is just a courtesy call," Hector told him. "We got to shut off the electricity for a couple of hours. I wanted to let you know."

"The fuck you do." A dog came out between his knees, a brown-faced pit bull, and the man took hold of his collar.

"Look," Hector said. "I should have introduced myself first. Hector Cantu—I live about thirty blocks up Van Dyke from here. My guys are just helping out a friend. This is Marny."

"Nolan Smith," he said but didn't shake our hands.

At this point the mailman came up the steps behind us. A big old guy with the kind of black skin that changes color around the eyes, like a sink around the drain. He handed Nolan a few bills and patted the dog.

"Mrs. Smith doing all right?" he said.

"Not too bad."

"We got off on the wrong foot," Hector said, when the mailman had gone.

"If you want to talk to a more mannerly person, you can talk to my mother." There was a cardboard box on the front porch, with the label peeling, and Nolan reached inside it to pick up a handful of dry food, which he dropped in a bowl by the door. The dog went over to eat. "But she's asleep."

"We don't want to wake her. We just wanted to let you know."

"If you wake her, I'll set my dog on you. Get you some water, Buster."

He clattered through the screen door with the water bowl. Hector and I waited on the porch while the dog ate, moving his jaws like dogs do, partly chewing and partly just catching the pieces of food in his teeth.

"Buster," I said to Hector.

Then Nolan came out again with fresh water and set the bowl down. "This is what's going to happen," he said. "If you need to shut down the street, you may do so at my convenience. Now is not a convenient time for me."

Hector said, "I got a permit here. I don't need to ask you. I'm just letting you know."

"If you shut it down," Nolan told him, "I will personally come by your house with a baseball bat and break windows."

We stared at each other for a minute on the front porch. It was a fresh sunny afternoon. There wasn't much traffic around but up and down the street you could hear the sound of people working with their hands; in its own way, quite pleasant. A spring sound. Nolan said, "You think I'm angry. I am not angry. This is how I talk."

"Look," I said. "I'm the one who's going to be your neighbor. Hector here's just helping out. I don't want any hard feelings."

"You are not understanding what I am saying. I don't have any feelings about you at all. Maybe you think I have some kind of Mexican thing against your friend. I don't. Maybe you think it bothered me that your representatives came by three four five six times to try to persuade me to persuade my mother to sell her house so that more white people could move in to the neighborhood. It didn't. If you want to move in here, that's your business. But if you interfere with my life I will interfere with yours."

"All right, okay. When would it be convenient for us to turn off the electricity?"

"I'll let you know," he said.

In the end, we waited all afternoon for the go-ahead. Angelo said he had other things to do, but in the morning, without asking me or telling anyone else, he shut down the street and reconnected the supply line running from my house to the mains. A few of his buddies stood in the yard with hammers, wrenches, shovels and tire irons, but nothing happened, and an hour later Angelo switched the lights back on.

9

That weekend Beatrice had arranged a launch party at Bill Russo's house on the shores of Lake St. Clair. A publicity stunt. There was a big barbecue on Saturday, with a band and a marquee, as the English call it. Basically a large tent. The idea was, so people moving in could meet a few representative members of "old" Detroit—community leader types, priests, schoolteachers, artists, businessmen. WDIV, the local NBC affiliate, had promised to send a van. The house was grand enough for some of Robert's "closer" friends to stay over, which included me, and Sunday afternoon was supposed to be a chance for us to hang out quietly before things got crazy. Robert's wife planned to fly in, with their son. Clay Greene was also bringing his family.

It's about an hour in the car from Detroit, and I drove up with Bill Russo and Johnny Mkieze and Beatrice, in Bill's old Cadillac, his father's car, a 1963 DeVille. Johnny and Beatrice squeezed in the back. I was kind of jealous of them, sitting on top of each other like that, with their legs pushed to the sides and their knees knocking. Johnny was a small guy, but physically strong and very dark-skinned—attractive to women. His accent was almost perfectly American, but he had a way of talking to women that no straight

American man could pull off, like he was one of them, but in a flirty way, too. He made them laugh.

I said to Beatrice, "You gotta have a woman up front," but she insisted: "You get carsick in the back." Which is true, I've got no stomach for tight spaces. So I said to Bill, "I guess you're stuck with me."

After five minutes, with the window down, I forgot about the two kids behind me, who couldn't hear us anyway with the noise from the road, and talked to Bill. Everyone seemed in a good mood. It was the first really warm day of the year, what I would call southern warm, where you don't have to worry about a little wind or shade. The air felt like an old towel fresh out of the dryer. I didn't know Bill very well though I'd known him for almost fifteen years. We had one of those funny relationships, intimate-flavored, kidding, natural, but also formal, polite and distantly friendly at the same time. There were basic facts about his life I was ignorant of, and vice versa. Like the fact that his sister was married to one of the producers of *One Tree Hill*, and lived in Hollywood, in Beverly Hills, in a house with a small Picasso in it.

"A small Picasso," Bill said again.

I was suddenly very happy to be there, with this young state rep, in a classy old car, driving out to some beachfront mansion, which he'd been going to since he wore diapers. It was great to hear him bitch about that Picasso.

In college I thought he was a spoilt little rich kid—one of those kids who compensates by digging latrines in Ecuador over summer vacation. But his friends were still private school friends and he wore his varsity wrestling jacket all over campus. Somehow, he hadn't changed but I didn't mind. It was also true that he spent his days doing good in the world, and rubbing shoulders with the kind of people I don't even like to shake hands with when they ask

me for change outside the lobbies of heated buildings. He visited
the Boys & Girls Clubs, talked to drug counselors (mostly reformed
addicts), pushed their case in the House, sometimes gave out of his
own pocket. Prison reform was his hobbyhorse. "People think I'm a
crazy fucking liberal, but I'm basically a practical guy. Most of those
bums deserve to rot in jail but it doesn't work. It just doesn't work."

He had passionate political feelings but also liked to chase
women and get drunk. Sometimes he used his political earnestness
to chat up girls—this was the sort of thing I used to dislike him for.
He missed doing "fun drugs," stuff like mushrooms, marijuana,
ecstasy and cocaine. We talked about all that in the car. In a couple
of years if he wanted to get serious about politics, he was going to
have to marry some nice girl. But not yet. You have no idea, he said
to me, what a turn-on it is, political power. I can get girls these days
who I couldn't even kiss without standing on a step. (He's about five
foot seven, a pink-faced, clean-shaven guy who still looks like the
boy next door.) The girls get turned on, aides, interns, secretaries
(never his own), he gets turned on, everybody gets turned on together, by his access to committee meetings and the governor's cell
phone number.

"I don't know why I'm telling you all this," he said. "I'll tell you
something else. There's a story that Matt Damon's coming tonight."

"What do you mean, a story?"

"Maybe Beatrice told me, I can't remember. My sister knows his
agent and Matt's in Detroit filming. I got my eye on him."

"For what?"

"To play me in a movie, what do you think. When I'm president."

After all this, the house, when we finally pulled up the drive,
turned out to be sweeter, smaller and quainter than I imagined.
Mud-gray shingles and crooked chimneys, with a screen porch at

the back. A couple of loose steps pointed down the garden path to the beach. His great-grandfather built it in 1913 when his shares in Ford Motor took off. He was one of the first people to pick this particular spot along the shoreline of Lake St. Clair. But the garden was large and beautifully, wildly kept, with rose hips and black-berry bushes, plum trees and tulips leading down to sandy grass. There was also a short rotting dock and a speedboat in the water.

Inside it was bigger than it looked, with lots of small bedrooms sharing bathrooms and corridors. From the bed my room had a view of the water, and I lay down and took a nap while people tramped around downstairs. I could hear men in the garden hammering in the stakes for the marquee. When I woke up it was maybe four o'clock, a very clear lakeside windy afternoon. I put on a jacket and tie and went out the back into the garden, where somebody in black tails handed me a champagne cocktail. There were maybe thirty people standing around; the women had to hold on to their hats.

The first person I recognized was Michael Carnesecca, Tony's kid. He hugged me around the knees and made me spill my drink. I like this kid; Cris let me give him a sip of what was left in the glass. He made a face and said "More," and then we played chase with the glass for a while—he jumped up and I held it out of his reach. He was a little violent; it got out of hand. At the same time I was looking around at the other guests, looking for Matt Damon, and Cris, misunderstanding me, said, "Go ahead, Marny, go find some pretty girl." But she had to pull him off me in the end, by force, and took him aside into the bushes to bawl him out—in un-dertones. It was the first time I saw her lose her temper.

So I refilled my glass at one of the white-clothed tables and ended up standing next to a woman with flowers, real flowers in her hat. Roses and petunias, I don't know. She was a ripe-colored black woman, almost eggplant-colored. Her lips were painted some glossy shade that made them look freshly licked. In her summer dress she stood the way a man stands in jeans—I could see her plump strong legs under the material. She was short, too, and looked about fifteen years old.

It was difficult to hear so we walked down towards the water, towards the sandy grass. The band was starting to set up by the back porch. Her name was Gloria Lambert and she taught art and computers at Kettridge High School—about five minutes by car from Johanna Street. In fact, she knew Johanna Street well. A good friend of hers lived on Johanna Street, and I started to laugh.

"I guess you met Nolan," she said.

"Yeah, I met him."

"His bark is worse than his bite."

"That doesn't mean he don't bite," I said, though why I said *don't* I don't know. "Is he a boyfriend of yours?"

"You ask questions. How many you think I got?"

"So how come you know him?"

"There's a program I run where local artists come in to talk to the kids."

"Is that what he is? So why did you get invited to this thing?"

"I won the Eliza Curtis Hubbard Memorial Award."

"Which is for what?"

"Teaching art. Let me ask you a question. This is what I don't understand. Those are some nice houses on Johanna Street, but what are you going to *do* when you get there?"

"I don't know. I'm drifting a bit right now."

"Well, what are you *good* for?" she said.

In the windy sunshine, everything looked very beautiful and real. Maybe I fell a little in love. I said to her, "You've got the most amazing skin I've ever seen on a human being. Do people say that to you?"

"White men. Usually they put it a little different."

I had just drunk two champagne cocktails on an empty stomach. There was a flagpole in the garden, about twenty feet high and made of painted wood. The paint was peeling but the Stars and Stripes hung out straight in the wind and sometimes dipped suddenly and folded over itself. That's how I felt all afternoon, coming and going.

Then someone said, "George," and pulled at my elbow. It was the German girl, Astrid, the hitchhiker, with a camera in her hand. She took my picture with Gloria, who afterwards moved away.

"How did you get here?"

"Your friend Robert likes blondes. Don't you remember, you sent me his email address?"

"What happened to Ernst?"

"He wanted to go, I wanted to stay."

This is how the afternoon went on. If I wanted to get out of a conversation, I said, "Have you seen Matt Damon? He's supposed to be here," and pretended to look for him. A video guy pushed his way through the crowd, with his face hidden by the machine. Whenever I saw him I carefully finished my sentences. There were speeches, too. Robert James said a few words; the wind made rough kissing noises and squeaks against the microphone. Bill Russo talked. "This is the house my great-grandfather built with money put in his pocket by the men who worked the line at the old Ford Motor factory in Highland Park." For maybe an hour, around six o'clock, I played quietly inside with some of the kids. Clay Greene had showed up with his two boys, and I met his wife, Helen, a very tall, handsome, likable, not at all graceful woman, who was trying to make macaroni and cheese. "There isn't any butter," she said. "Can you run to the shops to get butter?"

"There aren't any shops here. I'm too drunk to drive. I don't have a car."

Beatrice came in, looking for something, and saw Helen. The two big, good-looking women embraced, leaning over each other.

"I need to get a few things from the shops," Helen said. "Do you mind staying here with the boys? They're perfectly happy. I'll be back in a minute."

Beatrice said, "No, that's fine. Of course. Go."

"Are you sure? I can't face wrestling them into the car."

"Go."

So she went. One of the boys, the smaller one, started crying and going after his mother, so Beatrice with a certain rough familiarity picked him up in her arms. She was wearing a linen pants suit— working dress. The boy kicked and she dropped him and stood kind of flat-footed and unhappy while he cried.

"I'm no good with kids. These kids don't like me."

"They can hear you," I said.

"Fuck you, Marny," she said and walked out.

So I got some pots and wooden spoons from the kitchen and sat down on the floor, banging them together. The older one was reading books. After a while, they both got bored and tried to go into the garden, but I reached the door in time and shut it. The small one started to cry again and Clay Greene came in with Peggy James, Robert's wife. She had a baby wrapped around her middle in a kind of cloth.

Clay said, "Quiet, son, you'll wake the baby."

"He won't," Peggy said, "and anyway, it doesn't matter." She was pretty, too, less handsome than Clay's wife but more attractive and noticeably younger than us. She had a button nose and very expressive mouth—big clean healthy gums that kept her mouth open and smiling. Also, she was skinny as a boy, even after childbirth, and wore shorts, because of the hot weather, and her legs were tanned and smooth and strong and thin. She wore pull-up stripy sports socks and sneakers. She was like a sexy kid sister. Everything was okay with her, and when Helen Greene came back Peggy woke up her baby to give Helen a cuddle.

"You look fantastic," Helen said. "God, how do you do it. I bet you even get some sleep." And I went outside to find another drink.

The band was a sort of Supremes look-alike act, but shorter, older and fatter, and with bigger hair. They played an afternoon set and an evening set. Around seven o'clock the first bus arrived, to take the guests with kids back to Detroit. Then the lights came on, in strings, hung across branches and bushes and the undercarriage rope work of the marquee. Another round of champagne made its way among us, in bright groups, on the waiters' trays. Astrid and I went walking into the trees, glasses in hand.

"I've had a very bad time," she said. "It's only beginning to get better."

"What happened?"

"I don't want to talk. I talk about it too much."

We started making out a little. There was another wooden jetty farther along the shore, mostly hidden by reeds, which kids probably used for diving off. We sat on the wet wooden boards at the end, letting our legs hang and kissing, which isn't easy. I had a crick in my neck. Eventually she said, "I should tell you, I'm in a project at the moment where I'm filming everything, about me and my life here. So even if we end up going to bed together I want to film it. I don't know if you are comfortable with that."

"But you're not filming this now."

"I'm not stupid. Everything isn't possible."

"Where are you staying tonight?"

"I don't need to stay with you, if that's what you mean." Then: "Do you want to go swimming?"

"It's too cold for me."

A few minutes later we stood up (the seat of my pants had gotten wet) and walked back to the party. I kept looking out for Gloria but couldn't find her. I had never kissed a black girl and wondered if they tasted different. But maybe she had caught the seven o'clock bus. I had another drink. There were things to eat, too, but I wasn't hungry and had a kind of surging important feeling that it was possible to be more simple and honest with people than I usually was. I could say to Gloria, I want to kiss you and I could also admit that I had never kissed a black girl. Astrid was very honest, and even though she was also pretentious and I didn't like her much, I admired her for it. She was very pretty anyway. I hadn't had sex since coming back to America, over a year ago. The way all this frustration built up inside me is to make me think, nobody is very kind to me, and nobody knows me well, either. But I couldn't find Gloria, she had probably caught that bus. Beatrice walked past me, almost pushed past me, with a red face. I said, "Hey!"

"I need the bathroom," she said.

"I want to talk to you."

"You can watch me pee."

So I followed her inside (she was using the house toilet, not one of the porta-potties lined up by the air-conditioning units) and stood by the door. I could hear the loud stream against the porcelain and water, then it stopped and I could hear the contact of the toilet paper. She came out with wet hands.

"What do you want to talk about?"

"I'm worried about you."

"I'm worried about me, too. I'm worried about you."

I tried to kiss her and she pushed me off. We stood looking at each other, combatively. Good-naturedly, too. It was kind of fun, like playing squash and wanting to win. I tried to kiss her again and this time she let me and we kissed for maybe a minute before she pulled away.

"Marny," she said, "please, don't force it," and walked out into the garden again. Eventually I followed her, feeling pretty tremendously sad and drunk.

There were maybe fifty people still standing around, under the lights, though the second bus idled in the narrow roadway at the front of the house. I could hear it, and see it through the trees: "RedLine Motor Company, You're Halfway There." But the band sang "I'm Gonna Make You Love Me," and the microphone magnification made it sound like it was coming from somewhere else. Maybe the shore. The wind had died down; the night was clear, not very hot. The stars looked about as far away as the lights of a house across a lake.

I hadn't talked to Robert James all night, but I'd seen him. His wristwatch strap had broken, so whenever he wanted to check the time he had to take the watch out of his pocket and hold it softly in his hands. For some reason this was very endearing. But I caught him now alone, looking at a broken champagne flute in the grass.

"You wondering if you should pick it up?" I said.

"I don't want anyone to step on it. One of the kids, tomorrow morning."

"It's starting to get messy, isn't it?"

"What?" he said, and I waved behind us at the party. There were people dancing on the plastic parquet laid down under the marquee, but not many. Maybe five or six couples. There were also a few tables scattered underneath and people sitting around those. A queue outside one of the porta-potties—the other one had overflowed.

"You want to walk down to the water with me?" Robert said. "How are you doing anyway?" We reached the foot of the pier and stepped out onto it, and then Robert climbed down suddenly into the speedboat. "Don't worry," he said. "I'm not going to turn it on. I just want to feel the water."

"I'm thirty-four years old. I have no job or wife or kids or girl-friend. For some reason I've moved here, on your dime."

"Don't worry about that. I got a lot of dimes."

"I don't know, Robert. I'm having anxiety-sadness."

"What's that?"

"There's a hundred things I'm worried about, but what really worries me is that even if they all turned out okay I wouldn't be any happier."

"I'm a little caught up in temporary concerns myself," Robert said.

"What kind of concerns?"

He didn't answer for a while. Even in the half-light coming from the garden and reflected in different ways off the water I could see he was a very good-looking guy. Without making any particular effort. He wore chinos and a shirt and no tie. But he looked com-fortable in boats and like the kind of guy a woman could trust to pay for their kids' private schooling. "You know," he said eventually, "my father, before he died, started exposing himself. Mostly to his nurses, young women."

"I didn't know he was dead. I'm sorry."

"Partly it was just one of these mental degenerative things. Alz-heimer's, whatever you want to call it. And nobody got hurt. He wasn't threatening or anything. But it was like, all his life what he really wanted to do was take down his pants. And just show people, I don't know. You never met him or maybe this would mean some-thing to you. But when I was a kid, Jesus, this guy had all the an-swers."

"So he was old. He had a brain thing."

We sat there feeling the waves underneath us. "When was this?" I said.

"Maybe it started three years ago. He died last fall."

"So what are these temporary concerns?"

But he was done talking. "They're not important. They'll go away."

After a while he got out and I followed him (I kept following people) and we walked back up the faint slope into the garden.

"Listen," I said, taking his arm, "I just want to say good-bye to someone," because I had seen Gloria in the line of people making their way onto the bus. She was standing and waiting her turn.

"You going?" I said to her. "I want to talk to you. I've thought of a better answer to your question."

"I can't even remember it anymore. I don't remember your name."

"Marny," I said. "Can I give you a call?"

"You're drunk. If you can remember it you can call me."

And she told me her number and got on the bus. For several minutes I wandered around in a daze, repeating it, until I found a pencil in the kitchen and wrote the numbers down on the back of a *Sports Illustrated* subscription card, which was lying by the telephone. When I came out again Tony Carnesecca was standing in the porch light.

"What the fuck are you doing?" he said. "You were mumbling like a crazy man. Anyway, there's something I want to tell you. Cris is pregnant."

"That's terrific."

"She wanted me to explain why Michael's been acting up. She's weaning him. They've all gone to bed."

"That's terrific," I said again. "I think I'm gonna go to bed, too."

I felt a little sick, walking up the stairs, but then I saw a light un-

der Beatrice's door and knocked. She had the room next to mine—
we shared a bathroom. When there wasn't any answer I got undressed and went for a piss, but after brushing my teeth I couldn't
help myself, and knocked again on the bathroom door.

"What is it, Marny?" she said. "What do you want."

"I want to come in."

"I'm trying to go to sleep."

"Why can't you sleep? I don't want to be alone."

"Just come in for Christ's sake and stop shouting. It isn't locked."

So I went in. She was lying in bed with her hair spread out
against the pillow. The bedside lamp put half her face in shadow.
Her skin in the light looked tired. I thought, she's thirty-four years
old.

"What do you want?" she said.

"What were you doing?"

"Nothing, staring. I forgot my book."

"I want to sleep here."

"What are you, twelve."

I felt weird standing there in my pajamas while she lay flat on
her back, covered in bedclothes. I said, "I don't think you're very
happy either."

"I don't want to have one of your talks. I'm not in the mood. I
don't want to explain anything about myself and I don't want to
hear your explanations either."

"Beatrice, this is what I'm like. You used to like me. You used to
like me for being like this. So I like to talk. Sometimes I don't even
know if other people have intimate conversations with themselves
in their own heads or if what they talk about to themselves is the
same shit they talk about to me. What time their babies wake up
and how much their fucking kitchen is going to cost. For example,
I have no idea what you talk about to yourself. No idea. If that's just

adult life, count me out. There are things that became very clear to me tonight."

She didn't say anything so I went on. "I used to be in love with you. You probably know that but I thought I should tell you anyway."

"God, Marny. Is this how you talk a woman into bed?"

Suddenly she seemed in a good mood, she looked cheered up. "Come here," she said and I sat down next to her. "You can lie down if you want to. I'm not going to sleep with you, but you can lie down here if you want."

So, feeling dutiful, I climbed under the sheets beside her and lay on my back. Beatrice rolled over and switched off the bedside lamp.

"Come here," she said, rolling back, and held me. Her eyes looked right into mine, too close for me to see her properly. She kissed me on the face a little and then kissed my mouth. I kissed her back, trying not to kiss too hard.

"You're going to be okay. We're all going to be okay. Anyway, I'm not unhappy, just in the dumps. There's a difference."

"What's the difference."

"The dumps doesn't matter."

"Was it seeing his wife?"

"I've seen his wife before."

"But is that what it was?"

"I don't know," she said, and turned over again on her back. Then she said, "I don't mind if you stay all night, but I want to sleep."

I don't think she fell asleep right away, she couldn't have, but I didn't get another word out of her. I just lay there, not moving. I didn't want her to kick me out. This funny phrase came into my head: *you must be so happy*. I meant me. But the truth is, I couldn't sleep at all like that and the night stretched ahead. I got that feeling

I sometimes got as a kid of looking at myself through the wrong end of a telescope. Eventually she started breathing softly, one breath after another, and the fact that this big warm female animal, almost six feet big, was lying next to me and not wearing much started to take effect. An erection climbed up my pajama pants and wouldn't go away. I don't know how long I lay there, not sleeping—several hours. Sometimes my erection went down a little, but this made it touch my thigh so it came back up. Jesus, I wanted to rub it against her like a dog. But I also wanted to show her, Look what I got, what am I supposed to do with it. All kinds of crazy thoughts came and went. I thought about Robert's dad. I thought about Gandhi. I read once that he liked to sleep naked with naked girls, to test his chastity. And it occurred to me that all this sexual pressure, which had been building up all day, and not just all day but for months and years it seemed, wasn't building towards anything. It was just there and maybe what you did was learn to ignore it. I don't know how to put this without seeming crazy, but I started to have kind of saintly fantasies, I mean fantasies about a life of chastity and repression and so on, and this was the first test of it. I was doing okay. If you can get through tonight you're going to be okay, you might make it through to the other side of all that stuff.

Eventually I tried to sneak out of bed and she half woke up.

"Are you going, Marny?" she said and pulled at me a little so that she could kiss me. Her breath was warm, almost hot. "I'm sorry," she said, "I'm sorry," and let me go.

10

The next morning was Sunday. After church, Bill Russo planned to put on a caucus brunch for some of the big donors. (Russ is what Bill Russo's MDP friends called him, and since they knew him better than I did, I started calling him Russ, too. And then stopped.) Apparently these donor types like to meet each other, and the Michigan set wanted to rub shoulders with Robert James. After that some quiet time was scheduled. Maybe a ride in the speedboat and a little swim. Drinks on the sunporch, etc. But I'd had enough. Tony Carnesecca was driving back early, with his wife and kid, so I asked him to give me a ride.

They'd had a bad night, sleeping three to a room, in two beds. Michael was just getting used to being out of the crib. He woke up scared around two in the morning and came in with them. So Tony got out. Then Cris tried to sneak out, too, and sleep with Tony, but Michael heard her and cried, so Tony tried to get him down but couldn't, and eventually they all ended up together again. Only Michael slept.

"I know what you mean," I said. "I'm tired, too."

Cris told me to sit in front. And then, after buckling Michael in and buckling herself, she said, "You were kind of quiet-drunk last night. Are you hung over?"

"I don't know. I think I talked too much."

I closed my eyes and pretended to sleep. When we hit the highway, I fell asleep properly and only woke up when Tony pulled into his drive. Michael was also asleep and Cris very slowly and carefully lifted him out. I felt for the kid. She laid him out gently in his stroller and started walking him around. "I'll just drive Marny home and come straight back," Tony said and pulled out again.

"I'm supposed to stay in Johanna Street tonight."

"What do you mean, supposed?"

"Well, Walter's coming up tomorrow and that's what I told myself I was going to do."

But he dropped me at Robert's place because I had to pack up. Which is how I spent the afternoon: going through the house and collecting my things, sometimes from other people's bedrooms. There wasn't much, a couple of boxes of household goods, a duffel of clothes, a few books and CDs, some of which I had loaned to other people. Even though no one was home I knocked on their doors.

In Beatrice's room I sat down on her bed, which was fully made up, and then took off my shoes and lay down on it. I was still very tired. I could smell her on my skin from the night before then realized it was only her sheets. The novel on the bedside table had a bookmark sticking out of it—a postcard from her mother, with a picture of Frank Sinatra on the front, smiling into a microphone.

The note itself was prettily legible, effusive in a faintly foreign way. "Darling, how wonderful it was to see you . . ." etc. and then I noticed the date: the twenty-ninth of November 1993—a few days after Thanksgiving break freshman year. This was several months before I met Beatrice coming out of seminar on the way to lunch.

We stood in the melting snow, talking and getting colder; I tried not to show it. But it was like a window had opened up and let in some of that cold air.

Eventually I got bored of lying there and went round the rest of the house. Robert's bedroom was surprisingly messy. There were clothes all over the bed, shirts, pants, socks, etc., probably from when he was packing his overnight bag. There were papers all over his desk, too, bills, printouts, and a letter from Clay Greene. Clay once explained to me why he still wrote letters. Every time I send an email, he said, I imagine cc'ing the editor of *The Washington Post*, because it isn't going to disappear and sooner or later somebody will find it.

His letter to Robert was mostly about a guy called Stanley Krause, who worked at Goldman Sachs. Goldman had invested a good deal of money in Robert's consortium, and they were interested in some of the warehouses and factory buildings Robert had been buying up, for their own use. Stanley wanted to make sure they "had their name down"—this was Clay's way of putting it. "It's worthwhile humoring these people," he went on. I wondered if this is what Robert meant by temporary concerns. But there was also a picture on his desk of Peggy and little Ethan, swinging together on a swing in Central Park, with the tall blurry fence of the reservoir behind them. They seemed likely candidates, too.

AROUND FOUR O'CLOCK I THREW my duffel in the passenger seat, put my boxes in the trunk, and drove the ten blocks south to Johanna Street.

Every time I came back to the house I looked for signs of a break-in, but it seemed in good shape. The paint job looked almost sticky. Shrubs poked out of the beds in the front yard and the grass had the blue-green underwater appearance of a first growth. I brought my stuff inside, up the porch steps then up the hallway staircase to the second floor. The first thing I did coming in was check the wall phone in the kitchen for a dial tone. It flatlined, so I dialed up Robert on his cell.

"Listen," I said, "are you still at Bill's? Because I forgot something by the phone, a number. It's on a subscription card."

There was a wait and footsteps while he carried his phone downstairs.

"When did you take off?" he said. "I thought you were sticking around."

"Tony gave me a ride home."

He started reading out the 800 listing.

"Not that," I said. "There should be something else, maybe on the other side. In ballpoint— Wait a minute, I gotta find something to write with."

This turned out to be not so easy. The place was totally unlived in, but there was still the usual mess of junk mail and utility bills on the kitchen counter. Nothing to write with, though. No dried-out felt-tip or uncapped Bic, no golf pencils. "Hold on, hold on," I called out, "listen, I'm going to have to call you back," before I realized I could type it into my computer, which is what I did. Afterwards I said, "This isn't really why I called. I wanted to say thank you. I'm in Johanna Street right now. I'm moving in. It looks great. My first grown-up apartment."

"Take care of yourself, Marny. I don't want to see you on the news."

"You guys having a good time? Have you been swimming?"

"It's very relaxed," he said. "We're all very relaxed."

After hanging up, I poured myself a glass of water from the kitchen tap. All the appliances were brand-new. Hector and one of his cousins, a kid named Ziggy, had driven me out in his truck to the Ikea in Canton. We came back with a bed, a sofa, a coffee table, plates, pots, glasses, knives, forks, plants, etc. Ziggy helped put it all together, he was a real helpful kid. One of these guys who takes over this kind of job if you let him. So I let him. But he liked talking, too. When they hear you're a teacher or used to teach, people sometimes open up to you, a lot of our important decisions and failures involve school. So he worked and I asked him questions.

Ziggy spent a couple of years at North Texas, where he majored in merchandising. Then one summer he got his high school girlfriend pregnant, ex-girlfriend really, and instead of going back to Denton he stayed in Galveston. By this point anyway he was thirty grand in debt and three semesters short of graduating. Three fucking semesters. She had a job at Payless ShoeSource, which she quit, and the manager was a friend of theirs so he took her place. That was two years ago. They were living at home with her mother, in a two-bedroom apartment, the baby was walking, there was plastic everywhere, Ziggy spent his whole life kicking things over and picking them up again. He started getting acid reflux, which sounds like no big deal, but after every meal he wanted to lie down in a dark room. It's this funny thing about pain, he said. You want to be alone with it, you don't want to move, you don't want to do anything except hang out with this pain.

It's all in your head, his girlfriend's mother said, which is stupid. She's somebody who doesn't agree with or believe in simple scientific facts, but it's true he was depressed. So when his cousin said, come to Detroit, he said, okay. His girlfriend was still in Galveston with their son, but he kept trying to persuade her. Every day he sent her pictures of the house on his phone; he was building a hot tub in the garden. But he took pride in my apartment, too. "We did a good job," he said.

For some reason the thought of Ziggy put tears in my eyes. I was still hungover, emotionally drained, but with my feelings very close to the surface. Ziggy seemed to like me, we were both starting over, and already I had entered into new relations with people—the kind of people I didn't use to know. You're doing okay, I thought, keep going. Then the doorbell rang, and I looked out the living room window to see who was there.

It was Eddie Blyleven from down the road and another guy I didn't recognize carrying a six-pack of Sierra Nevada. So I went downstairs to let them in, and we stood on the porch with the afternoon light in my eyes and on their hair.

"I guess you're moving in," Eddie said. "This is Kurt Stangel, one of your neighbors."

Kurt was about my age, but fatter—bigger and stronger all round, with a big flat face and thick neck. "Well, it's good to have another body on the street."

"What do you mean?"

He was wearing shorts with pockets on the thighs. I could hear his keys in the pocket and see the weight of his wallet dragging them down. He also had on a short-sleeved collared shirt, half buttoned up. Sunglasses hung across his chest, which was completely hairless. "These houses don't look after themselves," he said.

"Do you want to come in for a beer?" And then: "Is there anything you want me to do?"

"That's up to you," Eddie said. "Some of the guys have signed up to a system, where we go out in pairs and just drive around, keeping an eye on things. There are three shifts a night and not enough guys. But listen, this is your first night, get some sleep. We can talk all this over in the morning."

After they left I got in the car and went shopping, which means a five-mile drive each way in Detroit. There are no supermarkets in the city. When I came home with groceries it was about seven o'clock—the light had changed color and the shadow of the house cut a wedge of brown out of the green backyard. I could see the garden from the kitchen bar, where I sat down to eat a toasted English muffin with sliced cheese. The food did me good. I hadn't had a bite since breakfast.

Everything seemed too quiet, so I turned on the TV and sat on the couch, working my way through the Sierra Nevadas. I thought about calling Gloria. I wanted to confess something to her: I'm in a transitional state. There were things I said to you last night I shouldn't have said. But I'm getting through it, I'm coming through it, I'm getting out on the other side. It struck me I was maybe a little drunk. Around ten o'clock I undressed and pissed and brushed my teeth, then read in bed for a while without taking much in. It was a summer's night in Detroit, my window was open, and I could hear leaves and sometimes traffic from outside.

Switching the light off didn't make me sleepier, and eventually I got up to shut the window.

A few cars were parked in the road. There were lights on in one of the houses, and the street lamps spread a thick glare over the asphalt and curbside lawns. Someone had left a bag of garbage out and the dogs had got at it. Diapers and soda bottles lay in the grass. Then a low-riding Buick swung by, driving slowly—maybe Kurt and Eddie were inside it, doing the rounds. I stood there for several minutes, watching, waiting for the car to come back.

11

I had seen Walter Crenna maybe two or three times since leaving Yale. Once over Christmas break several years ago, when I hung out with Beatrice and Bill Russo at Walter's place in Washington Heights.

It was just good luck that I happened to be in town—because of the AHA conference. My supervisor at Oxford, who was chairing a panel, invited me to give a paper on it, so Aberystwyth paid my flight. I say good luck because Walter had been having a hard time. Bill heard about it first and recruited me and Beatrice to cheer him up.

"Or at least make sure he doesn't kill himself," Bill said. The three of us met at Penn Station and took the subway up together.

"Don't be melodramatic," I told him.

"Well, judge for yourself."

This is the story. After graduation, Walter lived at home for several years, helping out his mother. His father had Parkinson's and needed a lot of care, and Walter, who was very close to his father, made himself useful: driving him to his medical checkups, shopping and cooking. His mother needed to keep working for the sake of their health insurance—she taught English at a local private school. Walter was supposed to be writing a play or, failing that, studying for the GRE and applying to grad school. In fact, he mooched around the house all day, reading his high school yearbook, playing piano, picking up novels and putting them down again. Cooking elaborate meals and leaving the kitchen a mess for his mother when she got back from work. They argued a lot, Bill said. She was pushing him to do an MFA or find a job, but the closest he came to either was substituting sometimes at her school.

When his father died, she kicked him out. Bill knew Mrs. Crenna fairly well. She even called him at the time to ask his advice.

"What did you tell her?" I said.

"I didn't tell her anything, I listened."

"What did she do?"

"She called in a favor with a friend of hers at Dalton. Anyway, he ended up getting a part-time job helping out in the theater program. Teaching a couple of classes, putting on shows. So Walter moved to New York—she found him an apartment, too. For these reasons, and a few others I won't go into, she blames herself for what happened. I had her on the phone last week in tears. Go see him, she said, he doesn't want to see me. He's ashamed. Which is why I called you guys."

"So what happened?"

"You can guess. He got mixed up with one of the students. His job involved a lot of contact with students, which he liked; they liked him, too. Then he took things too far with one of them, and the parents got wind of it. For a while there was talk of a criminal prosecution, but I think that's died down. Anyway, he's lost his job and can't afford to keep up the rent and doesn't want to go home anymore to face his mother."

"How old was the kid?"

"Sixteen."

"A he-kid or she-kid?"

"I thought you'd ask that. Turns out he's into girls."

"So what did he sound like when you talked to him?"

"We haven't talked. He's not answering his phone. I only heard about what happened from his mother, who called me on Christmas Day. But we had an email exchange."

It was snowing when we came out of the station, new snow on top of old—snowing and almost windless. The flakes held up in the glare of the street lamps. Aberystwyth never gets very cold, and I had on only my ordinary winter jacket, a thin fleece from Gap. I was shivering badly by the time we got to Walter's place, a ten-block slippery march over half-cleared sidewalks. Beatrice, thinking maybe of our night on the clock tower, said, "I don't care why we're here, it's fun to be out with you guys again," and put her arms through each of ours. In her boots, she was taller than me; Bill came up to her ear. So we walked like that, the three of us in step, through the snow-muffled streets of Washington Heights.

Walter wasn't feeling the least bit tragic or ashamed. I could tell that much as soon as he opened the door. But he didn't look well, either. He looked heavier than in college, when he was already heavy enough; and in the heat of the apartment his face had a red sweaty shine. There was a smell of onions coming from the kitchen. "I'm making tomato sauce," he said, "excuse me," and came back a minute later with glasses and a bottle of wine.

His apartment was nicer than I thought it would be, but messy. The rooms had high ceilings; the windowsills were big enough for flowerpots. In fact, Walter had several green plants lined up on each, but since the radiators sat under the windows, their leaves had turned brittle and gray. There were leaves scattered on the floor. Most of the furniture seemed to be left over from his college dorm room. Bill had to sit on a beanbag and I pulled over the stool for his keyboard piano. Walter clearly wasn't used to entertaining, but there were several empty bottles boxed up by the front door, for recycling. We all got drunk before dinner, which he didn't serve till half past nine.

I thought we might have a hard time getting him to talk, but in fact all he wanted to do was talk about this girl. He was still in love with her. She was in love with him, and once she turned eighteen and became completely independent of her parents, they planned to move in together. At one point he stood up to look for some paper she'd written for him. "An extremely precocious piece of work," he said. But there were papers, newspapers and books everywhere. He couldn't find it, and this was the first time he showed any nerves or strain.

"Don't worry about it," Bill said. "I'll take your word for it."

"I'm not worried about it," Walter snapped. "It's just that I can't find anything these days. I spend all day in this apartment *losing things*."

What *did* worry him was money. Her parents were loaded, but he didn't expect or even want to take a cent off them, and his own mother was struggling just to help him keep up the rent on his apartment. Dying is expensive, he said. His dad had put a certain amount by, but most of it got used up in hospital and funeral expenses.

"There's not much I can do to make a living," Walter said. "As it happens, I'm an excellent high school teacher, but I might have a hard time getting a job."

A quiet joke, which reminded me of the guy I knew in college. But most of the time his irony deserted him. Beatrice started questioning him about this girl. Somewhere along the way she had lost her temper.

"What's she like?"

"That's what I've been trying to tell you."

"I mean, is she tall, blond, dark, what? Is she jocky or nerdy or preppy? What's she into?"

"I don't recognize her from any of those descriptions."

"You mean, you don't know her very well. You haven't been paying attention."

"I know her intimately."

"What's that supposed to mean? Did you sleep together?"

"I did not."

"Then what's the big deal about?"

"We did other things."

"You fingered her, she sucked you off, what?"

"I don't like thinking about any of this the way you describe it."

"But you don't mind doing it to a sixteen-year-old girl?"

"Honestly, when it comes to what you are talking about, she was enormously more experienced and mature than I was."

"I don't doubt that." And so on. When we finally sat down to eat, at a foldout table in the kitchen, Beatrice asked, "So what's her name?"

"Susie Grabel," he said, and for some reason we all laughed.

Dinner was better tempered, and once we got off the subject of Walter's delinquencies, we talked about what you'd expect us to talk about: our bright college days. But I preferred the other conversation, it seemed to matter more. Around midnight, with nothing decided on or resolved (no plan of action, I mean), we stood up to go.

"I'll give you a call next week," Bill said. "And this time, answer the phone."

"Yeah, yeah," Walter told him. Then he turned to me: "Are you having a gay time of it in England? We haven't talked about you all night."

"I'm okay," I said. "I'm ready to come back home. I miss you guys."

"Nobody's living at home," he said.

After that Walter and I communicated mostly by email. The last time I saw him in the flesh was our reunion. He had booked a room at Mory's for four o'clock on the Saturday afternoon. That gave us a couple of hours' drinking time and we could head over to the cocktail party in a big group. It was one of those paneled backrooms with a large table in the middle and too many high-backed chairs, so that you had to squeeze behind several of them just to sit down. For the first half hour Walter and I had the place to ourselves. That was fine with me—I wanted to hear his news.

At that point Susie Grabel was just finishing up her junior year at Oberlin College. Walter had moved out there to be near her. She lived on campus; he had a room in some professor's house about a five-minute walk away. He made a little extra cash by tutoring students in composition but still depended mostly on handouts from his mom.

None of this embarrassed him; he had become unembarrassable. There was something very likable about his straightforward and essentially disastrous infatuation with this girl. I wondered whether Susie ever felt torn between her new exciting undergraduate life and her relationship with an older man, who could have no part in it. But apparently Walter had been embraced by most of her friends. He went to the movies with them, sometimes driving small groups in his car to one of the strip mall cinemas dotting the highways outside of town. He went to their parties, too, and was particularly useful in being old enough to buy alcohol.

"I'm having a great time," he said. "I'm in the best shape of my life."

That was last summer. Susie was graduating in a couple of weeks and planned to teach summer school, but after that they needed somewhere to live. Something to do as well. Walter had persuaded her to come to Detroit—they wanted to set up a theater workshop for kids. His background was playwriting, and she could handle the music side of things. We were all going to live together. I had the upstairs apartment, which had its own door. The only shared space was the driveway, the front porch, and the entrance hall; they got the run of the garden. I had never met Susie.

SUNSHINE WOKE ME UP EARLY that first morning—I hadn't yet put up curtains. There were trees in the street, but they didn't cast much shade; the leaves just meant that the light on my bedroom floor seemed to move with the wind. It was the first time I had slept in my own bed, in my own empty home, in years, and I spent a large part of the morning going from room to room and enjoying the loneliness. But I was also glad to know it would end pretty soon; Walter was coming.

He pulled up around lunchtime, in a rusty red Ford F-150 pick-up truck with everything he owned tarped in and tied down by cords. I thought this was terrific. I helped him unpack and we had something to eat afterwards, standing at my kitchen counter, then walked around the neighborhood together.

Already about half the houses looked lived in, and there was work being done on most of the rest. Even though it was Monday afternoon, there were people gardening in their front yards, talking on porches, messing around with cars. A guy called Joe Silver had set up a grocery store in his downstairs living room. He made cakes and sandwiches, too, and served coffee in dime-store mugs, which he brewed himself, in one of those Italian coffeemakers that looks like a 1950s scooter. Since the weather was nice, blowy but sunny, people sat and ate on his front steps. Joe came round in an apron afterwards and took their money. There were also several sets of tables and chairs in his front yard, and people seemed to hang around all day, chipping away at their laptop computers.

Walter and I walked out past East Jefferson to see the water. I really was very glad to see him and had a kind of almost gay reaction to his physical presence, just the fact that he was there and talking to me, and not over the phone either, but with his body, too. He's a big guy and sweats easily, he has these childish meaty thick hands, and at one point he stopped suddenly without saying anything to tie his shoes, and this took him a minute, he wasn't very quick at it. I waited for him, then we walked on. There was a list of things in my head I wanted to tell him, things I wanted him to ask me about because I couldn't tell him otherwise, and of course he never asked me what I wanted him to. But probably he had the same feeling about me.

There's a park at the waterfront by the bridge, and we sat under one of the trees, with our backs against the trunk. The wind was strong enough that we ended up shuffling round to the other side of the tree, for shelter. But the temperature was somewhere in the eighties; the warm dry air was full of dust.

"Is your mother still giving you money?" I said.

"Not anymore. That's part of what this is about—I want to get clear of all that. When you accept people's money you have to listen to their opinions about you. The last time I went home, I was sitting around with nothing to do, and my mother said to me, why don't I ever hear you playing the piano? You used to play so beautifully. It just sits there all the time and doesn't get any use. We had this argument about it. I found myself taking the position that I was never particularly good at the piano and didn't have any more talent for that than for anything else, which is probably true. But then I thought, what are you doing, why are you having this argument with her. She's your mother. What do you care if she thinks you used to have talent. Let her think it. I'm still too caught up in all that stuff, it doesn't matter anymore."

"What stuff?"

"You know, the precocities of youth."

"I'm glad you're here. You've put me in a completely different frame of mind."

"Robert told me you were in bad shape."

"That's not quite right," I said. "I go through these swings, and right now I'm feeling everything pretty intensely. But that can be good, too. You look well." In fact, he looked like he always looked, tired and overweight, and pimply around the mouth and by the side of his nostrils. His sneakers were white and very dirty. We walked back against the sunset, and when we passed Joe Silver's place, people were helping him carry the tables inside. So we helped, too.

On Friday evening, Susie Grabel came up from Oberlin. We all had dinner together. She wasn't very pretty. Her hair was straight and brown, and she wore it very long, halfway down her back, like a girl who can't let go of her childhood. Her skin was about the color of fresh yogurt, her eyes were pale blue and nearsighted, but she had one of those wonderful voices or accents that sticks to all the words. She had a deep voice. The dress she wore that first night was like the ones my mother is wearing in photographs of me as a kid. Down to her ankles with a sort of beaded pattern. She asked us if we thought it was dangerous, and Walter said, "It depends who you talk to."

Walter and I had gone out a few nights before with Kurt Stangel and a couple of other guys. There were five of us in the car—three first-timers, including Walter and me. We were supposed to be learning the ropes. Kurt had said to us, "If anybody has a gun, bring it," so I sat in the back in the middle with the Remington between my legs. We drove around from midnight until four in the morning. Kurt has two kids, a boy four years old and a girl just six months, and one of the other guys had a ten-year-old daughter.

"It turns out," I said to Susie, "that your average middle-aged, middle-class American Caucasian has deep-seated fantasies about protecting his children by means of violence. I mean, he dreams of putting his life at risk for the sake of his kids, because that's all Kurt and this other guy, a trade magazine writer named Todd McConnell, wanted to talk about. What they would do if somebody broke into their house."

"Did anything happen?" Susie said. "While you were out?"

"Around two a.m. we stopped off at Kurt's place for coffee and doughnuts. That was probably the most exciting bit. I asked Kurt if he'd seen any action. He said that we were just the scare-them-away gang. Mostly it's kids looking for TVs. They don't want to get shot and they don't want to shoot anybody. They're still young. But he's chased a couple of cars around the block; nobody wants to get out of their cars. So far the organized crime has kept away—people aren't sure why. He thinks there were deals cut with the police department, you know, with some of the gangs, and kept asking me questions about how well do I know Robert James. We had a good time. I haven't been out like that," I said, "with a bunch of guys since I was sixteen years old, coming back from debate in my teacher's minivan."

Walter said, "Yeah, he held on to his gun like it was soft and furry."

"What does Kurt do?" Susie asked.

"What do you mean?"

"Well, you said that Todd McConnell wrote for trade magazines."

"Kurt doesn't do much. He used to work for Nike in PR and put away some money, but it's like a cult around there. He was sick of selling stuff. Selling is lying, he said. That's something else they talked about—Todd offered to get him some freelance work. Put him in touch with a couple of editors. Those two guys were sitting up front and the rest of us just listened to them like a bunch of kids. Kurt pretended to be insulted. That's not why he got out of public relations, he said. That's not why he moved here. They seemed to know each other well. His wife's a lawyer, but she lost her job last year, which Kurt says she didn't care much about because of the baby. For her first child she got two weeks' maternity leave and didn't want to go through that again."

"Where did they used to live?" Susie said.

"Chicago, I think."

"But what's he going to do?"

"I'm not sure he knows. In college he wanted to be an actor, and there's a movement afoot to get the film industry going in Detroit. A lot of tax breaks. He thinks that if he hangs around enough he might get called up as an extra."

"What about Todd's wife?"

"He's divorced."

"Is that why he moved here?"

"Partly, I guess. He was working for *AutoTrader* in Atlanta. But then he got divorced, and his wife moved back to Madison, where her parents live. Then *AutoTrader* let a bunch of people go and he was one of them. He figured Detroit was closer to Madison anyway, and he could live on the cheap and write freelance about the car industry."

"People's lives," Susie said.

ON SUNDAY NIGHT, WALTER AND I sat up late in his apartment, talking. Susie was on her way back to Oberlin. It's about two and a half hours in the car, around the western shoreline of Lake Erie. I told him I liked her a lot and asked him how he got up the nerve to make the first move. I mean, you must have been sweating bullets, I said. You always were a heavy-sweating guy.

Walter was very matter-of-fact about the whole thing. She came by during his office hour once to ask him to decipher something he'd written on one of her papers. She was an excellent student; he used to write a lot of commentary. Without thinking much about it, he said to her, I'm very happy to communicate with you about your work, but I'd prefer to do it by email or in the presence of other people. I find you personally attractive and that makes me uncomfortable; I don't want to make you uncomfortable, too. She blushed and didn't say much, and left shortly after. But then she came by during his office hour again a few days later, looking determined, and it turned out to be easier than he expected. Does this mean you're okay with what I admitted to you the other day? he said. And she said, yes, and he said, because I think you're a knockout.

She was by some distance the smartest kid in her class, he said. "Much smarter than me. I told her it's a pity you're set on music, because as a cellist you're only eager and hardworking. But she knows all that. She wants to teach."

The more time I spent with Walter, the more I admired him. In college he was kind of a snob, and shy, and still hung up on stuff most people didn't give a damn about—like cocktail recipes and hi-fi equipment. You needed to "get" Walter. But these days he was good at making friends. He used to go around the neighborhood helping people move house. If someone invited him for a drink, he said yes. He never seemed to be in any hurry; he never had anything more important to do. That counts for a lot. People liked him even if they didn't understand him.

Once I complimented him along these lines, and he said, "I don't have much vanity left."

"That doesn't sound like a very happy condition."

He made a funny sort of throwaway noise, the sound my father would make if you told him that a kid you knew in high school was pitching for a minor-league affiliate. Like, you don't say. Not caring much about it.

12

Robert started paying me three hundred bucks a week to run a newsletter, which was mostly online and ran advertisements for neighborhood businesses: a dating service, a goods exchange, that kind of thing. Every Friday I printed out a heap of copies and stacked them at Joe's and a few other places around town. There was a Your Stories section, in which I interviewed people and asked them why they moved to Detroit, and what they hoped their new life would be like, and so on. Robert wanted me to write a history of the whole business eventually, and this gave me an excuse to keep records and start nosing around. Each week I sat down with somebody new and it's wonderful what people will tell you if you ask them.

There was a couple from Grand Rapids who planned to start a school, Bert and Ingrid Wendelman. Their relationship had an interesting backstory—it was Bert's second marriage, and she was about fifteen years younger than him, one of these blond red-faced Dutch midwesterners, not particularly sexy, but healthy-looking, friendly and kind of ageless. I sometimes find it hard to tell how smart these northern European types are, since I usually measure intelligence by degrees of sarcasm, and Ingrid played everything straight. But I think she was a tough cookie, capable and not to be crossed.

Bert taught English and drama at a Catholic school in Forest Hills. Ingrid was the third grade homeroom teacher of his son, Jeremy, by his first marriage. This was how they got to know each other, and when Bert and his first wife decided on a divorce, they sat down with Jeremy very reasonably and asked him who he wanted to live with. He picked Bert and Ingrid—he really liked his homeroom teacher.

Of course, that's not the whole story, and Bert also said that Jeremy's mother was a resident oncologist who worked unpredictable hours, so he often gave the boy his supper and put him to bed. The divorce settlement made it difficult for him to keep the house and give his ex-wife a fair shake, so they sold it. Both Ingrid and he needed a new start—their affair had soured a lot of their daily relationships. People took sides and most people sided against them. One of the things they both realized, Bert said, meaning him and Ingrid, is how little it cost them to give up the friendships, both at work and among their neighbors, that they had built up over the years. He was determined this time around to arrange his life differently.

I liked Bert a lot. He was a good-looking guy, a little over six feet tall, with a mustache and a faintly thinning head of brown hair. Back at the school in Forest Hills he ran the kayaking club, and still tried to "get out on the water" at least once a weekend. He seemed in good shape. He was also about to turn forty-five, and you could just see a little stiffness in him when he walked, not stiffness exactly, but a kind of brittleness or carefulness, if he had to run a few steps, for example, or stand up from a low sofa.

The school he planned to set up with Ingrid was going to be a homestead-type school in a single house, with only a couple of classrooms. One for kids up to the age of eleven, which Ingrid was in charge of, and the other to see them all the way through high school. I asked him if he needed a history teacher.

"Have you done any teaching?" he said.

"I spent about five years lecturing on colonial America at the University of Aberystwyth."

"Some of these kids will be twelve years old," he said. "I tell you what. Why don't you get a little experience, even if it's only substitute experience, at some local school. If you can teach at a Detroit public high school you can teach anywhere."

So I called Gloria. I wanted to call her anyway, but I used Bert's idea about substitute teaching as an excuse, which I half regretted, because the way she sounded on the phone received a slight adjustment when my interest turned out to be practical. She remembered who I was.

"You ask a lot of questions," she said. "And you get drunk like skinny people, kind of high energy. I thought you must have forgot my number."

"I wrote it down."

"Well," she said, "you took your sweet time calling it."

I told her I was thinking of becoming a teacher and eventually she invited me to lunch at her school—after the holidays. It was still mid-July, which gave me no excuse to see her for a couple of months. But we kept talking. For some reason neither one of us wanted to hang up, though I can't say I enjoyed the conversation much. I didn't want to say the wrong thing. When I met her the first time I was too drunk to care, but over the telephone I noticed a couple of times that I changed what I was saying because she's black. For example, she asked me what my neighbors were like, if everybody was excited by what we were doing, if we all got along. I told her about going out one night with a few of them in the car to patrol the streets. Somebody took a gun, I said.

"You took a gun?"

"Mostly we just drove around talking. About two a.m. we went to one guy's house and made some coffee and carried it back into the car. It was an intense way to get to know each other."

"I bet," she said.

It was a relief to get off the phone. Apart from anything else I wanted to look forward to seeing her again without anything getting in the way, like having to think of things to say. Gloria is a well-organized person and put a date in the diary for me to come by the school, a few weeks into September, but by that point Astrid and I were already sleeping together.

SUSIE WAS ONE OF THE reasons I went out more. By August she had started spending a lot of time at the house, and since Walter and I used to have dinner together every night, I tried to give them some space. This left a big hole in my life. Also, I was sexually lonely, and seeing Walter and Susie brought that home. For example, there were parts of my personality, like tenderness, that I didn't get to use at all, and which I saw Walter and Susie using every day.

I ran into Astrid at Slows—a barbecue restaurant by the old train station, where I sometimes went to eat by myself at the bar. She was there with a couple of girlfriends, German girls from home who were visiting her, and they were going on to a party at one of those half-abandoned warehouses in east Detroit and invited me along. Artists had turned the building, which had all kinds of problems with it, including faulty electrics and asbestos plastering, into studios. The party was partly a chance to show off their work, but they'd also rigged up an elaborate sound system and themed different studio spaces according to types of drink and music. But the walls weren't thick enough to separate the sounds, and the clash of noise fronts was really pretty powerful and unpleasant and hard to escape.

Astrid and I eventually took our drinks out into the parking lot. It was a hot August night, and I could hear the call of a Tigers doubleheader coming from one of the cars. There were several people, younger than me, sitting inside it, drinking and smoking pot. I could smell the sweet smoke drifting over towards us, towards the crumbly cinder block wall at the edge of the lot where Astrid and I sat down. She told me the story she hadn't wanted to talk about before, which explained why Ernst had left her. I later saw another version of this story, which she had written down. It also appeared in a different form in a film she was working on, and after that night, after we started seeing each other, I heard her talk about it several times.

A few weeks after I dropped them off, she was raped coming out of a nightclub on Woodward Avenue. She had gone to this club with Ernst to hear a new DJ, who mixed a lot of Motown in with other things, techno and more contemporary music. At one point she went outside by herself for a smoke. This was a couple of weeks before the Michigan ban, and the dance floor was full of smokers, but she wanted a breath of fresh air along with the cigarette. My guess is she had also had a fight with Ernst, though she didn't mention it. It was very late and the street was deserted; the bouncer had gone inside. While she was standing there, a young man came out of the glare of a street lamp and asked her for a smoke. He was dressed in clean new jeans and unlaced work boots; he had recently had a haircut. He was black. She took out her packet and reached it towards him and he grabbed her hand and started pulling her along.

"I was drunk, too," she said. "Not sick-drunk but enough to be confused. Also, it was still very cold, there was still snow on the ground, not much, and I was wearing only a small dress. At first when I went outside I thought how nice and cool it was, after the hot club, but when he gave me a shock, I felt suddenly very cold and shaky."

Woodward runs through a small park and he dragged her towards it. Even though it was two or three in the morning there were still a few people coming out of the restaurants and clubs. But nobody helped her and for some reason she wasn't screaming. She thought he might have a gun. She tried to explain to him that she didn't have any money, her boyfriend had her wallet and he was back at the club. "He'll give you whatever you want," she said. When they got to the park, he pushed her down behind a tree next to some bushes; the ground was very hard and also a little wet. When he lay down on top of her (he felt very strong and heavy), he said, "Fuck, it's too cold for this shit," and pulled her back up.

There's not much around there except tall commercial buildings, with shop fronts on the ground floor and offices above, but a few blocks from the park he found a row of parked cars and broke into one of them. They had to cross several large streets, almost as wide as highways, to get there, and even though it was very early, there was still some traffic. By this point she had started screaming. He held her around the waist with his arm and had also grabbed her other hand as if she were drunk and needed support. He had large hands with long fingers and smelled strongly of cigarettes and aftershave or alcohol. But everybody was in cars and no one heard her; at least, no one stopped.

Inside the car, he spent about a minute getting it to start. When she tried to open the passenger-side door, he struck her very hard on the mouth, breaking a tooth so that her mouth filled with blood, which she spat onto the floor. This is one of the ways they eventually identified the stolen car. Then they drove for about ten minutes, she has no idea in what direction, until they came to a dark street with several vacant lots on it, a few run-down houses and a medium-size apartment block. They went into the apartment block and he pulled her up a flight of stairs—she had stopped using her legs, and the next day, apart from everything else, she found her shins and knees covered in dark bruises.

He said, "Let's just hope my sister ain't here," as he beat on one of the apartment doors and then kicked it in. She doesn't remember much about the apartment. All the lights were off and he took her through a couple of dark rooms and then pushed her onto a bed, where he raped her, pinning her arms against the mattress with his elbows. She didn't resist him. When she woke up or came to she heard a woman saying, "What you have to break down the door for."

"You wasn't here."

"How'd you get here."

"Some car."

"What you doing now?"

"I'm a drive it away."

"Don't leave your ho with me."

"She ain't no ho."

"I ain't cleaning up after your white hos."

"She ain't no ho."

"What you doing now?"

"I told you. Taking the car."

And then he left. Eventually the woman came into the room Astrid was lying in.

"Well," she said. "What do you expect me to do with you?"

"I want to go home."

"You should a thought of that before."

"Please," Astrid said. "I don't have anything." She had left her purse in the stolen car.

His sister hadn't switched on any lights, but the curtains were open, and light came into the room from a street lamp outside. She had a mannish face, with very short hair; she looked yellower than her brother, who was very dark. Older, too. "Fuck this," she said. "Where you live?"

"I'm staying with friends in Royal Oak."

"No way I'm driving you out there."

Astrid said, "I'm very scared. You're a woman, too. I don't know what to do."

"Don't mess around with no niggers," the woman said. But she drove Astrid to the Greyhound bus station downtown. "Come on, get out," she said, with the motor running. "I don't expect you wanna see any of us again."

At least the station had a waiting room, with lights on, and a few people sitting around. But for the first few minutes Astrid sat on the bench outside, in spite of the cold. She wasn't yet ready to say anything to anybody. The station is about a block from the Lodge Freeway, which runs under Howard Street. By this point it was almost five in the morning, and the early commuter traffic made a continuous roar, which echoed off the bridge and surrounded her with noise. Dawn was about an hour away.

There was a bathroom inside, though it was very dirty. Astrid went inside to clean herself up before calling 911. The dispatcher sent an ambulance and a squad car—they took her first to the hospital and then to her friends in Royal Oak.

At the hospital a policewoman photographed the bruising on her legs and around her thighs. A doctor took several samples, including blood samples, and put her on a complicated course of medication. In the afternoon, she had another visit from the police. She wanted to see the photographs, but they weren't ready yet. Already the bruises on her legs had begun to change color, and after the policewoman left, she asked Ernst if he would take new photographs of her injuries. He didn't want to so she took the pictures herself. At first, she was just very anxious, because it seemed to her that her bruises were the only evidence she had, apart from the photographs, that something terrible had been done to her; and she knew that the bruises would go away. But later, as she did in fact begin to heal, and her skin turned yellow and then paler again, she started taking pictures as a way of recording the process, which seemed to her almost beautiful and even moving.

She soon realized, she said, that these photographs were the only actually "artistic" photographs she had ever taken, the only ones with any artistic *value*. It shouldn't have surprised me that Astrid was still the pretentious woman who had annoyed me in the car, but even as I sat on the wall outside the party, listening and saying, I'm sorry, I'm sorry, I felt annoyed. I also thought, you tough bitch. But I did feel sorry for her and wanted to kiss her, too, though we didn't kiss till later, after a few more drinks, when we went back into the party.

Later she asked me to look over the version of the story she had written down. She especially wanted my opinion about the dialogue, if she had gotten right the way black people talk, if it was offensive. I told her I didn't know any better than she did. Also, I wasn't there. "But you know what it's like," she said. "You remember only what you hear, and you hear only what you expect to hear, which is what prejudice is."

I shook my head at her. "I don't know."

Ernst left her, she said, for no other reason than that everything about them had become too unhappy. I'm not unhappy, she told him. Something terrible has happened to me but I'm dealing with it. (I liked it when she used American slang.) He said to her, Come with me, let's go home, I've had enough of this country, but she felt that America was just becoming interesting. She was becoming interested in herself—she was discovering new things. Also, they argued about sex. Already a few weeks after the rape she wanted to prove to herself, and Ernst, that she could be normal and okay about sex, but in fact, she admits now, she was a little crazy in this respect, and Ernst understood very well that she didn't want to be touched. But this is how she interpreted it, that he didn't want to touch her, and she accused him of stupid things, she said he didn't want to put himself where a black man had been, that she was stained and dirty and ruined, a ruined woman, that this was how he saw her. All of which upset Ernst very much, he was in tears, and somewhat pathetically tried to stroke her. But it wasn't just pathetic, he couldn't help himself, it was all too deliberate and unnatural, a little forced, and again she felt this childish feeling, that he was stronger than her, and when she pulled away in reaction, she had never seen him so angry before.

Why do you make that face, she asked me.

"I'm beginning to feel a little sorry for Ernst."

"I feel sorry for him, too. When you saw me that night"—she meant at Bill Russo's place in the country—"I was still a little crazy with everything that had happened. But you were smart. You ran away from me."

"I didn't run away. There were people I needed to talk to."

"No, I know when a boy runs away from me."

"Did they find the man who—raped you?"

"They found the car, and there were his fingerprints in the car, and they know who he is, but they haven't found him."

"But they found his sister?"

"Yes. I saw her again."

"What did you say to her?"

"I can show you one day. I filmed it."

For some reason, she hadn't brought her video camera to the party. But often, when I saw her afterwards, she had it along: a small black Kodak, which she wore around her neck like sunglasses. It took some getting used to. I found myself talking and acting unnaturally and hated watching the results. My voice sounded funny to me, which is what everybody says, more southern than it sounds in my head, and kind of complaining or sarcastic or gay. In the beginning, I often stared into the camera, which Astrid told me not to do, but I couldn't help myself.

Not that night but later I agreed to let myself be filmed having sex with her, which I came to regret. It started bouncing around the Internet at a bad moment, before the trial, when there was already a lot of media interest in my name. I learned firsthand the way private acts become distorted if they are shown in public. Because in fact it was a very tender scene. This was the first time Astrid had had sex since being raped, which is why she wanted to record it. We were extremely gentle with each other, and it wasn't so much about pleasure as about getting through it, though of course there was pleasure, too, especially on my side. She cried much of the time but also held on to me and in her own way seemed pretty insistent. But it didn't look good, and the sound quality was poor, which made it difficult to hear what she was saying. We filmed it at my bedroom in Johanna Street, and the way people took it was, this is the kind of thing they got up to there. But it didn't really have any bearing on the case.

13

Kettridge High is more or less on I-94, about thirty blocks north of Johanna Street. You can hear the traffic clearly as you walk up to the school entrance, and even inside there's a hum that isn't just kids. There was a security check inside the door, with one of those metal-detector portals. I passed through it minus keys and wallet, which I collected again on the other side. The guard wore a uniform that looked like a police uniform but cheaper, and he had a gun on a cord attached to his belt. He was sitting on a plastic cafeteria chair, and the table I pushed my wallet and keys across was a cafeteria table—a high school's makeshift version of airport security.

The guard was black, the secretary in reception (who I could see through a window in the office door) was black, and the kids I saw making their way to lunch were black. I shouldn't have been surprised, in fact, I wasn't surprised, which didn't stop me feeling like I'd entered another country, after an airplane flight.

Gloria had told me to come to her homeroom and the woman in the office gave me directions. The school itself looked like the school I went to in Baton Rouge, both inside and out—1960s architecture, one-story, with a couple of columns holding up the

entrance and yellow brick siding. The hallways had stippled parti-
tion walls and glossy floor tiles; everything echoed.

When I reached her room, Gloria was talking to a kid, so I
waited by the open door. The kid had to bend his neck to look
at her, though he also had a backpack over one shoulder, which
seemed to pull him down. He was about twice her size, with a kid's
mustache and his hair cut back in rows. Gloria stood up straight,
with her feet together; I wondered if she used to dance. She wore
high socks and plain blue shoes, a skirt and a buttoned shirt—the
prim schoolgirl look, which for some reason looks flirty on women.

"Come on in, Greg," she said, when she saw me. "This is Alonzo.
He's one of the good ones. He's one of the ones that makes it all
worthwhile. Greg is thinking about becoming a teacher."

"I didn't want to interrupt you."

"Nah, I was going," Alonzo said. And then: "So you got some-
thin' to teach me?"

"I don't know. A little history."

"Not too much, huh?" he said.

"Does he have a crush on you?" I asked, after he closed the door.

"I hope so," she said, but shook her head. "It's easier if they want
me to like them."

"I'm sure everybody wants that. So what makes Alonzo one of
the good ones?"

"Oh, I say that to all the kids," she said.

The classroom windows overlooked the school parking lot,
which had all kinds of cars in it, including some expensive-looking
SUVs, with tinted windows, and much cheaper cars, with smooth
treads and rusty hoods.

"I haven't been inside a high school in about fifteen years. I always tried to sit next to the window. There was a gas station just
off campus, and I used to watch people filling up. They filled up

and they drove off, all these grown-ups. I was jealous, because they could go where they wanted, and nobody bothered them. We went there, too, during lunch break, for potato chips and soda."

"Well, I'm a grown-up and I'm stuck here. Let me show you one of our projects," she said.

The classroom walls were covered in bright pictures, colored in by felt-tip or Magic Marker and pinned up with thumbtacks. Then I noticed that some of the pictures were photographs, computer printouts of digital images, done on the same white paper.

"This is something Nolan worked with me on," Gloria said. "It's ongoing. They keep bringing in new stuff. We call it *I See What I See*. He got Nikon to donate some cheap digital cameras, the kind you give kids. We told them to take a lot of pictures of stuff in their lives. Then we ask them to draw whatever they took a picture of. Mostly they try to make the drawings as close to the photographs as they can, because it's easier, which is fine, but that's not really the point."

She said "drawing" like "drawring." There were pictures of women's faces, and babies, and people watching TV, and dirty kitchen sinks. There was a picture of an old dead-looking man lying in a hospital bed. There were some cars and bicycles. I saw the odd gun, too, and a lot of posters of women or ballplayers or actors on bedroom walls. There were pictures of high school kids horsing around after school.

"What do you want them to do?"

"Well, they can do what they want, but I want them to use their imaginations. That's why we decided to use the school printers, which you can probably tell are very low definition. So that the photographs don't look too realistic. In class we talk about Impressionism and Pop Art and all that, but most of them don't make the connection. Their drawings are just like the photos, only worse. But it's only been a month; we're still working on it. Let's eat. Teaching makes me hungry."

"How old are the kids?"

"This is my freshman class, but some of them are a little older."

"Where are Alonzo's?"

She showed them to me. "This one's maybe more interesting than the others." It was a photograph of one those storefront churches, a brick facade painted white, with a barn door and a big purple cross above it going into the roof. A.M.E. was hand-painted on either side of the cross. The picture he drew to go with it showed something that looked a little more like a cathedral, with a spire and peaked roofs.

"He didn't make that one up either," she said. "That's the Central United Methodist Church, the one by the ballpark, where the Tigers play. A Michigan Historical Site. They had the first gay priest there, at least in Michigan. The first gay Methodist. It's kind of a hippie church."

At lunch, which we ate in the cafeteria, I saw a few white faces, all teachers. Two of them sat down with us, a man and a woman— Gloria seemed to be good at making friends with white people. The woman was blond and maybe forty years old, Jenny Schramm. She sounded like she was from Michigan, an accent I had started to recognize and which probably made her working class. She talked a lot. She was one of those talkative types who live their whole lives under the impression that they're helpful and well liked. Gloria set her off by saying I wanted to become a substitute teacher. Jenny told me what you need to do.

You need to get fingerprinted. You need to pass a few basic tests, including safety checks, most of which you can take online. Then you need at least to begin some kind of certification process. There are online courses for that as well. I wrote most of this down.

"How do you like teaching here?" I asked, and she talked some more.

"Sometimes I feel like salt in a pepper pot," she said at one point. "But I don't mind that." Gloria had gone for a coffee refill or maybe she wouldn't have said it.

The man had a leather jacket on, which he didn't take off, even at lunch, and gray stubble. His name was Eric Kaymer and he went out halfway through to smoke a cigarette. But before he went he flirted with Gloria, which I could only partly listen in on because of the woman. His accent wasn't as rough as his appearance. From what I overheard he went to a lot of theater.

Gloria seemed a very popular person in the cafeteria. Girls called out "Miss Lambert" from across the room, and stopped by our table on their way to class. The lunch ladies liked her, too. She had a quick natural smile and I wondered if it was sometimes a burden to her, if it was just something she could do.

"Were you a sorority girl?" I asked her at one point.

"Delta Sigma Theta," she said. "Why?"

"Do you keep in touch?"

"I keep in touch with everybody. Nobody gets away from *me*."

When Eric came back, Gloria said to him, "Greg's one of these guys living over in the new neighborhoods."

"Oh, I thought about getting in on that."

"But you decided not to?"

"They turned me down," he said.

"I only got through because I know the guy who started it."

"How's it working out?"

"I don't know yet. I've met a lot of strangers; people talk to each other. After college I went out of the country for about ten years. I only just came back. But the sense I get from the people I talk to is that they weren't very happy with their old lives. Not just because of money worries, though that, too. I read once that when people don't know what to do with themselves, when they reach a dead end, they dream about going back to school or becoming an actor. Those are the kind of people we get."

"Is that what you're doing?" Gloria asked.

"Maybe that's why they turned you down," I said to Eric. "We were looking for people who wanted to change their lives. You have a life here already."

"Is that what I have? So what's your excuse?"

"I'm one of these academic drifters. I spent my twenties trying to get a job I'm not gonna get, and now I'm not fit for anything else. But it's been good for me so far. You know how there are some basic facts about yourself that you don't know, because you don't want to face them or can't get the angle to look. I'm trying to look."

"That sounds like a full-time job," Eric said. "Does it pay much?" So I shut up.

After lunch Gloria walked me to the parking lot. "Did you find out what you wanted to know?" she said to me.

"Mrs. Schramm was very helpful."

"Yeah, Jenny talks a lot. Was there anything else?" She sounded a little combative.

"What's the graduation rate?"

"Depends how you do the accounting. If a kid doesn't show up for class but twenty days a year, does it mean he didn't graduate or he didn't attend? But it's about a quarter."

"And can they read and write?"

"Not as well as I'd like. Anything else? Well, I got things to do," she said, and I felt really pretty unhappy and ashamed when she left.

This is what I thought about on the way home.

One night at Yale, I walked into my college dining hall while some sorority party was going on. It was a Friday night, a little after ten o'clock, and I heard the noise of the party after coming back from the library. A dull thudding bass line and other sounds, crowd sounds and sometimes clapping. You could hear it from the courtyard, and since there was nobody at the door, checking tickets, I went in. Everybody inside was black, and they were almost all women, which I could see even though most of the lights were off—except for a disco ball or a spotlight, I can't remember which, maybe both, which shone or glittered in the center of the room. Underneath the ball or in the light two black men were dancing and taking their clothes off. When I got there they were shirtless and down to their jeans. After a few minutes they raised their arms and pointed at the women in the crowd, and a couple of volunteers eventually walked into the spotlight, or had to be pushed. The men picked them up and kept dancing—picked them up over their heads, I mean, and gently lowered them again, in time to the music, closer and closer to their faces, while everyone cheered them on. Even though there were maybe two hundred people in the room, which was hot with crowded bodies, I had the sense that something private was going on, and it was only after I walked out again, into the cooler evening, that I realized how that could be. What I had seen was somehow racially private, and even though nobody stopped me or asked me what I was doing there, I felt like I had passed through closed doors into a kind of family room where things could be said and done without embarrassment, which wouldn't be shown or discussed outside.

When I mentioned this to Beatrice at the time, she said, "Bullshit, it's got nothing to do with race, it's a gender thing, it's because they were all women. You don't think women want to have sex."

But I wasn't sure. "I don't know," I said.

I suddenly remembered this conversation, which I hadn't thought about for years, while walking home from Kettridge High.

This is strange, because at the time it made a big impression. I was still a virgin, sex wasn't something I liked to talk about, and the way those women cheered the two guys on was something new to me. The fact that they were black, the fact that everybody seemed to be having a good time, that no one looked ashamed, all that was part of the impression, and I wondered if it had anything to do with my attraction to Gloria.

14

Our neighborhood was probably the most middle-class neighborhood in the whole setup. Walter nicknamed us the "burnt ends." There was Hector Cantu's crowd, Latinos of one stripe or another, legal and illegal—Robert's lawyers had fixed things pretty well with the ICE. Everyone called their neck of the woods Little Mexico. Then there was a kind of global village, people from Iraq, Somalia, Sudan, most of them refugees, living cheek by jowl with each other, about twenty blocks east of Johanna Street in the Marina District. That was the smallest block. Probably the weirdest development was out by the old Wayne Conner plant, which had been bought up by a social networking company.

They turned part of the plant into a server farm and filled all of the surrounding residential streets with their employees, who moved from shitty and expensive apartments in the Bay Area to houses in Detroit. Then out by the old airport was another mixed bag of middle-aged dropouts, more burnt ends. People sometimes talked about the "five neighborhoods." Already restaurants were opening, food markets, street bazaars and bars—you met up in the places getting a reputation. Walter and I used to go for breakfast at a Somalian café in the Marina. It served cheap polenta porridge, which Walter had become obsessed with. We drank tea and ate the porridge and read the *Detroit Free Press*; Walter was looking for part-time jobs.

The last piece of the puzzle was a stretch of dead land around I-94, not far from Kettridge High, which a guy called Franklin Mayer wanted to turn into an urban farm. Franklin was a friend of Robert's. His father was somebody at Chrysler. He went to law school after college but dropped out and started using his moderate inheritance to buy up real estate. I met him once at Robert's place in New York. A big, bluff, red-faced, genial guy, rich-sounding and good-looking, a kind of American gentleman. He had the talking habit of somebody with not enough to do. If you needed to drive somewhere he was happy to come along. But he also had practical talents and saved money by fixing up his properties himself. He taught himself basic plumbing, a little carpentry, something about electrics and gardening. His hands were always chapped and dirty under the nails.

Franklin talked a lot about real estate, he thought about it a lot, and got out at just the right time, before the crash, and ended up with a big pile of dough. More than he needed or wanted, he said. He wanted to do something "real" with this money, something political that didn't pander to party. So he started this farm. A lot of people I knew made cash in hand by working on it, breaking ground, tearing down houses, building fences, etc. In the early stages there was plenty of work to go around. You showed up in the morning and somebody gave you something to do, and at the end of the day you got paid. Sometimes I worked there, too.

It served a useful community function. A litigator from Chicago might dig ditches with a factory hand from Kismaayo. The farm was one of the places where people from different neighborhoods got to know each other.

This was easy enough on your own street. Living opposite Walter and me was a gay couple, both in their forties. One guy used to work in IT but wanted to write plays; I think he still freelanced to pay the bills. Sandy Brinkman, from Seattle. His boyfriend, Tomaso, was Venezuelan by birth, a landscape gardener. Everyone on our block got to know him—he offered to help us with our yards.

Next door were the Mogfords, Hazel and Jayson. She was a post office administrator; he used to run a construction company. They were both black, she was maybe a little lighter-skinned. Jayson's company expanded too quickly in the boom and went bust in the bust, just after they moved into a new house, but they managed to get through all that without ending up on different sides.

"It got to that point you all read about," Hazel said to me. She had a soft southern accent, the kind that made me miss Baton Rouge, and wore her hair straightened and bright red lipstick. "We owed more than the place was worth. I'll tell you what we did. We packed what we wanted to keep in Jayson's van, then I walked up to the front door, I'll not forget this, and put our keys through the slot. Then we drove to my mother's house in Louisville. If we had stayed *there* much longer we'd have got divorced."

They had two kids, two boys, and sometimes their football ended up in our backyard. I played a little catch with them. Walter and I had dinner there, too, several times. When my washing machine broke down and started leaking through the ceiling onto Walter's bedroom, Jayson came by and fixed things up for us, for about fifty bucks. People helped each other out. We had time and didn't need much money. Their older boy was ten years old, but very advanced mathematically, and sometimes I gave him a hand with his homework. They both went to Bert and Ingrid's new school.

Robert insisted on keeping up a black presence in the neighborhoods, partly for PR reasons. But it wasn't just that. I talked to people who came back to Detroit because it meant something to them, as a black city. People had family here, they wanted to make it work. Jayson's great-grandfather grew up in Elmwood Park, just the other side of the cemetery, about a half-hour walk away. There were also a lot of mixed-race couples. Kurt Stangel's wife turned out to be Nigerian, but rich Nigerian. They met at Northwestern Law School. She was shy, attractive, very dark, and also quite religious; they spent their first few months in Detroit looking for a church.

Next door on the other side lived a Jewish family, the Rosens, a dentist and his wife with three kids, including a six-month-old baby. The dad was big, loud, fat and bald. He was one of those guys who looks funny in jeans, because they sit very high on his waist, held up by a belt, but he wore them every day, even when working. Along with New Balance sneakers and a Cornell sweatshirt. Sometimes he practiced "informally," as he called it, from an office in his den, but the truth is, they had made a reasonable return on selling their house in Orange County, New York. He wanted to sit on his ass and throw a baseball around with his older boy, and take him to Tigers games. Cynthia, his wife, was small, olive-skinned, shrill, with a faint, faint mustache over her lip and more soft hairs along her neck, under the jaw. Their kids were called Benny, Miriam and baby Solly.

Jack, the father, probably had the best description of what we were doing. "We're settlers," he said. "There were boys I knew from synagogue in Port Jervis, who when they were all grown up and sick of their American lives, said fuck this and moved to Katzrin, where they sit on their tushes and make more kids. With everything paid for by the Jewish state. I said to my wife, I want a piece of this action, and she said, there's only one problem. You're not a religious nut. But here it doesn't matter," he said. "Here you just have to be nuts."

But I talked to Cynthia, too—an intense woman. She said, the way they were living in New York, it's lucky nobody died. Just to pay the mortgage she started working as a paralegal in the city three days a week. (Apart from all her other degrees she spent a year at law school.) With the commute she didn't get home until ten o'clock some nights. There were basic things about family life, just to keep the ship running, that didn't get done. Her kids walked out of the house without a packed lunch. When Miriam was three years old, she caught whooping cough. But you have to have the energy to pay attention to the signs, you have to be prepared to get out of bed at two a.m., and get dressed, and get the kids dressed, and drive to the hospital. You have to be sane enough to recognize what needs to be done, and what can be put off until the morning. But nobody in that house was sane. This is what she wanted from moving to Detroit—she wanted to get more pleasure from her kids, while they were young and still essentially happy animals. That's the phrase she used.

In fact, most of us were proud of doing what we were doing, and talked about it proudly, which helped us get along. We wanted to say, here, at least, I know who my neighbors are. The Rosens moved from outside Newburgh, and there were a lot of ex-suburbanites on our block who didn't use to know anybody they could borrow an egg from. So we borrowed a lot of eggs.

Another curious feature was the political mix. You'd expect a lot of left-wing hippies, counterculturists, and we got them, too. But there was also a libertarian streak, and a number of Tea Party types.

Opposite the Rosens lived a childless married couple called the Adlers, Tina and Don. Don was a professional grumbler who worked in insurance and was forced into early retirement a couple of years ago. First they moved to Phoenix (from Kansas City), which was too expensive he said, and not his scene. So he said to

Tina, for once in our lives let's *do* something with our lives. He used to have political ambitions but the system was hopeless and corrupt. The trouble with any system is that it's designed to perpetuate itself. There's no point in getting into government if you want to get rid of government. That's not how it works. And so on.

He used to walk over the road when he picked up his newspaper and talk to me. He was kind of friendly-miserable. When he heard about this Detroit business, he thought, this is what I've been talking about my whole life. The idea of America is a small-town idea, Jamestown, Plymouth, it's a city-state idea. In his opinion the trouble started with the Constitution. There was nothing wrong with the Articles of Confederation—a confederation is what we should have stuck with. He read history books and liked to explain why he disagreed with them. He also watched a lot of TV and sometimes told me in the morning what he planned to watch later in the day.

Tina was one of these nice women who puts up with unreasonable men. Her whole personality was a defense against male-pattern craziness and also at the same time a kind of supporting act. She was small and made herself up heavily. Her hair was supposed to look blond but looked faded; it couldn't quite take on the artificial coloring, it had got too thin. In her own way, she was just as crazy as him. But they must have had guts, too, to move to Detroit in their sixties, when they didn't know anybody. She said to me privately that Don was much happier these days. There were days in Phoenix he wouldn't leave the house.

"I know he talks too much," she said. "You're a good listener. Don't think I don't thank you in my heart when I see you together. But he's one of those men, when he isn't talking too much it's worse."

But Don did more than talk. He started getting involved in the politics of the place. Robert and the rest of us hoped that something like a town hall mentality would develop, but there wasn't anything in the charter about local government. He thought it should spring up on its own.

In fact, what happened was this. The first community organization of any kind was the Neighborhood Watch, set up by Kurt Stangel and Eddie Blyleven and a few other early arrivers. (It's funny, but there was already a slight difference in status between the people who came in that first wave, in late February and early March, and the ones who showed up later, during the summer and after. Walter and I were considered second-wavers.) Eventually the Neighborhood Watch started concerning itself with more than just the roster for patrols. In August, there was a string of burglaries along the streets running off East Lafayette, more violent ones, involving guns. A kid, a nine-year-old boy, was briefly held hostage—forced at gunpoint into a car and then pushed out several blocks later, from where he had to make his way home in the dark. I think they just wanted to scare him, they wanted to say fuck you or watch out. He wasn't hurt but another time somebody *did* get shot, a Michigan grad student named Shreedhar Patel, who was fixing up a place for his family to move into. Maybe it was the same guys who took the kid, but Shreedhar had a gun, a Beretta 92 that his father had given him when he moved to Detroit, and which he didn't know how to work. Somebody saw it and shot him in the leg; then they took off. Eddie suggested establishing a couple of checkpoints at night, by the corners of St. Paul and Grand and Jefferson and Van Dyke, and closing off some of the smaller cross streets altogether. Part of the western border was the cemetery wall, and to the north and east the neighborhood opened out into the other new settlements.

For the first time, the meeting was widely attended. People crowded into Eddie's front room, and since the night was fine eventually moved out into the garden. There were strong feelings and real disagreements. The mother of that nine-year-old boy stood up to say something, one of these tightly put-together, anxious hippie moms, who bike their kids to school and go shopping in big cars. "These people," she started to say, "what you have to understand about these people," before someone shouted over her. What do you mean, these people, why don't you just say it, etc. You could hear us several blocks away.

Then Jayson stood up. He was short and chubby and even on his feet had to shout a little to get noticed, but when people saw his black face they let him talk. "Wait a minute, wait a minute here," he said. "This isn't a race thing. This is a class thing. You've got to understand the mentality. It's about you just moved here and what do *you* know. Let's get that straight."

The boy's mother said, "I will not be shamed out of saying what I want to say. If it was your boy— What you have to realize is that the first person I blame is myself."

This went on too long in my opinion, the righteousness and upset and self-explanation, on all sides. But we got through it in the end, and afterwards there was a kind of elevated mood, like, this is politics, this is how you talk things through.

The first thing we decided is that the Neighborhood Watch Committee needed to be democratically elected, which didn't make much immediate difference, since Kurt and Eddie got voted in by a show of hands. But Jayson also put himself forward and won a seat on the panel. So did Don Adler. And the motion was passed. We closed off St. Paul, Kercheval, Baldwin, Seminole, etc., after nine p.m., using old cars, and set up checkpoints along the rest.

ROBERT JAMES WASN'T TOO HAPPY about any of this. "You haven't got the right," he said, "and if something goes wrong there'll be big trouble. And something will go wrong."

He used to pick me up in the car on the corner of Johanna and drive us over the bridge to Belle Isle for a jog. Sometimes afterwards we came back to his place for breakfast, then I'd walk home.

"What do you want me to do," I said. "You need to increase the police presence."

"That's not a solution. They have enough to do."

"Then hire a security firm."

"For five square miles? This has to work because it works, because people want you there."

"I don't think they want us there."

We ran on silently for a few minutes, or almost silently—puffing a little and pounding our feet in the grass. "It doesn't matter what anybody wants," Robert said eventually. "No checkpoints."

"Well, tell that to Eddie Blyleven."

"I will."

"He'll tell you what I've been telling you, that you have to do something. So what are you going to do?"

"There are things we can try with the police we already have. I'll talk to the commissioner about stop-and-frisk."

"That's another way of pissing people off," I said.

When we got back to the house Robert had an email waiting for him that put him in a good mood. He checked his phone as soon as we walked through the door, and after that the atmosphere lightened a little.

"What is it?" I said.

"Nothing yet. I'll let you know."

His mother was staying with him—she came in at this point and we all sat down to breakfast in the kitchen. The last time I'd seen her she was wearing a boot cast. This time she had on a pair of house slippers and skinny jeans and a plain collared shirt, open-necked. She was one of those mothers who expresses affection for her son by flirting with his friends. But she hung on Robert's neck, too; she touched him a lot. Maybe she *had* changed a little, maybe she was needier, and wanted to talk more.

Robert seemed to put up with her. His wife and baby boy were still in New York. Peggy, he said, had a circle of friends now, of other mothers; she was having a good time. Anyway, she was a New York girl, by birth and education and inclination, it wasn't easy dragging her out of the city.

Mrs. James said, "I wish she'd come up to the house more. Whenever she wants to. I don't even need to be around—I'll clear out. But it's good for a boy to get a little country air."

"What have I just been saying," Robert said. "There's air in New York."

"You should come, too," she said to me. "Just send me an email. Whenever you want to get away. You and Walter."

"It's only thirteen hours in the car," Robert said.

"Where's Beatrice?" I asked at one point.

"I don't know. In her room."

"She's gone to see Franklin about something," Mrs. James said. "She's back for lunch."

Something about the way she said it made me sit up. They had known each other a long time—fifteen years. Ever since Robert brought Beatrice up sophomore year in college, to their house in New Hampshire, to meet his parents. Longer than she could have known Peggy, who was probably only in junior high at the time. But I guess mothers learn to put up with their son's changing relations.

They both had flights to catch in the morning, and Robert excused himself to make another call. This left me alone with Mrs. James. She refilled my cup from the pot sitting under the coffeemaker.

"Robert puts himself under too much pressure," she told me. "He never says anything, he never complains. But if this thing works out it will be big news. So he tells me. It will open a lot of doors. Poor kid," she said. "It's a funny thing how ambition creeps up on you. When he was a boy all he ever wanted to do was help me in the kitchen. I used to stand him on a chair by the counter with a wooden spoon. I let him stir the mix when I was making cakes. And now the president sends him texts. It's wonderful, I'm very proud, but I can't always take everything as seriously as he wants me to. Peggy's very patient with him, she's very good, but it's not easy having a small kid either. I don't care how rich you are. Their place in New York is spacious for New York, but I don't want to get in their hair. We're called mothers-in-law for a reason. So I came out here. He feels his duty to me, too. And I get to see Beatrice."

I didn't know whether to kiss her on my way out, so I didn't do anything. She said, "Look after each other."

Robert walked me to the electric gate. I was wearing one of his college sweatshirts, because it was cool out and my sweat had dried. "Listen, what are you doing for dinner?" he said. "Because I've got an extra ticket for this thing. Some conference on educational reform. Beatrice doesn't want to go."

So I saw him again that night, though we didn't talk much. I met a lot of rich men, guys from the Big Three, and representatives from the mayor's office, and other people who had flown in especially from DC. There's a whole education reform mafia, businessmen who want to put their money into something. Detroit is like ground zero for education. Robert loaned me a jacket and tie, there was champagne served in the lobby of the Westin Hotel, and afterwards a three-course meal cooked up by the head chef of the Rattlesnake Club. While dessert was going around, Robert and I ended up at the bar together, with drink orders, and I said to him, "So she doesn't mind, you staying here with Beatrice."

"She minds."

"Because most girls would find that weird, and with your mother as well."

"She's jealous of that, too."

"So what do you do about it?"

"Well," he said, "I take it into account."

At that point his drinks arrived and I didn't see him again for the rest of the night. It was a relief to get back to Johanna Street, where I could knock on Walter's door and take off my tie, feeling drunk, and make fun of the whole scene.

15

A few days later Walter told me that Susie was pregnant. They hadn't exactly planned it—they expected the whole conception business to take more than "a couple of shots." And she was only eight weeks in. Susie didn't want to tell anybody until twelve, so I shouldn't say anything to her about it. But he wanted me to know—he was very happy.

Maybe this is why Susie started to resent how often I stopped by. It was also a problem that she didn't like Astrid, who she thought of as a phony person. I didn't totally disagree with her, but there was something prim and old-maidish about Susie that riled me, given how she met Walter. She thought Astrid was an exhibitionist and a user of people and, I don't know what else, a slut. Whereas Astrid had nothing but warm feelings for Walter and Susie and didn't make any judgment about their relationship, not once, not in my presence, not even when we tried to talk each other to sleep, making the small talk of lovers in bed, which is often petty and hypercritical.

It turns out that knowing secrets about people makes them dislikable. I couldn't help noticing the slight extra gentleness in Susie's voice, and the way she sat down next to Walter on the couch when we watched TV. She and Walter used to go jogging together several times a week, and they kept that up, but I heard her once saying, coming up the steps, "I don't know what it is, but I get so tired these days." Even though she was only talking to Walter. This is the kind of thing that got on my nerves.

Not that I dislike kids. Tony and Cris sometimes came around with Michael, and Cris was starting to show. (Susie asked her a lot of questions about it.) And sometimes I even babysat for them, which probably means I did it twice. But I liked Michael. He called me Zio, and I used to hold him by his feet over my shoulders and pretend to look for him. "Where are you?" I said. "Behind you," he said. So I'd turn around and get pretend-annoyed. I thought you said you were behind me, and so on. But I worried about Walter. I thought he was a very likable drifter, but when you drift you don't want to accumulate too much stuff. And I felt jealous of his relationship with Susie.

I WASN'T QUITE SURE HOW to get in touch with Gloria, I mean, what excuse to make. We had left things on a purely practical footing. But I did what Mrs. Schramm said. I went down to the nearest precinct, at Beaubien Street, and got my fingerprints taken. This was a humiliating experience. While I waited, a cop brought in a group of high school girls who talked the whole time among themselves, very publicly, laughing and making fun of people. One of them looked at me and said, "What do you think he do?" and another one said, "He look like a rapist." Then the first one said, "Yeah, he got that rapist look," before their attention shifted to someone else.

Afterwards, I got a kind of receipt or notification, for being fingerprinted, which I sent along with the application form to Detroit Public Schools. I called up the registrar's office at Yale and had them mail a transcript over. I signed up for a first aid class. Then I waited. The city had to pass everything on to the Department of Education. None of this gave me a reason to see Gloria.

Then one day I had the bright idea of writing a neighborhood profile about Nolan. So I knocked on his door, and he opened it with the dog at his feet and a fat kid standing behind him. They were just going out.

"What do you want?" he said.

"I want to interview you for this newsletter I write."

"What about."

"Gloria Lambert told me about your ninth-grade project. We could talk about that. We could also talk about your own work. We could talk about the neighborhood."

"We're just taking the dog for a walk. If you come along, you can clean up his shit."

"What's your name?" I said to the kid.

"His name is Clarence. He's my son. If you talk to him the conversation is over."

Nolan took the whole interview business more seriously than I expected. He made two conditions, that the piece should include a link to his website and that I should clear everything with him before it came out. I didn't care much about these profiles so I agreed.

The kid seemed like a nice kid. He kept saying, "Dad, how come I can't talk to this guy? You're talking to him."

"Because I don't trust him," Nolan said.

"But *you're* talking to him."

Clarence had to run a little to keep up, not all the time, but at some point on every block he had to run a few steps. Nolan was a rapid walker, he didn't let the dog sniff around. When Buster shat against a tree he handed me a plastic bag.

"I can't believe you're making me clean up this shit," I said.

"I didn't make you anything. You just agreed to something."

I had to walk with the bag in my hand for about ten minutes, until we came to Mackowski Playground, where there was a garbage can. Then Clarence ran off to the slides and Nolan and I sat down. He took something out of his pocket and threw it on the ground, a biscuit for the dog, which was still on the leash.

The park was busy, the weather was white and cold, and Halloween pumpkins sat out on the porches. There was a lot of construction being done on the houses overlooking the park, and you could hear hammers and drills even on a Saturday afternoon. Guys were blowing leaves into the streets and sweeping them up, but the playground was still wet with leaves, and the climbing frames looked slippery and new. Kids had their gloves and hats on. There were kids kicking a soccer ball against a baseball backstop. Clarence had one of the few black faces. On the east side was the parking lot to a nursing home and a few old men and women came out and had a look at the weather and kids and went back in.

I knew a few people there, and a woman named Rita Fuentes came over to say hello. I introduced her to Nolan. I said I wanted to write a profile about him, and she said, "He did me, too, a couple of weeks ago. My name in the papers. I sent it to everyone I know. I sent it to my son."

She grew up in Puerto Rico but worked most of her life in Manhattan, thirty years for one family, as a child carer and then housekeeper. During this time she married and got divorced. Her own son was now a sophomore at Michigan State, and when he left home she decided to move with him. "Close but not too close," she told me. Somehow she had managed to save a little money. For the interview I took a photo of her new apartment, which she was very proud of. The garden was full of late flowers; she grew vegetables. But she still made money, on weekends and after school, looking after other people's children.

Nolan could be pleasant enough when he wanted to be, and after Rita left I said to him, "I guess you grew up around here. It must be changing a lot."

"I should tell you right now I consider this occupied territory."

"Most of this was empty land. The houses were in bad shape."

"How long have you lived in Detroit?"

"About six months."

"So you don't know a damn thing. Where did you meet Gloria?" he said.

"At some party, one of these fund-raisers."

"Why did you call her again?"

"I wanted to talk to her about teaching."

"That doesn't sound to me like a reason."

"What kind of art do you do?"

"Do your homework. Don't ask what you don't need to ask."

"What are you angry about? Why are you angry at me?"

"I'm not angry. This is just how I talk. People get used to it."

In fact, I did get used to it, and over the next few weeks we saw each other several times. Clarence knocked at our door on Halloween, not with Nolan but with three other kids and an old, slow-moving woman behind them, who I took to be somebody's grandmother. He was dressed as a football player. His helmet was mustard yellow and much too big for him—it said "Bulldogs" in cartoon letters. When I asked him about it, he told me his dad used to play football.

The next time I saw Nolan I said, "So how did you like Ferris State?"

"You've been doing your homework," he said.

He invited me in for coffee one day and I met his mother. "Properly," I said to her. "I saw you on our doorstep a couple of nights ago, with the kids."

She had the same broad shoulders as her son; her hips looked as if they were painful to her. A bright shawl hung around her neck, and she held it against her bosom, even indoors, and only let go when I reached out to shake her hand. The room she invited me into smelled of Pine-Sol or air freshener. The curtains were half drawn, probably against the cold, it was a cold November day, and there were a lot of lights on, standing lamps and table lamps, that made circles of light on the carpet and the blanket on the sofa. The TV in the corner was one of those old TVs with a wood-grain effect and gray knobs. From the kitchen I could hear the radio on.

"You've got a beautiful home, Mrs. Smith."

"Please, call me Eleanor."

"He can call you Mrs. Smith," Nolan said.

"Let the boy call me what he wants to."

"What do you want to call her, boy?"

"I'm gonna give you a word of advice," she said. "Don't let my son bully you."

"I think I'd like to call you Mrs. Smith."

Nolan was an obsessive coffee maker. We could see him from the living room messing around in the kitchen, there were steam sounds, we could hear cups on counters.

"I just want mine black," Mrs. Smith called. "I don't want any of that fancy milk."

"How long have you lived here?" I asked her.

"Forty-seven years. I raised two boys in this house, and now I'm raising another one. When I get the chance."

"Do you mind people like me moving in?"

"Oh, the things I mind . . ." She waved her hand away.

"Does Clarence live here full-time?"

"Clarence is not a topic of conversation," Nolan shouted from the kitchen. "You need to stop that."

"I wish he did. His mother is somebody a little goes a long way," Mrs. Smith said.

After coffee, she left us to talk, and Nolan talked. It turned out he was perfectly happy talking about himself—he had a professional-confessional mode. His older brother got killed in a gang shooting when Nolan was still in high school. That was one of the things that straightened him out. The other was music. There used to be a record shop on Charlevoix, run by a white guy named Jez Lansky, who'd been at that corner since the neighborhood was about a quarter Polish. Probably he'd have got robbed out of business or beaten up if people didn't like his records. But he played a lot of good music. Not just Diana Ross and Louis Armstrong, but Mable John and Billy Eckstine, Art Blakey and Horace Silver and Clifford Brown. Nolan's dad used to say, "Jez is all right, you can hang out at Jez's." When he died, there was a line outside St. Albertus three blocks long following the coffin, and about half of those people were black. It didn't matter that Jez was white and a homo and that he probably died of AIDS. Then they closed down that fucking church two years later, which had been there for about a hundred years, but this is Detroit.

"What instrument did you play?"

"I didn't play any instrument. I liked the music, too, but what I really liked was the covers. My heroes were Reid Miles and Bob Cato and Mati Klarwein. Jez put me onto all those guys. I wanted to be a designer."

That's why he went to Ferris State, apart from the fact that they gave him a football scholarship. Because of the Kendall College of Art and Design. Nolan had a lot to say about art degrees. What he took was a four-year course and you needed to write a thirty-thousand-word dissertation. It was a *degree*. These days you could get a master's for pressing a button on a camera thirty times. To change the subject, I asked him about his brother.

"He was like a low-level high school crack dealer. Not even a soldier, he was more like a small-business man, he was a kid with a lemonade stand. I don't even think he was using. But then someone shot him in the neck."

"Did they find out who?"

"Probably somebody owed him money. We don't know."

"Were you close?"

"White brothers are close to each other. He looked out for me, I looked up to him."

"I don't know that white brothers are always so close."

We talked about his art, too. Coming out of college he wanted to make some really big art, he was obsessed with Diego Rivera, he wanted to apply the techniques of illustration on a large scale. I had noticed one of these pieces, a jungle scene painted on the side of an old factory—about fifty feet wide and a hundred feet tall. Later he got into photography, which is what his project with Gloria was about. The kids were just a means to an end for him, he was using them. The problem of art is always the problem of realism, he said, the relationship to reality. Big art for him was all about being bigger than reality, like, if it was bigger, it might be truer, too, or more real. Photography was the same deal. He talked a lot in this vein and I wrote some of it down, not because I was interested but I wanted to keep him happy. Right now he was working on a piece about his brother, about the crack scene in Detroit, called *Looking for My Brother's Killer*. The point is the guy was probably dead, there was nobody to look for, but he was going to keep looking. He was hanging out with some pretty wrecked people and asking questions and taking photographs. Nobody remembered his brother. When you got people dying and going to jail at the rate they do, nobody remembers anybody. But photography was just a transitional phase for him. He wanted to push realism further, he wanted to make art that changed reality, that had an effect on it, and one of the forms he was looking at was legal art.

"What's legal art?"

Lawsuits, he said. He wanted to sue people, where the art was just the legal act, the court papers and documentation, the judge's ruling. But it cost money. A lot of what he did was apply for grants.

"Who are you going to sue?" I said.

"I ain't angry but I got a lot of grievances, a lot of things needing correcting."

I drove around Detroit with him, too—Detroiters were always driving me around. The first time it was just the two of us, and he took me around the old Black Bottom neighborhood, or what was left of it after urban renewal. "Negro removal," Nolan called it, a line I had heard before, which slightly lowered my opinion of him. So he went around with borrowed ideas like the rest of us. He talked about Joe Louis and Bishop Franklin, Mies van der Rohe and other people. We walked under the highway intersections, the Chrysler Freeway and Gratiot Avenue, right by Ford Field, it was a dripping, cold November morning, through to the park on the other side, and I felt about as wet and cold as the roads we walked on. At one point I thought maybe this is where the guy dragged Astrid, but I don't think it was. I asked Nolan if he knew her; he didn't.

Then he bought me coffee to warm up, at a place called Wigley's Meats. It was about eleven in the morning. We also ordered corned-beef sandwiches. Nolan told me a story about a crack house where he took some pictures. A lot of these places were whore houses, too, it wasn't just a question of drugs and customers, but clients and audiences, people hung out. People get pretty amusing when they're high or when they want to get high. One of the worst things he saw was a woman going down on her son, who was about fourteen years old, the mother was maybe in her late twenties, both of them needed a fix and guys threw money at them while they did it. Wigley's was an upmarket tourist destination, sort of blue-collar chic, though I guess locals went there, too, it wasn't particularly expensive. Nolan never lowered his voice.

"Why do you tell me this stuff," I said.

"There is no human nature, there's just law and economics. You set up people to want something, they'll do whatever it takes to get it. Supply and demand."

"That's not what supply and demand is."

"Fuck you, Marny," he said. "You like me, you're kind of scared of me, but you still think you're smarter than me because I'm black."

"That's not what I said."

"You saying it all the time, you just not listening to yourself."

Another time he even took me out with some of his crack buddies, guys he met while looking for his brother's killer. I felt nervous about this. Nolan wouldn't tell me what the plan was. He picked me up in his car a little after ten o'clock—it was a Sunday morning. I said, "What, are we going for brunch?" Then we drove around and picked up a few other people, mostly in east Detroit, and ended up driving to a football game. The Lions were playing, and one of his buddies, a dealer, had a box.

When we picked up this dealer guy, Ernie, I had to get out of the front seat and let him get in. So I sat in back with two other dudes, who made me climb over one of them to sit in the middle. It was like being a kid again, which made me feel bratty. Ernie kept complaining about where I put my feet, he said my shoes were dirty, and get them off his clothes. The two guys in back with me were called Marcellus and Taequan. "Is that like Tae Kwon Do?" I said, and he wrinkled his nose like something smelled bad. With these people, I figured, you have to give as good as you get.

Ernie was a skinny, nervous-looking guy, maybe forty years old. He had a little mustache and didn't wear anything but a nylon jacket, like a caretaker's jacket, over his shirt, and skinny cotton pants and cheap sneakers. His color was muddy red, and he had one of those faces that look hard to shave—there were a lot of rough patches, little bumps, some with hairs growing out of them. It was about thirty degrees outside, a white, cold day, on the edge of snowing. We parked by Eastern Market and there were guys outside grilling dogs and drinking beer. I said to Ernie, "Aren't you cold?"

"I regulate my own temperature. If I get cold, I run in place."

But he ate a lot, a slice of pizza, a couple of chili dogs, people were selling popcorn and he ate that, too. Eventually we walked over to the game, which was about a ten-minute walk, part of a stream of people, not exactly marching but dutifully going along, milling and pushing forward, but in high spirits. The Lions had sucked for about ten years, the season before they hadn't won a game, and nobody expected much. But people looked happy, everybody had a good time.

Mostly what we talked about was football. Detroit was playing the Browns, old rivals. Cleveland stunk, too, though not as bad as Detroit. I heard a lot of Cleveland jokes outside the stadium, on the walk over. Thousands of Browns fans had made the three-hour drive. But the queues were good-natured, and I was used to this kind of depressed kidding but also borderline angry cheerfulness, from growing up outside New Orleans and being around Saints fans. I didn't care much about football, but I mentioned the brown baggers to Ernie to pretend like I did, like I used to be one of them—guys who showed up at the Superdome wearing brown paper bags over their heads.

I said, "You guys need some brown bags, it's brown-bag time."

Detroit was like one and eight going into the game. Cleveland had won maybe three games. "What is this, the toilet bowl?" I said. Nolan had bought everybody a round of Jägermeisters at the tailgate. It was eleven thirty in the morning and I felt good.

"This asshole right here needs to shut up, that's what he need to do," Marcellus said.

Then the game started. Cleveland knocked in a field goal and then Detroit got one back.

"It's going to be one of those six-three games," I said. "Nine-six, twelve-nine, that kind of game." Then Cleveland scored three straight touchdowns, in about ten minutes, boom boom boom, and it looked like just another winter afternoon in Detroit, with the scoreboard ticking over, seventeen to three, twenty-four to three, one of those days. Somehow getting beat like that made everybody relax. They didn't have to care anymore.

But Detroit had this kid from Georgia named Stafford, a first-year guy, playing QB. Marcellus called him the pretty girl—he was going to be good. "Come on, pretty girl," he said, "put it in there," stuff like that. And Stafford started mixing it up, throwing it all over the field, guys made catches, guys broke tackles, it was two shitty teams going at it, and by halftime Detroit was only down three.

Ernie's box had heating and a minibar, and we were drinking the whole time and Ernie kept sending Taequan out to get the waitress. "Tell him what you want," Ernie told me, "get what you want, this whole thing's on me."

I said to him, "You're a good man, Ernie, thank you very much." But then the beer started talking for me and I asked him if he knew

Nolan's dead brother or who had killed him and how many people he had killed himself.

"Marcellus here's your killer," he said. "Ain't that right, Marcellus? I'm just a businessman. I do paperwork."

"Naw, don't put that on me," Marcellus said. "Don't believe what he tell you. He's cold-blooded."

"You guys are just fucking with me, aren't you?"

"If we was fucking with you, you'd be dead."

Then the second half started and it was more, Come on, pretty girl, make babies. This is what Marcellus called touchdowns. Stafford threw a touchdown pass and then got sacked in his own end zone. Cleveland scored again and got the ball back. Detroit was down six, but stuffed the Browns on fourth down, and then there were two minutes left and the pretty girl had the ball in his hands and was driving the Lions downfield. "Come on, you white Georgia motherfucker," Ernie said. "Be good."

Stafford brought the Lions to the two-yard line and then got picked off in the end zone as time ran out. But there was a flag on the field and the play got called back. Stafford meanwhile lay flat on his back with the medical team poking at him. He took a hit on the last throw, but he got up and ran another huddle, and with no time left on the clock, dumped the ball into the tight end, a little behind him, so the guy had to spin around into open space. But he caught it anyway. Everybody went fucking crazy around me, including me, but we had to wait for the extra point to go crazy again and make it official. The Lions had won. It was the last game they won all year.

On the ride home, Taequan heard Nolan calling me Marny, and he said, "How come people call you Marny? Is it because you a bitch?" When I didn't say anything, he said, "How come he laughing? How come he laughing when I call him a bitch?"

"Leave him alone," Nolan said. "He's all right."

"I'm just saying, how come he got like a female dog name?"

"Because he's *my* dog," Nolan said.

He dropped everybody else off first, and when Ernie got out, I climbed through the gap between the seats and sat in front. We drove like that, not talking much, until we got back to Johanna Street. He parked in his own drive and I walked home.

16

I started hanging out with Clarence a little, too. Walter and Susie had finally got their license from human services, to run a
children's workshop out of their house. So every day, a couple of
times a day, parents and nannies came by with their buggies and
scooters. There was a morning session and an afternoon session.
Mornings were mostly for toddlers, and afternoons became a kind
of after-school drop-off for five- and six- and seven-year-olds. Susie
sat down at the piano, I could hear her from upstairs, and taught
the kids songs, while Walter did crafts with them, designing cos-
tumes and stage sets. He was good with his hands, and good at getting down on his hands and knees, which I wouldn't have expected.
They were going to put on a Nativity play and wanted to get it
ready for just before Christmas.

By Thanksgiving I knew most of the songs myself, which drove
me nuts. "Away in a Manger," all of that. The religious element
surprised me, too, but Susie was raised High Church Episcopalian,
and Walter went along with her. How much he believed I don't
know. But he was very good with kids, patient, he got down to their
level, all that lack of vanity or ambition or whatever you want to call
it served him well here. Though I admit I also felt uncomfortable,

seeing him on the floor with these small boys and girls, when what got him into this situation in the first place was his inappropriate response to a sixteen-year-old student in his class.

The kids who came were mostly from our neighborhood, mostly newcomer kids, but Mrs. Smith sometimes brought Clarence along, and if she was late picking him up, he waited upstairs with me. I let him watch TV (Nolan was strict about TV) and gave him a glass of milk and we got along fine.

One afternoon Tony Carnesecca dropped his son at my house, because Cris was teaching a prenatal yoga workshop and he had something to talk about with Robert James. Michael would only get in the way. It was just for an hour. So I sat him down in front of the TV and about an hour later Clarence came up because Mrs. Smith was late, so I got him a glass of milk and told him to sit down next to Michael.

Michael stood up to make room, and I said to him, "You don't need to get up, there's plenty of space on the couch," and Michael said, "I don't like chocolate people." He was only three years old, he said it the way he might push away a plate of food, and Clarence, who was six, threw the milk in his face.

I said to Michael, "That's not a nice thing to say, I want you to say sorry," and then Tony walked in.

Michael was crying and Clarence was trying to push him down by the neck. It wasn't very easy for me to get him off, Clarence was a heavy kid, and Tony said, "What the fuck's going on in here?" and he pulled off Clarence himself, who started crying, too.

"I don't want you touching my boy, you understand that?" Tony said. "I don't want you touching my boy."

"It wasn't his fault," I told him.

"What the fuck are you doing, standing around with a paper towel?" Tony said. It's true, I had a paper towel in my hand. After

Clarence threw the milk I went into the kitchen to get something to clean it up with, and that's when he went for Michael's throat.

Tony took Michael to the bathroom to dry him off, and when he came out, he said, "I don't want this boy hanging around my son. Never again," and walked out.

Later that night I called their house and spoke to Cris, and then asked to speak to Tony. I told him what had happened, but he said, "You think this is just a kid thing, you think this happens all the time. But kids don't go for other kids' necks, not like that. His father is a violent angry Negro. I don't want my son hanging out with his son. If that's a problem, let me know, and I won't bring him by the house."

I didn't mention any of this to Nolan or Mrs. Smith, and maybe Clarence didn't either because he thought he might get in trouble, I don't know. But they never said anything to me about it.

THERE WAS A GENERAL FEELING in the neighborhood, which I didn't totally share, that the old Detroit blacks should be grateful to us, for pushing up their property prices and giving some of them domestic employment, mowing lawns, painting walls, that kind of thing, and bringing in stores and bars and restaurants where before there were boarded-up shops. But the stores weren't cheap and the truth is, you didn't see many black faces at Joe Silver's coffeehouse, for example. Most of the old residents kept to themselves.

One of the guys who took a more cynical view of the whole business was Steve Zipp, which is maybe why I liked him. We started hanging out a little. Every other weekend he had this baby to look after, which he didn't know what to do with, and sometimes he came by Walter and Susie's apartment, because Susie was very hands-on with other people's babies. He felt intimidated by actual parents, he said.

Steve was a funny guy once you got past appearances. He looked like an accountant and that's what he was. His clothes were too big, and he often wore his work shoes, which were black and shiny, under chinos on the weekend. When he was cold, he put his suit jacket over the top of his sweater. *From the country that brought you the pita chip!*—that's the kind of thing he said. I mean, he actually said it, in his football announcer's voice, when there was some stupid commercial on TV, selling something you never knew you needed and which probably wouldn't work anyway. A lot of things about America struck him as basically ridiculous.

He was also very suspicious of Robert James. He said the numbers didn't add up. Steve had gone to city hall and checked the public records, and somebody was either hemorrhaging money or there were private investors we didn't know anything about. You couldn't buy up two thousand houses in Detroit and sell them back at this rate without taking a big hit. Not if you were paying for health insurance, too, and contributing to the infrastructure costs. Unless you had some under-the-table deal, with the city or somebody else, to sweeten the pot.

The reason he had a baby was that an old friend of his from high school wanted to have a baby, and when she turned forty-two years old and wasn't married and didn't have a boyfriend, he offered her his sperm. He didn't expect to have anything else to do with the kid, he was kind of going through a midlife crisis himself, but it turned out having a baby was a full-time no-joke. So he volunteered to do his part. The kid's mother lived in Toledo; she worked at the university hospital there. Steve grew up in Toledo, which is where they both went to high school.

Three years ago, he'd moved back home to start an accountancy practice, leaving behind a fairly safe job at KPMG in Cleveland. Just a perfect time to start a business, he said. These days, of course, even KPMG was cutting working hours and asking people to take part-paid leave. Whenever he had any regrets, he reminded himself of these facts. His practice never got off the ground, the house he had just bought was losing equity, so he wiped out his savings by selling it and applied to Starting-from-Scratch-in-America. But the baby thing is what really set him off—you need to live in a manner you wouldn't mind passing on. One of the things that kept him busy in Detroit was Internet dating.

Steve introduced me to the E-change, which was set up by a kid named Nathan Zwecker, who used to work at the server farm. It was a kind of Craigslist site for everybody from the five neigh-borhoods, based on what Steve called the "Burning Man model." Basically, anybody who wanted anything or had anything to barter, from a secondhand car to an empty seat at a dinner party, posted it on the site, and because the community was really very small and interconnected and geographically concentrated, it got a lot of traffic.

Zwecker became something of a big cheese—I did one of my profiles on him for the newsletter. He was pleasant-looking, with a round face and pale hair, quite formal, tall, a little overweight. In another life he might have been a priest. Or a rabbi, I guess. When I met him he was twenty-three years old, a Pomona drop-out, who got hired full-time by some San Francisco tech company after a summer internship. One of the things he worked out is that people in the five neighborhoods wanted to respond very quickly to each other in specific ways, so he figured out how to map every post according to time and place and the kind of posting. The pro-gramming wasn't particularly complicated, he said, it was mostly a design issue. It needed to look good and easy. The point of the project, as he understood it, was to take a virtual community and make it real, give it real estate, fill it with people, etc., but that also put a certain pressure on the virtual sites to keep up, in real time.

Robert James invited him to some of their business conferences. Clay Greene consulted him about his book. They even started talking like Zwecker in TV interviews. "Basically," Robert said, "the idea behind the whole place, what got us started, is that we wanted to take a virtual community and make it real." He was sitting on a rigged stage, heavily made-up, surrounded by lights, with the cameras fixed on him, and looking totally natural and like himself. This was at the big MDP fund-raiser held at the old Wayne Conner plant, about a week after Thanksgiving. All kinds of people came, the mayor, Bill Russo and his crowd, some of the top brass from the UAW. Obama came, and was supposed to bring his wife and kids, but in the end only the president made it. But I'm getting ahead of myself.

Steve Zipp spent a lot of his time on the E-change. He was one of those people who could carry on a conversation while scrolling around on his phone. "You think I'm not making eye contact because of this thing," he once said to me. "I never used to look people in the eyes anyway." If some girl posted she was going to Ikea in an hour and needed muscle, Steve checked out her profile and volunteered to ride along. This way you got to meet girls without any date pressure. The E-change worked like an eBay site. People got ratings. So if you went along and creeped out that girl by making inappropriate passes over the meatballs, your ratings took a hit, and nobody would invite you along to anything else. Steve obsessed about his rating, which was high for somebody who made his kind of first impression. He was an amusing person to have around. "I only make appropriate passes," he said.

"What is this rating, like a sex appeal thing?" I asked him once.

Steve tried to persuade me it was more innocent than that. "It's more like, do they show up on time, can they keep up their end of a conversation, are they clean? Do they spend all their time checking their phones?"

"You check your phone constantly."

"That's because you're a real friend," he said. "I would never behave that way with a virtual friend. It kills your rating."

"Well, where do I get to rate you?"

"You only get to rate me if you respond to one of my posts. But you never would. You're a Luddite."

The truth is, my real life was filling out nicely, I didn't need a virtual one. I hung out with Walter and Susie, and babysat for Tony and sometimes looked after Clarence for a quarter hour in the afternoon. I wrote the newsletter, which got me out of the house and introduced me to people. Sometimes I had dinner with Robert and Bill, at fancy restaurants or at Robert's house with the whole thing catered for. Ridiculously pretty women in black skirts and white shirts handed around trays of champagne as soon as you walked in the door. About once a month, or maybe a little less than that, I met up with Tony's friend Mel Hauser, and we drove out to the police canteen and had lunch there and fired off some rounds. Mel persuaded me to buy a handgun; he said the Remington wasn't much use for anything but a drive-by shooting. If you wanted to protect yourself you needed a hand weapon, and he offered to get me one through the department. Retiring officers had the option of buying their weapons from the city, which most of them took, but some of them didn't, and then the guns became generally available for purchase by other officers. Mel bought me one of these, a Smith & Wesson M&P40 with a four-and-a-quarter-inch barrel.

Astrid and I met up irregularly but often stayed the night together, then saw each other several days running, buying groceries, cooking dinner, watching movies, living like lovers. We could also go weeks at a stretch without so much as texting. Nolan and I sometimes went jogging through the neighborhood streets. Some of his football muscle had turned to fat since he quit playing and he wanted to lose the weight. Once or twice a month, on Sunday morning, Robert picked me up on the way and we drove out to Belle Isle for a five-mile run. Tony and Cris had me around to their house for dinner, which saved them the cost of getting a babysitter. I saw Eddie Blyleven, Kurt Stangel, Jayson Mogford and Don Adler at Neighborhood Watch meetings, and I also sometimes went out on patrol with Eddie and Kurt. Kurt had started to get somewhere in the extras business. This gave him something to talk about—Sean Penn bummed a cigarette off him once, that kind of thing.

Steve Zipp had nicknames for a lot of us. Eddie Blyleven he called Insurance Eddie or Captain Eddie, because he was big and fair-haired and all-American and like everybody's big brother. He put his hand on your shoulder, he said encouraging general things, he called you buddy. In fact, he used to be a lieutenant in the Air Force Reserve and even did a tour of Afghanistan before being discharged for medical reasons. His life had fallen apart, he was drinking too much, his wife was in the middle of an affair. They eventually divorced and she remarried. Then Eddie sobered up and needed somewhere to start again so he came to Detroit. Some of these things he told me himself, without making judgments or excuses, and the truth is, when I knew him, he seemed like such a controlled likable guy that nothing he said about this past self seemed very relevant or revealing.

Sometimes we all hung out together, Eddie and Kurt and Steve and me, and Walter, too, before Susie arrived. We went fishing at the Roostertail together. Eddie and Kurt both liked to fish, and for their sake we got up at five on a summer morning and drank our coffee in the car. Steve called Kurt Stangel "the Strangler," for no good reason, apart from the name, I guess, and the fact that he was big in a different way—flat-faced and strong and kind of affectless, too. As it happens, Kurt did a great Orson Welles impersonation, with the almost-English accent and the slyness and the suppressed grin. Fishing involves a lot of time-passing techniques. But he could be pretty passive, too. I got the sense from Kurt that what used to be his personality (you know, funny and referential—he knew a lot of movies), which he could roll out effortlessly in high school and college, now took some effort. Because of parenthood and adulthood or whatever. So you only got glimpses of it. Kurt called Steve Zipp Big Thumb, like it was his Indian name or something, because of that damn phone. I don't know what they called me.

For some reason Beatrice had dropped off the map. I saw her at Robert's house but that was it. And maybe once or twice every couple of weeks, I substituted at Kettridge High and had lunch in the school cafeteria with Gloria Lambert.

17

The first day I got called in was early October, very cold and rainy, real Monday-morning-blues weather. Reception smelled of wet clothes and too many kids. Nobody cared what my background was in, they just gave me a textbook and the attendance card and sent me out to teach. By "they" I mean the assistant principal, Mrs. Sanchez.

"We're starting you off nice and easy," she said. "Ninth-grade math. Fractions."

I said, "I haven't thought about fractions in twenty years."

Mrs. Sanchez had long, artificial, brightly painted nails. Her office was full of spider plants. One window looked into the reception area, the other had a view of a corridor. She had her degrees on the wall, from Wayne State and Marygrove College, alongside photographs of kids—Mrs. Sanchez sometimes had her arm around them. The tube lighting on the ceiling cast no shadows, it seemed designed to grow the plants. You couldn't see any outside weather, and the office felt warm from all the lights.

She said, "I wouldn't worry overmuch about fractions."

When I got to the classroom, a few minutes before the bell, the door was open and kids were not only coming in but going out, too, talking in the hall, *visiting*—for some reason, all kinds of spinsterish words like that came into my head. Then the bell went off, as loud as a fire alarm, and I stuck my neck out into the hall and said, "Everybody get in who's coming in."

It was a relief to say something out loud. I was talking so much in my own head, talking to myself and looking at everything and feeling blank and tired. A few kids came in and I shut the door. Then about ten seconds later another kid walked in, and I said, "Okay, that's it, you're the last one," and stood by the door with my back against it. Then someone else tried to get in.

"Hey, what the fuck," came a voice on the other side of the door. Some of the kids in the classroom heard him and laughed.

One of them called out, "Hey, Nugent, you late. It's a lockout."

"What do you mean, it's a lockout?"

While this was going on, I stood there, pressing my back against the door and not saying anything.

"Sub's here and he's locking you out."

Then Nugent said, "What's he like?"

The kid talking to him had an Eagles jersey on, which was meant to be short-sleeved but came over his elbows on the arms and hung around his chair like a dress.

"Harry Potter," the kid said.

"All right, keep it down."

"You gonna let me in?"

"I saw you in the hall. I said, everybody get in who's coming in. You didn't come in."

"I had something to do."

"You were eating a candy bar," I said.

"I was hungry."

"So go get something to eat."

"You don't understand, I'm like on some watch list. I get one more absence, they give me detention and I got to come after school."

"You should have thought of that before."

"I didn't know we had no sub today with a stick up his ass."

"Well, now you know."

"Man, fuck this. This is unreasonable. No way I'm going to detention for this. I'll tell you what happen next. They put me on suspension for not going to detention. Then I'll drop out of school and be like one of them corner kids because of you. And all because you wouldn't open this damn door."

I let him in.

By lunchtime I felt like I was coming down with flu—physically sore and stiff. My head ached, the institutional-strength classroom lights hurt my eyes. I looked out for Gloria in the cafeteria and sat down at her table but not near enough to talk. After lunch, when she got up to bus her tray, I bused mine, too, and said, "Can I talk to you?"

"What about?"

"I just need a friendly voice."

"You can walk with me, I got class."

She seemed short with me, officially polite, and I wondered if somehow I had annoyed her. But the truth is, she was probably being friendly enough. I didn't know her well at all. Every time I taught at Kettridge I looked out for her in the lunchroom, and we found things to talk about or joined in the general conversation, and once I waited around after school by my car when I noticed it was parked close to hers. It was a Friday afternoon, the week before Thanksgiving, and a high-pressure front had cleared out the clouds. The big highway street lamps overlooking I-94 were already lit, and the sky had the almost white blue color of a late winter afternoon. It was cold, too; the metal of the car door felt chilly on my butt as I leaned against it.

"You waiting for somebody?" Gloria said, shifting the bag on her hip to look for her keys.

"I thought maybe we could go for a drink. It's Friday night."

"Most Friday nights I have a bath and go to bed. Saturday night's going-out night."

"How about tomorrow then?" But I remembered I couldn't. Astrid and I had a date. "Actually I can't tomorrow, let's just have a beer tonight."

It was rush hour, and the noise of the freeway gave a funny urgency to the conversation and made everything seem somehow temporary and important. The world outside was the world of traffic and commutes and stretched from here to Ann Arbor and Brighton and Auburn Hills, on 96 and 94 and 75 and 696.

"I told you I'm tired. I get cranky when I'm tired. If you want to ask me out just ask me out."

"I thought that's what I was doing."

"I don't know what you're doing. If you want to go out with a girl you don't have to start teaching at her school."

"But I wanted to do that, too. I'm not exactly overemployed at the moment."

"That's all this is. You don't know what to do with yourself. I can't even tell if you like me very much. All you ever do at lunch is try to argue with me."

"I argue with everybody."

"That's just what I mean. Listen, I told you I'm cranky. You got my number, if you want to give me a call give me a call."

"Well, how am I supposed to know if you like me?"

"That's one of those things you figure out for yourself."

There was something immature about all this, her tiredness and the way she got annoyed. Her face was very smooth and boyish, she was as short as a kid and acted like a kid in school sometimes, for the sake of her students. She had a lot of energy, but when it ran out, there was nothing left and this is what she was like. On Sunday evening I gave her a call and asked her to join me for the big political fund-raiser Robert James was putting on. Tickets were $300, but I could get in as a friend and bring a date. The Wrenfields were booked to play, along with Anita Baker and Chairmen of the Board. Obama was supposed to be coming with Michelle and the girls.

"Well, in that case," she said.

I TOLD NOLAN ABOUT THIS, and he said, "What you want to go out with her for?"

We were jogging around Butzel Park, mostly on the street because the sidewalks were covered in snow. Just after Thanksgiving a low-pressure front blew in and dumped a foot of snow all over the city. I opened the window one morning and looked out on countryside—white fields. But it didn't last, not like that. The only good thing to come out of all this, Nolan once said, is that the fucking streets get plowed. Even so, we took it pretty slow, since the asphalt was full of cracks and holes and some of the plowed snow had melted again and frozen overnight. Slow suited me fine; it was cold enough my lungs hurt breathing.

"What kind of question is that? The usual reasons."

"That's what I'm saying. You just want to go out with a black woman."

"I thought she was a friend of yours."

"She is a friend of mine."

"Did you used to go out with her or something? Is that what this is?"

"Naw, I'm not the kind of asshole she goes for."

"What kind is that?"

"White ones," he said. "Anyway, aren't you going out with some-body?"

"Not really."

We were kidding around, which suited me fine, since I wanted to let him know one way or another. Nolan reduced many things to black and white; it didn't mean he was more pissed off than usual. And we kept jogging along on flat feet, blowing steam and pulling our sleeves down over our hands. But somehow this put me in a bad mood and after the run I got into an argument with Nolan about Obama. He said he was just like every other president, a front man for big business. We were standing outside Nolan's house, in wet snow, sweating and cooling down. I don't care what else you want to say about him, I said, but to have a black man in the Oval Office makes you a witness to history. Am I supposed to be grateful, Nolan asked. Oh give me a break, I said, and started walking away.

18

Gloria lived about a ten-minute drive east of me, just at the border with Grosse Pointe, on the Detroit side. One block farther, and the mansions began—well, not mansions exactly, but big old suburban houses, with privately maintained lawns out front and publicly maintained trees shading the road. But on Gloria's street there were still boarded-up garages and empty lots. There weren't any trees, except growing wild in the lots, and the houses had cheap sidings and no driveways. They looked like kid-size milk cartons, one after the other, all lined up.

I crawled along the curb reading numbers and pulled up outside the only apartment block, a yellow-and-brown brick building, probably built in the 1930s, with dozens of small windows and a fancy entrance. There were pillars on either side and a kind of ziggurat pattern cut out of the brickwork overhead.

Gloria lived on the fourth floor. I rang the bell and she let me in and I walked up the concrete stairwell—three out of the four landing lights were broken. But her apartment was warm and bright, she had simple tastes, there was a rug on the floor and a couple of chairs, a coffee table, there were plants on the window ledges and a drop leaf table pushed up against one of them, where it looked

YOU DON'T HAVE TO LIVE LIKE THIS • 165

like she ate her meals. It was the living room of a single person who thinks, now I will sit here, now I will sit here. I knew what that was like myself.

"How long have you been in this place?" I said.

"Two years come Christmas. But I grew up in the building. My mom still lives in it."

"That's pretty close."

"Close enough. But there's another entrance. You got to go out and come back in." And then, "My daddy died. I'm the only child. I figured this was better than having her move in with me when she got too old."

Gloria wore a green wool dress, with long sleeves, and dark tights—it was like she had only two things on. She had pulled something up and pulled something down. Her lips were painted the same bright wet color she wore the day I met her, at Bill Russo's place in the country, and she had on a bright cheerful mood, too.

As we walked down to the car, she said, "What do you get to eat for three hundred dollars?"

"I think it's a Thanksgiving theme."

"That's all right," she said. "I'm one of those people that loves turkey. Leftovers, too. Turkey and gravy and mash potatoes, all of that."

It was just after noon on the first Saturday in December. There was overnight snow on the ground and tiny, almost invisible specks of snow or rain falling through the air like salt. But the roads felt powdery under my tires and not icy or slick. We made good time.

A black SUV blocked the entrance to the parking lot and then pulled out of the way after I waved the clearance badge, which came with my invitation.

The old Wayne Conner plant used to be run by General Motors, to make diesel engines, but they shut down their diesel division in

1979. For the next twenty years it got leased to different companies, mostly light-truck manufacturers. Then it went empty. Robert
James bought the plant in 2008 and rented it to a California web
company, which hired the Kraemer Group, a Detroit architecture
firm, to turn the factory space into office space.

It was a nice building. There were three lines of tall continuous
windows running the length of each floor, and around the corners,
too, and the brickwork was faded to a chalky shade of fall yellow.
The main entrance wasn't much to look at, just a couple of flat high
gates, with a smaller door cut into one of them, which is the one we
used. Two Secret Service guys in black suits and overcoats stood by
the gates, doing the eye-roll patrol, and another woman in a temporary booth sat with a space heater blowing at her feet and checked
our names against the guest list.

But inside was warm. We walked through a metal-detector arch
and somebody took our coats and gave us a ticket. Behind the coat-
check table you could see, through internal windows, row after row
of graphite-gray cabinets sprouting red and blue wires. The hum
was about as loud as the noise of the sea when you're sitting on the
beach. But the party was upstairs, in the open-plan office area, and
much louder.

Somebody had rigged a projector to one of the computers, to
show a football game against part of the white wall. Because that's
what you do on Thanksgiving, I guess, watch football . . . Michigan
was playing Ohio State and the band was still on the field when we
arrived, a few minutes before kickoff. Then the players ran out of
the tunnel, looking about ten feet tall and stippled like golf balls
against the office paneling. Even over the noise of the party you
could hear the trumpets of the marching band. I got a little buzz
off it and took a beer from one of the drinks tables, and gave one
to Gloria.

"See anybody you know?" she said, and I said, "I want you to meet an old friend of mine," because Beatrice was talking to Cris by the floor-length window.

"Listen," Gloria said. "If someone tries to introduce us to the president, I'm just saying if it happens, don't expect me to say a word. You'll have to do the talking. I don't think I could."

"I haven't seen him yet."

Cris and Beatrice seemed to be in midflow, but we wandered over anyway. Beatrice was listening and Cris was saying, "You know what I keep thinking about, I keep thinking about the fact that there are all these stories men have, you know, when they're confessing things to you, which is what they do to show they can talk to women, and it kind of works when you're just starting to go out and sitting in some nice restaurant, and it's exactly these stories which you can't bear to hear once you're married to them. Hello, Marny," she said. "I'm being disloyal for once in my life. It's wine at lunch. Don't grass on me. Introduce me."

"This is Gloria, she teaches at the high school where I sometimes substitute. Cris used to be a lawyer."

"That's a terrible introduction," Cris said.

Outside the snow started coming down heavier, the salt had turned into corn puffs, and the second-floor factory window showed all of it, about a hundred feet wide. Beyond the parking lot I could see a raised highway, and beyond that and underneath it some temporary storage facilities and container units half buried in snow. There wasn't much traffic on the highway but what there was kept coming just as steady as the snow. At one point I noticed a stream of black SUVs approaching and figured the president had arrived.

Tony stood watching the game, and I excused myself and went over to him.

"Who's that black girl you came in with?"

"Someone I teach with. Cris is on a roll."

"We had a fight," he said.

Clay Greene was there, too, with a glass of champagne in his hand. "You're a young man," he said, "and I'm going to give you a little advice, which you're not going to take. But it's good advice. Apologize. Tell her what she thinks you did wrong, and apologize for that. Do it now and you can still enjoy yourselves this afternoon." He seemed already a little drunk.

"Where did you get that?" I said, pointing at the champagne flute.

He looked at me vaguely. "Robert gave it to me."

So I left my beer somewhere and went over to find Robert. I looked for Gloria, but by this point she was talking to Beatrice alone, and somehow I liked seeing the two of them together. Anyway, I wanted to bring her back a glass of champagne.

The room was large and full of people, the ceilings were low and we had to crowd ourselves around the office furniture. I pushed past men in suits and women in cocktail dresses, and guys in jeans and girls wearing heels and jeans or heels and miniskirts. There was a smattering of black faces. Robert had invited local businessmen, community-representative types, but he'd also given free passes to some of the new immigrants. There was a lottery system. People from the five neighborhoods could sign up, and later they found out if their name was on a list.

Robert wanted to play on the story of the Pilgrims' feast; the Thanksgiving theme was his idea. Like it was native Detroiters who gave of their bounty to provide this meal, who welcomed us in. But the fact is most guests had to pay through the nose, and the money went to the Michigan Democratic Party.

Waitresses in white aprons and waiters in stiff white shirts served up little paper plates of food on silver trays. I ate a mini turkey burger with stuffing on top and ended up carrying around, then crumpling into my pocket, a salty paper cone that held sweet potato fries. In a side room, I saw Robert sitting on a rigged-up stage, with bright lights shining in his face that made him look powdered or rouged. He was talking to a guy with a mic.

"One thing we discussed," Robert said, "one thing that worried me, is how *big* to make these neighborhoods." His voice was gently amplified. There were people standing around, drinking and eating and watching. Robert sat in an office swivel chair; he looked very comfortable. "And in the end what I decided was, they should roughly add up to a midsize college campus. There's a reason people have such nostalgic feelings in this country about their four years of college. And it isn't just the football team. It's because college is really the only time in our lives that most of us get to live in the kind of small-town community that we still associate with the founding of this country. And by the way, the Pilgrims on the whole were young, they were a young group of people, some of them were starting out in life for the first time, marrying and setting up a household and raising kids, and some of them had been out in Holland and were having a second or a third chance at it, starting over from scratch. And when you look around you, not just here and today, but in those neighborhoods, and you can imagine that I sometimes like to take a quiet walk around them, what you see is more or less . . ."

I spotted Kurt Stangel, wearing a fat tie, and he came over to me and said in a low voice, "Have you seen Sean Penn?"

"Is he here?"

"They've got a documentary room, where people can go up and talk into a camera. Anyway, Eddie saw Sean hanging out there with Micky Dolenz."

"What do you mean, Micky Dolenz?"

"What do you mean *what do you mean*? The guy from the Monkees. All these LA types hang out together when they're in town. You wanna go see?"

So we wandered out again, and on the way I picked up another beer. A guy in a pale gray pinstripe suit said, "Who's running this show?" and somebody else said, "Robert James."

"Who he?"

They were standing together by the drinks table, in everybody's way, and when people pushed past they excused themselves very politely and didn't move.

"One of these hedge fund types. He retired at like thirty and doesn't know what to do with himself, so he does this."

"Throw parties?"

Pinstripes had psoriasis on the back of his hands and kept scratching at it; the other guy was shorter and looked Jewish.

"No, this is just a publicity stunt. I mean, the whole neighborhood thing. Premature gentrification. He's trying to get Obama's attention."

"So is he coming or not?"

"Don't bet on it. He's in Oslo for the Peace Prize."

Then we got our beers and Kurt asked one of the waiters where the documentary room was. But it wasn't a room. A kind of gallery overlooked the factory floor. There was a big open column of space in the middle of the building with a skylight on top made of small square panes. The afternoon light came in and fell like snow. You could hear the computers below giving off heat.

Somebody had put together an exhibition on the gallery walkway. (Later I met the guy, a German named Kellerman about my age, whom Robert had recently hired as artistic adviser. He dressed like a banker and spoke English English.) There were paintings and photographs on the walls, a lot of disaster kitsch, Detroit landscapes, burned-out houses and teddy bears in the snow. I found it depressing, the way artists go for this stuff, like it's any more real than daffodils. There were also found-object displays and video installations, not just by professional artists but by some of the locals, too—mostly kids, with their names and grades and high schools labeled underneath. I looked out for Kettridge High but didn't see it.

A long queue around one of the corners turned out to be the line for the documentary station. Kellerman had had the bright idea of inviting people to talk about what brought them to Detroit in the first place. So he set up a chair against one wall and pointed a camera at it. A chunky, short-haired woman in Doc Martens and a yellow floral dress kept people moving along.

I noticed Don Adler in the queue, but the rest of the crowd looked younger. The guy talking when we walked past said he graduated from the University of Chicago in 2005, then moved in with some friends who were renting a house by Wicker Park. For a while he lived off money from his dad, who worked for Aerotek in Maple Grove, Minnesota. His dad was an engineer, which was one of the reasons he studied engineering. But then his dad got laid off and couldn't afford to send him pocket money. By this point he was willing to take anything and signed up to a call center agency. They found him a job at a travel insurance company, which had some vacancies in the night shift. This meant leaving the house at ten o'clock in the evening and coming back at eight a.m. Then he slept till lunchtime, but often overslept, and found himself wandering out to buy milk at four in the afternoon and feeling weird.

Meanwhile, he and one of the girls he lived with got engaged. She worked as a teaching assistant at a public elementary school in Evanston, but they didn't have enough money to rent a place of their own and didn't know anyone in Evanston to share a house with. The commute was about forty minutes each way and she found it draining. Even before they got married, which was last year, she became pregnant, and they needed to think of some other arrangement, not even to make their life tolerable, but just to make it feasible. After five minutes a light came on and it was somebody else's turn to talk.

"Have you seen Sean Penn?" I said to Kurt, and he pointed.

It didn't look like Sean Penn to me and then I realized it was probably Micky Dolenz. He was one of those fifty-year-old guys with a little boy's face under the stubble and gray hair. Later I realized he was closer to sixty-five. Micky was sitting in front of a video installation, and Kurt and I took up a couple of empty seats in the row behind him. The video screen showed two women talking. One of the women was white and one was black, they were sitting on opposite ends of a brown couch, and suddenly I realized that the white woman was Astrid.

The credits rolled and then Micky got up and wandered off, but the piece was on a loop and I sat around to watch the beginning.

Kurt stuck around, too, and said, "The thing you have to realize about famous people is that they're famous for a reason. Sean Penn is smarter than anybody you've ever met, he's in better physical shape than anybody you've ever met, and he's got more energy and intellectual curiosity about the world than anybody you've ever met. These people make things happen. He flies over to Haiti, and boom, a hospital gets built.

"There's no wasted energy. If he's hanging out with Micky Dolenz there's probably a reason. Maybe he wants to make a Monkees movie. Not a remake, but a music-industry movie, about the whole publicity machine and the end of innocence. All of that crap. It's not a bad idea. So he calls up Micky and says, I'm in Detroit, come, too."

Astrid asked the black woman, "Do you remember when we first met?"

The woman shook her head and said, "I know who you are. I know what this is about. The only reason I agreed to this is because you paying me."

"Would you like to talk about that? Would you like to mention how much you're being paid?"

"I don't like to talk about nothing. It's your money, you axe the questions."

"Do you remember when we first met?"

"I thought the Monkees was an LA thing," I said to Kurt. "They were set up by the television studios."

"Yes, but in 1967 they were supposed to play a concert in Detroit with Jimi Hendrix. But Jimi walked out and one of his publicists put it around that the Daughters of the American Revolution forced him off the tour."

"I don't think that's why Micky Dolenz and Sean Penn are in Detroit."

"You can't make a movie about the American music business and not talk about Detroit."

Astrid said, "What did you think when you saw me lying in your bed? For me, it was a very powerful moment. I was very scared, I didn't know where I was, but to see a woman come in, after what had happened, made me think that what connects us as women is more important than nationality or race, it cuts through all that bullshit, when you came in, I knew it would be all right."

"I didn't do nothing but get rid of you."

"You drove me to the bus station."

"Well, if my brother came back I didn't know what he'd do."

There was a poster over the video screen that read *A Conversation About Rape, with Astrid Topolski.* Kurt said, "Listen, I'm gonna get another drink. This is downing me out."

"Okay," I said but after a few minutes stood up as well. Watching Astrid made me uncomfortable. As if I had done something wrong but didn't know what—as if I had done something to her. Or maybe it was more like guilt by association. I went looking for Gloria.

Along the way I passed the queue for the documentary station. There were people in line shouting, and the woman whose turn it was made a calming motion with her hands and said, "Well, I don't know if you're coming to this party or not, Mr. President, but there are people here with a few things on their mind. What you're doing to this country means that some of us got no choice but to set up on our own. If we have to do that in Detroit, we'll move to Detroit."

Her hair was straight and brown, she wore a suit jacket and jeans and looked maybe forty years old. She looked like she'd had kids, a little thick in the waist, and had to kind of perch on the edge of the chair. Her jeans seemed new, like she hadn't broken them in. Her accent sounded southern, what I think of as a Christian accent. Some of the people shouting tried to shout her down, but she had supporters, too.

Don Adler said to me, "I've been waiting my turn forty minutes and need to go to the bathroom. But these dumbos don't let anybody speak."

"I'm sure they'll keep your spot if you explain why."

He gave me one of his looks.

"I prefer to take my chances holding it in," he said.

The first person I saw as I came back to the party was Clay Greene, who stood in silk jacket and tie, leaning slightly, and put his hand on Astrid's arm. I walked up and said to Clay, "I didn't know you guys knew each other," and he said, "This charming lady . . . this charming lady . . ."

"I want to talk to you, too," Astrid said. She was wearing cow-boy boots and jeans and a plain white T-shirt.

"I saw your documentary."

"That's what I want to talk to you about."

"I'm here with somebody else tonight."

"I want to meet her," she said.

"No."

"Well then, point her out."

So we excused ourselves from Clay and started looking.

"Is it the black schoolteacher?" Astrid said.

"There," I said.

Gloria stood holding her beer bottle in two hands across her lap and watching the football game. Tony was with her and said something to her. He had to bend his neck; she kept her eyes on the wall.

"I'm glad it's her," Astrid said. "It's good for you. It's what you need."

"What does that mean?"

"The first time I met you I could tell, you are scared of this country, you are scared of people, you were scared for me . . ."

"Look what happened to you."

"And here I am. Anyway, you are a man. Are you sleeping together?"

"Does it make a difference? No."

"Why don't you sleep with her? Is it for me?"

"This is our first date."

"And will you sleep with her tonight? Excuse me, I want to know. For myself, I don't mind. But I think maybe she is the kind of woman who does, and I don't want to make trouble."

"Astrid, this conversation makes me uncomfortable and unhappy."

"Some things you don't mind doing, but you don't want to talk about them."

"I mind doing them, too," I said and went over to Gloria.

"What happened to you?" she asked.

The football game had gone to commercial and people wandered away to get drinks and food. It was an odd party—it felt like an office party, we were surrounded by office plants and there were brightly colored ergonomic chairs pushed up against the walls—except without the sense of release or shifting intimacy. Too many people stood around watching the game. That's what happens when you put a TV on: people stare at it.

"I got waylaid. Were you bored?"

"I love football. I went to Michigan. Go Blue," she said.

"We were having an interesting conversation about Nolan Smith," Tony broke in.

"What were you saying about Nolan?"

"Excuse me, do you know where the restrooms are?" Gloria asked and went off in search of them. I didn't know her very well but it occurred to me that when she got angry she became little-girl polite.

"What did you say to her about Nolan?"

"Nothing," Tony said. "I just told her what happened."

"What happened about what? Nothing happened."

"Well then, that's what I said."

I left him to find Gloria and when she came out of the women's bathroom she said, "If you didn't want me to come, why did you bring me?"

"I wanted you to come but I got caught up with stupid people."

She took this in for a minute. From where we stood, I could see the corner window wrapping around the building, so that the streets and the parking lot below spread out in two directions. Snow fell heavily now; the cars on the freeway went at half speed with their headlights on.

"We'll have a bad time getting out of here," I said.

"I'm not like your friends. You move in . . . high circles."

"What are you talking about? You're practically the only person I know who has a decent job."

"That's what I mean."

"And Tony's just an asshole. That's got nothing to do with circles."

"Tony was like the only one I could relate to. I know lots of Tonys."

"You mean Beatrice," I said.

"I don't think she's a good friend to you. She says things."

"What did she say?"

But this changed her mood a little.

"She said that at Yale you were voted most likely to become the next Unabomber."

"That's not even true. That's not even *her* joke."

"It wasn't about you, it was about me. It's like she wanted to keep me out."

"I'll talk to her."

"Don't talk to her."

"I'll talk to her. She's an important person to me but it's not always plain sailing. Our friendship has always needed a lot of adjustments."

"You know he did his PhD at Michigan," she said. "I took some classes in the math department and there were still people there who remembered him."

"Who?"

"Ted Kaczynski. He said it was the worst five years of his life. I guess I don't have such high standards. I like Ann Arbor."

A voice came into the room through a kind of speaker system. "I figured I'd wait till halftime," it said. "I know when I can't compete.

But now that everybody's in a good mood." And a few people cheered.

At first I thought somebody must have turned up the sound on the football game, but then I realized there was a guy with a microphone at the other end of the room. The office space ran the length of the factory floor, but the ceilings weren't especially high, they had those panels you stare at from the dentist's chair, and Gloria and I stood in exactly the wrong place, by the restroom doors. But then I felt her hand on my arm—Obama had come.

We tried to push our way a little closer, but the party, which had been loud and spread out, was now quiet and packed in. A few people at the back stood on tables to get a view, but Gloria didn't want to do that and in the end I managed to find her a chair. I climbed up next to her for a moment, holding her waist, and then stepped down again. This is what Obama looked like from fifty paces, a young Arab businessman. His head looked small and he seemed light on his feet.

Walking with the microphone in hand, he said, "We got in, I don't know, about eight a.m. this morning, and the first thing I said was, take me to these neighborhoods, take me to these streets, so we drove off, with about eighteen cars, one after the other, and by this point it was about nine thirty, and I knew we had got to the right place, because there were guys working, building, wearing those hard hats and dirty day-glo jackets, climbing on roofs and digging foundations, on Saturday morning, and the other half of the folks I saw were sitting in Joe Silver's café drinking lattes."

People laughed, but at the time I didn't hear all that, and only worked out from the *Free Press* website in the morning exactly what he said. Partly it was a problem with the acoustics. The office had been designed to cut out the flow of noise from one space to the next. There were also hecklers. Someone called out, "The United

States of Detroit," which didn't mean much to me then and doesn't now. But Obama stopped and started again.

"Now I know there are folks here today who don't agree with everything I do, and I don't expect you to. But there are things we can agree on. That the American Experiment ain't over yet. And that's not because we're sitting around on our butts, waiting for the results to come in. The people rebuilding Detroit, and some of you are in this room right now, are still tinkering with it, still adapting it, still moving forward. You have come here from Albuquerque and Chicago, from Queens and from Cleveland and from San Diego. You have come from Mexico and Poland and Sudan and from right here in Detroit. You have come because you lost your job or you couldn't get a job or you had to work three jobs just to put food on the table. Because your health insurance ran out or your mortgage was worth more than your home. Because the school you sent your kids to couldn't afford to buy books or because the part-time job you got in college turned out to be the best thing you could find after earning your degree. You have come because there was a voice in your head saying, *You don't have to live like this. There's a better way to live.* This voice has called people to America for over four hundred years. It calls to us now . . ." and so on. Eventually he said, "But stick around, I'm just the warm-up act. Am I right in thinking we got the Wrenfields coming next?"

Afterwards, though, the men in dark suits closed down on him pretty quickly, and a few minutes later I saw the herd of SUVs in the parking lot filing out. Maybe they were worried about the snow—it sat lightly on the parked cars about six inches thick.

I said to Gloria, "Did you get anything to eat? There were turkey burgers going around. I want to introduce you to Robert James."

We caught up with him shaking hands. There were maybe fif-teen, twenty people who wanted his attention, and he stood there in his open-necked shirt, looking the part but not saying much. He looked tired, too, like he'd been wound up and was winding down. "I've got to get this stuff off my face," he said at last and rubbed his palms against his cheeks and held them up. "I hate TV, please excuse me." He headed for the exit, but I chased him into the concrete stairwell.

"I want to introduce you to someone," I said. But Gloria had got stuck somewhere. The stairwell was empty, and for a moment we just stood there, the two of us, almost embarrassed. Robert had his foot on the stair—he was giving me time.

"We're going over to my house for a party," he said. "Obama's already there."

"Let me just get her."

"Come, too, I can put you on the list. I'd drive you over but I need fifteen minutes alone."

"It's been a good day for you," I said.

"It's been a terrific day."

So I found Gloria and we went downstairs and collected our coats, then stepped outside. The afternoon felt warmer. Snow reflected the cloud-filtered sunlight, and there was a kind of cold glow in the air. Cars driving out had packed the snow down in two ruts and we walked in those.

"It's stupid, I should have brought my other shoes," Gloria said.

I turned on the ignition and let her sit in the car while I scraped the windows clear. When the snow came off I could see her again, looking ahead but not looking at me.

There wasn't much traffic but I concentrated on the road instead of talking. After a few minutes Gloria said, "I still don't know what took you so long in there."

"I ran into Kurt Stangel. They had a camera set up, where people could tell their stories, and I listened to them for a while." Then I said, "The truth is, I liked seeing you with Beatrice. I thought you would get along."

"I'm not really into that sister act she tried to pull. Did you go out with her?"

"No. In college she went out with Robert James."

"Did you ever sleep with her?"

"There's a lot of things I could tell you about her but not like this."

"Like what?"

The drive was too short to talk any of this out. Robert's street was blocked off at both ends by security vehicles, so we had to park around the corner. It was a little after three o'clock in the afternoon and the street lamps came on while we sat in the car. They flickered and then burned, and the snow, which was still falling, made patterns against the rays of light.

"I shouldn't drink at lunch," I said. "It makes me depressed."

But she was looking out the window at the sidewalk. "I'm really annoyed with myself I didn't bring other shoes."

"I could carry you in. I said I could carry you in."

"I'm deciding if I want to be in a grouch. Okay, carry me."

So I stepped into the cold and opened the passenger door and she jumped into my arms. She put her legs around me. I could feel the strength in her thighs and managed to kick the door shut and get the key in while she hung on. Then I shuffled along through the snow—she weighed about as much as a ten-year-old kid. It just felt like an incredibly friendly thing to do, on both sides. She held her cheek against my hair, which had snow in it that melted against her skin and made her shiver.

"Be nice to me," she said, "when we get in. Don't leave me."

19

In fact, we soon got pulled in different directions, but it didn't matter much. Obama was there—I mean, he was in the house, in one room or another, and from time to time you could see him, smiling sometimes and sometimes holding back smiles. Gloria kept looking out for him and then we ran into Clay Greene, who had sobered up a little.

"This is Gloria Lambert," I said. "She teaches art and computers at Kettridge High. She's one of those teachers who wins prizes."

"Now I'd very much like to hear your views on something," he said to her. "I'm working on an article about class and race and education. Maybe you can help me. Let me get you a glass of champagne." And he picked one off a passing tray.

I left them to it and edged into a group of people talking to Robert James. They were standing in front of the living room fireplace, with their backs against the heat.

"May I use you as a fire screen?" I said to no one in particular. The conversation was about the mayoral election, which was a month old. The guy who lost used to work at Arthur Andersen. Some lady's ex-husband had a weekly lunch date with him at the

Yacht Club, oh, about twenty years ago, when people still lived like that. She couldn't remember what his impressions were.

"Have you seen Beatrice?" Robert said to me, when the circle broke up. "Apparently she's working on a novel. She's got an agent, Clay Greene's agent. He's here, too."

"Which one is he?"

"Some English guy. Not that old."

"Do you mind?"

"Why should I mind?" he said.

"Excuse me."

I felt a hand on my arm and it was the woman with the ex-husband. She was the underweight kind of elderly lady. Her skin bruised easily—I could see the marks on her wrists made by some of her bracelets. Also, she was drunk. Her head lay slightly lopsided on her neck.

"Excuse me," she said again. "Robert tells me you're one of these terribly brave young men."

"What do you mean?"

"He said you moved into one of these houses, these run-down houses, on those streets that everyone moves out of. Aren't you afraid?"

"I've got a shotgun for the car, and a standard police-issue Smith & Wesson at home."

"But you don't take it with you?"

"If I need to. Where do you live?"

"Oh, where we've always lived, in a little house, which needs such a lot of work, but I never got round to it, and now the children are away, and my ex-husband, of course, and there isn't any point. Just off Lake Shore Road. But what I've never understood is this business with needles. I used to sometimes smoke a cigarette, a very long time ago, when I was practically a girl, but I just don't believe that people would willingly put something into a needle and then—stick it in their arm. They must be very desperate to do that."

Beatrice came in, looking for somebody. She stood in the doorway in a black dress, which wasn't what she wore at the factory party. In heels she stood tall enough she could look over people's shoulders. I excused myself and went over to her. "What did you say to Gloria?"

"She's too nice for you."

"Is that what you said? You used to think I was too nice."

"I don't remember that."

"If you're looking for Robert, he just left."

"Thank you, I wasn't."

"He says you're writing a novel, he says you have an agent."

"Marny," she said, changing her tune, "can I tell you something even Clay doesn't know? He's not just my agent; we're seeing each other."

"How long has this been going on?"

"He flew in a couple of months ago to see Clay and stayed the night. That's when it started. He's supposed to be showing up here, but I haven't seen him."

"What's he like? What's this novel about?"

"One of these English guys who live in New York and end up being more English than the English, you know, charming and offhand and polite. But he's our age. His father's a lord but not a real one—he got made. He went to Eton."

"What's this novel about?"

"Oh, I don't care about that. That's just one of David's ideas. He thinks he can sell it." After a minute, she added, "I like Gloria, by the way, I like her a lot. What are you shaking your head about?"

"Nothing, I'm not. Is Walter here? Have you seen him? He was worried about Susie when I left. She's starting to look pretty big; she wasn't feeling too hot."

Beatrice hadn't seen him.

"I think I understand what it is about having kids," I said. "They've got kids at their house all day, really small people. After a while, after you've been through your twenties and thirties, you want to have simple relations again."

"What do you mean?"

"It's just something on my mind. This is the trouble with being a pioneer. You want a new life and you set up an outpost and soon it looks just like the life you left."

"I don't think what you'll have with Gloria is simple relations."

"Oh fuck off," I said and went to find her.

But I ran into Susie and Walter first, talking to Helen, Clay Greene's wife. They were standing in the dining room; the big mahogany table had been stripped of leaves and pushed into a corner. Helen said, "Why don't you sit down?" There were dining room chairs lined up against the wall. "No point in playing the hero."

"Everybody tells me to sit down. I don't want to sit down. I've been lying down all afternoon, and poked and prodded."

"Did they find anything wrong?"

"What they say is, it's probably perfectly normal or maybe it's not. I had a little spotting this morning. So I call up and they say, come in, we want to be safe. But then they can't tell me if it's safe or not."

"How many months are you?" Helen asked. I was standing just outside the conversation. I wanted to talk to Walter, but he was listening in, and I didn't feel I could interrupt.

"Seven months next week," Susie said. Her belly was at the pillow stage, but she looked fatter also in the neck by the lines of her jaw. Her face had that animal placid cud-chewing pregnant look.

She kept her hands on her hips and moved like she was carrying a full heavy pitcher of water.

"You'll be fine, everybody has one kind of worry or another. Believe me, it's worse when they come out. Everybody tells you, just get through the first three months. My boys now are eight and three and I'm still waiting to get my life back."

It occurred to me that Helen didn't like Susie very much, and this was her way of showing it. But maybe women her age can't help themselves. They have to say something if they see somebody pregnant.

Susie said, "Well, all I care about now is this little guy right here. I want to get a good look at him, I want to find out what he's like."

Then Clay and Gloria came over.

Around five o'clock she wanted to go home. She had seen the president, she had stood in the room with him, it was enough. So I went to find Robert and say thank you, good-bye. He was picking at the food in the kitchen, standing around with the chef and the waitstaff and some of the president's entourage. Obama was there, too, trying to get a game of three-on-three together. "Where there's a backboard there's a ball." He meant the Roof King backboard over the garage door. The snow had stopped, the evening was clearing up, Obama offered to do a little shoveling himself. He hadn't done a thing all day but eat small portions of food, the kind of food you can hold in one hand while you talk a lot of crap. "Come on," he said.

The impression he made on me was very strong, his fame and his restlessness, which was partly physical and partly in the way he talked—he interrupted himself and made little appeals to people around him, not just people he knew but also one of the waiters, a six-foot white guy who used to play point guard for Aquinas College in Grand Rapids. "Sam wants a game," Obama said. "Sam's up

for it, Sam wants to work off some of that gut you get in your twenties, when you work too hard and the rest of the time sit around on
your butt.

"Come on," he said again. "Who's in? I need some names."

Robert gave him a queer look. His shirt was unbuttoned at the
top, his sleeves were rolled up. He kept himself in good shape. "The
ball needs pumping up," he said.

"So pump up the ball."

Obama started pointing at each of us.

"You in? . . . What's your name? Introduce me."

"Marny's more of a squash player."

"I'll guard him then," Obama said.

About twenty minutes later, I found myself scraping a snow
shovel up and down the concrete drive. We took it in turns. Robert had loaned me a college sweatshirt, to pull over my undershirt,
but I was still wearing slacks and leather-soled shoes. Then Obama
took the shovel off my hands and pushed the last crumbs of snow
into the pileups on either side of the drive.

"How far is East Lansing from here?" he asked. "About two
hours?"

"A little less. An hour and a half," Sam said.

"Robert, Robert James," Obama called. "Did you invite Magic
Johnson to this thing?"

"I'm not sure."

"This is his kind of basketball weather. He told me once, he used
to practice his jump shot with mittens on."

Then there was a ball bouncing among the six of us, middle-
aged men, in dark pants and dress shoes, breathing smoke, as we
shuffled around, passing and shooting and chasing the ball under
the garage lights. About ten security guys stood along the spear-
topped iron fence, watching us, and the house itself was lit up like

a Christmas tree. People crowded into the window frames to get a look. But the court felt private enough.

"I'm about as warm as I'm gonna get," Obama said. "Come on, Reggie. Let's get it on."

Reggie was his assistant, one of those friendly-faced black guys, about six and a half feet tall, and bald as a cantaloupe. About a foot taller than Bill Russo, who played, too. Bill still kept a set of workout clothes at Robert's house and was the only one of us in rubber soles—he had on his wrestling shoes and started grabbing people by the waist and pushing.

"Get off me, Bill," Robert said.

But Bill was having a good time; he didn't give a shit about basketball. He guarded Robert, and Reggie guarded Sam, and the president guarded me. Mostly I tried to get out of his way. I didn't want to injure anybody, and the ground was cold concrete and slippery with snow dust. Obama put up a jump shot and missed, and Reggie grabbed the rebound and kicked it back to him, and this time he knocked it down.

"It's raining on a snowy day," Obama said. He had a quick, jerky left-handed stroke, which took a little getting used to. After each shot he held his hand out like a claw.

"You got to get on him," Robert told me.

We played to fifteen and then we played to fifteen again. Sam was still in good shape. His shot was rusty but he was strong and fast and could dribble all over the place; somehow nobody ever got in his way. And Robert had a nice little soft fifteen-footer—a whiteboy jump shot, Obama said. I don't think Reggie tried particularly hard. He picked up a lot of rebounds. We won the first game and then Obama got hot—shooting from the fences, he called it—and they pulled out the second. Obama and Reggie liked to talk. Sam didn't say a word, and Robert didn't talk much either; it took me a while to realize he was pissed off. Partly at Bill, who kept horsing around and taking out his legs. But partly at me, too.

"Rubber match?" Obama said, and when the third game started, Robert switched me onto Bill and guarded the president himself.

Afterwards I tried to work out what happened—I wanted to understand the buildup. Maybe it was a racial thing. Robert played varsity basketball for Claremont High. They had one of those teams where the uniforms don't show your name. The way Robert was brought up, you played hard and you made the extra pass and you didn't care how many points you scored, you cared about winning. And you didn't talk. But Obama liked to run his mouth. It didn't bother me much. But maybe it had nothing to do with basketball, maybe Robert was pissed off about something else.

Anyway, it was cold and people were tired, and still half drunk. I got the feeling on both sides that some guys really wanted to win. Then Reggie set a pick for Obama, and Robert pushed through it. I tried to help out and caught an elbow in the nose from somebody and sat down on the frozen concrete, trying to hold the blood in with my fingers.

Obama put his hand on my head. "You all right, kid?" he said. "Let's call this thing off."

But Bill ran in to get toilet paper, which I stuffed in my nose to stop the bleeding.

"Marny's fine," Robert said. "You all right, Marny? He's fine. If you start something you finish it."

"I don't mind," I said. So we finished the game.

Afterwards, I said to the president, "There's somebody who wants to meet you."

Gloria was waiting for me in the kitchen, with a wet, warm cloth. I took out the bloody tissue paper and held the cloth to my face. When she saw Obama, she kind of stood at attention, but he put out his hand and she shook it.

"I think you knew my father," she said. "I think you knew my father before I knew him."

Obama's high forehead was sweating under the kitchen lights; he started drying himself off with cocktail napkins. After a while, he had a handful of these napkins and nowhere to put them.

"Who's your father?"

"Tom Lambert. He used to work for the DCP in Chicago."

He put the napkins in his pocket. "I was very sorry to hear it when he died."

"That was a long time ago."

"Too long," Obama said. "He died too young."

"Thank you, Mr. President."

The kitchen was crowded, there were maybe thirty people in the room, including the caterers, waitstaff, security, and the rest of the guys who played. Obama put his arm around me and said, "I want you to know something about this guy, he's not a whiner," and then the other conversations took over. Somebody brought the president a glass of mineral water. He turned to Robert, who was drinking tap water by the sink, and called out, "You ever seen the shower they got on Air Force One?"

"You can use the showers here."

"If I leave now I can kiss the kids good night."

The sense I had of unreality was strong. Robert had left his shirt over one of the chairs and put it on again, buttoning it slowly; his fingers were probably cold. He didn't look very happy—we lost that last game by six or seven points, and I got this funny feeling that Obama was talking so much because he won. But then I couldn't read him at all. His face was very expressive. Of course, he was used to being looked at, and maybe the best way of covering up what you think is to show a lot of expression. But then at other times his face went blank, he stopped paying attention, and people around him had to repeat their questions. Robert I knew a lot better, but he was strange to me, too, and I wondered if they had been working on some deal that didn't come off.

Gloria said to me, "Take me home."

"You ready to go?"

"If you can't make it with me now, you never gonna make it with me."

So I took her home.

20

Gloria was one of those people with a confession to make. I don't mean confession exactly, but something she has to tell you if you're going to get to know her. There were probably twenty people she'd told this story to, a couple of high school friends, a few of their parents, one of her teachers, someone from camp, her roommates at Michigan, a few other college friends and most of her boyfriends.

When she was seven years old she learned to ride a bike. Her father used to take her out on Saturday mornings. He worked as a lawyer for the UAW and didn't see much of Gloria in the week—mostly he got home when she was in the bath. But Saturday morning was Mother's morning off (on Sunday the whole family went to church), and Gloria could pick whatever she wanted to do with her dad, eat pancakes, go to the zoo. That summer she mostly felt like riding her bike.

Sometimes they rode through Jefferson Chalmers to Lakewood Park and looked at the water, or they rode over to Chandler Park or they went into Grosse Pointe, which started just across the road from their apartment block. Gloria liked to look at the big houses, and the streets of Grosse Pointe are wide and quiet. There isn't much traffic.

They were biking along Whittier Road one day, just off Char-levoix, when her daddy came off. He just leaned over slowly and the bike leaned with him, and turned to the side, and since there isn't much of a curb on Whittier he fell into one of those patches of grass between the road and the sidewalk, and lay there next to a tree. She laughed at first, but then she had to turn around and go back to him, because he didn't get up. The bike was still between his legs, he was still breathing, his eyes were open, but he didn't do anything or say anything when she shook him or shouted at him. It was about nine in the morning. Even as a kid Gloria liked to get up first thing, and her daddy made her breakfast on Saturdays and sometimes they set off while her mother was still in bed.

For almost an hour she sat by her father in the grass. After a while she even stopped crying. A few cars went by and there was a jogger on the other side of the road, but nobody came out of their houses to see why a little black girl was sitting next to a fifty-five-year-old black man in the grass by the curb with their bikes on the ground. The reason she didn't knock on anyone's door to ask for help is because she was scared they weren't supposed to be there and she didn't want to get her daddy in trouble.

The front lawns on Whittier were bigger than any yard she'd ever played in. The houses were made of those bricks they build schools out of, with white plantation shutters on either side of the windows. Once or twice her father had invited one of his colleagues from the UAW back to their apartment, a white guy, another law-yer, but her parents didn't do much entertaining, and the people they had round were mostly family or from church. In other words, when she was seven years old she didn't know any white people to talk to.

There are sidewalks on both sides of Whittier Road, but they don't get much use. Everybody drives. A few people must have got in their cars while Gloria was sitting there, but nobody stopped by or said anything until a cop pulled over by the side of the road.

By that point her father was dead. When the ambulance eventually came they took Gloria to the hospital with him and checked her temperature and gave her something sugary to drink. Her father lay on the gurney with a blanket over him, as if he was cold. That seemed weird to her; she was sweating. Then her mother came to the hospital and a few hours later took her home again without him.

Years later she got into one of those stupid teenage arguments you get into with your mother. Here's what her mother said: that if Gloria had gotten help sooner, her father might still be alive. At Michigan Gloria looked into this a little—one of her roommates was premed. Her roommate told her that they probably had ten or twelve minutes to respond, after the coronary event. In other words, unless the first door she knocked on had a doctor in the house, or somebody who knew CPR, there was probably nothing that Gloria could have done to save her father. Even if they called an ambulance immediately it would probably have come too late.

But Gloria still thought about why she hadn't asked for help. When the cop came over she was just sitting on the side of her bike spinning one of the wheels. She had wet herself and still remembered the feeling of not being able to hold it in and letting go. It was a hot July morning and getting hotter. By the time her mother drove her home she was totally dry—she didn't even get changed. If they had gone biking that morning in Jefferson Chalmers or Morningside, she's pretty sure she would have knocked on somebody's door when her father fell over. But she didn't because she was shy of white people, and nothing any white person had ever said or done to her was a good enough excuse.

I said to her, "There's another way of reading this story. I can't believe nobody came out to see what was going on."

"When a kid screams, how often do you check to see what's wrong? Even if you do look, you see a man lying down beside her."

"If you were white," I said, "somebody checks. Some mother would consider it her responsibility. Some busybody, some neighbor."

"Where he fell down was next to a tree. So from one side you couldn't see us too well, and from the other side was across the road."

"If you were white, somebody stops the car, they get out and look."

"I know you mean well," Gloria said. "But I don't want it stirred up like that. Please stop."

We were sitting in her living room, on two of the chairs. Gloria felt hungry when we got in from Robert's party—she made us something to eat and lit candles and all that. Afterwards we sat over a bottle of wine.

The conversation was a mood killer, but I spent the night at her place anyway. I don't sleep well in other people's beds, and her bedroom was small. It was kind of a good little girl's room, very plain and neat. She had a single in it, and I lay on my back all night with my eyes closed, trying not to move and wake her. Then when it got light she made me take off. On Sunday mornings she had a weekly date with her mother to go to church. The early morning service started at nine a.m. This is the one her mother liked to go to, because there weren't any kids, and afterwards the two of them had breakfast together. So I said, "Can I call you later?"

And she said, "Please, call me."

Then I put on last night's clothes and carried my tie in hand and walked out. It was cold in the stairwell, I could see my breath in the one landing light still working, but outside didn't feel much colder. The air was still, and snow had fallen overnight and covered the roof of my car and tufted the side mirrors. I palmed off the snow with bare hands. The sun hadn't made it yet over Gloria's apartment block, but the rest of the street, up and down, showed the line between sunshine and shade very vividly. On the west side, on the Detroit side, the milk-carton houses sat in brilliant light.

Snow lay about a foot thick in the middle of the road, so I decided to leave the car and walk home. It took much longer than I thought. I ended up on Mack Avenue, where the storefronts and service stations and jury-rigged churches eventually gave way to concrete sidings topped with chain-link fences. By this point it had become a six-lane highway. There were train tracks running underneath it and some kind of industrial plant spread out alongside. But the parking lot had no cars in it, just heaps of garbage, rubble and tires, and pileups of snow. I started to feel scared. I was also hungover and sleep-deprived. The world seemed very large around me, not just the planet itself but the number of people, the scale of buildings and the general infrastructure, highways and tracks and office blocks and container depots. It's almost impossible to keep your sense of proportion, you come out too small, so you have to combat how little anything matters with your most unreasonable voice, saying, it matters, it matters, it matters. These are the stupid thoughts that went through my brain. I could still taste Gloria's mouth in my mouth, my feet were wet and numb, and then I passed the twenty-four-hour McDonald's on the corner of Conner Street and went in for a pancake breakfast and Styrofoam cup of tea. Later I got Walter to drive me back and picked up the car.

21

There was a message on my answering machine, but I didn't listen to it till I went to bed, which was early, about nine o'clock. My brother wanted to know if I was coming home for Christmas. He couldn't get away with the kids (he has three of them) and the house in Baton Rouge was too small. Andrea had put her foot down, and Mom didn't want to commit to Christmas in Houston until she had heard from me. Of course, I was welcome to sleep on his couch if I wanted to, but regardless, I should let Mom know. I should call her anyway, just give her a call, he said. She's building this whole thing up into something it's not. It's stressing her out.

My father offered to pay for my flight. Walter and Susie had also invited me to spend Christmas with them, but life seemed pretty tense downstairs. She was under doctor's orders to stay in bed until the baby was born. Her due date was six weeks off and Walter not only had to run the kids' workshop himself but also look after her—clean house, go shopping, bring her meals. She was taking this bed rest thing very seriously and shuffled around instead of walking, when she had to go to the bathroom, for example. I said once, how do you feel, do you feel weak, does something hurt, but she said, looking up, I just feel worried. Worried people can walk,

I thought, but didn't say anything. Walter looked strung out. So I took my dad's money and flew home.

Home felt weird to me, too. My mother made meat loaf the night I got in, because it was my favorite thing to eat when I was twelve years old. After she went to bed, my dad offered me a shot of Jim Beam. We sat up watching TV and both got a little drunk. That's what we did every night—watch TV. I didn't tell either of them about Gloria, but all week long I had this *Guess Who's Coming to Dinner* fantasy going around my head. For some reason I liked to imagine their reaction.

Gloria and I called each other practically every night. I sat in my old bedroom like a teenager, with the door closed, talking quietly, except when I was a teenager I didn't have a girlfriend. One night I even went through my bedroom closet, looking for shoe boxes—the ones I had stashed my lead soldiers into a couple of weeks before going to Yale. They were still there. I unwrapped a few of the figures from their squares of kitchen towel, feeling a sort of abstract sadness. It struck me that all of my childhood interests and enthusiasms could be explained as displaced sexual energy.

On Christmas morning, while my mother got the dinner ready, my dad and I drove down to the racquet club and played squash. I could beat him easily these days. His hair, which was yellow, had become yellow-white. At least he hadn't gotten fat, he was never particularly skinny, but he had these skinny legs. And since his feet didn't bounce off the ground anymore, his running looked like a kind of sprightly walking. Especially since he held himself uncomfortably upright, even chasing balls. There's a history of back trouble in my family. I felt sorry for him, beating him, but he didn't seem to mind.

Afterwards, in the showers, he said, "Are you having an okay time up there?" His chest was broad and muscular. It had faint white hairs, almost the color of his skin, running between his breasts and down to his navel. He was still physically vain and soaped himself off with pleasure, but his hair looked thin under the water. "Are you living the way you want to live?"

"Getting there."

"Because I know that was always very important to you."

"Whatever that means," I said.

The club was pretty empty on Christmas morning, there were only a couple of old guys in the showers, but my dad knew one of them, so we had to put off our stupid argument until the drive home. Then he started asking questions about the setup in Detroit—what had happened to the people who used to live in these neighborhoods. Really he wanted to impose on me his Greater Knowledge of the World.

"You don't need to talk to me about these people. I've thought about them more than you have, believe me."

"Give me a break," he said. "I used to be a union rep."

"You represented a bunch of journalists. The oppressed middle classes."

"What are you talking about, I started out on the docks, with the ILA. Don't talk to me about racial tensions. I only got out when you kids were born, when we moved to Baton Rouge. So it shouldn't surprise me I have suburban middle-class kids. But this isn't what I wanted to talk about. One of my boys wants to make money, and gets it; and the other one wants something else. I just wanted to know if you were getting it."

"I don't know what you mean by *something else*. You make it sound like a kind of luxury."

"Well, for most people it is. If we're talking about some philosophical idea of happiness here. People in my experience live much more for pleasure, they're forced to."

"That's a terrible thing to say. That's not even true. I don't even think you know what you mean by the distinction."

"That's three different arguments," he said. "Pick one."

But we all tried our best when we sat down to eat. Christmas is a lonely meal for three people. The food outnumbers the company. There was turkey and two types of stuffing, cranberry sauce and greens, a salad and mash potatoes, and gravy, and a bottle of wine, which only my father drank much of. I never felt comfortable drinking in front of my mother.

"Why didn't you want to go to Houston?" I asked them.

"Your mother doesn't like Andrea's cooking."

"She's a fine cook."

But my mother said, "It isn't her cooking. She has no sense of ceremony. The children should get a sense of what Christmas means."

"You mean, they should get a sense of the effort you put into it. They should feel guilty."

"Putting a little effort into something is nothing to be ashamed about. The fact is that Andrea is not a great coper, which I don't understand at all, because she has much more help in the home than I ever had."

Afterwards my mother and I cleared up and my dad went out to smoke a cigarette. "Did you have a fight about something?" she said, over the dishes. "What about?"

"I don't really know."

"Who won?"

"You mean the squash? I did."

"You know that's not what I mean."

The next day my brother drove down from Houston by himself, about a five-hour drive. We had a late lunch together and afterwards Brad and I went out to throw a football in the street. It was about sixty degrees out, there was no wind, and even through the endless white cloudy sky you could feel the heat of the sun.

Brad was a couple of inches taller than me, bigger in the chest and better looking, with fair hair and a blond face. But he'd also grown a gut, sitting on his ass and billing time. Mostly he threw and I chased the balls down, running routes down the middle of the road.

At one point he said to me, "So you getting any action in Detroit?"

"I think I got a girlfriend," I said. "A real Detroiter."

"What does that mean?"

"Someone who grew up there, not someone like me. She's black."

"I meant, what do you mean, *think*?"

"It's early days."

You couldn't talk like this throwing a ball back and forth, but sometimes a car came by, and then we stood around together by the side of the road and carried on a conversation. We wanted to talk and sometimes flipped the ball between us for an excuse.

After a while, he said, "I think Dad's got a girlfriend."

"What makes you say that?"

"He keeps calling me up. He wants to talk. He wants to make me like him before he tells me."

"I don't understand."

"This is why Mom's stressed out."

"I don't understand, did Mom say something to you?"

"She's been saying stuff like this to me for the past twenty years, but this time she says it's true."

"And you believe her this time?"

"I believed her some of the times before."

"How come Mom doesn't tell me any of this stuff?"

"Come on, Greg. You're her little boy. She loves you more."

He drove home before supper, around six o'clock. My mother tried to put something on the table for him, but Brad said he planned to eat on the road—it would keep him awake. So this was the last real conversation I had about anything until I got back to Detroit. But that was partly my fault. I don't know why I didn't tell them about Gloria.

A FEW DAYS INTO THE New Year, my dad moved out and I started spending a lot of time on the phone with my mother. She didn't know for sure if he was seeing somebody. At first all he did was rent a room from some friends of his in New Orleans, the same place I moved into briefly after quitting my job at Aberystwyth. My mom had bad things to say about these people, whom she once considered friends of hers, too, but I also felt implicated in the business. As if I'd been giving him ideas.

"Look," I said. "It's not like I was particularly happy there. I mean, I didn't last long."

"I'm sure he's having a ball."

"Are you talking to each other?" I said.

"He tries to call me about every other day, but I don't want to talk to him so I hang up the phone."

"What did he say to you when he moved out?"

"He said he wasn't very happy. He said he'd been trying to talk to me about this for some time, which is true, but that I didn't want to hear it. That's true, too. I never could see the point of analyzing what you can't change, which is that we were more or less stuck with each other. But apparently he didn't see it that way."

"So what did he say? I mean, did he explain what he thought he was doing?"

"He said, the way we were living, it didn't seem to him any violation of our marriage for him to get a room somewhere in New Orleans and spend a little time there."

"What did he mean by that?"

"You know what he meant. Don't make me say it," she said.

It was very hard for me to tell how much I cared. I don't mean that I didn't seem to care at all, just the opposite. I talked about what was happening to Gloria and sometimes it felt like a kind of offering to her. She had told me her terrible story about her father and so I was telling her mine. Gloria turned out to be a good sympathizer. She had the kind of sympathy people want more of. But what I was doing using this material, which was more or less the story of my life, the people who made me, my whole childhood, and feeding it into a relationship that was about a month old, like it was some kind of fuel, to raise the temperature, I don't know.

A week after New Year her classes began, which knocked her out most evenings, but we saw each other on the weekends. She introduced me to her mother, who was an attractive, elegant, not very nice woman, in her early fifties. She had long straightened black hair, with some white in it, and a long sort of French-looking face. I guess her coloring was what people in books call high yellow. By this point I had started reading a lot of African American literature—*Black Boy* first, then *Another Country*. I figured I may as well educate myself, but I was also a little ashamed, since it seemed I had a taste for it, and I didn't want Gloria to know it was a taste.

Her mother was named Eunice; her stage name was Eunice Ray. She used to be a singer and was moderately successful in her thirties, when Gloria's father met her at Cliff Bell's jazz club. It wasn't called Cliff Bell's then, but something else. I heard this story from Gloria first, and then Eunice. Tom Lambert seems to have been a well-known, well-liked figure in his community. People came to him with their legal problems, he listened to everybody, he worked hard. But he also liked to have a good time, even if he didn't drink, he liked pretty women. "I was one of them," Eunice said. "Gloria takes after her father. What?"

"Nothing," Gloria said.

But she showed me a few photographs. Her father had one of those innocent happy dark-skinned white-teethed black faces that probably cover up a lot of private opinions. He must have been fairly old when they had Gloria. I got the sense that she was his darling girl, and maybe Eunice used to resent it, and still did.

The first time I met her she gave us brunch in her apartment. It was all laid out when we got there, on her number one china. Eunice was dressed in a thin floating dress or robe, which had an African print on it, made of different browns, but you could also see through it to her gray silk underclothing. I was incredibly nervous, but Gloria told me not to worry. My mom's a big snob, she said. And in fact we ended up ganging up on Gloria, making fun of her.

Afterwards I saw her around the building occasionally. She always looked heavily made-up, even when stepping out with the trash. I offered to carry it down for her once—she seemed the kind of woman who doesn't mind a little gallantry.

Gloria and I talked about our parents a lot. At the end of January a letter from my father arrived. He had called a few times while I was out, but I hadn't called back. This is what he said in his letter, or the gist of it anyway. He said he hadn't been happy since he retired. There are men who like retirement but not that many in his experience. He used to argue with my mother about moving back to New Orleans, but the truth is, she never liked the city very much, and her life was the house. But he didn't have anything to do.

"This is why I watched all that TV," he wrote. "Even when you were kids I watched a lot of TV. Instead of getting up to no good. I thought, better stay on your ass and watch TV. Keep out of trouble. And I don't regret the time I spent on the couch, because I wanted to be a good husband and father. And believe me, the TV helped. But I've been playing that game now for almost forty years, and after a while I thought, who are you doing it for anymore. You kids don't need us anymore. And I don't make your mother particularly happy. You're sixty-five years old, and all your so-called domestic virtue is really just another name for laziness. So get off your ass. I don't have any illusions about going it alone either. Men of my generation weren't brought up to it. But I've got a room at the Wenzlers', and there isn't a TV in it. If I haven't got a reason for going out I lie in bed and read books. When I was your age, or maybe a little younger, I loved to read. Of course, there's another side to my life here but I don't expect you want to hear about it so I won't tell you. But this is what I want to say. From the outside I look like a worse man now than I did two months ago. But it doesn't feel that way from the inside, it really doesn't. For the first time in years I feel like a moral agent again. I'm a human being, and people coming into contact with me are bumping into somebody who is actually there. They get some response. For years, and this is literally true, I didn't say a single thing I hadn't said before, not to anybody, not even to your mother. Now I say something new every day. All this is kind of a long-winded apology. But what I really want to apologize for is that dumb fight we had over Christmas, when I was still dealing with this shit. Maybe I was jealous of you. Your brother understands a little better what I'm talking about, he has three kids of his own. But he's also got his own reasons for staying mad, which you don't have. So next time I call you pick up the phone, don't play these answering-machine games. They're beneath you. And let's talk."

And he signed himself with his name, "Your father, Charlie."

I showed this letter to Gloria, but for once she gave me the wrong kind of sympathy. I'm sorry, she said, this is the craziest excuse I ever heard. A man walks out on his wife to make himself a better man. And for something to talk about. You've got to be kidding me. She got too angry on my behalf; she was also a little angry at me. But we didn't have a fight about it—I kept the lid down.

22

Walter knew my father a little, they met at graduation, but he wasn't around to talk to. When I got back from Baton Rouge I found a note under my door. Walter and Susie had decided to fly home—they were going to spend New Year with his mother. I was surprised the doctors let her fly. And then one night Walter came back alone. I heard his taxi idling in the street and went down to say hello. Susie had stuck around in New York and was trying to mend fences with her parents. I carried one of his suitcases inside.

He offered me a cup of tea and I went upstairs to get some fresh milk. Then he told me what had happened. Just before Christmas they lost the baby. For two days Susie didn't feel any kicking. She was getting more and more panicky, so Walter told her to go in, just so the doctors could calm her down. But the heart had stopped. There was a problem with the placenta, blood clots; the truth is, they were surprised the placenta had lasted as long as it did. Then they doped her up with Pitocin so she could push the baby out. Susie found the whole thing not only unbelievably awful but tremendously embarrassing—to go through all the special attention of labor for the sake of this dead thing. So afterwards they flew home. She needed a change of scene and couldn't face anybody who knew her pregnant. They weren't telling people yet so I should keep quiet. And I didn't feel like bringing up my father with him. He looked fat and sweaty and unhappy. There wasn't much to eat in his apartment, but he found an old box of Entenmann's powdered doughnut holes and kept popping them into his mouth while we talked.

I told him about Gloria, but the first time we appeared in public together was Jimmy's baptism. Cris had had her baby, another son, and Tony asked me to be his godfather. This surprised me. I didn't think we got along very well anymore. But Tony was one of those confident abusive types who act that way only in front of people they like. He could be pretty quiet with strangers. It's also possible that his best friends got pissed off with him after a while, so he had to keep making new ones.

Walter came, too. We put on our jackets and ties, and Gloria met us at the house, wearing a cream-colored dress and a cream-colored hat with black spots, and a rose on top. Her overcoat was a hand-me-down from her mother, with a black fur trim. She looked great. Going to church was one of the things she really dressed up for.

I couldn't tell what impression she made on Walter. He had a funny way with women he didn't know. He simpered and half shut his eyes; he talked very gently. And Gloria made a real effort. "This is what happens when a man dresses himself," she said, and tightened the knot of my tie. Then she offered to straighten out Walter's. I could feel her hands on his shirt, my first little flare-up of sexual jealousy. It wasn't till we pulled up outside the church, which had a parking lot big enough for a football field, that I realized how painful the whole business must be for him.

There was a sign fronting the road, like a football scoreboard, which read:

ST BARNABAS WELCOMES INTO CHRIST
JAMES CARNESECCA
WILLIAM HOFSTEDTER
LUCY TEMPLETON

Underneath that it said:

SPAGHETTI DINNER
JAN 20 7 P.M.

Gloria knew about Susie but wasn't supposed to. She was the only black person in the church and I walked in holding her arm and feeling self-conscious. Everybody would assume we were sleeping together, but the truth is we weren't.

On the second night I spent with her, Gloria explained to me what the deal was. She wasn't a virgin, but the two or three times she'd had sex with her boyfriends she ended up regretting it afterwards, when the relationship ended. It seemed to make ending it more painful. So I was going to have to take it slow. It was early days so I didn't argue with her. But even though we started spending many of our weekends together, nothing changed. I called what we did the hug-and-spoon race, which nobody won. She liked the phrase and I was stuck with that, too. On nights she stayed over I got very little sleep—I couldn't sleep. We fooled around a little and did other stuff. Her thighs were like a strong boy's, muscular and warm brown and totally smooth. She had these short little powerful legs. Her body was longer; her breasts sat up high on her chest; her nipples were rough and large. Once she took pity on me (the whole thing seemed to amuse her somehow) and gave me a hand job, but I didn't like that much. It made a mess and left messy feelings, too. I felt kind of sticky all over, and she seemed to resent it afterwards.

So we had a fight later about something else. I didn't ask her again, but whenever she stayed over I couldn't sleep. Sleeplessness makes me obsessive; I lay there next to her body all night obsessing.

Church was a funny place to have these thoughts. Two other kids were being baptized that day—all the parents sat together in the front row. Mostly it was just a normal service, but then Cris and Tony walked up with baby James, and I walked up, too, in front of everybody. The priest had black hair, combed up at the front like Elvis's. His skin was very pink, though he probably had to shave a lot, because the black hairs came through darkly. He wasn't very tall. Then he took the baby and dipped his head and Jimmy didn't do anything but just lay there stupidly with a wet head. He cried when Cris took him. Cris and Tony said their bits, and I had to cast out the devil. Then we walked back and sat down. But the devil felt real to me then, I must say.

The priest, whose name was McAndrew, read out: "Just as Christ was raised from the dead by the glory of the Father, so we too might walk in newness of life."

For some reason Brad wasn't baptized but I was. My mother must have insisted, and for the second-born son my dad didn't put up a fight. So I was once a baby with a wet head. Tony and Cris were sitting in front of me, and I could see Jimmy trying to push his nose into her breast. Cris had on a dress you can't lift up, and he was crying and butting his nose against her. I remember thinking, Don't be greedy.

Afterwards we all filed out. The Carneseccas had invited everyone back to their place. For once it wasn't snowing. The sun shone bright enough the snow hurt your eyes, and most of the guests wore sunglasses as they walked to their cars. We were all dressed up and out of the house early on a Sunday morning, and people had a relaxed easy air, like it's time to get drunk. Gloria said to me, "I been to church twice today already. Aren't I a good little girl?"

"A very good girl."

She said, "You know, you don't have to hold my arm all the time. I'm okay."

Then Walter caught up with us and drove us to Tony's.

Everybody arrived at more or less the same time, but Tony had paid for caterers. Pretty soon the house was full of people and it wasn't a big house. I ran into Mel Hauser.

"I didn't see you in church," I said.

"Oh, I don't know. When are you and me going to hit the range again?"

I introduced him to Gloria, but he wandered off to get another drink. He seemed a little drunk already.

There were flowers all over the house. Cris had banged in nails and hung flowers over the front door and the kitchen door, and by the stairs. The television set was hung with ivy.

Robert James was there. So were Clay Greene and his wife. Their kids were there, too, and one of them said to Helen, "May we go outside?" He looked tall for his age and well brought up—he had short dark brown hair, parted in the middle. It looked recently cut. Afterwards I noticed him alone in the garden, rolling a snowball down the snowy slide. But it was only the angle of the window. Another kid, maybe his brother, rolled it back up again.

Cris sat in the kitchen, nursing Jimmy. "Wasn't he a good boy?" she said to me.

"I've never been a godfather before," I said. "What do I do?"

"Just pay a little extra attention, that's all I ask. It doesn't matter so much now but later on. You're a good influence on Tony. The boys could use a man in their life who isn't their father."

"I find it hard to imagine my life more than a couple of months in advance."

"You're not going anywhere," she said.

A waitress in a short black dress squeezed her way around, filling up wineglasses. I asked her name. Desiree, she said; she was a student at Wayne State. "What are you studying?" I asked, but she didn't hear me. There was also a bar set up in Tony's study, which is where I found him, talking to Mel Hauser. Mel said to me, "Do you want a cigar?" They were both smoking.

"I've never had one of these before. What do they do to you?"

"They make you feel sick," Tony said. "Don't tell Cris. She doesn't like it in the house."

But I lit one anyway. "What are you drinking?" I said.

"Scotch."

Mel poured me a glass. "Hey," he said. "I may have heard something about that girl you asked me to look into."

"What girl?"

"The German kid, the one who got raped."

"Well, what is it?"

"Come out to the range and I'll tell you. I want to get my facts straight."

Something about his tone got on my nerves. "What happened earlier?" I said. "You disappeared pretty quick."

"What do you mean?"

There were scabs of skin on his bald head and his cheeks looked gray and heavy. I decided not to pick a fight and went to find Gloria.

Maybe I would have got drunk except we ended up having to leave soon after. Gloria was talking to Walter and Helen Greene.

Helen said, "Where's Susie?"

"She's still in New York. Her parents live there."

"Is that where she wants to have the baby? It's funny, isn't it, how when you have a kid yourself you want to come home to Mommy."

"Yes," Walter said.

"So what's the plan? Are you going to fly down?"

"I guess so."

"I'll tell you something nobody tells you about having kids. It's like this closed shop. We all have to toe the thin blue line. Because the truth is, having kids is not only awful, but it exposes as basically pointless your relations with everybody else. So you learn to put up with the kids."

"I'm going to get a drink," Walter said, and then he pulled at me a little, and I went with him and he said, "You have to get that woman away from me."

"It's not her fault."

"If she says one more word to me I'm gonna sock her."

"You have to tell people, Walter. Because this is going to keep happening."

"Back off, Marny," he said. "I'm leaving. You can find your own ride home."

But in the end, he waited a little and we left with him. Robert couldn't drive us because he was taking Clay and Helen and the kids. Anyway, Gloria was ready to go and I felt strangely worn out. So Walter hung around, standing on the front porch by himself, while we said a few good-byes.

Tony asked me, "So are you guys going out?"

"I guess so."

"What happened to the German girl? Does Gloria know about her?"

"There's nothing to know. Stop it. Don't look so amused."

"You kids," he said. "I got to get my kicks where I can."

Everybody was pissing me off but Gloria. I found her talking to Cris in the kitchen and took her away.

It was a quiet car ride. Some of the snow had melted in the sunshine, but it was cold, too, and you had to watch out for black ice.

Walter dropped us off at Gloria's apartment, but before we got out he said to her, "Marny probably told you, didn't he?"

"Told me what?" she said. "Yes. And I prayed for both of you."

"Did you really?" Walter said, and that was that.

Gloria liked to go to the movies on Sunday afternoons, so that's what we did. We saw *Up in the Air* at the Shores Theatre in St. Clair. She fell asleep for part of it, and afterwards, we got cheeseburgers and milkshakes at Achatz Burgers. Then she took me home, around nine o'clock. Walter's light was still on so I knocked on his door instead of going up.

"You pissed off at me?" I said.

"Not really. Come in."

So we stayed up late talking, till one in the morning. We did this a lot when we first moved in, before Susie arrived. Walter's grandfather, on his mother's side, came from Port Ellen in Scotland, and he always kept a bottle of Laphroaig around—this was one of his affectations in college. But he brought it out now and we drank that.

The cheeseburger and malted shake were still working their way through my system. Mel's cigar didn't help; I'd also had popcorn at the movies. My first drink of the day was at eleven a.m., at Tony's house. It had been a long day. But the whisky woke me up again and I felt fine, okay, until the next morning.

"I got the sense that you didn't like Gloria," I said.

"Listen, don't listen to me. What I think about people right now isn't very rational."

"If you want to talk about that, we can talk about that, too."

"I don't want to. It isn't just that we lost the baby. There were other issues all the way through. Susie didn't want to worry anybody, she didn't want me to talk about it, but it's been a long year. The lining of her womb is abnormally thin. The doctors said there's a risk to her, too, if we try again, but this is something we haven't discussed yet. So I don't much feel like discussing it with you."

I shook my head. "Are you worried she'll stay in New York?"

"What does that mean? I told her to stay. She hates her parents. I told her, you have to make friends with these people, because they'll die when you don't want them to."

"I didn't tell you this, but my dad walked out on my mother."

This is how we talked. I felt a kind of fever of intimacy, which wasn't just the whisky. The heating shut down in his apartment at ten o'clock, and we stayed up for another three hours. By the end I was almost shaking with cold. But I didn't want to say good night. There was something thrilling about speaking openly like this, and digging up several years' worth of buried conversations. You can only fight like this with old friends, and even with them you can't do it very often. But it makes you think, the rest of your life, you're wearing thick gloves.

"That was a long time coming, wasn't it?" Walter said.

"I don't know why you say that. You hardly know him."

"I met him once, I've heard you talk about them. You said yourself, she's a very passive-aggressive woman."

"I would never have used that phrase, I don't even know what it means. That's a bullshit phrase. Some people are aggressive and some people are less aggressive, so you call them passive-aggressive. Big deal."

"That's not what it means. It means some people say what they want and other people get what they want by not saying it."

"My mother says what she wants all the time. She wants him to come back."

"Is he coming back?"

"I don't know."

"What do you care? You're thirty-five years old."

"They're my parents. It feels like my whole childhood is at stake. I liked my childhood, I was happy, and it turns out the whole time that my father was miserable."

"You're not a kid anymore. And none of this means they didn't love each other."

"You should hear him talk. He's been waiting to do this for forty years."

"Remember, you don't have to take anybody's side."

"What does that mean?"

"And by the way, you never struck me as such a happy kid. When you got to Yale you were repressing a lot of angry feelings."

"Don't give me this repression line. It doesn't mean anything."

"It means you were weird about sex. You were always weird about sex."

"Are you kidding me, Walter?"

"Look, I got over it. I saw a girl I liked and repressed my feelings for her. And then I realized this is crazy. Susie was sexually active three years before she met me. In junior high the kind of thing her classmates did for fun was go down on boys. What she did instead was have two serious relationships with guys from the upper school, which didn't work out."

"It's not just her. Everybody at Yale figured you were gay."

"Well, I'm not gay."

"You just took a long time to make up your mind."

"I knew I wasn't gay in college."

"What, the girls you met were too old for you?"

"Mostly they were too young. I didn't want to get slammed on Friday nights and hook up. I also didn't want to have stupid conversations about Nietzsche at three in the morning."

"Give me a break, Walter. That's not why you didn't go out with anybody."

"So why didn't I?"

"I don't know. You tell me."

Later we got on to Gloria. "What's with the little-girl routine?" he asked. "Are you sleeping together or what?"

"What. She stays over but there are lines we don't cross."

"Is it a Christian thing?"

"She's not a virgin, if that's what you mean."

"That's probably what I mean. I knew teachers like her at Dalton. The kids love them, they're lively and sweet, and they haven't quite grown up. Or if they have, they revert."

"Walter, you should know how you come across right now. You seduced one of your students. So forgive me if I don't take what you say about sex very seriously."

"I'm just telling you so you know. There's some damage there, that's all I'm saying. You need to be careful."

"I can't believe I'm having this conversation with you."

"How old is Gloria? Thirty, thirty-two? And she expects to spend the night at your place and not have sex? I'm sorry, I never did anything as kinky as that."

"So how long did you wait before you had sex with Susie?"

"We waited until she was seventeen. Because that's what the law is in New York."

Maybe all this reads angrier than it was.

"I don't really mind not sleeping with her," I said. "Did I tell you I spent the night with Beatrice? Last summer, after Bill Russo's party. We ended up in bed together but nothing happened. She fell asleep and I just lay there. A lot of things became clear to me. Sex is a distortion. It changes what you feel about people. It makes you like people you don't really like and dislike people you don't really dislike."

Walter asked me if I had heard about Beatrice's novel. "Apparently we're all in it. Susie had dinner with Beatrice in New York.

She's worried what people are going to say. You, me, the whole gang, everybody we knew in college."

"What's it about?"

"Beatrice wouldn't tell her."

"Have you met this English guy?"

"Robert has. Your classic gay Englishman, he says. But then her boyfriends always pissed him off."

By one o'clock my eyes hurt. Maybe two inches above them, behind my forehead, some kind of vein was pulsing; it felt backed up with blood. I stood up to get a glass of tap water from the kitchen. Walter wanted one, too, so we stood by his sink, knocking back glasses of water. We were still in the thick of our conversation, in the heat of it, but I guess we both knew that whatever we had said might change color overnight. Like when you pull a muscle in the middle of a squash game, and keep playing, you feel fine, but the next day you can hardly walk.

"When's Susie coming back?" I said again.

"Wednesday."

I went up to bed.

23

A few weeks later Mr. Pendleton, one of the history teachers at Kettridge High, slipped on the ice outside his house and broke his leg. Mrs. Sanchez asked me to take over some of his classes and I started going in three days a week.

This totally changed the complexion of my daily life. I got up early, I went to bed early, I worked hard. On the days I wasn't teaching I prepared my lessons. On the days I was I had lunch with Gloria in the school cafeteria. Kids gossiped about us in the hallways. Sometimes they caught us holding hands. At first we were worried what they might think. Once a girl asked, "Dr. Marnier, are you doing it with Miss Lambert?" I blushed and two of her friends said, "Oh, he is, he is." Later they said, "Do you like black girls then? Is that what you like?" But this was only teasing, they didn't mind. Going out with Gloria was good for my reputation. I think it was harder on her.

The job also made a difference to our relationship. Instead of the guy from the social experiment across the freeway, I was now a part of Gloria's working world. I knew the kids she liked and the ones who gave her a hard time, the kids she sometimes dreamed about at night, worry dreams, and wanted to talk about over dinner until I said, stop. We never spent the night together during the week, but sometimes she slept at my place on Fridays and Saturdays.

Once I even went to church with her and her mother. To the Glory of Zion Baptist Church on Carlton Street. I said I was interested. Outside it looked like a prison; there were high brick walls and small windows. But inside it felt like the hold of a ship, hot and crowded. There was a lot of singing and hand clapping; people stamped their feet. I couldn't bring myself to do any of these things. Afterwards we went out for breakfast. "Was it interesting?" Mrs. Lambert asked me. Another time Nolan invited us to his mom's house for Friday-night dinner.

Nothing particularly noteworthy happened, but I remember it for a couple of reasons. It was the middle of March, the first warm-ish day of the year. Roads were clearing, and the pileups of snow on the sidewalk shone with puddles.

Since I didn't teach on Fridays I went over to Joe's Café and sat there much of the afternoon. For a while it was even warm enough I could sit in the front yard. Spring birds sounded hesitant and strangely clear in the mild air. Joe had just got his license and after a cup of coffee I ordered a gin and tonic and then another. Partly just because I was in a good mood, the week was over, and I was going out with Gloria later, but partly because I was nervous about seeing her with Nolan. I don't know, maybe it was that. Gloria had never said so but I suspected that they used to go out. Not all girls make me jealous but Gloria did. And sometimes, if I let my mind drift that way, I began to imagine stupid things. That she was only going out with me because I'm white or that that was why she wouldn't have sex.

After a couple of G&Ts I felt sharp and nervous, kind of buzzing, when Gloria met me at Joe's and we walked over together. You could hear snow dripping off the roofs onto the porches below. I had a girlfriend, a job, an apartment, spring was coming, I'd been living in Detroit for almost a year. I felt like you do in the middle of the beginning of something, which is just about when you realize it's the beginning.

Clarence was going to bed when we arrived. He had his PJs on—Nolan carried him in his arms, so the boy was sitting on his forearms and looking frontwards. Clarence was a big kid; Nolan had strong arms. He kind of pointed him towards us and said, "Say good night, Clarence," and Clarence said good night. Then they disappeared for a while and Gloria caught up with Mrs. Smith in the kitchen. I sat in the living room with another couple, Byron and Tamika. She worked for the Lutheran Adoption Service in Southfield. He was training to be a chef at the Art Institute of Michigan. But this was only his latest idea; he'd spent his twenties trying to get a band off the ground. They said, what do you do, and for once I had an answer.

"I'm a high school history teacher. Gloria and I work together."

When Mrs. Smith came in she said to Byron, "I better watch what I'm cooking with you around." She wore an apron and high-heeled shoes; her hair was pinned up on her head. Her coloring was paler than Nolan's, and she'd put on some lipstick in a rush, making her look a little windblown. She was sweating from the kitchen; her cheeks were red.

"Well, what are you cooking?" Byron said.

I felt like I had been let into a room that is usually closed to the public. Baton Rouge is about 50 percent black. My high school was maybe 65 percent black—it was a magnet school, and people from my neighborhood got bused in. I didn't have one black friend, not one. Even as a kid I had a sense of some world that was everywhere around me, which I couldn't get into. My school bus drove past front yards with cars broken down in the grass, and other kinds of junk. People sat out on the porches, even in hot weather, talking.

"I guess you all have known each other for a while?" I said to Byron.

"I was Terrell's friend first, back in high school. Nolan was just his dumb brother." Mrs. Smith had already gone back to the kitchen.

Nolan liked his wine and brought out wine at dinner, which was a sweet potato stew, made with chicken thighs and pinto beans. The health care bill was just about to come up to the House for the last time, and Gloria said, after tasting her food, "But Nolan, I haven't told you yet. I met him, I met him."

"Who?"

"Obama," she said. "I can't believe I haven't told you. He almost broke Marny's nose."

"I don't know it was him," I said.

"Oh, come on. They were playing basketball, and he got him right in the face."

"I don't understand anything about this story," Mrs. Smith said, so Gloria told her.

"What did you do?" Byron asked me.

"He got beat's what he did," Gloria said. "I watched the whole thing. And afterwards I get this towel from the kitchen, to clean him up, and Obama says to me"—she tried to do his voice, but it came out wrong—*"This man's not a whiner, this man's not a whiner."*

"That's more Jesse Jackson," I said. "Obama sounds more like me."

"Oh please."

"What do you mean, *please*. I've got more in common with him than you do."

"Like what?"

"An Adam's apple," I said. "You want me to go on?" This is something I'd been thinking about a lot. "I mean, his father's from one place, his mom's from another, and he grew up somewhere else altogether. My dad's Canadian. He spoke French as a kid. My mother comes from the Pacific Northwest. They brought us up in the Deep South, except that the suburb we lived in wouldn't look out of place in Indiana. Obama and I are the kind of Americans who have to choose what to sound like."

"You're crazy," Gloria said.

But we talked about the health care bill as well. I told them that I had campaigned for Obama in New Hampshire. This was in my tender serious boyfriend's voice, the one you use for intimate strangers. The people I came across were mostly working-class whites, I said, not quite rural or suburban, but the kind of people who live on the outskirts of poor small towns. The only thing Obama's election would do is give them an excuse to dislike a black man publicly. Because everybody's allowed to dislike the president—he's fair game. They could say whatever they wanted about his health care policy.

"Those people say what they want to anyway," Nolan said. "You think they give a shit, Marny? You think someone like you's any better? For people like you he isn't black, he's just *a Harvard guy.*"

After dinner we sat in the living room, and I asked Mrs. Smith who played piano. There was an upright piano pushed between the windows. "My husband bought that for the boys. But they never really played. It's a shame, Nolan got those musical fingers, nice and long, but all he ever cared about was drawing and throwing that football up and down the block."

Eventually the wine kicked in and I said, "There's something I've always wanted to ask about the inauguration. You know, when Obama's kids were standing there, and the Reverend Rick Warren said their names? Sasha and Malia. Like they were some kind of tropical fruit he wanted to take a bite out of. I mean, was that commented on?"

"You mean by black people?"

"I guess so."

"Yeah, it was weird," Nolan said. "It was kind of weird."

Gloria and I walked home together afterwards, about a hundred yards. It was cold enough by that point that she let me put my arm around her; a nice clear end-of-winter night, pretty starry.

"Did I do okay?" I said. "Did I embarrass you?"

"I'm not always testing you," she said.

"Did you ever go out with Nolan?"

"Oh, please," she said. "For about a minute. He's not really my type."

But I didn't ask her if she'd slept with him. We spent the night together and the next day together and the next night together. It was all very innocent and low-key. I felt like I was falling in love but maybe not just with her, with something else, another world, but maybe that's always what falling in love is like.

24

That was on Friday night. Gloria stayed for the rest of the weekend. On Sunday a seventeen-year-old kid named Dwayne Meacher, riding his bike, stole an iPhone from a man talking on the sidewalk. Not far from Johanna Street, in fact; two blocks away. Meacher got hit by a car immediately afterwards and cracked his head on the asphalt. The roads were still slick; he didn't have a helmet on. There were differing accounts of what happened, including a disputed confession by the driver to a cop who showed up at the scene three minutes later. For whatever reason, the ambulance took another twenty minutes to arrive.

The first I heard about it was on the local news. Gloria had gone home and I watched the Sunday-evening roundup by myself.

Meacher was knocked out by the fall and remained unconscious in the hospital. The TV report listed his condition as critical; the *Detroit Free Press* described it as a coma in the morning. I usually took a copy of the paper to class with me, to show my students that history is not only happening all the time but happening locally. Meacher made the front page, but I can't say anybody mentioned him in the cafeteria until Thursday lunchtime, after *The New York Times* ran a leader on the story. The *Times'* piece, if you read past the jump, had as much to say about Robert James and his "development model" as it did about Dwayne Meacher. Then *The Huffington Post* picked up on it, *Slate* ran something, *NewsHour* did a story, and the whole shooting match started.

Part of what attracted the talking heads was easy symbolism: the kid on a bike, the vintage car (an old Saab 900 convertible), the iPhone. The fact that the kid was black and the driver was white. Everybody at the scene turned out to be white, except for Meacher and the cops. Columnists and editorial writers used the story to talk about New Jamestown—which is apparently what some people called the new neighborhoods. But after this the name stuck. Robert got a lot of publicity, not all of it bad.

The trouble was, too many people saw something. It was the first warm weekend of the year. There was a yard sale on the block and somebody had put the Tigers game on the radio, probably to show that the radio actually worked. Spring training. People stood around and listened to the game. The guy whose phone was stolen shouted, "Hey, hey you," and everyone turned to look. Several eyewitnesses insisted that Meacher, trying to escape, biked straight across the road and in front of the car, which swerved to avoid him. Other people said the car swerved into Meacher.

The driver, Tyler Waites, described himself as an "Internet entrepreneur." We ended up learning a lot about him.

One of the cops reported that Waites had said to him, "I was just trying to get in his way." But Waites denied this. He said the cop was confusing him with the other guy, whose phone was stolen. I happened to know him—Sandy Brinkman, the playwright from Seattle. Sandy was pretty torn up about the whole thing; his boyfriend was Venezuelan and could pass for black. He said to me a couple of weeks later at Joe's, "Look, I know what discrimination is."

"So did you say that Waites was trying to get in his way?"

"Who knows what I said, I was distraught. You know the first thing I did when the kid got hit? I went and picked up my phone—the screen was broken. I'm an *asshole*. Maybe he's right. I said to Tomaso, it's time to atone, baby; it's time to change our ways. I should fast, I should do something. When you pick up your fucking phone instead of going to the kid. Whatever the papers say about me is right. But I should shut up at least—I'm not supposed to talk about the case."

But the cop insisted it wasn't Sandy, it was Waites who told him, "I was just trying to get in his way." "I know what I heard," the cop tweeted, after the story ran. He got in trouble for that and was eventually suspended with pay. What nobody wrote about, but what you couldn't help noticing, was the extra police cars on our streets, driving slowly, even in the middle of the afternoon. The atmosphere was changing, people were taking sides.

GLORIA AND I HAD A drawn-out fight about the whole thing. I mean, it just simmered away, and sometimes it boiled over.

There were all kinds of stories coming out about this Waites guy. His father was a Bircher, a lawyer in Memphis, which is where Waites grew up. He went to law school in Memphis, too, but dropped out after a year to go into real estate. His business partner was another law school dropout, an African American, as it happens, who used to play power forward for the Memphis Tigers. They had big-name backers, including some local sports personalities, ex–NFL players, and they made some money at first and then overextended themselves. Waites and his partner had a falling-out; the company was still involved in litigation.

Then Waites launched an Internet business, a website that organized people's online lives. The idea was, you set up one account with him and used it to access and pay for all other services on the web. You had just one username, one password, one set of payment details. In practice, it turned out to be a front for people who wanted to look at hard-core pornography and cover their tracks. The *Times* quoted Waites as saying, "You can't blame me for the human condition. I offer a service. What people use it for is their business." He was still running this site from Detroit and the *Times* piece gave him a lot of free publicity. (They ran a follow-up story about it.)

The implication was, these are the kind of people who moved to Detroit. Law school dropouts, shady businessmen, porn pushers; rich kids who couldn't make it on Daddy's dime. Life's unattractive failures. Steve Zipp knew Tyler Waites—he helped him out with his accounts. What Steve said to me is this. Once the press starts looking at your life, forget about it. We all look like jerks. Tyler's not so bad.

But would he run down a black kid in his car? That was the question, and for some reason people wanted to answer it biographically. They made a big deal about the Bircher connection. For Gloria, it was the end of the story. Of course, he ran him down.

"You can't have a daddy like that and not be poisoned by it. It's a split-second thing. You hear somebody shout, Stop, thief, and you see this black kid, and he's getting away. So you put your foot on the pedal, a little bit."

"But he didn't shout, Stop, thief," I said. "He shouted, Hey, you. There's a difference. Who knows what *hey, you* means. And Tyler wasn't on speaking terms with his father."

"Oh, that's just because— That's not because Tyler hated him, or anything like that. That's just because his daddy thought he was a loser and a borderline criminal. He didn't want to have anything to do with Tyler, not the other way around."

"How can you say such things so confidently about these people? You never even met him."

"Believe me, I met a few Tyler Waites."

"And the reason his father wouldn't speak to him is that he went into business with a black guy. And dropped out of law school. So what if he did. I've quit a few things in my time."

"That's all this is," Gloria said. "You think I'm mad at you."

"Aren't you?"

"Little bit," she said. "For taking his side."

"I'm not taking anyone's side."

"Sure you are. You just don't know it yet."

There was a columnist at the *Chicago Tribune* who argued that anyone who had moved to the "Communist-style society of this Detroit development" must be considered "innocent of any connection to the Birchers." He went on: "In this place, the State (by which I mean one Robert James) controls all the rents, heavily subsidizes the local bus service, offers universal health care and even employs a number of its citizens on a nationalized urban *farm*. They may as well put up a sign on the Freeway exit: No Bircher Need Apply."

I wasn't so sure about that, either. A lot of my neighbors were left-wing hippies, it's true, potheads and Marxists and VW-caravan kind of mommies and daddies. But there were some NRA nuts, too, Tea Party types who thought the only solution to America's problems was to get out and start over. One of the things I liked about New Jamestown is that most of us got along pretty well.

My real argument with Gloria was this. You can't ever know why anybody does anything and this was a crime that depended almost entirely on motive. Did Meacher run into Waites's car or did the car run into Meacher? Witnesses on both sides were willing to swear one thing or another. The simple fact was, car and bike had collided, and they might just as well have hit each other if

Waites was trying to swerve out of the way and misjudged the angle. Which is why the whole thing came down to motive. To mens rea, as they put it in the papers: a guilty mind.

But what kind of guilty mind were we talking about? Could Waites have *planned* to knock Meacher down, for the sake of some preconceived idea of long-term personal advantage? Of course not. So what do we mean by guilty mind in this case? A racist inclination? Because every white American male of his generation who grew up in a town like Memphis was going to have something in his past, a connection or relation or association, something he did or said or somebody he knew, that suggested a "racist inclination." If that was the test then Waites was always going to be guilty, then we were all guilty, even if Waites had tried to slam on the brakes he was guilty. And a test that everybody fails is no test—it doesn't help you sort anyone out.

So what else could guilty mind mean? A spur-of-the-moment impulse to bump the kid? But how can you measure an impulse? Even if Waites *did* say to the cop, "I was just trying to get in his way," that doesn't mean he was right. This is the kind of explanation we come up with after the fact, but motive isn't a fact, it's an interpretation, the only fact in this case is that Meacher got hit.

"Please," Gloria said. "This is starting to upset me. And last time, when it was just the same kind of thing, you took my side."

"What do you mean, last time? About your father? Of course I took your side. But you're the one who's flip-flopping. In that case you tried to tell me it *wasn't* about race, those people would have left a white man dying by the side of the road just the same."

"Don't bring him into this," she said. "Don't use him like that."

"But you brought it up."

"I guess you didn't understand me because that's not what I meant. I was talking about me. If I hadn't a been scared, I'd have knocked on somebody's door and got help. It's all about race."

"That's not what you said. You're changing your tune for some reason."

"Are you seriously telling me that if Meacher is white, if the kid on the bike is white, that Waites would have *hit him with his car*? Because he stole somebody's phone? Are you telling me that?"

"I don't know."

"*Changing my tune*. What does that mean."

"It means you're picking a fight with me about this for some reason."

"Oh, you haven't even seen me pick a fight."

"I have to be able to say what I think to you. You have to trust me."

"You can say what you think, you just got to think better. Or put up with the consequences."

"That's not what I'm talking about. You're holding back on me. What you're saying to me is, watch your step. You can go this far but no farther."

"Are we talking about what I think we're talking about?"

"I don't know. But at some point I want to talk about that, too."

"Because I thought we were talking about Dwayne Meacher."

"Okay, all right."

"Tell me this then. How come it took three minutes for the cops to come and twenty-three minutes for the ambulance to arrive? Let's talk about that."

"But Gloria, you're mixing everything up. I don't know why the ambulance took so long, but that's not Tyler Waites's fault. That's not my fault. But you're acting like it is."

"That's right," she said. "*Because you taking his side.* And don't speak to me like that again, not now, not ever. Tell me I'm mixing— things up. Get out of my sight and don't come back till I've calmed down."

"How will I know that you've calmed down?"

"Because I won't throw something at you when I see you."

SOME FACTS STARTED TO EMERGE about Dwayne Meacher, too. He was a junior at Macomb, another 4A high school, and a basketball rival of Kettridge. A solid B student, he played trumpet in band, which is what I used to play. His father was serving a fifteen-year sentence for voluntary manslaughter at the Mound Correctional Facility—he got in a bar fight and killed someone with a bottle. Dwayne lived with his mother and three sisters. His mother had medical issues and didn't work; she was described in the papers as a former nursing assistant. One of the sisters was quite a lot older and studying health care administration at Wayne State. The other two were still at home.

The principal at Macomb, Dr. Selena Brown, characterized Dwayne as "kind of a nerdy kid, but popular, a tech-head." But he had a history of extracurricular "issues." She had to keep the police from intervening when Dwayne got caught selling prescription painkillers to his classmates. He agreed to do forty hours' community service, at a substance abuse treatment program, which meant in practice visiting people in prison and going around with one of the caseworkers to make sure guys on parole showed up for their drug tests. His caseworker described him as "always very punctual and respectful, pleasant to be around, a nice kid."

It probably wasn't the first phone he stole either. iPhone theft was getting to be a problem downtown. There was a much-mocked op-ed column in the *Free Press* called "Why Stealing a Phone Isn't Just Stealing a Phone." The point of the piece was to explain why people got so attached to their phones. "It's where you keep not only your bank details but your text messages and your photographs of family and friends. It isn't just a technological gadget or status symbol. It's your home, it's where you live." But the truth is, as one police officer said, "These gangs aren't interested in your bank details, and they don't care about your photographs either. They wipe the instruments clean and ship them to Africa. The phone Meacher stole has a street value of about fifty bucks. Fifty bucks is what he was after, that's what the risk was for."

There were daily reports in the paper and on the news of his condition, which didn't change—critical but stable.

25

A few weeks after this incident Robert James called me up and said, "It's getting nice out, let's go for one of our Sunday jogs." But this time he didn't mean Belle Isle. He wanted to run around city streets, he wanted to see the neighborhood.

We worked up a sweat together and afterwards sat down at one of Joe's front tables to cool off. Joe himself came out to serve us, in a bright yellow apron.

"I know who you are," he said to Robert. "I've seen you on TV."

"That's me."

We sat there for a good hour while the sweat dried, drinking ice water and then coffee and eating Danishes.

"You're not around much these days," I said.

"No, I've been in New York."

There was something about the way he spoke I always found attractive. He thought about everything he said, even basic things like that, and came out with them slowly.

"You washing your hands of us?"

"I'm in and out. I'm in now. I've got a lot of things going on that need attention."

"But you're here now because of this Meacher business."

"That's part of it," he said. "I want to hear what you think."

We talked about Meacher and eventually I said, "What happened with Obama, by the way? I've been meaning to ask you."

"What do you mean?"

"I got the feeling there was some bad blood."

He frowned a little, in a good-looking way. "I wanted to let him know that what we were doing in Detroit could be reproduced."

"So now he knows."

"That's right."

Kurt Stangel walked over with a Frisbee in his hand. His T-shirt had a picture of Mel Lozano on it, in a sports bikini. Robert put up with him for a while, then when Kurt went inside to get coffee Robert said to me, "Listen, Marny. I've got a favor to ask you. You're friendly with a guy named Nolan Smith?"

"Who told you that?"

"Tony told me. Is it true?"

"I know Nolan."

"The thing is, he's starting to cause us a little trouble."

"Oh, Nolan's all right. He just talks a lot."

"Well, now he's talking about Meacher. There's a criminal process, which I'm not especially worried about. But Smith is talking to his family, too, he's making promises to the mother which I don't suppose he'll be able to keep. There's going to be a civil suit, which we expected, but Smith seems determined to make it into a public event, which won't necessarily help their case."

"What do you care?"

"I have a duty to the people who come here . . ."

"Come off it, Robert."

"What's happening right now to Tyler Waites is ninety percent to do with the situation we put him into."

"So far as I can tell, Tyler Waites is doing fine."

"That's because you haven't thought very much about what this kind of public legal process can do to you."

"It's Dwayne Meacher I'd be more worried about if I were you."

"I am worried about him. The people who really lead the field in brain trauma are the US military, but there are good people in private practice, too, who work closely with the military, and I've brought them in on it."

"I haven't seen anything about it in the papers."

"I didn't want it in the papers. But if you're willing to talk to Nolan Smith about what's going on, we can fill you in."

"Why don't you tell him yourself?"

"We've tried. There've been some misunderstandings."

"Robert, I don't want to be your middleman. Anyway, there's not much I can do. He's been looking for a chance like this for a while."

"Tony tells me you're pretty good friends. He says your girl-friend's an old friend of his, too."

"That's enough of that," I said.

"Marny, I don't think you appreciate how delicate our position is. In Detroit generally. We really don't want to turn this into a racial thing."

"It *is* a racial thing."

We sat in silence in the spreading sunshine for a few minutes. The reflection off the metal tables was bright enough to make me squint; salt kept getting in my eyes. But it was nice to dry up in the sun, I felt good.

"What happened with you and Obama?" I said. "Is this the kind of thing he was worried about?"

"Yes."

"Because it felt to me more personal than that."

"He's suspicious of people like me. He thinks we don't like him."

"What do you mean, people like you?"

"Hedge fund guys," Robert said. After a minute, he went on: "Tony told me something about this Nolan character. He says he's a very forceful personality."

"Why don't you just say it? He's an angry black man."

"Oh, get over it, Marny. You got a black girlfriend, and now you're standing up for all the brothers?"

For some reason, this made me blush. "Fuck you, Robert," I said.

He gave me a minute to calm down—he went to take a leak, and moved like a thirty-something man after his jog, feeling his weight on the steps. "We're all paid up," he said, coming back.

I stood up stiffly and Robert walked me to my front drive, which is where he'd parked his car.

"This is not how I wanted the conversation to go," he said. "The thing about you, Marny, is that you're the kind of guy who falls in love with guys. I don't mean like a gay thing, but you get ideas about them and you can't see straight. You were the same about Tony at first. This guy could do real damage if we don't watch out."

I said I'd talk to him.

BUT I TALKED TO STEVE Zipp first. I sometimes helped him look after his boy. The kid was about a year and a half now and fun to be around. He looked like Steve, pale and serious; his hair was cut like Steve's, too, and he had skinny red knees and walked around like a guy late for work. Neil Lyman—Lyman was his mother's name. Neil was a bad napper and Steve often drove him to sleep in the afternoon. Sometimes I drove with him. Then we sat in the car and talked or parked by Joe's and got a cup of coffee with Neil in the car.

"Tell me about Tyler Waites," I said.

"He's one of those loud guys people like. Like in high school he would have been the class clown, but the kind of class clown even the teacher got along with. Funny, not mean. If you go around with Tyler he talks to everybody and you just stand around and watch him work."

"Is he a racist?"

"Let me put it this way. I'm willing to bet that around the wrong people he's gone along with some jokes that are a little off. Maybe he even makes these jokes himself. But it's also true that if you walk into 7-Eleven with him, and the lady working the counter is one of these big black ladies, with five-inch fingernails and artificial hair, you know, someone you and I have basically nothing to say to, he'll have a fifteen-minute conversation with this woman, where she laughs her head off, and you have to drag him out of the store."

"What's he look like?"

"Too tall. Good-looking, but doesn't mind looking stupid. Slightly preppy. I think he's a decent golfer. I like him. He calls me Nerd Man. Why do you want to know?"

"Gloria and I have been fighting about this whole thing." I also told him about Nolan Smith, that he was planning to raise a big stink about Tyler Waites. "Robert James asked me to talk him out of it."

"Okay, well," Steve said. "Tyler's got a thick skin. Let me show you something about Robert James, though. I maybe figured out why the numbers add up."

We were driving around in his Oldsmobile, not really going anywhere but just driving around. Neil had just about fallen asleep in the back. It was another fine blue May afternoon, with a bit of breeze to make it cool in the shade. But the car got hot in the sunlight, which was clear and direct. Those big leather front-row bench seats get hot pretty quick.

At one point he pulled into the parking lot of the twenty-four-hour McDonald's at the corner of Conner and Mack. "I had breakfast here once," I said, "the night after Gloria and I got together. There were all these guys coming off shift, and me with zero sleep, you know, when you feel real cold and it was cold as hell out anyway. For some reason I walked back from her place and got lost. Then I came across this McDonald's and just sat there feeling kind of spaced out and at peace with everybody."

"How's that going?"

"I don't know. It's all new territory. I keep doing things I haven't done before and saying things I haven't said before."

He turned the car around and drove back slowly the way we had come. "I'm happier now than I've ever been in my life," he said.

"How much of that is to do with the kid?"

"Some of it. And it doesn't hurt I only have to see him every other weekend. But the main thing is I'm not working very hard, life is cheap, and there are people around who want to have a good time. The Internet is a beautiful thing. I get to have sex with actual women, it's amazing."

"I can't tell when you're being serious anymore."

"Look, my whole life I lived conventionally. I got an accounting degree, for Christ's sake. And it turns out this is a crazy, crazy way to live. Because there's all kinds of stuff you want to do, let's face it, there's stuff you're actually doing, that you can't say anything about to the people who love you. So it starts to get weird—you start to get weird. This is how I came across. I don't want to give all the credit to coming here. There are things I'm doing now I couldn't have done if my mother were still alive. A couple of months ago, for example, I had a date with a guy—he posted something on the E-change along the lines of, if you haven't tried it, you can try it with me. Some gay guys get their kicks out of turning you around."

"So what happened?"

"You see that, you're paying attention now. You want to know."

"So tell me."

"Well, this is something I can do, gay sex is something I'm capable of. But it wasn't for me. I'm too competitive. I don't mean physically. Emotionally the kind of person I want to be intimate with is the Other. I want differences, I want allowances, I want explanations."

"Maybe you didn't meet the right guy."

"Well, I tried it once, maybe I'll try it again. But I don't think so. You don't get points for scoring guys, that's not what you dream about. I mean, when you're thirteen years old and covered in zits. At least I didn't. I wanted girls. And then you get to college and girls are everywhere, they're in your bathroom, taking a dump, they're coming out of the shower, they're eating food, and none of them will look at you. I still didn't have a chance. Now I do, that's all. But what I want to know is, who's paying for all this? It's the accountant in me, I can't get rid of him. Look, this is what I wanted to show you."

Neil was asleep by this point, and Steve parked by the gate of the big industrial plant under the bridge. There was still a pile of garbage in the forecourt, rubber tires, shopping carts, dirty clothes, but there were also a couple of cars, including a security vehicle with a siren on the hood.

"What's security doing in this dump, right?" Steve said.

"There's nobody there."

"Just stay in the car," he said.

I watched him get out and walk up to the fence. In spite of the sunshiny weather, he wore long pants and a buttoned-up white-collared blue shirt. Pants always looked too big on him. He needed to belt them in and his legs showed up only at the knees.

There was a locked chain holding the gates shut, and he tugged on that a little, but they wouldn't budge. The fence had barbwire on top but the gates didn't, and for a minute he tried to climb up the vertical bars—he jumped and tried to pull himself up. When that didn't work he started calling out, "Hey, hey, anybody home?" But nobody came. I saw him looking around in the dirt and then he picked up a loose brick and threw it over the fence. When it landed a few pieces broke off.

Eventually a side door opened, and a guy came out.

"What the fuck you doing?" he said. He was black and about six foot three and maybe fifty pounds overweight.

"Just fucking around," Steve said.

"Well, go fuck around somewhere else."

"How come they make you work Sundays?"

"Because of assholes like you."

The car window was rolled down so I could hear all this. The guy had a Triton Security cap on, loose blue jeans and big white brand-new sneakers.

"What's the plan for this building anyway? They gonna fix it up?"

"Look. I get paid to sit here so I sit here."

"Is there something inside? I just want to see."

"I'm gonna go back in now. If you're still standing there when I sit down, I'm calling the police."

Steve walked to the car and got in. "Let's just sit here. He's not going to call the police."

"What the fuck are you doing?"

"I bet he won't," Steve said, but he turned on the ignition anyway and backed out.

On the way home, he explained himself. Neil sometimes woke up very early in the morning, as early as four a.m., and to get him back to sleep Steve put him in the car and just cruised. A couple of weekends ago he drove past this place—another Sunday morning, predawn. The gates were open and there was a container truck backing in. So he hung around to watch them unload.

"So what was it?" I said.

"Aluminum. I'm almost certain. There were wooden shelves and bins, which is what they usually store aluminum in, to prevent scratching. But I couldn't see anything else."

"I don't understand."

"The price of aluminum has gone up almost two hundred percent in the past year. Partly because of new technologies. But it's also one of those commodities people buy up in a recession. So I started looking around for storage depots—empty office buildings, factories, warehouses, that kind of thing. I don't need to tell you how many there are. You think the police presence is for us? Somebody's buying up aluminum, and they've done a deal with Robert James to store it. After all, that's what Detroit is good for, cheap real estate. And it's all going in—nothing's coming out. They're driving up prices. We're just the window dressing here, what's really going on is big business."

I couldn't tell anymore how crazy he was. Indications from various quarters suggested that my view of reality was pretty limited.

LATER THAT WEEK I DROVE to Linwood Street to fire a few rounds with Mel Hauser. We had lunch first in the canteen and I heard a lot of cop gossip. Nobody had much sympathy for Dwayne Meacher.

"Look," one of them said to me. "There's no case there. You steal somebody's phone, you're on a bike, you're trying to get away. Then you get hit by a car. If the kid isn't black, believe me, none of this is even an issue."

He had a good head of gray hair and a spongy old-guy's face. His nose was bulbous; he had trouble getting food out of his teeth. I had my first Coney that day, a hot dog covered in chili, which tasted like it sounds.

"What do you think?" Mel said.

"It's school-lunch food."

"This isn't a particularly good example."

"The civil suit is more baloney," the guy went on. "Michigan has a no-fault law, which basically means, since the kid didn't have insurance, the driver's insurance has to pay damages. It doesn't matter whose fault it was—that's what no fault means. Everything else is just a publicity stunt."

"But the kid is black," I said. "So it is an issue."

"You're the guy who lives around there. As far as I'm concerned that's looking for trouble. When they burn down your house I'll say the same thing. You asked for it."

"Do you think they'll bring charges against Tyler Waites?"

"Is Larry Oh up for reelection?"

Mel's old buddies were all white. But I liked them; they liked to piss each other off in a friendly way. I asked Mel how his kids were and one of them said, "What does he know?" A few of the other guys had retired, too. They didn't talk as much as the rest, they seemed happy to be there, they went up for seconds. Mel didn't talk much either.

Afterwards, on the way to the range, I asked him why it took three minutes for the cops to arrive and twenty-three minutes before an ambulance showed up.

"How do I know?" he said. "There was probably a car on patrol."

There were five or six guys ahead of us, but the duty officer brought out a couple of Smith & Wessons and Mel took me through the process of cleaning them. Since the weather was fine, we went to the outdoor range, which looked like a parking lot surrounded by concrete walls. But over the walls you could see trees, already summery with leaves, blowing back and forth. The clouds in the sky got pushed along at a good clip, but it wasn't cold. *Pop pop pop*—the background noise was full of gunshots, but the open air made everything sound a little farther away.

"So you don't think it was a racial thing?"

"This is Detroit," Mel said. "Nothing works. We don't have enough ambulances, which is why for some parts of the city they use private companies. It's up to the dispatch operator when you call 911. They have to make sure everybody gets to the scene on time. Police, ambulance, fire services. And let me tell you something else. Nine out of ten of the people on the phones are black."

"What about the cop. The one who said that Tyler admitted to him he tried to hit the kid. How come they suspended him? Doesn't that look a little like a cover-up?"

"You know why. For fucking tweeting about it. They should have fired him. Blame him if you want to blame anybody."

"Do you know him?"

"I know guys like him. There's a real hot dog element to these people. But he pissed on his own doorstep this time. And by the way, twenty-three minutes is par for the course. Twenty-three minutes is nothing to ask questions about."

Shooting handguns is fun. But you need strong arms—just holding your arms out straight is heavy work, and Mel suggested I put two hands on the gun. I did okay in the beginning and managed to pepper a few in the chest area, but after that the holes started spacing out. Even with my earmuffs on I could hear the contact with the cardboard, a kind of *thwuck* sound after the pip of the shot.

You put one foot in front of the other. If you're right-handed that means your left foot first.

Mel said, "Keep your eyes open. Both eyes."

Apparently I'd been closing one of them. But it's like I could feel different parts of my brain getting tired. After a while I started seeing double images, or silhouettes around the figure lines, and my hands and the gun waving gently in front, superimposed. When I breathed they moved; I could hear my heart in my ears. Five minutes is a long time to stare at something. We were standing in direct sunlight, and the ground was a pale gray concrete, which reflected it back. By the time we stopped I had a light sweat going.

There was a soda machine by one of the benches and Mel asked me afterwards if I wanted some pop. They had Welch's grape. So we sat on the bench drinking and burping and watching some of the guys.

"Everybody's fat these days," Mel said. "When I was a kid I looked like you."

"So what do you have to tell me about Astrid?"

"Well, you wanted me to look into it so I looked. You said they knew who his sister was so why couldn't they find the guy. Rape is a big deal; we take rape seriously. And in this case we had a name and at least one address where the suspect was known to hang out. It didn't make sense to me either. So I asked around a little. There were complicating factors. For one thing the guy in question had paid to get in—to the club, I mean. It was ten dollars at the door and the bouncer remembered him. He wouldn't swear to it but he also thought they might have come out together. There's a camera at the door, which was broken that night, but cameras inside showed Astrid dancing in the vicinity of a well-built African American male in his late twenties. The image quality isn't good enough for a positive ID. It was pretty dark in there."

"I don't understand."

"It looks like the suspect was probably known to the girl."

"What does that matter?"

"For one thing it means she hasn't been telling the truth—at least, not the whole truth. Rape is almost always my word against yours. Where the victim is the only witness, and there's a good reason to question her credibility, it's very, very hard to get a conviction. Plus in this case another interpretation suggests itself. That she had a fight with her boyfriend and left the club with some guy she just met and afterwards, maybe when she sobered up, regretted what she did and tried to pin the whole thing on the guy. I'm not saying it wasn't rape. This guy has previous convictions, including domestic assault, and maybe she changed her mind before they got back to the apartment. Maybe he got a little rough, maybe he even raped her, but if he did, it's going to be hard to prove because there's a pretty good case that she lied about the rest."

"So that's why they didn't do anything."

"That's why. Are you finished with this?" he said, and took my can and his and threw them away. On the way out he asked me: "What's your relation to this woman anyway?"

"I picked her up hitchhiking when I drove to Detroit."

"It all figures. Let me give you some advice you probably don't want to hear. Everybody lies. This is what you learn from forty-six years as a cop. And victims and witnesses have just as much reason to lie as the people it's your job to lock up."

"How is that advice?" I said.

26

Meanwhile, my life went on. The school year was coming to an end and Gloria and I arranged a field trip together. We took a group of ninth graders to visit Franklin Mayer's farm, which was only about a five-minute drive by rented bus from Kettridge High. Most of the kids had seen the barbwire fence around it. There were security issues early on, people stealing equipment and fertilizer, and Franklin had instituted an ID system. But I wanted these local kids to get a look at what was happening on the other side of the barbwire.

It rained in the morning but cleared up enough for us to get out on the fields after lunch. A lot of the people who worked the farm came for just a few days or maybe a few weeks, and Franklin didn't expect them to buy their own clothes. There was a changing room with lockers full of gear. So the kids got to put on rubber boots and wade out on the soft earth.

Franklin took us around. I liked this guy, but he wasn't somebody you had to listen to. He talked a lot, his big good-looking red face looked a little sunburned, too, and he wasn't at all shy leading forty homegrown Detroiters through what used to be one of their neighborhoods. We started out with the cucumber patch and the kids put down a few seeds. "Man, it smells like shit here," one of them said, and Franklin said, "It smells like three different *kinds* of shit."

"I never met a white farmer before."

"What do you mean?"

"I thought it was all like Mexicans."

"It's interesting you should say that," Franklin said, "because one of my uncles, one of my great-uncles, was an attaché to Heinrich von Eckardt. You know von Eckardt? He was the German ambassador to Mexico in 1917, the one who received the Zimmermann Telegram. They wanted to get Mexico on board in case America entered the war, which of course we did."

This is how he talked, and most of the kids got a kick out of him.

He pointed out squash beds and potato beds, tomato plants, rhubarb patches, and zucchini vines strung up on posts and wires. There were also young peach and apple orchards; the trees looked like twigs stuck in the ground. He walked us along the side of wide grain fields and stopped to have a word with a couple of guys. "If any of you wants a summer job," Franklin said, "talk to Pete."

Pete was Pete Chaney, a former high school English teacher, as it happens. I knew him slightly; he was a recovering alcoholic and had two teenage girls back in Billings. His wife still worked at the *Gazette* and couldn't decide whether or not to divorce him.

There were animals, too, a handful of cows, three pigs, chickens in a coop, even a horse named Toto, which Franklin kept for no other reason than that he liked to ride it around the farm. Just at the end he let us dig up a few early potatoes, which were still very small, to show us what they looked like.

"I ain't eating nothing I have to dig out of the dirt."

"Where do you think French fries come from?" Franklin said.

"McDonald's."

The kids had a good time but Gloria didn't seem comfortable or happy. "Okay, I get it, it's very funny, ha-ha," she said to me at one point.

"What's wrong?"

"He's hamming it up."

"That's just what he's like," I said.

We could hear the traffic on I-94 over our heads, competing against the noise of birds, grackles and jays on some of the trees and crows in the fields. The whole visit took two hours; most of what we ended up doing was crowd control. Afterwards the kids changed out of their muddy clothes and washed their hands. There was a shack next to the changing room where you could buy whatever was in season, lettuces and radishes, etc. Just as we were leaving the young guy behind the counter accused some girl of stealing asparagus. He said, "Hey, where you going with that," and Gloria grabbed her and spun her around.

"I didn't do anything," the girl said, but we opened her handbag and found about half a dozen stalks.

"The man said I could. I said what's that and he said, take some."

"I didn't tell her that." He had a paper-white foreign-looking face; his accent sounded flavored by the movies.

But the girl meant Franklin, who came out of the bathroom drying his hands and said, "It's true."

"Why you jump on me like that, Miss Lambert," the girl said. Her name was Mabelle Johnson. She was one of these bony-butted black girls and wore her hair real tight on her head, in pigtails. "You know me better than that."

On the bus ride home Gloria apologized to her, but she also said, "I don't care who said what. You make sure the people who need to see what you're doing are seeing what you're doing. That's just common sense." But Mabelle just pushed up her lip and turned her shoulder. She was one of my kids, an okay kid, but a talker in class, who was hard to shut up because maybe 20 percent of the time she had something to say.

Gloria seemed disproportionately upset by the whole thing. We drove back to my place after school, in two cars, and did a little shopping together. Then I cooked while she graded papers.

"You're a little quiet," I said to her over supper.

"I didn't have fun today. Why didn't I have fun? I always used to think I was having fun."

"It's a field trip. The teacher isn't supposed to have fun."

"No, but I like field trips. That's not it."

"You want to tell me what is?"

She shook her head.

Later that week we talked about it again. She stayed over on Friday night and sometimes when I pushed a little hard in bed she got out of it by starting emotional conversations. We went to bed early but then kind of wrestled for a bit and gave up. But I was too frustrated to sleep, and then my restlessness woke her and we talked. It was around one in the morning.

My bedroom was on the top floor. Robert James made a big deal about getting little things to work, like neighborhood street lamps, and the light from the street came in through my curtains, bright enough I could see her dark face. But her expression was hard to read. Her eyes looked very large and white.

We said all kinds of things to each other. One of the things I remember is that she said, "I don't always know who I am. Isn't that weird?"

"When do you know who you are?"

"When I'm not with you."

But we got to sleep eventually and had a nice weekend together.

I DECIDED FOR A COUPLE of reasons to call Astrid. What Mel Hauser had said kept worrying me. It seemed that whenever I had sexual relations with people I started to get paranoid thoughts, I started to think I didn't know these people I was sharing my bed with at all. I mean, that's basically what Gloria had told me, that I didn't understand her. But in this case I had third-party information that Astrid had lied and lied in a kind of spooky way. So I phoned her up and we arranged to meet after work at that bar by the train station. The bar was her idea.

It turned out to be a bad day at school. We had one week of class left, the exams were done, everybody seemed to be feeling their oats. It didn't help that the air-conditioning broke down. Even with the windows open I could feel my shirt sticking to me and unsticking. When a breeze blew in it was like a little taste of vacation.

Since we were just killing time, I taught a few classes on colonial America—something I actually know about. This was a mistake; the kids didn't care and I got annoyed.

One of the interesting things about the early colonies, I told them, which you don't get much of a sense of, say, from *The Scarlet Letter*, is that even though the Pilgrims would probably be considered religious fundamentalists by today's standards, they actually had to make quite a few concessions to civil liberties. They just didn't have enough people, certainly after the first couple of winters, to keep up the old social structures.

Mabelle Johnson said, "Explain to me why I care." She had been acting up consistently since the visit to the farm.

"Well, for example, unmarried women had the right to own property."

"You mean 'cause I'm like an unmarried woman? What about black women? How much property did black women own?"

"I don't know. The first blacks came to Virginia in 1619, as indentured servants. Some of them eventually owned land, but I don't know about women. Some of them owned slaves."

"You made that up."

"Look," I said. "The line between servant and slave wasn't always easy to draw, especially at the beginning. People talked about servants in terms of money, but they also had contracts, which could be worked out."

"What do you mean, *money*?"

"I mean they left each other servants in their wills. They traded servants, they put a value on them."

"Like how much?"

"It varied. But about twenty, twenty-five pounds."

"How much is that?"

"In today's money?"

"In dollars."

"That's hard to say, but it's a reasonable amount of money."

"For a black man? I'm a tell Miss Lambert you said that."

"That's not what I meant. We're talking about white servants, too."

"Why don't you say what you mean?"

And so on. I didn't know what to do about her; there was nothing I could do. But I felt angry for the rest of the day and didn't get to see Gloria after school, except for three minutes in the parking lot. I told her I was going to meet an old friend for a drink.

ASTRID WAS LATE AND I sat at the bar long enough to finish a beer. Just as well, I thought, since I didn't know how to say what I wanted to say to her. But then she came in and I couldn't believe how nervous I felt—my heart beat unpleasantly.

She wore jeans and cowboy boots, which was like her uniform. In the air-conditioned bar her pale skin quickly goose-pimpled. "You called me," she said.

"I wanted to ask you something. A friend of mine's a cop, and I asked him to look into what happened to you. He told me something I wanted to ask you about."

"I should warn you, I'm not interested in any of that anymore. I've talked about it so much it doesn't feel real. And anyway, it wasn't important. You only have to open your eyes to see that what's happening all around you is so much worse."

"What do you mean?"

"Everything in my art was about me. But this is boring and stupid. So I started talking to other people. It's amazing, if you ask people things they tell you."

We ordered bar food, but I wasn't very hungry, I didn't eat much. The hamburgers came and she got her fingers dirty with ketchup. Even though she rubbed her hands on paper napkins, I could see the marks they made on her white T-shirt. I picked at the fries and drank another beer. One of the things we talked about was Tyler Waites. I said I knew Sandy Brinkman, the guy whose phone got stolen; Astrid seemed interested. Afterwards, she invited me back to her place—she wanted to show me what she was working on.

There was an artists' commune near the train station, a short row of houses that had been saved from demolition and turned into studios. People lived there, too, for a few months at a time. It was somewhere to find your feet. When a space came up, Astrid jumped at the chance. It's more like what she was used to in Berlin, she said. Everybody shared a kitchen; you cooked together. It didn't matter what your apartment was like. You lived for seeing friends.

It was a two-minute walk to her house, but we didn't go to her room at first. She took me to the studio, which was in another building. I had to put up with being introduced to other people, a Belgian PhD student, who was interested in modern ruins, and a black guy from East London. They were making pakoras in the kitchen. The black guy did most of the cooking. He wore high-tops, army pants and a Mookie Blaylock jersey under his apron. I could see the name when he turned around.

"What do you do?" I said.

He recorded house parties, mostly audio recordings. Basically, he was interested in the music being played, but he also took photographs. On Friday nights he just drove around the city.

I felt like the guy who hangs around the girl and was glad when she took me upstairs. Her studio was pretty basic; it had some video equipment and a cheap two-seater couch. Astrid immediately opened both windows—the whole house smelled of frying oil. Then we sat down and watched one of her films.

"Do you want something to drink?" she said, hitting the pause button. "All I have is Jack Daniel's."

So she poured some into coffee mugs and started the film again. The first thing I saw was a framing shot of a playground basketball court. There was a game going on and music in the background, but you couldn't tell if the music came from the park. Then it got louder and too loud, somebody rapped angrily—

All of my brothers live by the trigger
But nobody care so long as nigger kill nigger

—and the screen suddenly turned into a black talking face with a white wall behind it. The music stopped and you could hear him:

—I tell you something happened the other day. I went down to the park to play a little ball. Corey got next, so I said to him, can

I run with you, Corey? And he's like, you come to play? Because this little punk's been running his mouth. I'm fixing to shut him up. And D'Andre hears him, and he's like, yeah, shut this, and knocks down a three. Game over. You know, everybody having a good time, just talking a little shit. So we get in the game and they start going at it. Pushing and shoving. Bitching and moaning. A lot of ticky-tack calls. So I say, come on, fellas, let's play the game, I came here to play basketball. We usually run to twenty-one, twos and threes, winner stays. And after a while it's like nineteen up. Then D'Andre takes it to the hole, and puts up some weak shit, and I slap that shit away, and D'Andre's like, *and one*. Which pisses me off now. So I say, you gotta make the bucket. It can't be *and one* if you don't make the fucking shot, and Corey's like, man, he didn't foul you, bitch, and everybody saying, honor the call, honor the call, and D'Andre's like, ball up. He's one of these skinny hyped-up guys who got like twice as big in two months, and has to wear a T-shirt all the time to cover his back. So he takes the ball out and jacks up a three, which bangs off the rim, and Corey says, ball don't lie. Ball don't lie. And D'Andre goes over to the benches, like he's getting a drink. So I turn my back and run down court. And then I hear everybody saying, hey, hey, hey, watch out, and Corey's lying on the ground. Fuck me. And D'Andre's got a knife in his hand and is jumping up and down, and everybody says, get the fuck out of here, and he takes off.

—So what did you do?

—Man, I took off, too. But this is what I'm saying. Black man isn't being killed by Tyler Waites, not in this city, not in Detroit. Black man being killed by another black man.

—So why didn't you stay to help your friend?

—If the cops come, everybody guilty.

The other voice was Astrid's. She used subtitles for the man's speech but not her own, which annoyed me. And then the music came back and the screen went dark. The words *A Conversation about Race* started moving across it.

"I'm not interested in this kind of thing," I said. "It's banal. The only interesting thing is ordinary life. The rest is boring."

"The people I talk to, for them, this is ordinary life."

"I mean people living well, how to live well, that's the question."

"You don't want to see the rest?"

"How long does it go on for?"

"Thirty minutes."

"Okay, I'll watch it. Give me another drink."

There were six or seven other interviews, with a crack dealer, an auto worker, an elementary school teacher, a single mother, etc. Afterwards the camera zoomed in on Astrid's own face, with the white wall behind it. Her bottle-blond hair looked dark at the roots and carefully messed up.

"These stories are our stories," she said. "Everywhere is Detroit. We all risk transforming ourselves into human monsters, at any moment in our lives. And everybody is responsible, because we let it happen."

She turned off the TV and we sat looking at it. By this point it was close to midnight and the air coming in through the opened windows felt almost cold. I was shivering slightly.

"I may be too drunk to drive home," I said.

"Do you want to sleep on this couch? It's small," she said.

"I don't know."

"Do you want to see my room?"

I felt a little frightened of her. I couldn't tell if anything she said was true. At the same time, there was something glowing or burning in my stomach, like the blood in your hand when you shine a flashlight against it.

"You don't have to come if you don't want to," she said.

"Why are you talking like that? It's not a big deal. Fine, let's go see your room."

I almost hoped that we'd run into somebody downstairs, so I could sober up or change my mind, but we didn't. When we got there she said, "You can sleep in my bed, it's big enough. I don't mind." She undressed in front of me, she let me use her toothbrush, it was all very normal. But in the dark, when the lights were off, I couldn't help myself, I started touching her, and she responded quickly. It was strange, I felt very gentle towards her, when all night long we'd been scratchy and sarcastic. But afterwards I slept okay.

In the morning I had to pick up my brother from the airport. My car was still parked in the road outside the bar, and I worried something might have happened to it. But it was fine, and I drove to meet him in last night's clothes.

27

Detroit's got a nice airport. It's on the way out to Ann Arbor, and it has a kind of New South vibe—like money's been recently spent. These days you can't meet anybody at the gate, so I waited by the baggage claim for my brother to come out, and then he did, wearing Dockers and a pair of crappy deck shoes and no socks.

"What do you look like?" I said.

"You mean the shoes? This is one of the all-time great pairs of shoes."

Brad either wore a suit and tie or he dressed like a frat boy on Spring Break. It didn't matter he was thirty-eight years old and had three kids.

His ten-year law school reunion was in Chicago that weekend, and he planned on renting a car in Detroit and driving to it. Then dropping off the car and flying home from Chicago. I told him over the phone this is a crazy idea, it's like a five-hour drive, but he said, look, when you don't have the kids along, any kind of travel is a holiday, and he wanted to see me. I figured he wanted to check up on me, and this was his excuse.

In fact, he wanted to persuade me to move back to Baton Rouge.

"Listen," he said, when we got in the car. "I'm just going to say this now, to get it out of the way. And then we can talk about it or not. But I think you should go home to Mom. She's not doing so hot. Dad has moved out of the Wenzlers', he's got an apartment in the Quarter, and Mom says he's living with some public health student at Tulane. She's like twenty-five. Meanwhile Mom feels too ashamed to see their old friends. She says they mean well, but they're basically embarrassed by her, and the truth is, when Dad was around, everybody wanted to talk to him. She was just dead-weight. That's a direct quote."

"Why don't you move home if you feel so strongly?"

"Come on, Greg. I've got three kids in school. I've got a life in Houston. I've got responsibilities. As it is, I've been driving back a couple of times a month, which isn't fair on Andrea. She's got the kids all week and then she has to take them on the weekend, too. I don't want to make a big deal out of this but it's putting a strain."

"What are you trying to say, that I'm just playing around? I've got a life here, too. I've got a job, I've got a girlfriend. I'm actually a part of something, for once in my life."

"Okay, then. Show me," he said.

He arrived Wednesday morning and left on Friday afternoon. Thursday I had to teach, and Brad had some clients based in Detroit he wanted to see, but the rest of the time we hung out and talked. He slept on my sofa bed and turned out to be a good guest. The only thing he traveled with was a garment bag, in which he kept his suit for Saturday night. He borrowed my toothpaste, he wore the same clothes every day, he took up very little space. And he was curious about everything and asked smart questions. Mostly he liked what he saw.

"This is a great neighborhood," he said. "Solid middle-class turn-of-the-century American architecture. They knew how to build. What do they sell for now, do you know?"

"Nobody's selling. At least if you do the consortium takes most of the money. It's part of the deal."

"So when do people make money out of this?"

"It's not about money."

"Okay," he said.

On Thursday night Gloria came back with me after school, and the three of us went out to dinner. There was a Polish place in Hamtramck I wanted to try, but since it didn't take reservations, we had to wait half an hour at the bar. I got a little drunk, I let them talk.

"Can I ask you a question?" he said to her at one point. "What are you doing with this bum? You're clearly much too good for him."

"Is this like a big-brother thing?" she said. "I never had a brother. Is this what they do to each other?"

"Well, what does he say about me?"

"Oh, he never talks about you."

For two days I had felt like the tagalong kid, even while I showed him around. I liked hearing Gloria stick up for me, but I'm not sure the comparison did me any favors. Afterwards, when the bill came, I said, "Give it to the big shot here. This one's on him," and Brad took out his wallet.

"Come on, Marny," Gloria said. "This is our treat. He's the guest."

"No, he's good for it. He likes throwing his money around."

We had a quiet fight about it but Brad just paid. They gave us vodka shots on the house. I drank Gloria's, too. She decided I wasn't sober enough to drive home, so she took the keys and I ended up sitting in back while she talked to Brad. My thoughts felt a little soft-focus, but I liked listening to them talk. Gloria said to him, "How's your mom doing?" and Brad said, "That's partly what I wanted to discuss with Greg. Not great."

"I know what it's like," Gloria said, "when you feel responsible. I had it my whole life. I don't know if Marny told you, but my father died when I was seven, so it's always been just me and Mom."

"He did tell me. He said you live in the same apartment building. He said it mostly works out."

"That's pretty much accurate," she said.

It's a twenty-minute drive to Johanna Street and I fell asleep. You go about five miles on I-94, and in the dark and the highway noise I just closed my eyes. Gloria dropped us off, then switched to her own car and drove home. She had to teach in the morning and didn't want to get in the way of our catching up. But it seemed to me something else was going on, too—that she didn't want to sleep in the house while my brother was there, for some reason.

"Come on," I said, "it's his last night."

"That's why."

"What are you teaching tomorrow anyway. The school year's basically over."

"There's a lot of stuff I still got to take care of. Just hang out with your brother. I'll come over tomorrow night."

This put me in a bad mood. I was annoyed with her and didn't want to talk to Brad about it. I didn't want to explain or justify my annoyance but I couldn't think of anything else to talk about. So we went to bed early. That short nap in the car made it hard for me to fall asleep. I just lay in the dark shifting around.

Brad couldn't sleep either. I heard him turn on the television, and then I heard him on the telephone, talking to Andrea—Houston's an hour earlier. Eventually he got off the phone and turned off the TV.

It seemed strange to me that my brother was lying about fifteen steps away. Until I was eleven years old we shared a bedroom and

I used to fall asleep watching him read. Sometimes he woke me up in the night by going to the bathroom; afterwards, he made more noise, looking through his closet for new pajamas. Later I realized he was probably having wet dreams. Even then, when we were kids, we had these private lives, which we didn't talk about. Sometimes I got scared in the night and wanted to climb into bed with him, but he always kicked me out. Then my parents built the extension and I moved into it, and a few years later he left for college. But we were never as close after I moved out.

In the morning, I walked to Joe's to get a newspaper—there was one of those sidewalk dispensers outside his café, which carried the *Free Press*. I bought a few pastries, too. We sat around my kitchen table drinking coffee and reading. There was a front-page story about the Wayne County prosecutor. He hadn't decided yet whether to bring criminal charges against Tyler Waites.

"We're still taking evidence," he told a reporter. "In some cases, you don't have to rush into anything, and this is one of those cases. It's not even clear yet what the charge would be. We have every hope that Mr. Meacher will make a full recovery."

But the article was really a profile of this guy, Larry Oh. He was the first Asian American to serve as Wayne County prosecutor. And the piece focused on his ability to "present himself as a compromise candidate, whose appeal could cross the color line between the suburbs of Wayne County and the city of Detroit itself." The writer quoted a freelance political consultant who said: "This Meacher case is the last thing he needs, with the primary coming up. If he charges Waites, he loses his funding base. But if he doesn't, then the black vote disappears. He doesn't need much but he needs a little, and last time around he got fifteen percent."

I gave the front page to Brad and said, "This might interest you.

Maybe you can help me out. There's a guy I know stirring up a lot of publicity and I'm supposed to talk him out of it."

Brad took the paper and read for a few minutes. "It amazes me that people still consider this news."

"What are you talking about?"

"One of the Ford heirs just gave a lot of money to SETI. You know, the intelligent life in outer space people. Harvard scientists, and so on. Anyway, he's on the board at Concordia, and some Christian group wants him to step down."

"I don't understand."

"I mean, of course there's life in outer space. Do they think we're the only ones?"

"No, I meant the piece about Larry Oh."

He read that, too. "What are you supposed to do about it?"

"A friend of mine has been agitating against Waites. Robert James wants me to talk to him."

"Who is this guy?"

"Some artist, a friend of Gloria's."

"I wouldn't worry about it."

"Why not?"

"Nobody mentions him. I'm going to take a shower." And he threw me the paper.

But I looked through the rest of it and found a piece about Nolan in the Arts section. He had recently won a $50,000 grant from the Kresge Foundation to "pursue a civil law suit, on behalf of Dwayne Meacher and his family, against Tyler Waites." It was the first award of its kind, arts funding for a legal action. But a spokesman at the Kresge Foundation said they had no knowledge of the grant and did not support the views or the activities of Nolan Smith. The money had been channeled through Art in Action, a community group based in Detroit. The Kresge Foundation planned to review their support of this organization.

"Ignore it," Brad said, when he came out. His body looked like my dad's, pale fat muscular and blond. His cheeks had gone pink from the heat of the water, he looked like a big happy boy. "Nobody reads the Arts pages."

"Well, I promised to talk to him. Do you want to meet him or not? He lives just down the road, literally. He's one of those guys who grew up here."

"Sure," he said. "I got nothing else to do."

So we went to see Nolan. It was humid out, the air felt wet. The sky was not so much cloudy as vague, and the sunlight had a kind of depth to it. It looked like rain in the afternoon. Summer storms in Michigan can be pretty bad, and my brother had a five-hour drive to Chicago ahead of him.

The doorbell didn't work so I knocked on the door, which was a screen door and clattered in the frame. Mrs. Smith came out, moving slowly.

"Is Nolan around? This is my brother, Brad."

"You boys want to come over and play?" she said. "Come on in."

"Is Nolan around?"

"He'll be back this minute."

She led us into the kitchen and made some coffee. It was hot in there, too. One of the windows caught the sun directly. There were fruit flies on the bowl of grapes by the sink.

"If you like Nolan's coffee you won't like this," she said. "I make it so you can drink it."

When Nolan came in with the dog, he said, "Who is this?"

"My brother."

He smelled his mother's coffee in the pot. "I'm going to pour this out and start again."

"I'll be upstairs if you want me," Mrs. Smith said. "I'm taking a nap."

"Nobody wants you," Nolan told her. He started fussing around with coffee grinds, tamping them down in the filter and making a mess. The dog kept getting in his way; his paws made slippery tapping sounds on the linoleum floor.

"I met a friend of yours yesterday," Nolan said.

"Who?"

"German girl. At least she said she knew you. We had an open house at the studios, and she came by."

"I don't understand. How did she know you know me?"

"You know who I'm talking about?"

"Yes."

He started steaming the milk and for a minute we just listened to the machine. "How come your brother doesn't look like you?" Nolan said afterwards.

"What does he look like?"

"The Dutch Boy paint kid."

"I still don't understand how you figured out the connection."

"She asked me where I lived and I told her and she said her ex-boyfriend lived on the same street. She seemed like the kind of girl who gets excited by coincidences."

"She's a very bad artist."

"I believe that."

"She makes videos. She made this film about race relations in Detroit."

"I believe that, too."

Mrs. Smith had left the radio on, and you could hear the talk show voices arguing and laughing underneath the other noises. Nolan switched it off.

"There's this rap she uses as a voice-over," I said. "Maybe you can tell me where it's from. *"All of my brothers live by the trigger. But nobody cares so long as . . ."* I stopped. "I can't remember the rest."

"What, you don't want to say it? Pussy. What are you smiling at, Dutch Boy?"

"I'm just enjoying the pregame show."

"Whatever." He kicked Buster into the garden and said, "If you want some real coffee you can make it yourself," and carried his cup into the living room.

"I guess we follow him. What are you smiling at?"

"He got you whipped, boy," Brad said.

"Where'd you learn to talk like that? River Oaks?"

"You can sit here," Nolan told us, when we came in. "But this is what I'm going to do. I'm going to finish my coffee and then I'm going to do some work."

The living room was shaded by the balcony over the front porch, so that even on hot days it felt pleasant. The windows looked bright, though, against the daylight. They were open, too, and you could hear some of the trees outside.

"Robert James asked me to talk to you about something," I said. "About this Meacher business. If there's racial tension, the people who get hurt won't be the people you want to hurt. You should lay off Tyler Waites."

"Tyler Waites isn't the problem, Tyler Waites is the symbol. You people are the problem—Goddamn colonizers."

"I don't want to start an argument about the whole thing. But you have to admit, your life has got better since we moved in. Just ask your mother."

"Give me a break, Marny. Somebody's making money off of this, and it isn't the people of Detroit. Meacher's just a way to get us a piece of the pie."

"Nobody's making money, it's not about money."

"Then what the fuck is it about?"

"That's what I've been trying to ask him," Brad said.

"Not everybody wants to live the way you live," I told my brother.

"What's that supposed to mean?"

"Private schools and country clubs. A hundred-hour week. And then on the weekends, just to relax, a couple of rounds of golf, so you don't have to see the kids."

"Of course that's how people want to live." Then he said, "Okay, big shot. Tell me what the people want."

"Small-town life, free time. People have this idea that they hate big government. But what they don't like is national government. It's a category mistake. And if you keep things local, if you pool together, if you help each other out, you can live pretty well without chasing the buck."

"Somebody's always paying."

"Why? What you've got in Detroit is cheap real estate. And the rest doesn't cost that much. What else do you spend your money on? Private school? That's probably sixty thousand dollars a year. A live-in nanny? Another thirty grand. Andrea doesn't work; she can look after the kids. What do you bill people? Three hundred dollars an hour? How many hours is that?"

"Three weeks. You just bought me a three-week holiday I don't want."

"Brad, I don't understand this. You're a smart guy, you have general interests. When's the last time you read a book?"

"I don't want to read books. I want to relax, I want to play golf."

"So how much golf do you play?"

"Not enough. You know what I do on my weekends. I drive five hours to Baton Rouge and five hours back on Sunday night. And then on Monday morning I get up at six and go to work."

"And this makes you happy?"

"I don't expect to be happy. The happiness is for my kids. I expect to make money."

"This is what I'm trying to tell you. What people want is basically pretty simple. That's why kids are happy, they don't worry about everything else. Shelter, food and community. None of these has to cost much. You read *Walden* in college, you know what I'm talking about."

"That's not what people want," Brad said. "They want to make money, and they want to make more money than their neighbor does. That's how you know you're winning. And you're kidding yourself, Greg, if you think that Americans want to help each other out. That's not what I pay my taxes for. I pay my taxes so that other people are not my problem, and I pay as little tax as I can get away with. Have you met my neighbors? That's why we invented the automobile, to get away from them. That's why we move to the suburbs. That's why we spend half our lives in cars and the other half watching TV. If we wanted to see our neighbors we'd move to Europe."

"This guy makes you look good," Nolan said. "He's like a first-rate asshole. This guy makes you look second-rate or third-rate."

"And by the way, Thoreau didn't have any kids."

"That's not the point," I said.

"And he didn't give a damn about community."

"Do I have to stand here listening to this shit?" Nolan said. "Do you guys need like an audience or something?"

"Well, I promised Robert I'd talk to you."

"You talked. Now fuck off. I don't mean that in an impolite or angry way."

It was hotter than before when we got outside, and I noticed that the shadows of things, trees and cars, kept coming in and out of focus. There was a bit of wind, too.

"What happened there?" I said to my brother.

"You know he's flaming, right?"

"What are you talking about?"

"He's gay."

"He's got a six-year-old son."

"Of course he does. He's an African American male who played football in college. You don't expect him to come out in the locker room?"

"Are you saying he's out now?"

"What the hell do I know?"

"Then what are you talking about?"

"I'm just giving you a heads-up."

I was too pissed off to say much at lunch. We made mustard-and-salami sandwiches and ate them with slightly stale potato chips in front of the TV. The second round of the US Open was on. Brad seemed in a good mood—he was looking forward to his reunion. There was a drinks party at the Art Institute on Saturday night and dinner afterwards at the Peninsula.

"I haven't taken time off like this in five years," he said. "I mean, when I wasn't on some work thing or looking after the kids. It's good to see you."

"Obama was there, wasn't he, when you were at law school?"

"We overlapped a couple of years."

"Did you take any of his classes?"

"Con law. I liked him. He was a young guy, he knew when we were bored."

Afterwards I drove him to the Hertz outlet on East Jefferson. I parked and waited with him at the counter, then carried his garment bag to the rental car. In certain public spaces, airports, for example, you can sometimes see people you love the way a stranger would. Brad looked like the kind of guy waitresses and flight attendants start a conversation with. Like somebody who makes good money but also knows how to have a good time. His deck shoes flopped a little on his feet; they looked comfortable. But his Dockers were clean and new and sat tight on his ass. He wore an Astros T-shirt and Ray-Ban sunglasses.

I gave him a hug and he said to me, "You got a nice setup here. I'm going to leave you alone. It wouldn't kill you to call your mother once in a while. Dad, too."

"One of these summer storms is coming in," I said. "If you get tired just pull over. There's no point in doing it all at once."

When he left I felt sick, just sick. The mess I was making of my life. I couldn't even pay for his dinner. But what really threw me was this business about SETI. My brother is a smart, educated guy. He went to Oxford on a Rhodes and made the law review at Chicago. But he also has practical instincts; he likes to be reasonable. And it seemed to him obvious that there were other worlds and forms of life. He paid his mortgage, he went to the country club, maybe he even slept with his secretary, I don't know. But he could take it in stride, the idea that there might be something else out there. It didn't bother him at all.

28

The weather broke around six o'clock, and by the time Gloria came by after work, it was raining so hard she had to run from the driveway to the porch, and still came in the house soaking wet and laughing. Her hair when it got wet showed all the beads of water. I gave her a towel and we watched the rain flatten itself across the bay window.

"It's over," she said. "It's over. Another fucking year." She almost never swore.

"What do you want to do, you want to go out to eat? There's not much in the house but I can make pasta."

"Let's stay in and watch TV and go to bed."

We made out on the couch after supper. With my eyes closed I could sense her by taste and touch, and my skin had a hot-cold feeling; a cold drop of sweat ran along my ribs. The rain kept coming down. At one point Gloria went to the bathroom and I got up to turn off the lights. The room went dark and the outside world reappeared. Even at nine o'clock it was still bright out. The windows streamed and shimmered and let in a lot of green. I turned off the TV, too.

"I hope my brother's all right," I said, when she came back. "He should be checked in to the hotel by now."

"I got you something." Gloria held up a condom packet. "I want to apologize. I just get so stressed out, I don't even know what's stressing me out. But it's always the kids, it's the school. And I never realize what's going on until the year's over."

We went upstairs to bed, feeling kind of formal. She really seemed like an innocent kid, it was like a wedding night. We fooled around for a while and eventually Gloria said, "I can't tell if you're into this or not."

"I'm into it. I'm just surprised."

"I meant it to be like good surprise."

"I feel like there's something I need to tell you."

"So tell me." But already the mood had changed. I tried to kiss her again but she pushed me away.

"I love you," I said, for the first time.

"No, you don't. You just like me a lot."

I had too much time to think about what to say. "What are you talking about?" I said eventually.

"Everybody likes me."

"This is ridiculous. You've been sexually rejecting me for six months. And then you come on like this and I'm supposed to jump through hoops."

"I just feel hurt. I thought this is what you wanted."

"It is what I want." After a minute, I said, "Can we try again?"

But the wedding-night feeling had gone. I began to stroke her hair and then her face and her shoulder and her side; at least she let me. "I don't know what you see in me," I said. "You're a beautiful woman."

"I know what I am and it's not beautiful."

"Then you don't know."

But she turned on her elbow to look at me. "I'm like a type," she said. "There's a type of man who thinks I'm his type. Guys who like girls who look like boys. This is a bad-news kind of guy—I had a lot of bad experiences. So I take it slow. But Marny, baby, I liked you first time I met you. You were honest with me, you didn't spin me a line. You want to talk everything out. I get that. But you need to learn to shut up, too."

We kissed again and started up again. I kept thinking, you can tell her about Astrid later, when it won't matter so much. For a while it was like a refrain in my thoughts, you can tell her later, but then I forgot about Astrid and forgot about Gloria, too, to be honest. Afterwards, she said, "I didn't think it would make a difference, but it does."

The rain had stopped; we could hear the roof dripping. It was only about ten o'clock at night. We hadn't shut the curtains and the cloudy sky still held a little daylight.

"Are you tired? I'm not that tired. Do you want to read maybe?"

But she shook her head. "Let's just lay here."

"What difference does it make?" I said.

"I don't know. Don't make me say it."

"Is it because I'm white? Is that why you weren't sure?"

"Don't make me angry, I don't want to be angry again. Why do you say things like that?"

"Did you sleep with Nolan?"

"Marny, you don't even know how ridiculous you're being."

"I don't know, I think about you too much. I was really obsessed with you."

"Shush shush shush shush shush," she said.

BUT ON MONDAY MORNING SHE had to drive to Harsens Island. The Detroit Institute of Arts puts on a summer camp there for city kids. There used to be an old school on the island, which closed down. Then somebody turned it into a resort and restaurant, and when that failed, the DIA stepped in and converted the buildings into a campsite and retreat for artists in traditional media—painting and sculpture, that kind of thing. There's a lot of wildlife on Lake St. Clair, turtles and snakes and birds, and you can sail from Harsens to a dozen other islands.

It's about an hour's drive from Detroit. You have to take the car ferry. I said to her, "You just got done teaching for the year, what are you doing to yourself."

"I didn't know about you when I signed up. This place is amazing. Most of these kids have never been in a boat. They think nature is trees and grass. They don't know about all the colors."

"But Monday morning."

"You have to get them right after the school year ends, otherwise they don't show up. They lose momentum, they start stacking shelves. The difference between rich kids and poor kids is what they learn on summer vacation. I get on my students all year long to sign up for this thing. I like saying to them, see you next week. It's fun, I want to go."

On Sunday night, after supper, she said, "I have to pack."

"Let me at least stay over with you," I said.

"I want to clear my head and work out what I need. Baby, it's only a week. Not even that, five days."

"I'm not thinking straight right now. I don't know what's going on."

"Nothing's going on," she said. "I'll see you next weekend."

So she kissed me and drove off. That night I called Astrid, but she didn't answer her phone. I wanted to explain to her what the deal was, that I couldn't see her again.

I called my brother, just to catch up.

"Did you see that bit on *NewsHour* about Detroit?" he asked.

"About the Meacher case? When did it run?"

"Friday. I thought that's what you were calling about. Apparently a few people have started to sell up, and one of them is challenging the terms of his contract. He says the house is worth a lot more than he bought it for. He put in the work, he wants to see the profit. If he wins his case the whole landscape's going to change."

"How can he win? He made a deal, we all did."

"It depends how well the contract was drawn up."

"My guess is Robert has good lawyers."

"But that wasn't really the point of the story. They wanted to find out why people are trying to move."

"I don't know anyone who's leaving."

"This Meacher business could drive down property prices, if the situation isn't resolved in the right way. It's a good time to sell."

"But you can't sell, that's the deal. I don't know what the right way is supposed to mean."

"That's one of the questions."

I hung up in a worse mood than before. This was just my big brother throwing his weight around, showing me that he knows what's what. But the truth is, some of my neighbors *were* worried. Bert Wendelman's school had just been broken into. Ordinarily, there wasn't much to steal, but Bert had persuaded Texas Instruments to donate twenty new tablets as part of a low-budget promotional campaign. Things to do with New Jamestown often made it into the news. Anyway, the tablets got stolen. Their street value was about $3,000, which isn't much, but people are sensitive to break-ins at schools.

On Monday, I ran into Don Adler outside the Spartan grocery store on McIntyre. I asked him if he had seen the report on *News-Hour*.

"I stopped watching when MacNeil retired. It's not the Wendelman burglary that worries me," he said. "This is a big city, that kind of thing will happen. It's the not-for-profit crime. The sense-less destruction, this is what worries me."

"What are we talking about here."

"They're burning cars."

"Who is?"

"Who do you think? They just break windows and spray the insides with gasoline and light up."

"I haven't seen it," I said. But this wasn't quite true. In fact, I had noticed more broken glass on the street, and other remains, burned strips of rubber and melted CDs.

"That's because they clean this stuff up. This isn't what they want people to see."

"Who's they?"

"Oh, come on. Detroit has always had a certain amount of pointless crime. That's what they should have called one of the ball clubs. Not Pistons or zoo animals. The Detroit Arsonists. But it's getting worse and it's getting closer to home. At least to my home."

I spent too much time on my couch reading the papers, and not just the Detroit papers, but whatever I could find online. Larry Oh called a press conference for Thursday afternoon, and then on Wednesday night the story went around on Twitter that Meacher had died. The *Detroit Free Press* reported this fact on their web-site—I sometimes checked the home page while cooking supper.

Around ten o'clock, my doorbell rang. I was in the middle of unloading the dishwasher and went downstairs drying my hands on my shirt. Don Adler stood on the porch.

"Don't say I didn't tell you so," he said.

"What's going on? Do you want to come in?"

"I think you should come out."

It was a warm, humid night; the summer storm hadn't quite

cleared the air. I had a T-shirt on, and running shorts, which I sometimes wore around the house at night for comfort.

"I was just about to go to bed."

"Go put your shoes on. There's a fight—your friend Kurt Stangel is mixed up in it. Him and the black guy."

"What am I supposed to do? Call the police."

"If the police did their job, we wouldn't have to."

"What does that mean?"

But I followed him out in bare feet. The sidewalk was still partly wet, and I walked a little gingerly. There was a car parked sideways in the middle of the road, outside Nolan's house. I could hear people shouting. Mrs. Smith stood on her porch steps, in her bathrobe.

"What's going on?" I said to her.

She was in tears. "Marny, Marny," she said, grabbing my shoulder, "maybe you can talk some sense into somebody."

Six or seven people stood around the car, whose front window was broken. One of them said, "Come on, guys," and Mrs. Smith called out, "Nolan, Nolan!" I took hold of her hand and then let go of it. There was a strip of dirty lawn between the sidewalk and the road, and I walked over the grass but stopped at the curb. You could see glass on the asphalt under the street lamp light.

"Nolan!" I said and Eddie Blyleven walked over to me. He's one of these likable good-looking guys, big and responsible, who doesn't take anything too seriously.

"They've kind of punched themselves out already. It's basically over."

"What happened?"

What happened was this. When the story about Meacher started going around, guys from the Neighborhood Watch decided to set up a few roadblocks in case something kicked off—including one at the end of Johanna Street. People in other neighborhoods were doing the same thing. Eddie wasn't there but apparently this big black dude came out of his house with a baseball bat and told Kurt to fuck off. Kurt started explaining himself and the guy took out his windshield with the bat. So Kurt tried to take his bat away and they got in a fight. Kurt's a pretty big dude himself, Eddie said.

"They called me over but I said, leave 'em alone. The last thing we want is a bunch of white guys standing around beating the crap out of somebody. But I took the bat away, you can do some damage with a bat. We're too old for this bullshit. You have to be in pretty good shape to throw punches for more than two minutes, and these guys aren't in great shape. They're just wrestling now. What worries me is just the broken glass."

"Can't you step in?"

"It's like with kids," he said. "If you step in it just takes longer."

"Marny," Mrs. Smith said, and I went back to her. "What's he saying? Can't you get him away from those men? I want to get him inside."

"I don't have any shoes on. Did you call the police?"

"What am I call the police for? To arrest my son? I got more sense than that."

"I'm sorry."

"I don't know what to do. He gets so angry about everything. I say, what do you want me to do? That's how it is. He says I go along with everything, I'd go along with my own funeral. And that's right, I will, when the time comes, but now is not the time. Even when he was a boy he got angry. He wasn't one of these kids you can make it better."

Eventually Nolan just stood up and walked towards us. We were still on the porch, he didn't even look at me. His shirt was bloody and his nose had bloody snot coming out of it. "Baby, baby," Mrs. Smith said, but he pushed her off a little and left handprints on her robe. Kurt looked in bad shape, too, he had to pull himself up by the front seat. The door was open and he started brushing glass off the upholstery. People helped him out. Then Nolan turned back, as far as the sidewalk.

"That's my fucking bat," he said. "Give me my fucking baseball bat."

"I'll drop it by tomorrow," Eddie told him, "and we can talk."

"The fuck you will." But his mother pulled at him and he went back to the house.

"Do you want me to come in with you, Mrs. Smith? Is there anything I can do?"

But she ignored me. "Have you been taking your Capoten?" she said to Nolan. "Do you want me to get you a pill?"

"It's not like aspirin." He opened the screen door.

"Well, I'll get you an aspirin then."

Then the police showed up. You could hear the sirens coming along East Vernor, but Don and I didn't stick around. We walked back together.

"It's going to get worse if Meacher is really dead," Don said.

"Do you think he's dead?"

"Let me put it this way. My wife has relatives in South Bend. Tomorrow morning, that's where we're going. This is her mother's side of the family, it isn't something I do lightheartedly. But we'll stay a couple of days. We'll see what happens with this press conference and then make up our minds."

29

In the morning, I checked the *Free Press* website for news about Meacher, but there wasn't much. Then I started googling around. I found something on the *Voice of Detroit*, an "independent" news site set up by ex–*Free Press* journalists, former city administrators, union organizers, etc. A lot of their content came from citizen reportage. They ran a story about Larry Oh and Robert James. Apparently these two had had lunch together over the weekend, at Zingerman's Deli in Ann Arbor. Some law student took a picture of them on his phone and wrote it up for the *VoD*. (One of the comments asked, "So what did they order?" It turns out that Robert had a "Dinty Moore.")

I also found an op-ed piece in *The New York Times* about the history of the citizen's arrest. The byline said Anthony Carnesecca. This is how it finished:

Let's imagine that Tyler Waites intended to impede Dwayne Meacher, even at the cost of running into him. Could this constitute a justifiable *arrest* under Michigan law? Arrest is defined as the "stopping or restraint of a person," and the law establishes three conditions for the just use of this power: that a felony has actually occurred; that the fleeing suspect against whom force is used must be the person who committed the felony; and that the use of force must be necessary to ensure his apprehension. In Waites's case, all of these conditions have been met. In a city like Detroit, whose tax base has been decimated by population flight, *taking the law into your own hands* is not just a phrase from some Lee Van Cleef movie, but a necessary feature of a citizen's obligations, to himself and his neighbors. You may not like it, but you don't live in Detroit.

About an hour later, Tony himself stopped by. He had his Number One son with him, as my father used to call it. Michael stood a little behind his dad and tried to reach a hand into his pocket. If I didn't see him every couple of weeks he turned shy with me. Relations with kids take work, I had to keep starting over.

"Is it too early for a treat?" I said to Tony. "I don't know what I've got in the house. Maybe ice cream in the freezer."

It was already about eighty-five degrees outside, and the shade of the porch didn't make any difference. The sun couldn't beat the clouds but the heat got through anyway, a kind of damp heat. I was tempted to switch on the AC just to clear the air.

"Let me take you to lunch," Tony said. "I want to celebrate."

"I saw your piece in the *Times*."

"That's what I mean, I'm in a good mood."

But it was only eleven a.m. and we swung by Robert's house on the way. "I'm touching all the bases," Tony said. We took his car, I didn't have anything else to do. I said to myself, you're turning into the go-along guy. The gates stood open when we got there. Some guys were working on them, and we had to park in the road. Tony rang the doorbell several times, and eventually Robert's wife, Peggy, answered it.

"Sorry," she said. "We were just coming in from the garden. It's too sweaty out there. Robert bought Ethan this inflatable pool. He buys it, but we have to blow it up."

We followed her into the kitchen, where her son was playing.

"How long are you in town for?" I said.

"Just this week. We're having work done on the apartment, so I thought, let's get out of here."

She had brought the nanny with her, one of those women who puts makeup on her face to look unhappy. Maybe because she's not pretty enough. Her coloring was dark; you could see sweat on the hairs around her lips. But she seemed perfectly nice. Peggy said she was studying at the Tisch School but needed a break—she was two years into a PhD in cinema studies.

"What's your subject?" I asked her.

"Contemporary Scottish film, Andrea Arnold, Lynne Ramsay, those kinds of people. But I'm not in any hurry. I mean, they keep making movies. It's hard to get them in focus, they won't sit still."

Peggy said, "It's intense having a nanny. I mean you're around these people all day, just you and the kid. I couldn't do it with somebody who didn't have a brain."

"We have fun," the woman said. Her name was Fran. She picked up the boy and carried him to the sink to get water.

Michael said, "I'm thirsty."

"Well, ask the lady," Tony told him. "You've got a tongue."

The kid walked over and Tony turned to Peggy. "Is Robert around?"

"In his office. He's talking to Zwecker."

"Do you mind looking after this guy for a minute?"

"Sure."

"What are you doing to the apartment?" I said.

"It's very boring. Painting the walls."

"It's not boring, it's your life, it's where you live. All these stupid decisions."

"Tell me about it."

"Colors are tricky if you don't stick with white."

"We've got these big windows in every room, it's not a loft, but loft-style windows. But they're north-facing. It makes me depressed on sunny days, so I want to splash some color around the place."

We went on like this and eventually I said, "Do you have any aspirin? I've got like a weather headache."

"Sure," she said and went out. I watched her legs. She had these teenage legs, skinny and tanned and loose at the knees. Whenever I saw her she had shorts on, but like fashion shorts. Somehow it hurt me to look at her. My high school was full of girls with legs like that, but I never did anything about it. Then she came back with a pill and a glass of water.

"I know, it's terrible until it rains," she said.

"It's not always much better after it does. You guys are lucky, this is real air-conditioning. All I got is a window unit."

"We have to with Ethan, otherwise he can't sleep."

So we stared at each other a bit, two likable people, being likable, without much to say. There was no point of contact between us. This always amazes me about human beings—we become such specialists. Even the essentials get filtered through our particular interests. But I didn't want to talk about kids or paint jobs, and Robert seemed off-limits. I said, "Tony promised to take me out to lunch. I'm going to make him pay for once."

"Uh-huh."

"Maybe I'll go find out what they're up to."

At the bottom of the stairs I ran into this Zwecker guy. I hadn't seen him since the fund-raiser. It was hard to say what he dressed like these days, somewhere between a wise man in *Star Trek* and a medical orderly. He wore loose trousers and a tight mandarin-collared shirt made of synthetic material. He was a big guy; it showed his weight.

"So what are you and Robert cooking up?" I said.

"Virtual policing. We're working on an app right now. The idea is that people can use technology to police each other. It's already happening with journalism, but we want to take it a step further. People these days carry phones that do everything you need to do, from a policing point of view. They track your position, they take photographs and videos, they record sound. The guy who filmed Rodney King getting beat up is everywhere right now, he's you and me."

"I have one of these cheap convenience-store phones."

"Show it to me. It probably does more than you think."

"I'm not that interested. It sounds a little spooky."

"Look," he said. "You can make it out to be a police-state issue if you want to. But this isn't the state I'm talking about, it's the people. What we're really harking back to is the idea of the small town, where everybody looks out for everybody else but keeps an eye on them, too. What do you think the Pilgrims did to keep law and order, they didn't have a police force."

"Of course they did."

"That's not my understanding. They had a witness system. You needed two witnesses to get a conviction."

"I don't think any of us wants to live in Plymouth Colony."

"That's not my field. What it really comes down to is money. You can talk about rights all you want, but the fact is, everything costs something, even rights, we have a limited budget, and have to figure out what to spend it on. Right now the policing in this city can't get the job done, the tax base just isn't there to pay for it. So we've come up with a cheap way to fill the gaps."

"You could call it the Stasi app."

"All right."

"I'm not trying to give you a hard time. A good friend of mine pretty much lives by the E-change."

"You mean he uses it for sex."

"More or less."

"The trouble is people don't use this technology to make them happier. They use it for pleasure. Whenever you get an advance like this, the first thing it appeals to is the lowest common denominator. We have to evolve with the technology and that takes time."

"What do you mean?"

"For example, dating services. We have at our disposal this incredible tool for arranging marriages, but people are still using it in this unbelievably basic way. Even the people who aren't just after sex, who want committed relationships, who invest a lot of serious time in finding a partner, treat the search capacity of the Internet the way Jane Austen would. They look at education, they look at looks, they look at hobbies and interests. But we're starting to find out so much more about people. For example, we make incredibly short-term decisions about attraction. We act like attraction is something that can only be measured in the moment, as if the window of attraction that matters is a couple of years. The number two reason for the breakdown of marriage is sexual infidelity, and the truth is, this can be predicted, this can be guarded against. We're starting to get DNA information about the way people age, about their sex drives, that should form the basis of any serious decision about compatibility. I know from my own experience that I'm attracted to pale-skinned, black-haired women, Irish types. I also know that pale skin tends to suffer sun damage over time, that pale-skinned women who don't take enormous care of their appearance turn either reddish or look bleached-out, and that neither of these qualities is attractive to me, that pale skin and blue eyes is a recipe for skin cancer, etc. All of this is a matter of medical record, you can look at the photographs if you want to. So I adjust my attitudes towards attraction. I know about myself that I have a moderate sex drive, probably in the bottom half of the range, somewhere in the second quartile. And we're learning to connect sex drive to genetics and make predictions over time about, let's say, the expected sex drive of a twenty-two-year-old woman when she reaches her fifties. But this is only one aspect of what I'm talking about."

Tony came down and I said, "Are you ready for lunch?"

"You coming?" he said to Zwecker.

"Is Robert coming?"

"No."

"Then I think I'll pass. I've talked this guy's ear off already."

Outside the house I said to Tony, "Haven't you forgotten something?"

"Oh, Jesus. Maybe we can leave him here."

So we rang the bell again, and this time Robert answered. His shirtsleeves were rolled up to his elbows; he had bare feet.

"I forgot my son," Tony said. "Marny and I are going out to lunch. Do you mind if I leave him here for a couple of hours?"

"This is not my department," Robert said. "Talk to Peggy."

Tony went into the kitchen and Robert said to me, "Come inside. The air condition's getting out." So we waited in the entrance hall, with the piano and the fireplace and the twenty-foot ceilings. There was a vent by my feet, and I could feel the cold air blowing up the legs of my jeans.

"We should go for a run sometime," I said.

"I'd like to. My back isn't great. When it feels better."

"What's wrong with it?"

"Nothing you can really fix. At some stage you realize, you don't have to fix it, you don't have to make it right, you just hope it lasts—it sees you through."

"Well, let me know. What do you think Larry Oh's going to say?"

"We'll have to wait until he says it."

"Didn't he tell you anything at lunch?"

Robert looked genuinely surprised. "What are you talking about?"

"I thought you guys had lunch together in Ann Arbor over the weekend."

"Who told you that?"

"I read it online somewhere. You're like a famous man."

"Not that famous," he said. I tried to wait him out, but he changed the subject. "I hear your brother was in town. I'm sorry I missed him."

"He didn't stay long."

"But you had a good time?"

"He's a brother. It's like an old marriage. A lot of familiarity, a lot of contempt, no sex."

"Marny," he said.

"I don't know. I feel kind of weird, I feel a little drifty."

"What's going on?"

"Not much. Gloria took off for a week. She's got some camp thing."

"So you're batching it. This is why you're hanging out with Tony."

"I guess. I don't know how you do it, going back and forth. You've got to be two people, one with them and somebody else on your own."

"You get used to it. They blend after a while."

"That's not what I mean," I said. But then Tony came back, followed by Fran and Peggy and Ethan and Michael.

"Just give him a ball to kick around," Tony said. "He'll be happy."

Peggy picked Michael up. He was an armful, but she swung him around on her hip, the way mothers do, and stuck out a leg. "You want to wave bye-bye to Daddy? Wave bye-bye."

Fran asked Tony what his son liked for lunch, but then Ethan started complaining. He didn't like seeing Mommy with another boy. So Fran scooped *him* up, but that didn't help much; he squirmed and pushed against her face. Peggy kept holding Michael, who looked quietly at his father. "He'll eat what you give him," Tony said. "Come on, Marny, let's get out of here. Before the shock wears off."

"You go ahead." There was something in the air making me sneeze, so I went to the bathroom and tore off a few sheets of toilet paper. Tony was waiting for me in the car.

"Wave bye-bye," he said, when I got in. "What the fuck is that about? He's four years old."

"What's Cris doing?" The leather seat felt hot on my back, where the shirt rides up.

"She's running one of her baby yoga classes. It's okay to take Jimmy, that's kind of the point, but Michael gets bored. What do you want to eat? I want to eat somewhere you can have a drink."

We ended up at the Elwood Bar & Grill, by the ballpark. The Tigers were on the road, it was midweek, so the place was pretty empty. A Wurlitzer Music sign, lit up in neon, stood over the bar. There were a bunch of TVs on the wall, showing different games, Cubs-Mets at Wrigley, Rangers-Brewers at Miller Park, but the angle was bad, I couldn't get a good look.

"My dad used to take me here," he said, "before it moved. It's a different crowd now. I don't like it much but I still come."

Tony ordered two Bell's Oberons, which were on tap, and a Cobb salad. I had the tuna melt. When the beer arrived, I said to him, "So what did you want to talk to Robert about? Citizen's arrests?"

"Partly. I feel like I'm climbing out of a black hole, I'm writing again. People are taking me seriously."

"Is that what you're working on? Virtual policing?"

"Not really. You know, I published my memoir at the wrong time, about five years too soon. The *Times* piece had a link to it, and I checked my Amazon ranking this morning. It's still somewhere in the hundreds of thousands, but yesterday it was in the millions. You can reach people these days, if you want to, if you make the effort. It's a simple numbers game. How many email addresses do you have? About a thousand? So when a book comes out you write to everybody, asking them to buy it and spread the word. Even if the take-up's only five percent, that's still fifty people. And then they send it to another thousand, and so on."

"I don't know anything like a thousand people."

"To email? Come on. Even if my numbers are way off, it still adds up. You just need a critical mass."

"So what are you working on?"

"Another memoir, about being a father this time. There's this thing that happens when you become a dad. They should cut off your dick but they don't. Because that's basically what happens to the woman. All the sex organs get turned into something else. You know, their vagina turns into the birth canal. Their breasts turn into milk bottles. Cris just lies there in bed leaking and then Jimmy wakes up and comes in with us and sucks at her. And it's natural and beautiful. But all this time I'm lying there trying to sleep. And you know what happens to a guy. Your dick goes up and down all night long. You get these erections. And kids don't have a clue, they jump all over you. So you're stuck with this thing that is totally inappropriate but you can't do anything about. And you feel sick about it. Even in the morning, you're so sleep-deprived, you get these erections coming and going whenever you sit down—that's how tired you are. What happens in the night keeps happening in the day. It's like being a teenager. And you feel really weird about it. Dads don't talk about this kind of thing. Mothers spill their guts to perfect strangers, people they hardly know. But we don't talk to anybody. And the fact is, while all this is going on, you're probably not having much sex. Anything that walks by on two legs gets your attention. And you feel sick about that, too, because you just saw what she went through for you, and it's no picnic. And the whole point of babies, the point of kids, is that they're sexually innocent. That's what you love about them. I mean, Jimmy goes right for his pee-pee when you take off his diaper, but it doesn't mean anything, it doesn't hurt anybody. Kids reduce everything to the same kind of pleasure. But for grown men all that's left is one kind of dirty pleasure, and everything else is responsibility. So right from the beginning fathers have these feelings of guilt, which nobody has time to address. And six months later, or five years later, or twenty years later, the marriage starts paying the price."

"How's Cris?" I said.

"She's fine, we're doing fine. And Jimmy's great, he's starting to sit up, he's starting to eat solid food. That's just my first chapter, that's the premise. I want to talk about the new economy, too. Dads stuck at home with the kids, because they got laid off. Moms working."

At two o'clock I asked the bartender to switch one of the TV stations over to the local news. Eventually he found what I was looking for—Larry Oh's press conference.

He sat behind a table in some windowless room, with microphones bunched up against his face. You could see the effect of his white genes. His mother was a Catholic-school girl, when there were still Catholic girls' schools in Detroit. I remembered this much from the newspaper article. Oh had one of those ageless Asian faces, but a little tired-looking, a little crumpled around the eyes and mouth. I had to stand up and walk over to the TV set to hear him.

Dwayne Meacher came out of his coma yesterday morning, around three a.m. He's weak, but he's talking, Oh said. The EEG shows no sign of brain damage. In the light of which, they had decided not to press charges against Tyler Waites.

"What about charges against Meacher?" a reporter asked.

"We have no plans of pressing charges against Mr. Meacher."

"Okay," I told the bartender. "You can switch it back."

"Cris is basically fine," Tony said, when I sat down again. "She identifies totally with the kids, she's a great mother, I love to watch her with the boys. We used to fight about Michael. How long are you going to nurse him for? If he can spell breast, he's too old. But Jimmy's made a lot of that easier."

"I'm glad you said that. I didn't always know where to look."

"I could have told you where to look."

Tony paid for lunch. Both of us needed to take a leak. On the way out I asked him if he was okay to drive.

"Do you want to drive?"

"I had as much as you."

"I'm fine," he said.

There's nobody on the streets in Detroit anyway. About fifteen minutes later, we pulled up outside the gates of Robert's house; the workmen had gone. By this point it was maybe three o'clock in the afternoon. The sun had burned the clouds away, but the sky looked hazy, not quite blue. Tony had misjudged the angle, so I got out to tap in the entry code. With the bushes blooming and the grass recently cut, the air smelled almost tropical.

They must have changed the code. We couldn't get in and Tony backed up to park in the road.

I kept ringing and ringing the bell by the intercom. "Maybe it's broken," Tony said, but eventually Robert himself buzzed us in. Then he opened the door for us and stood in the doorway.

"I don't know where anyone is," he said. "Probably the garden."

So we went through the air-conditioned house, and into the kitchen, and out into the garden again. I was sweating already, just from the contrasts. Peggy lay on a blanket in the grass, trying to read on one elbow, under a hat.

"Where are the kids?" Tony said.

"Fran's just getting Ethan to sleep. He refuses to nap unless you put him in the stroller."

"Did Michael go with them?" he asked, and Peggy sat up.

"I think so."

"Which way do they usually go?"

Peggy had taken off her shirt. She was wearing a swimsuit top, but she put her shirt on again and stood up. "I'll go with you," she said, buttoning it.

"You sure he's not in the house?"

"I don't know."

But he wasn't in the house, and it took us half an hour in the car to track down Fran. Her phone was dead, and she had stopped on Charlevoix at an ice cream parlor that had just opened up. We saw her pushing the stroller out again; Ethan was still asleep. Peggy and I got out. Tony was driving. Peggy said, "Where's Michael?"

"I thought he was with you."

"Why would he be with me?"

Fran thought for a minute and said, "The last time I saw him he was watching TV in the kitchen. You were talking on the phone."

"You're right, that was me," she said.

"What do you want me to do?"

"Just take him home."

We got in the car and Peggy told Tony, "It was probably my fault. She doesn't know where he is. The last time anybody saw him was in the kitchen."

"He can't have gone far," I said.

So we drove back to the house, and Peggy ran in and started calling for Robert. Tony said to me, "I don't feel well, I shouldn't have drunk. I need to clear my head. I need some water." Peggy got the number of the repair guys, but it was a company number, and she had to wait on the phone to get through to a human being. So we looked around the house again; it was a big house. I went into the garden and ran around it once, from back to front, then walked back the other way, already out of breath. My eyes itched, I couldn't stop rubbing them, but I didn't find anything except his soccer ball, under a bush.

30

When I came back in everybody was in the kitchen, Robert and Tony and Fran and Peggy. Mrs. Rodriguez, the cook, was there, too, preparing supper. It was cool in the kitchen, the air tasted nice and artificial, I could breathe again. Fran said into the telephone, "Give me a fucking break. I just want a phone number. We're looking for a kid." Apparently the human being was reluctant to give out personal information, and Robert took the phone away and walked out of the room with it. I heard him say, "Nobody's angry with you, she's upset."

I said to Mrs. Rodriguez, "When did you get here?"

"About a half hour ago. I didn't see the boy. Maybe I left the gate open, I don't know. Sometimes I park in the driveway to bring something in, but I don't leave the car there, I park in the road. Today I had a little shopping, so that's what I did."

"He was missing already, a half hour ago," Tony told her. "We went out looking for him. It wasn't you."

Robert came in. "She's going to call back. She doesn't know their private numbers. The next thing we do is call the police. Peggy, give me your cell. I don't want to use the house line."

"I can't sit here," Tony said. "I can't just sit here."

"Do you want me to just drive around with you?"

"Okay." He gave me the keys. "You drive. I'll look."

We went outside to the car. It was like walking into a bathroom where the shower's been left on. My hay fever came back, my throat ached, my nose started running. The only thing I had to blow it with was a balled-up sheet of toilet paper. For the rest of the afternoon I had this uncomfortable drip.

Tony kept the windows rolled down. We crawled around the neighborhood. It all looked terrific, the big houses, the old trees, the front gardens, it looked like a million bucks. But we didn't see anybody to talk to.

"Look," I said. "Nothing's going to happen to him. He went outside and got lost, that's all. There aren't even any cars around." Later I said, "Maybe we should take both cars. That way we can cover more ground."

"I don't want to be alone right now," Tony said. "Okay, all right."

So we drove back to my place, which wasn't far. Outside the house I pulled up and left the keys in the car and got out, and Tony got out, to switch sides. Nolan was standing on the porch.

"What do you want?" I said.

"I want to talk to you."

"Not now."

"I want to talk to you now," he said.

"Tell him to fuck off," Tony said, and got in his car.

My car was parked in the drive, with the driver's side facing the porch. Nolan had a big blue medical bandage on the side of his neck and face. The whites of his eyes looked bloody, his nose was scratched up.

"Where have you come from, the hospital?"

"I got the kid."

"What do you mean, you got him?"

"I mean I got him, I took him."

I called out to Tony, "It's all right, he found Michael."

"I didn't find him, I took him. I got him."

"Well, where is he?"

"I want to talk to Robert James. I want you to call him for me."

Tony came out of the car, and it went from there. Eventually I managed to get them in the house—they were shouting at each other on the porch, like a couple of drunks, you could hear them up and down the block. But there was nobody around. I had a hangover coming on, a faint one, starting from the inside of my eye sockets, by the bridge of the nose. I felt thirsty and light-headed, almost dizzy, but Nolan looked excited, too, he didn't make sense. First I pulled Tony inside and up the stairs and then Nolan followed.

"Let's just sit down and get something to drink. It's too hot outside. I don't understand what's going on."

But nobody sat down. "I want to talk to Robert James," Nolan said.

"Where the fuck is my son?"

"What do you want to talk to him about?"

"He's got to understand what this is about. We're not fucking around here. He can buy up our neighborhoods and there's nothing I can do about it. But this is due process, this is the law."

"What's Michael got to do with it?"

"I'm just making him sweat a little. He needs to understand what political pressure is. This is political pressure."

"You're not listening. I need to know where he is."

"He's fine. He's not the one you should be worried about here."

"Tell me where my fucking son is, you fucking—"

"Tony, shut up for a second. Let's everybody calm down. I just want to understand what's going on here."

Afterwards it occurred to me that maybe Nolan thought Michael was Robert's kid, maybe that's why he took him, in protest, when he wandered into the street. I don't know if Nolan ever met Michael. When Clarence came by our house, his grandmother picked him up. But even Nolan must have realized his mistake. At one point, Tony said to me, "This is stupid. Give me your phone. I'm calling the police."

"The fuck you are," Nolan said and took the phone away, grabbing it out of my hand—he had big hands. Suddenly it was like this very obvious fact about all of us, which nobody ever mentions, had just been mentioned. He wasn't just stronger than me but maybe two or three or four times stronger. Tony had left his cell in the car but then Nolan stood up to block the door, and I remember thinking, he's scared, too, Nolan's a big guy and Tony is scared. "Haven't you got a gun, Marny?" he said. "Go get your fucking gun."

"That's right, Annie. Get your gun."

"Go to hell, Nolan."

"Just get it," Tony said.

So I went upstairs, which I was glad to do anyway, to get away. I had two guns, the Remington from Walmart, which I kept under the bed, and Mel's Smith & Wesson, a handgun, standard police issue. That lived in my sock drawer. The shotgun was plainly ridiculous, but then the Smith & Wesson seemed ridiculous, too, and I sat on my bed fighting a strong sense of unreality. I felt like I had to fight the unreality if I was going to get back to some kind of normal state of affairs, because if I didn't get back to normal, bad things might happen, things outside the human range I was accustomed to, which I had read about but which I had mostly preserved myself from.

The best way I can put this feeling is this. Once, driving through South Carolina with a couple of college friends, on the way back from Spring Break, we struck a rock in the road and popped a tire, and had to pull across the lanes of traffic to the hard shoulder. It was about one in the morning. The highway wasn't particularly busy, there were a lot of trucks, but the noise they made was terrific— more than terrific, frightening—as soon as you stepped out of the car. When you're in the car your own noise drowns much of the traffic sound, but as soon as you stop, as soon as you stand aside to observe it, you hear and feel the violence of the machinery passing by. And bad things can happen to you. Someone might run into you, someone might pull over and rob you. Until you get back in the car, on the road, in the traffic again, you feel helpless, and I sat on the bed until I heard Tony calling out to me so I went downstairs.

They were wrestling and punching each other on the floor, punching but not really hitting. They were both worn out. Nolan was almost on top, on his knees, and Tony lay on his back trying to hit him. "Get this— Get him off me," Tony said, but I just stood there, watching. Both of these guys were my friends, I didn't know what to do. Tony kept clawing at Nolan, openhanded, and then he caught him in the face and Nolan's bandage kind of dragged away. All his human mess, the inside stuff, started leaking out.

"Fuck me," Tony said. "You're fucking gross." He rolled away and pulled himself up by the sofa cushions. Nolan tried to stand up and got as far as his elbows, but Tony started kicking him, in the shoulder area. Not hard, but still, kicking. Nolan kept trying to get up but then he fell back again and hit his head on the floor; it kind of bounced. "What have you done with my kid?" Tony said. "Where is he?"

But Nolan was out cold, and I had to pull Tony off him.

"What were you doing up there?" he said. "Taking a nap?"

"I was trying to work out what to do."

"Well, you didn't do shit."

He picked up the phone, which was lying on the floor, and started dialing. There were faint handprints on his shirt, one of those short-sleeved collared shirts you wear to go bowling, red with a black stripe down one side. It said *Pearson's Auto Parts* in white italics, and then, underneath, *Mayflower Lanes* and *Summer League 2006*. The color of the shirt hid most of the blood.

"Who are you calling?" I said.

"Who do you think, the cops." But this took a while—he stood there giving answers. Yes, no, his name, his son's name. What's the address, he wanted to know, I don't know the address. Everything pissed him off. He turned to me, waiting; everything distressed him.

"Tell them to send an ambulance."

"Send an ambulance," he said and hung up. "Where does he live?"

"He lives with his mom. The house on the corner."

"Maybe she's got Michael. What are you doing?"

"Waiting here till everybody comes."

Tony took off. He had to step around Nolan, I heard him running down the stairs, and then I heard the front door bang. After a minute the door clicked open again and I heard him calling, "Marny, Marny!"

He was standing at the foot of the stairs, almost in tears. I went down and he said, "Which corner."

So I showed him. I didn't mean to go all the way, but he was walking fast and wouldn't stop. It was about four o'clock, the real baking point of the day. School was out, and we didn't see anybody. When I pointed out the house, he started running and then I ran after him and caught him on the steps and rang the bell.

Eventually Mrs. Smith waded into the hall. She opened the front door and looked at us through the screen. "I suppose you come to collect him."

We both had to catch our breaths, but I said, "Is Michael here?"

"They're in the garden, playing with the hose. Anything to cool down, it's one of those days. I hope you don't mind."

"No, that's fine," Tony said.

"Would you like some lemonade? We've been making lemonade from scratch. It might be a little sour. They used a lot of lemons."

"I just want to see my son."

"He's been fine, he's been a good boy."

Tony walked through the house and into the kitchen and out the back, which had a screen door, too, that clappered behind him. Mrs. Smith poured a glass of lemonade into one of those mottled translucent plastic cups, and gave it to me. We could see the garden through the back door. Clarence had the hose in his hand, and pointed it in the air, spraying the water upwards with his thumb. It fell down in a soft arch. Michael waited and then ran through the mist, squealing. Tony tried to pick him up but he wriggled out of his father's arms. We couldn't hear what Michael said but Tony put him down and Michael ran through the mist again.

"Those two just found each other, it's a beautiful thing."

"I wouldn't mind a turn."

"When I was a girl," Mrs. Smith said, "when I was a teenager, my mother used to run a Bible study group on Wednesday afternoons, and all these old women, it was mostly old women, though I don't suppose they were any older than me, came by the house and sat on my chairs and my sofa. Because I wasn't permitted to disturb, my mother kicked me out. Being the youngest, most of the time they sort of gave up with me, I got the run of the house. But not on Wednesday afternoons. And all these old women talked about their grandkids. I got five grandkids, I got seven grandkids, I got three grandkids and another one coming. They were big on the numbers, it used to make me laugh. They talked about grandkids the way my brothers talked about home runs. But now I know. It's hard work. You got to make them normal, not too much, you got to make them so they can love somebody, and you got to do it again and again and again. If I had five grandkids I'd count 'em, too."

Eventually Tony picked up Michael and carried him in, and Clarence came after them, leaving the hose spilling into the grass. "Turn off that water!" Mrs. Smith called out and he went back and turned it off. He got his shoes wet in the spreading water, and Mrs. Smith said, "Take off those wet shoes," when he came in.

"You sure I can't get you a glass of lemonade?" she said to Tony. "You can put a little extra sugar in it."

"We're all right, we better get going. His mother is waiting for us."

"Thank you," I said. She held the door open behind us. Clarence stood beside her in wet socks. There were sock prints and Michael's wet shoe prints all over the floor. The boys looked at each other but didn't say anything; there were grown-ups around and they didn't want to talk.

"Anytime," Mrs. Smith said. "You can drop him off anytime."

When we got down to street level, Tony took Michael's hand and the kid kind of dragged himself along the sidewalk until Tony picked him up. "Are you okay? What happened?"

"Put me down," Michael said. "I want to walk."

"Well, hold on to my hand."

"I don't want to hold your hand."

"Just tell me what happened and I'll let you go."

But Michael scrambled loose and ran ahead. Then he turned around to look at us and ran ahead again.

"I am unbelievably angry with you right now."

"What did I do?" I said.

"I told you to keep Michael away from that boy. I told you some-thing would happen."

"I did keep him away, I don't know what you mean."

We walked on, it was only about a hundred yards to my house, and at one point Tony kind of laughed, and I said, what, and he said, "I bet that's one angry bee."

When we reached his car he opened the door and told Michael to get in. But Michael wouldn't. "Get in the car!" Tony shouted suddenly.

"You can't leave me like this," I said. "What am I supposed to do with him?"

"There's no way I take my kid in that house, with him like that. You got to be kidding me."

"So leave him in the car."

"There's no way I leave him in the car."

"Just lock the door. If something happens, he can honk the horn."

"No way."

"I don't know what to do," I said and sat down on the porch.

"Is Walter around?"

But Walter and Susie were out; we tried the bell.

"Just sit here and wait for the police. It will take me half an hour to drop off Michael and come back."

"I'm hungry," Michael said.

"Just get in the car."

"I don't know what to do," I said. "It will take more than half an hour this time of day. Five o'clock traffic."

But Tony drove off anyway and eventually I changed my mind and went inside. "Nolan, Nolan," I called out, from the stairs. There wasn't any answer. We had left the front door open, at least it was open when I reached the landing, and I walked in. Nolan lay on his side, with his legs swiveled over, so that both of his shoes and both of his shoulders touched the floor, but his hips stuck out. Lying like that he looked a little fat, like a strong middle-aged black man who had put on weight. The bandage from his face had stuck to his shirt. He was never very dark-skinned, and his skin had a washed-out whitish look, like when you put too much milk into a cup of tea. There was a crust of drying spit around his mouth.

"Nolan," I said again, then sat down on my knees and felt his neck for a pulse. Some gestures are tender just because the motion itself needs gentleness. I had trouble at first, there's a lot of loose skin and tissue, and the cords in his throat were stretched by the angle of his head. But he was breathing, his lips moved, and then I found his pulse, which was steady enough and felt like a small gulp of blood, one after another. The human machine was operating fine and the rest of him couldn't get in the way of whatever I felt for him. I sat like that I don't know how long, until I heard the sirens coming nearer.

31

The cops came, the ambulance came, doctors did their business and loaded Nolan up on a stretcher—he's a big guy, you could feel how heavy he is, the way they carried him down the stairs. One of the cops rode along in the ambulance, they set the sirens off, the squad car followed, and another car drove me to the station to make a statement. I called Beatrice from the road, and about twenty minutes later, Tony showed up with Mel Hauser.

I'd been to this station before, on Beaubien Street, a big square grand old building, like a town hall. It's where they took my fingerprints for the education board. This time they emptied out my pockets and checked my wallet and removed my shoes. They took my fingerprints again and lined me up against a blank wall and photographed me looking different ways—mug shots.

Tony got the same treatment, but he liked these guys or at least pretended to. These were working-class Detroit city cops. One of them had a buzz cut and glasses, his face was reddish, his hair, too, and his chin ran down his neck in tough folds. A fat strong medium-size guy named Lisicki. Mel knew him—it was a good idea bringing him along. They gave me my shit back and pointed to a row of plastic chairs. It was like waiting in a hospital waiting room.

Then Beatrice came in with a lawyer, Dan Korobkin, a skinny Jewish guy with quick expressions and a reasonable amount of hair. Robert James wanted somebody around to talk me through the legal process. It turned out this lawyer knew my brother a little, Brad was two years ahead of him at Chicago. At least, this is what Korobkin told me. He sat next to me, on one side, Beatrice on the other.

"Is there anybody you want me to call?" she said. "I can let them know."

Korobkin said, "What happens now is a lot of procedural stuff, a lot of paperwork. They'll take a statement. You don't have to answer anything you don't want to answer, and if you feel like talking something over with me first, we can find a space. After that my main priority is to get you home."

At one point he went to the bathroom, and Beatrice leaned over and said, "So what the fuck happened." Along with the makeup, which she hadn't taken off, she had a strong scent of perfume on her, which was mixed in with her own smell—also strong on a hot day. God knows I must have stunk, too.

"Nolan saw Michael wandering around, you know, Tony's kid, and got him into his car somehow, because he thought he was Robert's. This was at Robert's house. Tony and I had gone out to lunch and left Michael behind. And then when we came back he was gone. So we got in the car and started looking for him. Anyway, Nolan ended up at my place, because he knows I'm a friend of Robert's, and I guess he wanted to make some kind of communication— some kind of threat. He's pissed off about the Meacher thing. I tried to explain that Michael was Tony's kid, he had nothing to do with Robert, but by that point everybody was shouting. I got them inside, into my place, but they kept screaming at each other. I tried to call the police but Nolan took the phone away, physically, by force, and then Tony and Nolan started going at it. I didn't see the whole thing, I had to step out. But when I came back they were rolling around on the floor. Nolan's already a little beat up, and Tony caught him in the— He had this bandage on his face that came away, and that must have hurt, because he just kind of lay there and Tony started kicking him, and I had to pull him away. Because by that stage Nolan was out cold. He lives with his mom just down the road and I figured he might have left the kid there, so we went to look, and the kid was there, and we took him away. Then Tony drove him home and I kind of sat with Nolan until the ambulance arrived. That's the best I can piece it together. The whole thing's a big fucking mess. Where were you? You look all dressed up."

"Downtown. I had a meeting. Some guy called Krause from Goldman Sachs."

"I think we got lucky, it could have been much worse. I think it's going to be okay."

"For who?" she said.

Tony kept talking, he seemed in a good mood. "The motherfucker took my kid," he said to Lisicki.

"I don't want to hear it. Mel, tell him to shut up."

"Shut up."

"Look, I didn't do anything, he was beating the shit out of me. But what I'm saying is, he had it coming. The son of a bitch definitely had it coming. Don't expect me to feel bad about it."

"I don't give a fuck what you feel. Keep it to yourself."

"Does anyone know how Nolan is doing?"

"What's that?"

"Does anyone know how Nolan is doing?" I said again, as loud as I could, but I don't think it came out clear. I was all talked out.

Lisicki said, "Nobody knows."

I felt like I was coming down with a cold. My bones ached, and there was a flat pain, like a low noise you can't get out of your head, running from my butt to my knees. A loose wire of nerves that kept shorting. Beatrice put her arm around me, to warm me up, she said. I must have been shivering—on a hot June day that was still waiting for rain. I had the sense for the first time in years, since I was a kid maybe, that my face was something physical. That the bones of my face were a wall and my mouth was a door and I didn't have to come out if I didn't want to. Nobody could force me.

But then they called me in to make a statement, and I remembered my brother's old joke about my stories. How I said, this and then this and then this.

AS SOON AS I GOT home I called Gloria, but the cabins they were staying in didn't have phones—and her cell had no reception. It went straight to voicemail. So when she came back Friday night I had to tell her about the whole business. The story had been kind of accumulating in me over the past few days, and I knew it would come out rehearsed, I knew I would sound formal and underemotional and overconsiderate, and that's how I sounded. But I had to tell her anyway. The other problem was she came back brimming with her own hard-to-follow stories, about people I didn't know and which didn't seem very important, relatively speaking. But I waited for her to tell them anyway, patiently. She sensed my patience, too, and that pissed her off even before I started.

So right from the beginning we fought about the whole damn thing.

"I don't understand what happened," she said. "Nolan passed out?"

"Yes."

"And you left him there, for how long?"

"About ten minutes, fifteen minutes."

"You've got to realize how upsetting this is for me," she said.

"What do you mean, for you?"

"This is personal for me. You understand that. Nolan's my friend."

"He's a friend of mine, too—"

"Apparently not. But that's not what I'm talking about."

"You mean your dad."

"Don't say it. I mean you, I mean you . . ." She was crying and kind of hitting me, which I recognized as a good sign, because if she could take it out on me, she could probably let it out, too. But all of this sounds more calculating than I felt. I was very upset. I tried to tell her this, I wanted to make it clear, but it came out as more of a statement of fact than I would have liked, not an outburst of feeling, and she had limited sympathy.

I said to her, "It seems to me that your first port of—concern should be me, should be what happened to me and what I'm going through . . ."

"What are you going through, Marny?"

"This, for one thing."

"You need to toughen up then. If you think this is bad."

She had cried herself out, but underneath the softness was more hardness. I got a sense of that, too. You live with somebody, in a state of real intimacy, you sleep in her bed (we were at Gloria's place; she was unpacking), you watch TV together, you leave the bathroom door open, and then you realize she can step out of this intimacy if she wants, she can make decisions about it. At least since I was at her place she couldn't go home. And she couldn't bring herself to kick me out either, that was a bridge too far. So I knew that at some point that night we would lie down in bed together, in close proximity, with the light off, which gave a reasonable chance for our actual real affection for each other to come out, like some kind of hedgehog in the dark. Which is what happened.

"I'm sorry, baby," she said. "I'm not really mad at you. I'm just worried about Nolan, I've known him for a long time, and it's confusing for me that you're in the middle of this. I feel like I have to take sides, and somehow I'm on the wrong side. Just lying here like this with you."

"So let's not have sides," I said.

32

Nolan turned out to be okay—medically, I mean. He regained consciousness in the ambulance; the diagnosis was severe concussion. I didn't think Tony kicked him that hard, but who knows. Nolan used to play football, free safety, he had a history of concussions, and this is one of those repetitive things, where the more you get it, the more vulnerable you are. It's a complex field; the damage isn't always structural. At least, the doctors disagree about that—a lot of what goes on is at the micro level. Synapses. Neuropsychiatry. You become predisposed. I started reading up on all this stuff; there were stories in the newspaper, too.

I tried to remember exactly what had happened. Nolan was kind of getting up, he was halfway up when Tony kicked him. His head snapped back when he hit the ground. This was an image that replayed itself in my mind. Apart from anything else because people kept asking me about it. Korobkin, Lisicki. Beatrice and Robert James. When you describe something often enough you remember what you describe and not what you saw.

They kept him overnight at the hospital, under police guard. His medical problems weren't the issue. Undressing him, the nurses found a gun. It wasn't loaded, but it wasn't licensed either, and

Korobkin said it could add a minimum of two years to his sentence. If he was convicted, that is. In which case there would be a lot of technical code to work through, a complicated points system. It was like scoring ice skating, except instead of medals they gave you months and years. The worst-case scenario was life in prison with the possibility of parole, but there were mitigating circumstances. Michael didn't get hurt and the whole thing played out very quickly. Little details, like leaving the kid at his mother's house, were likely to sit well with a judge. But the gun didn't help, and Nolan also had a criminal record. One count of disturbing the peace, and a misdemeanor drug charge he picked up in college. That didn't help either. Korobkin figured he could be looking at ten years.

When the doctors released him, the cops took over, and a judge set bail—$100,000. Nolan didn't have access to that kind of money. They couldn't even raise 10 percent for the bondsman.

I wanted to visit him in jail, but Korobkin advised against. I saw a lot of this guy over the next ten months, because what happened next happened in different stages, it took time, there were court appearances, things to sign, meetings with lawyers. It became an aspect of my life but not my whole life, though it affected the rest of my life, too.

Korobkin liked to talk baseball to me. He had Tigers season tickets, and every time I saw him, we spent maybe half the conversation on baseball. For a while it looked like the Tigers had a chance of making the playoffs, Cabrera was having a great year, knocking it all over the park. And Verlander put up his usual strong numbers. He got called up for the All-Star Game at the last minute. "What you need in this league," Korobkin said, "is a slugger and an ace, and we have both." But then guys got hurt and the White Sox put clear water between them, before the Twins pulled away. I had to listen to his complaining, too.

He offered to take me to a ball game, but I said no.

"You can talk about the game," I said, "but don't make me watch it."

"You know who you should have heard call a ball game? I'll tell you who." Korobkin was a big Ernie Harwell fan, the old Tigers broadcaster, who'd died in May. "He was one of those play-by-play announcers they should study in high school English classes. When a guy struck out looking, Ernie used to say, he stood there like a house by the side of the road."

The case was slowly taking shape but all of this takes an unbelievable length of time. The first thing you realize is, you want this thing resolved so you can move on with your life, but you have to live your life anyway because this thing is about to become a part of it. Kidnapping is a felony offense, even if the whole business doesn't last but a couple of hours, even if no one gets hurt, and the political context looked bad for Nolan. I mean, what he said to me, "I'm just making him sweat a little," which went towards motive. Korobkin asked me repeatedly about this line, and what Nolan said afterwards, about applying pressure. I had motives, too, operating at cross-purposes to each other, and from the beginning I decided to drown out the noise by concentrating as much as possible on telling the truth. But for reasons that slowly became clear this was unsatisfactory.

I kept trying to understand what had happened, and the law was one way of understanding it. But I felt like you feel when you're a kid and your parents tell stories about you at the dinner table. That's not the way it was, you want to say. Even if it's all true. Just because Nolan picked up some kid in his car, who was maybe wandering in the road or in Robert's garden (this fact was still under dispute), and brought him to his mother's house, where we picked him up a few hours later, Nolan was looking at ten years in jail. Maybe a quarter of the life he had left. There seemed to be something disproportionate—I don't just mean about the sentencing guidelines, though that, too. I mean about the way some stupid impulse, some spur of the moment thing, can become a permanent feature or scar in somebody's life. I guess I don't like the way facts become facts. I remembered the feeling of that hot afternoon, it was muggy, too, Tony and I were both a little drunk, and I had a hangover coming on, but what I mean is I felt like I was operating the whole time at some slight remove from reality, I didn't have great access. We were all just floundering around, trying to get a grip on something, and now, one month, two months, three months later, that floundering turned out to be the reality, and that other thing, the thing we needed to come to terms with, might as well not have existed.

The first sign of things to come was Nolan's release—someone posted bail. This was great for Nolan, but it meant people were raising money on his behalf, there were powerful donors, and the case was turning into a political football. People on every side kicked us around. There was a guy named Simon Kaplow, a law professor at Wayne State, who had been involved in local politics for years. He wrote an op-ed piece in the *Free Press*, he showed up on Channel 7 news. There was a vacancy on the city council, Dee Dee McIlvane had just stepped down, and Kaplow tried to turn the election into a referendum on the five neighborhoods. He backed a woman named Molly Brinkley, a former superintendent of schools; Gloria knew her a little bit. She said, "Publicly I like everything about Molly. She's got a lot of good ideas, I think she's honest, she works hard, she stands for the right things, but she's also personally a real mean little person, she's petty, she bears grudges, she's manipulative, she's not somebody I'd like to have any kind of business with."

It seemed like every couple of days we saw her face on TV, making her pitch. Detroit has got to get better, but who's it got to get better for? Who are these neighborhoods really helping out? All of this started out innocent enough, but somehow the tone changed. A group of Turkish immigrants had converted an abandoned church into a mosque and community center. There were stories about where the funding came from, there were complaints about the calls to prayer. People said they felt shut out from the community center. Maybe they did, I don't know. They felt uncomfortable. Molly Brinkley ran a political ad, about the old church and the community it used to serve. There were photographs, interviews with old ladies. She didn't say anything you could pin against her, she was very careful, but she got her point across, too. If it's a choice between these two groups of people . . . that was her point. Even Gloria said, "Something is happening to this woman, I don't recognize her."

Then Nolan filed charges against Tony, for assault. The only one off the hook was me.

I felt guilty about that, too. And kept thinking about what Tony said to me, "You didn't do shit." Like it was some kind of failure of courage or character to stay out of the way of the legal battle. Because in some way, and I felt this strongly, it seemed to me I was in the middle of the whole thing. Yet nobody wanted to take me on. Korobkin was one of Robert's guys. Apart from anything else Robert worried about a civil suit and wanted somebody checking up on me, on what I said. Everybody had lawyers, Tony had his lawyer, Nolan had lawyers, we had acquired these representatives and advocates and stand-ins who spoke their own language and managed to fight our battles in such a way that we hardly had to be present at all.

Korobkin asked me not to make contact with the other parties, but it seemed to me there were human things going on here I had to pay attention to. So I went to see Mrs. Smith.

By this point it was mid-July, a dripping, not very hot or cold but uncomfortable close overcast summer afternoon. Just after lunch— Gloria was seeing one of her sorority sisters. I had my lunch and then I thought, screw it, and walked the hundred yards to Nolan's house.

His mother answered the door. "I was wondering when you would turn up," she said.

"I've been meaning to."

We went into the kitchen and Mrs. Smith put the coffee on. "Clarence is getting into his baking," she said and pushed over a tray of sugar cookies cut into half-moons and stars. I took a mincing little bite. She fussed around with the coffee and then she poured me a cup and poured herself a cup and sat down. "Let me say first things first. When Nolan dropped that boy off, I had no idea. He said he was helping out a friend. So let me apologize for that. Let me apologize for getting you mixed up. When I heard what he did, I wanted to say, excuse me, I'll handle this, you come here, son. You are in big trouble. But it's not up to me. I got no say, and they talking about a life sentence. It doesn't add up. Nolan swears to me that boy was walking in the city street. He says the kid didn't know his way home. I can't bring myself to disbelieve him. Now I am mad as hell about what he did next, but the only one who got hurt here is my son. That's a fact."

"I don't know if you blame me for that."

"I'm done blaming. I don't even blame the other guy, Carnesecca. If somebody took Clarence, what do you think Nolan would do. Everybody needs to calm down. But these lawyers, they don't let you talk."

"That's why I came here today."

And she took my hand, which was on the table, in both her old-woman hands, which were very dry and warm. There was flour on them, that's partly why they seemed so dry. After a minute she let me go.

At one point Nolan came in with Clarence. They had just been taking the dog to the park. "What's he want?" Nolan said. Almost two months later, you could still see the scar on his face, a patch of lighter skin, as if it was dusted with flour, too. But that wasn't me or Tony, that was Kurt Stangel, when they fought over the baseball bat.

"He doesn't want anything. He's paying a visit."

"The lawyer tells me not to see you," I said.

"I guess you're all grown up now. Come on, Clarence. Wash hands."

"Don't listen to him, Greg," Mrs. Smith told me, while they went to the bathroom. "He's just worried. If he goes to jail, how old is Clarence going to be when he gets out."

In fact, I started seeing Nolan more regularly after that. We even went running once. I had this idea, maybe it was a stupid idea, that Tony and Nolan could work out their differences personally, and leave the law out of it. Korobkin explained to me, the law isn't interested in them personally. But I had an answer for that, too. The best way to fight cynicism is with deeper cynicism. These guys all know each other, I said. Everything's personal. Robert and Larry Oh have lunch together, they have mutual interests, they talk about trade-offs. I just have to persuade all the different parties what their interests are. But Korobkin shook his head. You've been watching too much TV, he said. And the truth is nobody wanted to work out their differences, they wanted to fight them out.

We jogged around the neighborhood, past Butzel Park, as far as Mack Avenue. I liked seeing the houses at different stages of being worked on, the gardens in progress, guys painting fences or washing their cars on a Saturday afternoon, women outside with the kids and the plastic toys. Of course all this set Nolan off. We didn't talk about the case much but we talked around it. I wanted to know what made him so angry; I didn't get it. These places were scary places before people like me came along, the houses were standing empty, nature was taking over. It's kind of terrifying, I said, how quickly weeds grow; certain trees as well. All of this architecture, which seems like such a permanent feature of the landscape, needs constant updating, home improvement, middle-class pride and ambition, or the landscape swallows it up. After a few years.

"Who said I'm angry?" Nolan said. "You got some guy setting up a roadblock outside my house, and when I complain to him, he beats the shit out of me. Some other guy kicks me in the head. And I'm the one going to jail. But if you want to talk about architecture, let's talk about that."

"You complained to him with a baseball bat."

"Don't get me wrong, I like these houses. When you all move out, we can move in."

"Who's we?"

The truth is, Nolan wasn't in great shape; he looked heavy, his color was bad, his breathing sounded anxious. When we got to Mack and Conner he had to stop, so we went into the McDonald's for refueling. I had a cup of coffee but he needed some sugar in his blood and ate two or three little hot apple pies.

We sat outside at one of those metal tables, sweating in the August heat, in the traffic noise. I said, "This city wasn't always a black city."

"When the white people made enough money, they moved out."

"So now they want to move back in. And by the way, it isn't only whites."

"How much money have you people brought to this city that you didn't spend on yourselves? On your schools and your houses and your neighborhoods?"

"You live in it, too. There have been jobs."

"Mowing lawns. Security."

From where we were sitting, we could see the old warehouse across the parking lot; a black guy in a brown uniform sat on a folding chair outside the office door, in the sunshine.

"That's not just security," I said. "It's big business—they're storing aluminum there. How long was that place sitting empty?"

"And who makes money from that? I don't see a lot of jobs in watching metal. And where does the money go to? Let me ask you a question. If this thing works out, how many people from Detroit will be able to afford a house in one of your neighborhoods?"

"I don't know, Nolan. But let me ask you a question. How much is your mother's house going to be worth?"

"Only if she sells it, only if she moves out."

On the walk home (Nolan wasn't up to jogging back), I wanted to say something else to him, something that communicated part of what I felt, sitting with him on the floor and waiting for the cops and the ambulance to show up. Instead what I said was, "You don't have to lump me in with the rest of them. I don't need their house anymore. I could move in with Gloria."

33

In fact, Gloria moved in with me—just for a while, while she was having some work done on her kitchen over the summer. This was two weeks before the start of school. The job wasn't supposed to last much longer than that. But you know what kitchen renovations are like, they drag on, they become something else, and sometimes I tell myself that part of what went wrong was just that fucking kitchen.

So she moved in, with Walter and Susie downstairs, and we read the paper over breakfast, and sat in the garden, when it wasn't full of other people's kids, and ate lunch at Joe's, that kind of thing. "So this is what the big deal is," she said. "This is why people move here." Most years she taught summer school, she's one of those people who can't put up with an empty hour, but for my sake she didn't, and we had a lot of empty hours. Sometimes I worked on the newsletter, she had a little administrative catching up to do, but basically we hung out together like people in love.

I had worried about living with Walter and Susie. Gloria's first experience of Walter's charm wasn't a tremendous success, Jimmy's baptism and the party at Tony's house afterwards. Walter could be weird around women, gentlemanly and politely sinister, and sometimes he was honestly weirdly polite and sometimes it served as a mask for ironic superior feelings. Even I couldn't always tell the difference. But it turned out that Walter didn't matter much, because Gloria and Susie got along so well. They both have that little-girl thing going on, in a practical good-girl way, not pink and princessy; and they shopped together, and cooked together, and worked in the yard. Walter and I drove them out to some nursery in Rochester Hills, and they came out with armfuls of plants and had to put their seat belts on between the pots. They talked the whole time. Walter and I didn't say much. If we said anything it was probably negative-sounding and dismissive, a cover for laziness, but the truth is we were both happy to listen in—like men dependent on the women in their lives to keep up their daily interest in the world. I don't know how much of it was phony or for show—Susie and Gloria's friendship, I mean—or a way of getting back at us for something, or excluding us. But it wouldn't have mattered because we were all basically pretty happy.

The first piece of trouble came when school started and Mr. Pendleton returned to work. His leg was fine; he walked with a slight shuffle, that's all, but then Mrs. Sanchez let Gloria know there probably wouldn't be any substitute work for me.

"Why are you telling me?" Gloria said. "Tell him yourself."

Mrs. Sanchez must have felt awkward. I remembered her spider plants, the heating on overdrive, her framed photos of the kids. She tried to explain herself. "I thought you were in contact."

"What does that mean?" Gloria said to me afterwards. "*In contact* is not a good phrase for this. Either it doesn't mean anything at all or it means something that's none of her business."

She was sort of making a joke of it, but it pissed her off, too, and somehow the funny side of it started losing out to the other side. "I mean, what does she have to say anything for? She can say something when they need you. Why does she have to tell me?"

"I got a letter, too. She probably figured it's better to say something to you than nothing. Because I was teaching pretty much full-time by the end of last year. They had to let me know."

"That is not what this is about," Gloria said.

She thought it had something to do with Nolan's trial, and maybe she was right, maybe it did. Every week new stories came out. I was mixed up in the case, there were racial overtones, and if I were Mrs. Sanchez I wouldn't want me teaching at the school either. The classroom of a public high school in Detroit is hard enough to control anyway, but if the kids have something on you, something they can use, you're finished. But Gloria took my understanding as a proof of laziness or, worse, a confession of guilt. And the truth is I did feel guilty about something and spent a certain amount of time trying to figure out what.

Tony was my friend, Nolan was my friend. I wanted to stay neutral. But the press didn't help—they made it hard to stay on the fence. In those first weeks and months, *The Detroit News* ran a number of articles, mostly about Nolan. I guess they wanted to own his side of the story—for a lot of people, this was an opportunity. The gun Nolan carried with him belonged to his dead brother. He kept it for sentimental reasons; it was never loaded. There was also speculation about what knocked him out, and the long-term health consequences. Nolan had a heart condition. Apparently, this is one of the reasons he quit football. The standard physical exam, which every college athlete goes through, revealed hypertrophic cardio-myopathy. African Americans have a high rate of this disease; athletes are particularly at risk. One piece suggested that maybe he was having a heart attack while Tony and I were at his mother's house, drinking lemonade.

Other things came out, too. The *Free Press* published a story about Clarence's mother, a woman named Martha Brett, who wanted to move to Arizona and had petitioned the court for permission to relocate her son. Her husband (she had a husband) worked for Daikin AC and had just been promoted to the office in Sun City West. Two days before Nolan kidnapped Michael, the court granted Brett's petition. On the following day, Nolan filed an appeal and later that night he took a baseball bat to Kurt Stangel's car. The picture painted in the *Free Press* was of a guy whose life was going off the rails.

"Let's not take sides," I kept saying to Gloria, but she said, "Sometimes you have to."

Robert James said something funny to me about all this. His mom was in town one weekend, and they had me over for brunch. Mrs. James was worried about me, she thought I looked skinny, she wanted to feed me up. Gloria came, too; we ate pancakes. Everybody was on best behavior. We talked about the case in these abstract terms, as if the only thing it touched on was our political opinions. At one point Robert said, "You know who I blame? The air-conditioning companies. They're tearing this country apart. Who moves to Sun City West? The only way these places are remotely habitable is air-conditioning and irrigation. But there isn't enough water, which everybody knows. Detroit is a terrific city. So are Buffalo and Cleveland and Pittsburgh. There's water, there's transportation links, there's history and culture, but because you can't go golfing twelve months a year, everybody is moving to Arizona. These cities they are building aren't cities, they're brochures. But air-conditioning is going to wipe them out again, global warming is going to wipe them out. In fifty years' time we'll all be heading north."

"What are you talking about?"

"Nolan's baby mama. They tried to take away his kid, this is what set the whole thing off."

"Have they moved already?"

"I don't know."

Afterwards, on the way home, Gloria said to me, "Baby mama? Where does Robert James get off talking about baby mamas?"

In fact, Clarence moved out at the end of October. I spoke to Mrs. Smith about it; she was in tears. "That woman," she said, "that woman has a lot to answer for. And her husband is the worst kind of father. They baby that boy, they give him whatever he wants. All he gets is pizza and ice cream in that house. I said to her, this family has a fat problem, we get fat. You need to cook real food, you need to show him what eating is. But she's one of those mothers who looks at her fat boy and thinks it means love. Like the fatter he is, the more he loves her."

"How often will you get to see him?"

"Summer and New Year. Two times a year is nothing. Two times a year is just enough to make him mad at you, for trying to knock some sense into him."

After Clarence left, Nolan basically shut down our relationship. I hardly saw him, except sometimes at his mother's house. And even then he found a reason to leave the room, he took the dog out, he went upstairs.

But Tony came in for a hard time, too. The *Chicago Tribune* ran a piece about his Detroit memoir, which gave a big boost to sales. Tony himself showed up at my house one morning, waving a print-out of the Amazon page—he'd gotten to 133 in the charts. But the case put his memoir in a strong light, and people started looking at it for other kinds of information. There was a *Slate* blog that picked out three or four passages and considered them for racist content. Tony's line on all this is that we're all racist and it's better to be open about it; that was the point of the book. He didn't present himself as an authority, he presented himself as kind of a fuckup. There was a confessional element. But that's not how the excerpts came across.

Tony always said he liked being disliked, he was used to it. But some of what showed up on social media sites was pretty scary. There were threats, and a guy from the Eastpointe police department came by the house to talk to Cris and Tony about security. What kind of threats they took seriously, the kind they let go, what they should tell their kids. It was very upsetting for her; for Tony, too. At least, the male protective instinct allowed him to express some of his anxiety by directing it at his family. "I'm just glad Michael is four and not six," he said to me. "At six he might start taking shit in the playground. But at four he doesn't have a clue. He just knows that Mommy and Daddy keep fighting about something. I mean, go figure. The guy takes my kid and I'm the guy all the trolls want to take a potshot at. I guess the world is full of motherfuckers."

But it didn't look good—Tony kicking Nolan in the head, knocking him out. There was a lot of national news interest. Robert, for example, was worried that pictures of me and Obama playing basketball might reach the Internet. Afterwards, under the garage lights, Bill Russo got one of the catering staff to take a group photo. That was easy enough to track down. But these days anybody with a mobile phone can turn into a problem. People take pictures they don't even remember taking. Robert went through the guest list, making phone calls. He called Gloria, too.

"What did he say?"

"He wanted to know if I had any pictures of you and the president. He wanted me to delete them."

"Do you?"

"Just one. He's boxing you out."

"Did you delete it?"

"What do you think?" she said.

But they came out anyway. You can't keep these things down anymore, and suddenly there was a picture of me on the cover of *USA Today*: in a half crouch, looking up at Obama, while he squared to shoot. Snow in the background, the lights reflecting off it, and Secret Service guys ranged along a fence. Robert's driveway. The press didn't know what to make of it. It's an odd story. Witness in a racial confrontation played basketball with the president at a Thanksgiving fund-raiser. "In Detroit, the lines are being drawn, and crossed, and redrawn," the article said. I spent a lot of my time online, reading the news.

Gloria thought the case was taking over my life; this was another one of our fights. She went back to work and I stayed home, screwing around on the computer. And often when she came back she found me on the computer, too, sitting at the desk in the living room, which overlooked the front yard. She could see me on her way up the steps, around six o'clock at night, with my face in the digital glow. I tried to explain myself to her. That this thing had put me in a moral dilemma, the kind you read about, where you have to do something, you have to make a choice. I've got loyalties and duties on opposing sides. I'm trying to think all this through.

"If you've got to do something," she said, "how come all you do is stare at that screen?"

And it's true, there was something unhealthy about my curiosity. I kept finding out new things about my friends, about Nolan's ex-girlfriend for example, in the public media. Clarence's mother used to work at the Hooters in Troy—she was one of these women ballplayers date. And in fact her current husband started out pitching for the Lansing Lugnuts, a Class A affiliate of the Blue Jays, before moving into sales at Daikin. (Korobkin: See, it all comes down to baseball in the end.) But Nolan never mentioned her to me, or the fact that his kid was moving to Arizona. And here I had another source of information.

The media puts people in interesting lights. It shows you angles you don't usually get to see, but there's a kind of glare, like flash photography. Everything looks a little lurid. And you try to square what you find out with what you already know, and it never adds up. So your friends become contradictions, and let's face it, a part of you is always willing to suspect even your best friend of any kind of dubious past or practice. You've got all these grounds for resentment anyway, little doubts and uncertainties, and the news seems to justify them. Tony once glassed somebody in a bar fight and spent the night in jail. The charges were eventually withdrawn. In his journalism days, he got caught up in one of these plagiarism scandals, and lost his job at the *Pittsburgh Post-Gazette*. Pittsburgh is where he went to grad school, his dissertation was on Emerson, he dropped out after two years. These are the kinds of things I learned.

But I was also looking for something else, stories about the five neighborhoods, about Robert James. Because a number of commentators took Nolan's trial as a larger trial of the whole idea. Nolan stood for the old black Detroit, Tony stood for the old white Detroit, I stood for the new guys. It didn't go unnoticed that I was the only one in the clear. There were stories about my guns, too, the Remington and the Smith & Wesson, and my connection to Mel Hauser, and Mel's connection to Tony. But Robert James was like the icing on the cake—since Nolan thought it was *his* kid, and the whole thing started at Robert's big rented house in Indian Village. We saw photographs of this place dressed up in party mode, with the lights on and guests arriving, and pretty waitresses standing in the floor-to-ceiling windows. And I would stare at these photographs, trying to recognize people.

This is a kind of self-obsession, and part of what pissed Gloria off. I wish I could write what happened from her point of view, because something was happening to her, too. For one thing, she got stuck defending me at work. The stories about my guns were particularly upsetting. She didn't know about them. One of them lived under my bed, the handgun was in my sock drawer, but when she stayed over I had no reason to bring them out, and I never mentioned them. I guess I was ashamed. And then there's the fact that I retreated to my bedroom while Nolan and Tony were fighting. People wanted to know what I was doing. Getting a gun? No, just sitting there, keeping out of it. But this didn't look good either. And what about when Tony kicked Nolan in the head and knocked him out. What was I doing then? Nothing, watching, I was too slow. And why did I leave Nolan like that, lying unconscious? Because Tony didn't know the way to his mother's house. Who called the police, who called the ambulance? Tony. What was I doing?

Gloria asked me this, too. She said, "I have to ask you. I get it from all sides. It's what everybody wants to know."

"Trying not to make things worse."

"How much worse could they have been?"

"I've been thinking about that, too. Worse."

"Marny, I don't want to talk about that. I don't want to think about it. You find out things, and you think, who is this person, do I know you?"

"You know me. You know me better than these people who write these stories."

"That's what you keep telling me. But I'm not sure. How come they knew about the guns and I didn't?"

"They weren't important."

"They seem important to me."

All of this might have been easier if she weren't living with me. Sometimes she came out the front door to find photographers in the street. You sort of get used to that but not really. She needed somewhere else to go, she needed to go home, but her home was a construction site. I guess she might have stayed with her mother, but she never got along with her mother, and these days they got along even worse because of me. Her mother was an unusually so- cially conscious person. She cared what strangers thought of her, and her daughter's association with a guy who was in the news for the reasons I was in the news upset her sense of family class. But look, this is all from my point of view. Maybe Eunice just thought I'm an asshole, that's possible, too. Either way, Gloria didn't really want to stay with her, at least while we were still together.

The other problem, and this seems petty in the general context, but I think it mattered, too, was just that damn kitchen. Gloria was under a lot of stress, and she took some of it out on the con- tractor, who was a likable and basically hardworking guy, but not very well organized, and not very good at communicating with clients. So, for example, she ordered a stained beech worktop, but there was a problem with the distributor. It was going to put the job back weeks, so he cut a deal on a stained oak worktop instead, and started cutting it down to size. And told her about it afterwards. This is the kind of thing. Gloria made him go back to square one and refused to reimburse him either for costs or la- bor. Then there was an issue with the gas supply. Her apartment was in an unmodernized and badly maintained building from the 1930s, held together by spit and plaster. When he took out the old oven he started a leak that meant he had to shut down the supply in the whole building to fix it. Which pissed a lot of people off— at Gloria, not at him. After a while he started taking a tone with her, the tone of a reasonable man doing his gentlemanly best with an unreasonable woman, which drove her crazy. And as I say the whole thing dragged on and on.

I don't want to take sides here, maybe I should have taken sides. Workingmen, contractors and plumbers and carpenters, carry a kind of male threat and appeal, which makes it difficult for some men to insist on terms and conditions. I guess I'm one of those men. Also, it wasn't my kitchen, and maybe some part of me felt that Gloria was building her escape hatch or something, I don't know. But you can't stand around watching a guy working hard and competently, doing things you don't know how to do, and then start complaining to him about the difference between stained beech and stained oak, and quibbling over prices. At least I can't.

Gloria wanted from me a little more interest and cooperation, but that's not really what the problem was. The problem ran deeper and didn't have anything to do with the kitchen. People always liked Gloria, she got along with everybody, and suddenly here she was fighting battles on all sides, with people who clearly considered her a difficult personality. With her mother, herself a real professional piece of work. Sniping back and forth with Mrs. Sanchez at school, mostly for my sake. And now she heard herself nagging away at Kevin the Contractor, the kind of slightly shifty good-natured overweight man who usually flirts with her. Somehow she had backed herself into a corner where just to go anywhere in any direction she needed to get her claws out. And I can't help thinking that at a certain point it occurred to her that the corner she was stuck in she was stuck in because of me.

But I don't want to paint everything in bleak and dismal. And the truth is, when I look back on our relationship, these two months stand for what I miss—I mean the months we were living together, in the house I shared with Walter and Susie. At first, over the summer vacation, we all had time on our hands. But later, when Gloria started going back to school, I used to walk her part of the way just to make sure I got out of bed in the morning. When the weather was nice; otherwise she drove. We kissed on a street corner and I watched her go, my working woman, dressed in her own version of a school uniform, the simple skirts and high socks, clean shoes, a collared shirt or blouse. I say uniform because I knew her well enough by this point to realize that even her natural modesty, good humor and kindness were a form of protection, against strangers and kids, against the world, against anybody who didn't love her, which makes up a high percentage of the total. So my heart went out to her as she kicked through the leaves.

On my short walk home I thought about what to make for dinner and sometimes picked up a few things on the way—from Annie's Corner Store, some hippie-dippie hole-in-the-wall grocer that had just sprung up. Or I got in the car and drove out to Greenfield Market, which was more of a hassle but cheaper and took up more of my day. That was the main benefit. Money didn't worry me much at that time. I had put a lot by from teaching the previous year. And I also had some vague sense that the way we were living couldn't last. So I thought about money like it was food on a plate, something you enjoy and finish off.

Fall came late and mild. Detroit always has a summer mosquito problem, but Gloria and I kept getting bitten deep into October. At night the street lamps shone like sunshine in the yellow leaves. We left our bedroom window open, but the reading lamp attracted bugs, and Gloria had sweet blood—she got bitten more than I did. At least the mosquitoes still like me, she said. She got bitten once on her chest, just where a pendant might hang, on the visible skin between her breasts. Gloria didn't want to scratch it because the scab would show, but sometimes when we were in bed together, making out, she got this unbearable wriggly kind of itch. She made me scratch it for her, and it was kind of a sensual delight, and also kind of not. It was more childish than that and a distraction from the other thing. So when I tried to kiss her she just said, no, don't stop, scratch it there, there, there. I mention this just as an example. We didn't always fight.

And even our fights felt like the real thing. We were living together, we were lovers, and we were working out some deep strife between us, which is what lovers should do. Gloria wanted me *not* to testify against Nolan. She wanted me to take sides—against the whole idea, against the rest of us. Let Tony and Nolan fight it out; it's their fight. I said the only thing I can do is tell the truth, anything else will get me into trouble. "It's not that simple," she said, "and don't take this the wrong way, but I'm not that worried about you." It wasn't just a question of what had happened. There was a context, there were consequences. "You have to work out what *you* want to happen," she said. "Because what you say is going to have an effect on that. You have to work out what you think Nolan deserves."

"This is too complicated for me, Gloria. They're going to ask me some questions, I'm going to give them some answers. That's all. It's really not up to me."

"Excuse me, no. That's like a Yalie's point of view, because you basically trust the system. You think, all I have to do is tell the truth, so help me God. But the system doesn't work, so it's a question of getting from it something you can live with. I mean, what's Nolan looking at? Life with parole. Ten years. Four years. Think about Clarence. Because whatever it is, he'll have to live with it, too."

"You want me to lie for him."

"I want you to make the right thing happen."

"That's not my job. They've got judges and lawyers working this thing out."

"You mean, the people who let Tyler Waites hit a young black man with his *car*. For stealing his *phone*."

"I can't talk to you when you're like this," I said. "You're identifying me with people I've got nothing to do with."

"These are the people asking you questions. I just want you to think very carefully about your answers."

"I'm thinking, I'm thinking."

"Think harder," she said.

I told myself, this is just the friction that produces the heat. We were working out whether to align ourselves. It's supposed to be painful, like a slipped disk—you have to learn how to move again. I said this to Gloria, too, but she wasn't convinced.

34

Nolan's trial moved from the district court to the circuit court. There was a motion hearing, to determine admissible evidence, and I went along to see what everyone had to say. The Frank Murphy Hall of Justice looks a little like a parking garage built in the 1970s, concrete with horizontal windows and those broad courthouse steps you need in the movies, to show the defendant tumbling down them into freedom or trapped halfway up by reporters.

Inside the place was done up in brown and beige. Everything was carefully coordinated, brown tables and chairs, beige walls, brown carpeting, nothing that shows stains. I guess the idea is to depress people into submission. The judge was an overweight black woman; her accent ranged from sonorous to nitpicky. A placard on the table in front of her had her name on it: Judge Liz Westinghouse. It seemed funny to me that she used her nickname—I tried to work out what that meant. Maybe her full name didn't fit. But she had also clearly acquired what the self-improvement gurus try to sell you, strength of personality. When she came in people rose, when she sat down people sat.

Mostly what happened was procedural stuff, and not very interesting. There wasn't much evidence in dispute. Nolan's lawyers wanted to argue that the kid was in the street, wandering around—not in the house or the garden or the driveway. Apparently one of the cops overheard Nolan in hospital saying something about the guys working on the front gate, which seemed at least an indication of his general vicinity. But his lawyers wanted to rule these comments inadmissible—the guy had been kicked in the head, he was just waking up. There was also some dispute about whether or not the cop had read him his Miranda rights before or after Nolan said what he said or what he was alleged to have said.

I found the whole business both depressing and impressive. All this attention to detail. You realize pretty quickly that you are in the hands of massive but at the same time small-scale forces. It's like being overrun by ants. Afterwards what you get is not facts exactly or truth or anything like that—there's no reason to think that the real facts or the real truth is best adapted to surviving this process. I mean, I was there, I saw a lot of what happened, but I don't know how much of what I saw or thought would have counted with these people, the lawyers. But there are certain kinds of information that do survive. It's like those urban myths about nuclear holocaust, the only thing left is cockroaches. But that's not quite what I mean either. There's a kind of reproach you feel, in seeing firsthand these competent, expensively trained people do their work. Like, on what basis do I live my life? Can it withstand this kind of scrutiny? No, not really. But I also heard in the back of my mind what my brother might have said if he were watching—that some of these guys were second-rate.

Nolan was there, too. I saw his shaved head. Even he seemed cowed. Sometimes he turned and whispered something in his lawyer's ear. And afterwards, on our way out, I caught his eye, and he gave me a look like, here we go, buddy.

A FEW DAYS LATER THE aluminum story broke in the business pages of *The New York Times*:

Hundreds of millions of times a day, thirsty Americans open a
can of soda, beer or juice. And every time they do it, they pay a
fraction of a penny more because of a shrewd maneuver by Goldman Sachs and other financial players that ultimately costs con-
sumers billions of dollars.

The story of how this works begins in a complex of warehouses in Detroit where a Goldman subsidiary stores customers'
aluminum. Each day, a fleet of trucks shuffles 1,500-pound bars
of the metal among the warehouses. Two or three times a day,
sometimes more, the drivers make the same circuits. They load
in one warehouse. They unload in another. And then they do it
again.

This industrial dance has been choreographed by Goldman
to exploit pricing regulations set up by an overseas commodities exchange, an investigation by *The New York Times* has
found. The back-and-forth lengthens the storage time. And
that adds many millions a year to the coffers of Goldman,
which charges rent to store the metal.

The writer was a guy called Kocieniewski; I looked him up. A
Buffalo kid, he used to work at *The Detroit News*. Most of his article was about the London Metal Exchange, its corporate structure
(Goldman used to be on the board), and the protocols for storing
precious metals. "Industry rules require that metal cannot simply
sit in a warehouse forever," Kocieniewski wrote. "At least 3,000 tons
must be moved out each day. But most of the metal stored in Detroit is not being delivered to customers; instead, it is shuttled from
one warehouse to another."

Two days later someone at the National desk picked up the story
and connected it to Robert James. The headline was gently tongue-
in-cheek: "Detroit Scheme Makes Profit, by Sitting on Its Assets."

Robert James describes it as the "Groupon model" for gentri-fication. "We take a virtual community and make it real," he said last year at the shiny new Wayne Conner Server Farm, at a fund-raiser attended by President Obama. There were ques-tions from the beginning about how the economics stacked up, but now it appears that Goldman Sachs, one of James's "team of investors," has been buying warehouses in the devel-oped neighborhoods to store aluminum . . .

So Steve Zipp was right. Maybe he was crazy but he was right. Then *Time* magazine ran an article on us, "Utopian Vision Faces Real-world Politics and Problems," which covered not only the aluminum scandal but also the Meacher incident and Nolan's trial. The journalist wanted to know whether the Goldman deal was funding the neighborhood project or whether the neighborhoods were just window dressing for a commodities scam. Beatrice didn't worry much about the difference—the article quoted her. "This maybe matters to you people," she said, "but I don't have time for philosophical distinctions. We're trying to do something good here. If Goldman broke the law, then the law should step in. Otherwise, I don't see what the problem is."

The problem was, as she explained to me herself one afternoon, that regulators planned to change the law and close one of the loopholes—three thousand tons turns out to be a pretty low min-imum for the amount of metal warehouses have to shift each day. "Goldman's one of our biggest investors," she told me. "If they lose their financial incentive, we're screwed."

"Why are you telling me all this?"

She hadn't stopped by the house in months, I figured she had given up on me. So if she came by now there was probably a motive—she wanted something. "I'm just keeping you in the pic-ture," she said. "It's your picture, too."

"Look, I should tell you something. I knew about this beforehand. I may have mentioned it to Nolan."

It was a cold prewinter day. I like this time of year, two weeks before Thanksgiving. The trees were leafless, the sun came in from every angle. Through my kitchen window, you could feel the light being translated into heat. Gloria had lent me her Gaggia, until the work was finished in her apartment, and I made some coffee. Beatrice looked important and attractive, a busy person, while I stood around in my jogging shorts.

"Nolan's not the problem here," Beatrice said. "But we need this money. If Goldman backs out, we have to make up the difference somewhere. And that will probably mean selling houses—speeding up the process. Which takes away control, it turns the whole thing into an open market. People will start selling, they'll start buying, you'll be living on a street with real estate signs in the yard."

"Is that a problem?"

"It depends what you want. But I don't think it's what you want. This place isn't ready yet. You need a culture—markets depend on cultures. But markets don't make cultures, you have to engineer them. That's what we've been trying to do. The health care, the ratio of shops and houses, the parks and schools, but you know all that. Handpicking tenants, different kinds of people, getting commitments from them. If they sell up now, in two years' time we'll be back where we started. At least, that's my best guess. There's also concern about what happens if this case goes to trial."

"What do you mean, if?"

"The only thing that makes sense, and I mean that from Nolan's point of view, is a plea bargain. Otherwise he's looking at some very scary possibilities."

"So he should make a deal."

"His lawyers say he doesn't want to—he wants his day in court.

And we've got our own concerns about that. This case has already attracted a lot of bad publicity. The last thing anybody wants is a courtroom drama."

"Except for Nolan."

"In that case, Nolan has a very limited conception of his self-interest."

"Is that what you want to talk to me about?"

"Marny, we're talking because we're talking. I'm worried about the trial, but I didn't come here with motives. I'm proud of you. You're one of the success stories, you're one of the people holding this thing together. Teaching at a local high school, living with Gloria."

I looked at her and she said, "You know what I mean."

"Well, I haven't been teaching this year."

"I heard that, too."

Afterwards I went for a run and tried to work out what she wanted from me—that I should talk to Nolan. Or maybe she didn't want anything, I was just being paranoid. Running gives you a mild high, thoughts dislodge themselves, things occur to you, and it occurred to me that I had come a long way from the kid I was, that I was doing all right. Beatrice had spotted this and pointed it out. Either way that's what she meant. I had become a point of contact between opposing views, somebody she could turn to for help. And maybe she was right about Nolan's self-interest, too. You can't dismiss an argument just because you don't trust or share the motive of the person who makes it. Also, I basically *did* trust Beatrice. She always left a scent behind in a room, not just her perfume. She was somebody you naturally wanted to please, and that had a kind of aftereffect.

GLORIA TRIED TO BREAK UP with me as soon as her kitchen was ready. "You just used me for my appliances," I joked. But that's not really what was going on. There was a coincidence of events. Without telling me Astrid had uploaded the video of us having sex onto her website, along with a lot of other stuff: more of her videos, photographs of Detroit, etc. Maybe she told me, maybe I knew, I don't know. Later she said, which was true, that the deal always was, whatever I video, I can use. Anyway, I stopped thinking about it. In some ways I'm not a very private person. There's a lot of stuff you're supposed to care about that I don't. But somebody found the link and tweeted it, at which point the video went twittering around—a really inexplicable number of people watched it. I could write down a number but it keeps changing, even now. Gloria came home from school one day and showed it to me. Some of her kids had seen it.

"I don't know if I'm more embarrassed or upset," she said.

"I think you're more upset."

"That's a very stupid thing to be a part of. Don't tell me what I feel. You don't want to know what I feel. I'll tell you what I feel. You spend all day trying not to shout at the kids and then I come home and try not to shout at you. When I got in the car I just thought, that's enough. Nobody's happy anymore. What's the point."

"I'm happy," I said. "This is my happy face."

"Don't play games, Marny, I'm not."

We talked a lot more than that, we said stupid things. She started packing up to go home. Just give me a couple of weeks to get my head on straight, she said. But she kept thinking about that video—she wanted to know when it was shot.

"Listen, Gloria. Don't think about it. It's upsetting, but it's got nothing to do with us. I know you've had sex with other people, you know I've had sex with other people, but we don't want to think about it. This makes you think about it, I understand that. But it's not important."

"It's not just this, it's Nolan, it's everything. I just need a break. I don't want to fight you all the time."

We held on a little longer after that. She stayed the night and left in the morning and moved back into her apartment. But we kept seeing each other—a little less often than before.

The last thing we did as a couple was try to talk Nolan out of standing trial. It's strange that on this major source of conflict and disagreement, we ended up briefly on the same side. It was like an intervention; his mother was there, too, and we sat in their kitchen and one by one we said, please don't do this thing. Everybody (except for Nolan) was extremely emotional. I felt very close to Gloria, to all of them. I was really at the heart of something, sitting in that family kitchen and debating with these people something so important and intimate, where the decisions you reach collectively have real consequences. But we didn't reach any collective decisions because Nolan shut us out. He sat there, he took it, but he didn't say much.

The best deal he could get was four years, which might mean closer to two in practice. That's what Larry Oh was offering him. If the case went to trial, he could end up with a life sentence— maybe he gets out on parole after fifteen years. Nolan was pissed off, among other things, that Oh had decided not to press charges against Tony for assault. He planned to sue Tony, after the criminal case resolved itself, for medical damages and general psychological suffering. But he was having a hard time finding a litigator to take on the case—Nolan saw a conspiracy in this, too.

Gloria was often in tears; Mrs. Smith was in tears. She brought out cake and coffee, but I was the only one who ate anything. Nolan made his own coffee.

"I don't need to tell you this," I said, "but there's a big difference between two years and fifteen years. Right now every option looks bad. I know it must be hard to choose between outcomes you don't want and can't even really imagine. But that's what you have to do. Two years means Clarence is nine when you get out. Fifteen years means he's twenty-two. The difference is basically his whole childhood."

"You haven't been reading the papers," Nolan said. "Clarence is in Arizona. And seriously, what chance do you think I have to get him back if I go to jail?"

"I don't think you have a chance now."

"I want to know what lawyers you're talking to—where you get your information. Did Robert James talk you into this? Because he doesn't want to see me in court, I can tell you that. A trial gives me a platform, it gives me a voice."

"Nolan, you know what it's like in there. Everything gets twisted. You never get to say what you want to say, and even if you do it won't come out the way you want it to."

"We'll see about that. This is really just a game of chicken. Larry Oh says four years or life, but they can do better than that. Robert James won't let this get to trial."

"I don't think Robert has anything to do with it."

"Please, Marny. He sent you here, didn't he?"

"No," I said.

But afterwards Gloria told me, this is one of the things that made up her mind. Not because of what Nolan said. He was going crazy, she could see that, he didn't make sense, he was fighting all kinds of battles he didn't need to fight. It's hard when you go through something like this to pay attention to what matters. But for her it was simple. We were all sitting around the kitchen table, and she realized (about me), he's not helping, I wish he wasn't here.

Everything had an effect. There was a lot of unpleasantness in the news. Somebody picked up on Walter's story, too, on the situation with Susie, and the fact that we were living in the same house turned into another couple of paragraphs on *Gawker*. What had happened to Meacher and Waites and Nolan and Tony was happening to me—when the news cycle spins you around, everything gets dirty. Then one Saturday morning a photographer papped Gloria coming out of my house and she just started running, crying and running until the end of the block. She knocked on Mrs. Smith's door, and they talked and then she came back for her car. That was the last time she came to my apartment. When I saw her again that night, at her apartment, I carried over a shopping bag of her stuff.

Breaking up is one of those dramatic things you do, it brings out a lot of grandstanding. It's like a license to say things. So I said some things I half regret.

My dad once told me, you've got this confessional streak, but no real desire to explain yourself. (A friend of mine broke the garage window by kicking a soccer ball against it, and I went straight in to take the blame.) Gloria was leaving me anyway, so I told her about my one-night stand with Astrid. I didn't want to give her the impression I had nothing to be ashamed of. It was complicated. The video was stupid and pointless, and I told her it didn't mean anything, but if she found out later what had happened, it could do real damage—I mean, after all that protested innocence. So I told her now. I said to her, look, this is over, you've made that clear, but I want a clean break, because I plan to win you back, that's my plan. I figured she was already disgusted with me; a little more couldn't hurt.

But I miscalculated. "Why are you telling me this?" she said. "I don't want to know, I don't want to know." And later, "I made myself very vulnerable to you." That seemed a weird way of putting it—it stuck in my mind for a long time.

35

Christmas was next, and this time my mother came to stay. To cheer me up, she said. A year ago everything looked better, everything was starting out. I had a girlfriend, I had a job, and my mother was married to my father. Of course, she had her own reasons for getting out of Dodge. She couldn't face Brad's family, Christmas with his wife in Houston, waking up in the spare bedroom, and watching her son go through what we all went through together, when she had a central role to play. So she came to me.

I gave her my bedroom and slept on the couch. But we got in each other's hair. Mom was scared to go out in Detroit by herself, even sightseeing, even in the afternoon. Nothing will happen to you at the Institute of Arts, I said. But she answered, "I've heard the stories." So she dragged me along with her, because the truth is, I didn't have anything else to do. We saw the Rivera murals, the Moscow Ballet was in town, so we went to *The Nutcracker* at Caesars Windsor, I took her around Belle Isle. Being a tourist is tiring, but when you go with your mom you kind of reenact the old relationship, even if it isn't true or real anymore. Anyway, none of this lightened my mood.

While she was staying I got another letter from my father. It was mostly about himself, this was turning into his big subject; he wanted to explain himself again. In the past six months, ever since moving out, he had realized the burden my mother placed on him. She's a very negative person, he said, and he hadn't realized until it was pointed out to him, by a very smart younger person, what family life had done to his personality. Young people these days, he went on, don't have the hang-ups I did, they don't feel any false obligations. And so on.

"What's he say?" my mother asked.

"Nothing much, just day-to-day stuff."

"If he's unhappy I want you to tell me, I want to know."

"I think he's all right," I said.

One night I went to see Astrid—I had to get out of the house. I'd been trying to call her for several weeks, but she didn't answer her phone. Finally, I sent her an email, and she wrote back. Her phone was dead; she had closed out the contract. She was leaving in the morning, flying to Germany for Christmas and not coming back. But I could watch her pack up if I wanted to. So my mom made me supper, and afterwards I drove over to Astrid's apartment, in one of those survivor row houses by the old train station.

All night long there was this stream of people coming through. It was a very unsatisfying visit. I guess I was hoping to pick a fight but she wasn't in the mood. So I just sat on her two-seater couch, drinking red wine and offering the bottle to newcomers when they walked in. Astrid was stressed out but also clearly on a kind of high, kissing everybody, crying lightly, giving things away—paintings, DVDs and CDs, bottles of alcohol and clothes. "I want to go home with what I can carry in a duffel bag," she said, again and again and again. I'm sure that some of the people coming through recognized me from the video link. It was embarrassing and depressing and every time I saw this woman she annoyed me and attracted me at the same time.

"I don't understand how you can just leave," I said to her at one point.

"I have had my experience here. It's like when you work on a picture, and then you say it's done, you have to do something else."

This is the kind of thing.

I wanted to have some real conversation with her, about the video, about Gloria, about something. I wanted to tell her, we can't see each other anymore, we can't hang out. But this was obviously pointless, and at least I figured that out. When I left she gave me a *Sesame Street* kid's book, the tiny hard kind you can loop to a baby stroller. *Bert and Ernie's Sleepytime Book.* "I bought it for my niece months ago; she's really too old for it. That's what happens when you go away. They grow up. My sister says, she walks everywhere now. You can have it," she said and scribbled something inside the cover with a felt-tip pen.

In the bleak overhead car light, feeling drunk, I read her inscription: *From Astrid, for the long nights . . .*

My mother was asleep when I got home, so I turned on my computer and started messing around online. After a few minutes, I looked up the video link. I sat on my sofa, with the computer on my lap, and watched us make love. Astrid was crying and I kept going and afterwards we held on to each other. I don't know what I felt looking at her, you could see her breasts hanging down a little shapelessly, she had small breasts and sat on top. But one thing I did feel was turned on. It was a stupid physical reaction, but I was also very lonely at the time, and I needed some outlet or expression for my intensity of feelings. And this was it.

All night long I left the windows open, but in the morning the living room still smelled of bedclothes.

"What are you doing to yourself?" my mother asked, over breakfast.

My heart skipped a beat. "What do you mean?" I said.

"It's freezing in here."

On Christmas Day, Walter and Susie invited us downstairs. Everybody else got along, but I behaved badly. It was kind of a make-fun-of-Marny party. Susie did most of the cooking and she wasn't a good cook. The turkey was dry in places and pink in others; the mash potatoes tasted salty and lumpy. There was too much food as well and it sat around on the dishes afterwards, and on people's plates, showing the oil. I don't think anybody cared. They just got drunk, even Susie, and there was an atmosphere of conviviality based on the idea that Walter and I were good friends, and Susie loved Walter and my mother loved me, so we all loved each other.

But I was in a bad way. I wanted to be elsewhere, and rejected all conversational approaches and offers of sympathy. Also, it didn't help seeing Walter and Susie together, basically happy.

That night my mother said to me, "I don't think you realize how much work it takes to put together a meal like that. It's getting everything into the oven at different times, and getting them out at the same time. You could have showed a little appreciation."

"I said several times how delicious everything was."

"That's not what I mean. It's not what you say, people just want you to have a good time."

"Some things are outside my control."

"You can make an effort. And maybe after a while it won't feel like such an effort anymore."

"What you don't realize is, that was an effort. That was me making an effort."

"What I saw is you picking fights."

And it's true, at one point I lost my temper. Walter said something about Gloria; he had spoken to her on the phone. He remembered that I once met a friend of hers who worked for an adoption agency in Southfield. Susie and he wanted to adopt.

"What kind of kid? A black kid?"

"Is that possible?" my mother asked.

"With these guys, it is," Walter said. "They're Lutherans."

"And what did Gloria say?"

"She was very obliging."

"Don't call her again," I said.

"What did you do to her?"

"Nothing. I just don't want to hear about her, I don't want you to talk to her. I don't want you people to have any relations with her when I don't."

"Well, why don't you?"

"Oh, leave me alone," I said.

Afterwards, my mother was always first to make up. She nagged at me, she niggled at me, but she couldn't stay mad for long—she felt too anxious. That was probably bad for me, too. I started indulging myself in teenage sulks.

But it was too much, her sympathy. I couldn't breathe. She looks like me, too, pale and earnest, like someone who doesn't understand a joke but is trying her best. Explain it to me, her face said. Instead I watched TV or I watched her cook and after two weeks she couldn't take it anymore.

"What I can't bear is the idea that this was a failure."

"Two weeks is a long time," I said. "We're not used to each other now."

"That's just what I mean."

But she flew home on New Year's Eve—the flights were cheaper. "I'll come back for the trial," she said. And after she left I felt surprisingly cheerful, cheerful in the old way, I mean. Like a college kid flying back after Christmas vacation, to his dorm room or apartment, to his old new life. But I had good days and bad days—good weeks and bad weeks.

One night, my brother gave me a call.

"You survived her," he said.

"She was all right. She loves me."

"Even I love you. Did you know all that about Nolan?"

"What," I said.

"I talked to Korobkin. It's not just the kid, Nolan has credit card debts. There are lovers, he's been leading two or three lives. Irreconcilable lives. I see this stuff all the time in my pro bono work. Immigrant families, fucked-up dads, guys under a lot of pressure doing fucked-up things. What you have to realize is that for some people private life is a different kind of reality."

"What's that got to do with anything."

"I thought I should warn you. This thing is going to get personal, they're going to come after you."

"Who is? I don't understand what you're talking about."

"His lawyers."

"*Whose* lawyers?"

"Listen, Greg. There's only one way this goes to trial—if Nolan's lawyers think they can make a reasonable case for his innocence. They have to turn this into a misunderstanding. Tony says one thing, he says another. The problem is you—you're the only real witness. And if you don't tell the story the way they want you to tell it, they'll come after you. That's all I'm saying. You should be prepared."

"Okay, so you told me. I'm prepared."

But he changed his tone. "What are you going to do now?"

"What do you mean?"

"I mean, what do you do with yourself these days?"

"I'm going to clear up the kitchen and turn on the TV. Then I'm going to bed. That's what I do."

But the truth is I was watching a lot of porn. I had never done this before, at least not online, and didn't know where to look. In high school one of my D&D buddies had access to the Playboy channel through his father's account—his parents were divorced. But it didn't interest me much; I felt embarrassed, especially in front of the other boys. But this time there was nobody around. I started out with Tyler Waites's website and that led me to other things. It was amazing, the variety on offer, all these sophisticated tastes. I remembered something Nolan said. There is no human nature, just economics. Supply and demand.

The picture quality was usually pretty bad, but that seemed part of the appeal—you could never get a good enough look. You always wanted to be closer. And between you and what you wanted was this screen.

One of the things you learn growing up is that adult pleasures are more complicated than they look. Even beer is an acquired taste; it takes getting used to. And watching porn turns out to be hard work. Most sexual imagery is pain imagery; the sounds are also sounds of pain. For some reason I could concentrate on these images. Because concentration is what it was: the rest of the time I felt distracted, I tried to read and put down my book, I fell asleep in front of the TV. But at two a.m. I could stay awake, watching a woman lying naked on her back in bed, with her legs up in the air, while a man pressed himself between her legs, so that you could see his buttocks instead of her pubic hair. I was very unhappy, that was clear to me even at the time, but I also felt some kind of connection with people. Not just with the women, the actors. All across America, and not only America, there are men on their own occupying themselves in this way—looking for something and straining towards it, unsatisfied. And I was one of them.

If you go to bed at midnight and get out of bed, after a broken night, at ten or eleven in the morning, that still leaves thirteen or fourteen hours of waking time to account for. Eating doesn't take long if you eat alone and I never felt hungry—I ate out of a kind of duty to something. But I didn't feel many duties. The pressure to appear a certain way to other people had started to fade. I almost never saw anyone, apart from Walter. The things he went through for Susie, not just with her but on his own, the decisions he must have come to, his private battles—I began to get a sense of them. He had come out on the other side. But I was still in the middle. Something important had failed or was failing and I needed to deal with it, I needed to think it through.

I lived like this for three months, hardly leaving my apartment. Going quietly crazy, Walter called it, but making progress. I started reading again, with more attention. I read *Walden* again, I read *Invisible Man. Native Son, Go Tell It on the Mountain, Stover at Yale.* High school staples like *The Awakening* and *Huck Finn.* Walter gave me a 1942 edition of *Say, Is This the U.S.A.* and I spent a week looking through the photographs and reading the captions, frequently in tears. The men and women in those pictures are probably dead now, even some of the kids. There were passages in each of these books that seemed tremendously important. I thought, other people need to know about this. But they'd obviously been given the chance and it hadn't made much difference.

When you don't do much, when you don't go anywhere, you notice small changes. In yourself and other people, in the world outside your window. The snow that started in late November kept accumulating—one inch, and then another, and then a few more. Mild fall, harsh winter. None of it had anywhere to go, it just piled up. I used to watch the kids play in the street. After particularly heavy nights, school would be canceled, the cold and ice made everything resound, the whole world seemed like their temporary playground. But then on other days, everyone stayed indoors. Cars sat parked on islands of frozen slush; the snow on their roofs was the last thing to stay white.

The Adlers moved out in February. Don knocked on my door, while Tina finished packing. There was a U-Haul van in his driveway.

"We're getting out now," he said. "We're not going to wait around for bad news."

"What bad news?"

"Whatever form it takes. I've got that prestorm feeling. This time I'm going to listen to it. Also, it's too cold here. It's just too cold."

"So where are you going, back to Phoenix?"

"I never liked it there. Somewhere else. Maybe Austin, but it's expensive now. These hipster types have a lot to answer for. Everywhere you used to find a decent quality of life, they come and drive up the price. The first place we're going is South Bend, where the in-laws are. Then we put some things into storage. I've got too much stuff, I don't use any of it. Then we make up our mind. Okay, well. So long," he said, and I watched him cross the road flat-footed, taking care on the ice.

36

Nolan's trial came at the right time for me. It snapped me out of myself, it forced me to make contact with people.

A form letter arrived from the prosecutor's office: "Being called to testify in court may make you nervous. This is a natural reaction . . ." One of their suggestions was to ask for a copy of my police statement and read it over beforehand. Which I did—it gave me a buzz to see my words officially documented. They had an air of authority, and I found it hard to remember what had actually happened, as opposed to what I had sworn to. There are all these processes that remove us from the past, step by step, and writing is part of the process. "Dress neatly," the letter said. I shaved, I wore my leather shoes, I tucked my shirt in. And for three days, the days of my court appearances, I woke up each morning as if I had a job to do and left the house looking presentable.

My mother offered to fly into town. I told her, "Mom, you don't have to do this, you don't have to hold my hand."

"What else do I do with myself?" she said.

"You were just here a few months ago. Come some other time. Come when I have time to see you. I'll be at the courthouse all day, waiting around."

"I can wait with you."

So we went back and forth like that, and after a while I said, "Let me do this alone," and she said, "Okay."

Robert picked me up on my first day, which was day three of the trial. Somehow he had gotten a pass for the courthouse parking lot. He honked outside the house in his Saab 9-5, on one of those pissy cold transitional mornings, not freezing but thawing, where it sort of rains off and on but it doesn't make much difference either way. Robert had the heating going pretty well; he sat there with his shirtsleeves rolled up to the elbow. You could see his forearms— instead of rowing these days, he worked out on an erg machine. There was a car seat in the back and food wrappings and bits of food all over the floor. I sat down on an empty bag of baby wipes.

"How's it going?" I said.

"Oh, this is just what it's always like. This is just the usual chaos."

"No, I mean the trial." He thought I meant the state of his car and life.

"Mostly what I've seen is procedural stuff. It's not like I hang around all day. Jury selection, that kind of thing. The truth is, I don't know what his lawyers are thinking. It's their job to make sure this doesn't come to court. If you've got a client who wants to have his say, you let him say it to you. You don't let him say it to a judge and jury, especially given the way Nolan is likely to come across."

"What does that mean?"

"Look, Marny. I'm sympathetic to him. But if he were my client, he's not a guy I'd like to put on the stand."

"He always struck me as pretty persuasive."

"All right," Robert said. "Let it go."

The downtown traffic is never very heavy in Detroit, but there was some buildup along Gratiot, and even more when he turned onto St. Antoine: a queue of cars outside the parking lot, which was separated by a chain-link fence from the road, and already half full. We got stuck for a minute behind some media van, whose driver had pulled over to unload equipment. Eventually Robert drove around him and down a side street and parked in one of the spaces slanted against a bay in the building.

"There's something else I wanted to talk to you about," he said. "You're going to notice some extra security around. I don't want you to worry about it. There are people I pay to give me advice, and this is the advice they give me, so I listen. But I'm not really worried."

"What kind of security?"

"A few extra patrol cars, private security cars. As long as the trial lasts, there'll be two guys in chairs on either end of your street. Just to see who comes and goes. That's all. Well, here we go."

Robert took me inside by a back entrance, through the metal detectors, up some steps and around some corners, down through administrative-looking hallways and then into a slightly grander hallway, where one of the news crews was setting up. I left him by the entrance to the courtroom—he wanted to get a good seat. But there were officers of the court I had to show my papers to, and I ended up, about a half hour later, in some waiting room for witnesses.

I spent a lot of time in that room. It wasn't very big and had carpeting and stippled paneling on the ceilings and one of those water kegs that glugs from time to time. There were two posters on the wall: *River in a Mountain Landscape*, by John Mix Stanley, which showed not so much a river as a kind of swampy dead end or pond in front of a couple of hills. The other poster was a team photo of the '88–'89 Detroit Pistons, who won the NBA Championship when I was fourteen or fifteen. It made me feel one of those weird overlaps or crossovers or connections between selves, and I started going through the roster to see who I could remember. There were three names I didn't know, Jim Rowinski, Pace Mannion and Fennis Dembo. When I got up to stretch my legs I often walked over to this poster and tried to work out who was who.

People in the room came and went—they got called up, they walked out, they came back. The prosecutor's office had assigned me a witness coordinator, who checked in from time to time. She was an attractive, disorganized woman named Sharia. Mostly when I saw her she had coffee in one hand, papers in another, two tote bags on the same shoulder, that kind of thing.

I said, "Sharia, like the law."

"Nobody ever said that to me before."

But I liked her; we talked. She had dropped out of law school after getting pregnant. Now the kid was two and she wanted to go back to school but couldn't afford it. I heard a lot of her life story— she spilled that out, too. I had time on my hands and didn't much like my book. That's another thing the prosecutor's letter told me. Bring reading material, but I should have brought a pack of cards. I felt too distracted to read. Sharia had other things to do. "I can't stand around all day shooting the breeze," she said. It's amazing how time continues to pass even if you don't have the mental attention to occupy yourself. It passes anyway.

Then Tony showed up, in a suit and tie—black shirt, maroon tie. I hadn't seen much of Tony since the arraignment. It's not like we felt guilty or complicit or anything. It's more like we'd had a kind of gay impulse, which we both experienced but were embarrassed by afterwards. I don't mean that that's what happened but that's what it was like. But I was glad to see him. He looked well, skinny and strong. His suit looked tight on him, and I said, "You look good."

"I've been hitting the weights."

"I don't think that's what you need."

"What do you think I need?"

"I don't know. Nothing."

There was a joke on the tip of my tongue, anger management, but it was a stupid joke and anyway I didn't want to piss him off. I said, "This whole thing has taken up a surprising amount of head space. It must have been worse for you."

"Cris is the one who's really on edge. We've been fighting a lot. She doesn't know who to get mad at, so she takes it out on me. But Nolan is high on her shit list, too. She's mad at all of us, and it was just getting better, it was just getting like we could forget about it, when this comes along."

We broke for lunch, and then we came back and waited some more. Tony and I talked desultorily, as they used to call it in the books. At first there were uncomfortable silences but we waited so long they got comfortable again. I could say things to him if I wanted to or not if I didn't. He felt the same. At one point he said, "This is what everybody dreams of. My day in court. What kind of society do we live in, where this is something people want?"

"Nobody wants this."

"I'll tell you something, Marny, I do. I want to say my say."

A little while later the sheriff or orderly or whatever the hell he's called called him in, and I had to wait out the afternoon by myself, and another morning, I had to sit through another catered lunch, before I could say mine.

WHEN THEY CALLED ME IN, I can't deny it, I felt excited; it was like stepping up to the plate in a softball game. They led me through a corridor into a room. My impressions at this point became a little confused. There seemed to be a lot of lights and people. You could feel their body heat and the wattage heat, and since the room itself wasn't very big, the atmosphere tasted low on oxygen. I looked for windows but there weren't any, just some kind of vinyl wall paneling, which went with the plastic/wooden tables and desks, and the beige carpeting.

Liz Westinghouse was the first face I recognized. She sat at the front of the room, a little raised up, in a leather office chair; she was leaning forward, resting her weight on a lectern. But I also saw Robert James on my way in, against a wall. Beatrice sat next to him; I kept turning my head. The truth is, there wasn't much room, there weren't that many people. Nolan was sandwiched by a couple of lawyers, one white, one black. They had their papers on a table. Nolan wore a gray suit. There was a cop by the witness box and a cop by the exit, and for the first time it hit me (I don't know how to put this without sounding stupid) that we had taken up our official positions. Nolan was on trial, I was a witness, and when I sat down I noticed Gloria in one of the rows of chairs.

Then everything happened like it happens on TV. They gave me a Bible to hold, they swore me in. You say the words and wait for something to change. It's like you believe in magic. In fact, there was a little magic. I felt nervous before, and afterwards somehow the nervousness deepened, which made me calmer on the surface. Then there was a kind of administrative pause. Some of the lawyers looked through their papers, they talked to each other, not in low voices; the judge said something to a woman sitting a few feet below her and typing at a computer. And I tried to get my head on straight. I looked at Gloria and she looked back at me, but without communication. Her look had the privacy of a stranger, and the distance between us was big enough (with the lights in my eyes), she might have figured I was staring into space. But if it was a staring contest, she won, because I turned away.

On my left hand, against another wall—it was an odd-shaped room, with six or seven sides—the jury sat in rows. Two black guys and one black woman, a total of eight women and six men—I counted. There must have been a couple of alternates. The youngest-looking juror looked like Steffi Graf, but not as pretty. She had worse skin. The oldest had cornrows. He sat up real straight and looked strong and frail at the same time. The overwhelming impression made by everything—I don't mean just the jurors, but the public, the lawyers, the judge, the cops, everybody in the room, the furniture, the lighting system, the vinyl paneling—was a kind of intense boredom, a careful, painful, necessary boredom, which only the lawyers seemed used to. That's why they talked in their ordinary voices and sometimes laughed at office jokes.

Then Larry Oh stood up—he had decided to take on the case himself, instead of farming it out to one of his staff. He shuffled his papers and put them down, and walked over to me, like you might walk over to someone you know in a bar. In fact, I did know him slightly. We had worked on my witness statement together, but I saw him first on TV at the Elwood Bar & Grill. After a while, when this kind of thing keeps happening, the lines get blurred, everything feels connected. What you read in the papers, what you see on TV, your life. Larry Oh wasn't fat exactly but had one of those boyish faces that suggests a boy's figure, which he didn't have. But he moved pretty well and dressed to hide his weight.

He asked some questions, I answered them. It was like dancing with a guy who can dance, you just follow his lead, and Oh took me slowly through the day. Tony picking me up, dropping his kid at Robert's house, coming back from lunch to find him missing. Driving the streets, running into Nolan at my house, getting everybody inside. Then he said, "I want you to explain what made you leave the room."

"Nolan wouldn't tell us where the kid was. We tried to call the police but he took the phone out of my hand, by force. And then when Tony wanted to leave Nolan blocked the door. It was a physically threatening situation. Tony said, don't you have a gun, and Nolan said something like, that's right, Marny, get your gun. I keep it in my bedroom, next to my bed, and went upstairs to get it."

"And then what happened?"

"Nothing. I mean I went upstairs and sat on my bed and didn't do anything. I think Tony called out, I couldn't hear what, and when I came back down they were fighting. You know, punching each other and wrestling on the floor, with Nolan on top. But Nolan was already pretty beat up and Tony caught him in the face, where he had this bandage, and kind of pulled it away. After that he managed to get out from under. Nolan was still on the ground, on his knees, and when he tried to stand up Tony kicked him. That's when he hit his head on the floor."

"Is that what knocked him out?"

"Objection, Your Honor. Counsel is leading the witness." It was one of Nolan's lawyers, the black one, who stood up politely to make his point and sat back down.

The judge said, "Sustained. Let him say it for himself, Mr. Oh."

So he tried again. "What happened after Nolan's head hit the floor?"

I looked at Nolan, who was sitting between his lawyers and leaning back in his chair. His arms were folded, which made the shoulders of his suit ruck up against his neck.

"He was out cold," I said. "I don't know what knocked him out. Tony kicked him, too. But I think it was probably the floor."

"And after he passed out, what did you do?"

"Tony called the police, and I told him to send an ambulance, too. I thought, maybe Nolan left the kid with his mother. So I told Tony to look there, but he didn't know the way."

"Did you show him the way?"

"I tried to describe it for him, but nobody was in any kind of shape to follow directions. So I went with him."

"How long did you stay at Mrs. Smith's house?"

"I don't know. Five minutes? It could have been two minutes, it could have been ten. I really wasn't in a normal frame of mind."

"If Mrs. Smith testified that you stayed at least fifteen minutes, would you have any reason to doubt the accuracy of her testimony?"

"If that's what she says, I'm sure she's right. Because at that point for her it was just, you know, an ordinary visit."

"Can you tell me why you left Nolan unconscious in your apartment for more than a quarter of an hour, while you sat around with his mother drinking lemonade?"

"She's very welcoming. If she gives you something to drink, you take it. I didn't want to appear rude. I know this doesn't make much sense, but I didn't want her to know what Nolan had done. It would have upset her. Also, we couldn't get Michael away. Everything takes longer with kids."

A few minutes later Judge Westinghouse called it a day. What surprised me is this: already I was reluctant to get off my chair. For someone who likes to talk, who cares about the difference between one way of saying something and another, who thinks of speech as the best kind of action . . . it was like, for sailors, being in a high wind. People were paying attention, my answers mattered. Whereas that evening, I made myself dinner alone and had nothing to do but go over these answers in my head.

37

Every morning the steps of the courthouse were packed with reporters and television crews. There were protesters, too, waving placards: *Free Nolan Smith*, with a picture of Nolan, based on one of his mug shots. Some guy held up a handmade sign that said *It Isn't a Crime* on one side and *To Live in Detroit* on the other. And the next day I had to push my way through these people. All of which reinforced what I felt the day before, that I was an important person, out of all proportion. This time I didn't have to wait in the waiting room. When the judge called me up to the witness stand, I felt very conscious of the way I walked—about fifteen paces from my seat, around a table and up a few steps. It was like going on stage.

The heating was on, and since it had rained all morning the smell of wet clothes was strong. But you couldn't hear the rain outside; there were no windows.

Judge Westinghouse took us through the motions. And then Nolan's lawyer, the black guy, stood up to cross-examine me. He looked fifty, maybe a little older—he had short, well-cut, grizzled hair and rimless glasses, he wore a bow tie, I don't think he could have been taller than five foot seven. His name was John Barrett; he introduced himself.

"Mr. Marnier," he said, "I'm going to start by asking you a few general questions. I want you to bear with me for a moment." He looked at his notes and put them on the table and walked over to me. "How long have you known Robert James?"

"I don't know, fifteen years, a little more."

"Can you tell me where you first met?"

"At university," I said.

"And which university is that?"

Larry Oh stood up. "I don't see how this is relevant," he said. "Mr. Marnier is not on trial here. Robert James is not on trial."

So Barrett wandered over to Judge Westinghouse. He didn't do anything in a hurry. "Judge," he said. "I'm going to show that what happened that day happened as a result of a misunderstanding. You had at least two, maybe three, angry people who weren't listening to each other. Now, there's a context to that misunderstanding, there's a history to it, and I plan to show what that history is."

"All right," she said. "I'll let this go for now. But it better go somewhere."

"Yale," I said.

"When did you move to Detroit?"

"About two years ago."

"Had you ever been to Detroit before?"

"No."

"Do you have any connection to the city, any kind of family history here?"

"No."

"Can you explain to me why you moved here? Was it for the job opportunities?"

"No, sir."

"You don't have to call me sir," he said. "Mr. Barrett is fine. So why did you come?"

And it went on from there. I found him hard to read. For one thing, his accent shifted sometimes, he changed his voice, too, usually to make a joke. When he asked me again why I moved to Detroit, I told him, "Cheap real estate." He said, "Come to Gary. We got a lot of empty houses," and a few people laughed. It doesn't take much in a courtroom, people are nervous and bored, it's tension laughter, but still, there was something in the way he said it, like, you and me, buddy, we come from different sides of the tracks. Later I looked up Barrett online (there was a profile of him on legalnews.com), and it's true, he grew up in Miller Beach, Indiana, and was raised by a single mother. But she was superintendent of the Gary Community School Corporation, and he majored in economics at Notre Dame before going on to Michigan Law. I mean, his background wasn't that different from mine.

Eventually he said, "Can you describe for this court your first encounter with Nolan Smith?"

So I did my best. I told him some guys were working on my house, and there was a problem with the grid connection, so we had to shut down the street. Anyway, I knocked on people's doors, I wanted to give them a heads-up. That's how I met Nolan.

"Did he threaten you on that occasion?"

"Isn't that a leading question?"

So he smiled at me and said, "I'm cross-examining you, Mr. Marnier. I'm allowed to lead. But I'll put it this way if you prefer. What was the nature of his response to this information?"

"He wasn't too happy about it."

"How did he express this unhappiness?"

"I was with a friend of mine, the guy who was supervising the work. Nolan said that if we went ahead he'd break this guy's windows with a baseball bat."

"Did you feel threatened?"

"I don't know. Nolan talks a big game."

"Did you go on with the work?"

I thought about this for a minute and said, "Not immediately."

I couldn't understand what Barrett was driving at. A lot of what he asked put Nolan in a bad light. But he was also interested in the time Michael told Clarence that he didn't like "chocolate people"—and Clarence poured milk in his face. It's amazing the information these people get access to. Maybe Gloria told him. Every little thing becomes a fact.

"What was Tony's reaction to this incident?"

"Well, he came in right in the middle, when the kids were fighting on the couch. And Clarence is bigger than Michael. Tony wasn't best pleased."

"Did he say anything to you about it?"

"Of course he did. We had to break them up."

"Well, what did he say?"

"I don't know. We talked about it."

"Was he angry with you?"

"Yes."

"Why was he angry?"

"He thinks I should have stepped in."

"Did he say anything else? Did he make any kind of request?"

"Yes. He did. Tony said he didn't want his son hanging out with Nolan's son anymore." I looked at Nolan, who was looking at me, so I looked away. "I don't know why you're asking me about all this."

"You let me worry about that. Did you tell Nolan what happened?"

"No."

"Why not?"

"I don't know. I wouldn't have told Tony, except Tony walked in."

"Is that the whole reason?"

"I don't know." After a minute, I said, "I didn't want to get Clarence in trouble."

"Do you think Clarence would have got into trouble?"

"I didn't want to make Nolan any more pissed off than he already was."

But we talked about Robert James, too.

"Did he ask you to say something to Nolan about the Meacher case? Did he ask you to intervene?"

"What do you mean, intervene?"

"Were you aware that Nolan was talking to Dwayne Meacher's family, that he was talking to lawyers and trying to drum up publicity?"

"I guess so."

"Did Robert James ask you to intervene?"

"I still don't know what you mean by intervene."

"Did he want you to stop Nolan from doing the things he was doing?"

"You can't stop Nolan from doing something if he wants to do it. I told Robert that. But Robert just wanted me to pass on some information."

"What information was that?"

"About the medical attention Meacher was getting."

"Did you pass it on?"

"I don't remember."

"Did you or didn't you?"

"I went to see Nolan about it, but I don't know if I said what Robert asked me to say. I guess when I saw him it didn't seem— appropriate."

"What about this case?"

"What about it?"

"Did Robert James ask you to communicate something to Nolan about this case?"

"No."

"Did he ever express any opinion to you about it?"

"Of course, he's a friend of mine. This case is a big deal in my life."

"I'm glad to hear it. So what did he say?"

"He said that it's the job of Nolan's lawyers to make sure it doesn't go to trial."

There was a little laughter at that, and Barrett smiled when he said, "And why was that?"

"Because he didn't think Nolan would win."

"Did he have any other reasons, do you think?"

But here Larry Oh stepped in and I didn't have to answer. Barrett kept pushing, though. He asked me about Beatrice, too. He wanted to know if she ever told me to talk to Nolan.

"I don't know," I said.

"What do you mean, you don't know?"

"We had a conversation about Nolan, and maybe she wanted me to say something to him, but it wasn't clear."

"But she had, let's call it, misgivings about the trial, which she expressed to you?"

"Yes."

"Can you describe for me what those misgivings were?"

Larry Oh stood up again, but the judge overruled him. It gave me a minute to think of an answer, and eventually I said, "This isn't the kind of publicity they want for what we're doing here."

There was a lot more on these lines; it's all in the transcript. When I was talking to Gloria about my testimony, I had this idea that all I had to do was tell the truth. She thought I needed to do more than that. I needed to edit and shape what I said, for Nolan's sake. The fact is, I found it hard enough just answering the questions. Answering them honestly, I mean. Partly because there were things I wanted to be dishonest about, but also because the answers seemed so limited, they left so much out. I was too caught up in the whole thing to exercise any control over how I came across. I wasn't telling the story, Barrett was. I didn't get to say what I wanted to say.

"Tell me about the guns," Barrett said. "How many you got?"

"Two. A Remington and a Smith & Wesson."

"Can you tell me why you bought these weapons?"

Larry Oh tried to step in again. "Objection, Your Honor, to this whole line of questioning. The witness is not on trial here . . ."

But Judge Westinghouse overruled him and I said, "That's all right. I want to answer this. I want to address this. When I came to Detroit, I didn't know anything about it. Just the stuff you see on TV, I read the news. People said to me, do you have a gun. I thought I needed one."

"But after coming here, you got better information, is that right?"

"Something like that."

"After you came to Detroit you realized you had nothing to worry about. Did you register the guns?"

"Yes."

"The Smith & Wesson. That's a police gun, right?"

"Yes."

"Why did you get one of those?"

"A friend of mine is an officer, and you can pick up used guns pretty . . . cheaply, if you're in the loop."

"And you registered that one, too?"

"Yes, he helped me."

"How did you meet this guy? What's his name?"

"Mel Hauser. He's a friend of Tony Carnesecca. He lives on Tony's street."

"And when did you meet Mel Hauser? I mean, after you came to Detroit?"

"Towards the beginning."

"What does that mean? How long after you came to Detroit did you register the second gun?"

"Maybe six months."

"Six months? Mr. Marnier, these are legal documents. Do you want me to look them up?"

"Maybe eight months."

"All right, all right."

It wasn't just that I felt manipulated, though I did. After a while, you start to lose track of what you actually think—I mean, they begin to persuade you. Barrett said, "There's a few things I need to get straight in my own head, there are a couple of things I'd like you to clear up for me. When everybody was standing around in your apartment, shouting at each other. You and Tony Carnesecca and Nolan Smith."

"I wasn't shouting at anybody."

"That's fine. Tony and Nolan. And you said, Nolan was barring the door."

"I don't think that's what I said."

So Barrett asked the court stenographer to repeat what I said, and eventually she found her place in the transcript and read it out. "And then when Tony wanted to leave Nolan blocked the door."

"How do you know Tony wanted to leave?" Barrett said.

"I don't know; you know."

"Did he try to leave?"

"He couldn't. Nolan was blocking the door."

"I guess what I'm asking you is, how did you know Nolan was blocking the door?"

"I don't understand."

"I'm trying to get a sense of what the difference is, in your mind, between standing in the doorway and blocking the door."

"I don't know what the difference is. You're asking me these questions like I can watch it on instant replay. I haven't seen it again, I don't know what happened. I know what it felt like at the time, I know what it seemed like. Nolan's a big guy, he was angry, you just have to be in the room with him to realize . . . and Tony was pretty pissed off, too. I'm not sure you can blame him. I don't really know what you're getting at."

"I'm not getting at anything, and I'm not blaming anybody. I leave that to the prosecution. I'm just trying to understand what happened here. That's hard enough. But this is what it looks like to me: you've got two guys with a history of antagonizing each other brought together by someone with a history of miscommunicating between them."

Afterwards, after he was finished with me, Larry Oh pushed himself up, with both hands on the table, and walked over. He looked at me for a minute and said, "Nolan is a friend of yours."

"Yes."

"Can you tell me what you feel about what happened?"

"Not really. There's a whole side of my life that's being closed off. I used to go out with a good friend of Nolan's. We all had dinner together, that kind of thing. I like his mother a lot. Will she want to talk to me now? I don't know."

"Can you tell me what you did after leaving Mrs. Smith's house?"

"Well, Tony took his kid away, they drove off, and I went back home to wait for the ambulance."

"What did you do while you waited?"

"Nothing. I just sat there. I checked his breathing, I checked his pulse. It took me a while to find his pulse, but it seemed okay, and I just sat there with him. It's like he was sleeping, I just sat there with my hand on his head."

This is true, it's what I did, but saying it felt like lying. Larry said, "No more questions," and the judge dismissed me. So I got up out of my chair. People were looking at me, but I looked straight ahead. I had to walk past Nolan and Gloria and Robert and Beatrice and everybody else. Walter was there, too, I suddenly saw his face. Then I was out of the room, in the hallway; the light was dimmer, it was cooler, too. Sharia met me with a cup of coffee—we could talk out loud. "Put some sugar in it," she said, handing me a couple of packets. "You can probably use a little sugar." I wanted to sit in one of the public rows and watch, but she told me I couldn't—

in case I got called back in. "We don't want you getting confused by what other people say."

"I can't wait in that waiting room anymore," I said, but it turned out I didn't have to, I could go home.

For a couple of minutes I sat in the hallway and drank the coffee. There was a bench pushed up against one of the walls, under a row of portrait photographs, judges and officers of the court. People walked past. There were other cases and trials, and a janitor took a mop to the marble floors.

Then Robert came looking for me. He was wearing what he usually wears, clean jeans, collared shirt, a North Face jersey—the rich man's modest uniform. The only thing he spent money on was his wristwatch, a Patek Philippe. Sometimes you see ads for these watches in glossy magazines, a handsome middle-aged father and his son waiting at a train station in black and white. The caption says: "Make your own tradition." Robert had a little boy now. His curly hair receded slightly, but it didn't matter, his face hadn't changed. Even in college, his skin looked weathered—from sailing, you couldn't help thinking. The truth is, I always found his presence comforting, like one of those magazines. The world of the rich, everything's going to be okay.

"What are you going to do now?" he said.

"Go home."

"You need a ride? I need some fresh air anyway. God, people stink after a while. I probably smell, too." In the car, he said, "They gave you a pretty hard time in there. I'm sorry about that. I thought they might."

"Yeah, well."

"Don't worry about it, Marny. You did okay, you did good."

"I don't know what I did," I said.

For the next two days, I mooched around at home, reading the news. There was a lot of media coverage. Nolan had become like a minor-league celebrity in Detroit. He was an artist and activist and publicly associated with protests against the new neighborhoods. I saw more pictures of Nolan, photographs taken in the hospital, showing open wounds, a real beat-up guy, a guy who had been kicked in the head and was now standing trial. While prosecutors refused to charge the man who kicked him.

There was speculation about what had actually happened. One theory went that Nolan drove over to Robert's house, with a gun in his pants, to confront him or threaten him or shoot him, because of the Meacher case. But I also found a few things out about Nolan's defense. Barrett was claiming that Nolan ran into Michael in the street and thought it was Robert's kid. So he picked him up, he told him to get in the car, the kid looked lost. But Nolan was worried about showing up at the house with the boy, just like that, given the nature of his relationship to Robert James. So he took him to his mother's house and waited for me to act as a kind of intermediary. What happened afterwards was the result of a misunderstanding— two angry guys refusing to listen to each other. But there was no kidnapping. That at least was the claim.

A few days later the phone rang, some time after lunch—there were still dirty dishes in the sink. I hadn't cleaned up yet. It was Tony. Cris and he were throwing a little party, to celebrate, just the fact that it was all over; he wanted to pick me up on the way.

"So what happened?" I said.

"Guilty," Tony said.

38

Cris gave me a glass of champagne when I walked in the door. She was crying, not particularly unhappily. Her breasts were full of Jimmy's milk, she wore a soft cotton dress, which you could pull down for easy access, even her tears looked like maternal overflow.

"I don't much feel like celebrating," I said.

"He took my son, he attacked my husband. And he's going to sue us now, you know that, don't you? Don't expect sympathy from me. I'm having a moment, all right? Just for today we can say, it's over, until the civil stuff starts up again."

It was wet outside, the garden had melted into mud. The house was overwarm and overcrowded. The kids kept getting between our legs. Jimmy could walk now, he was a late walker, and wanted to chase Michael around, which Michael kind of liked. But it also meant, whenever he stopped running there was Jimmy all over him, with chocolate icing on his hands and face. It was five o'clock and cake had taken the place of supper.

At one point Robert picked up Jimmy and said, "Hey, fella, what are you, the chocolate monster?"

Peggy was back in New York. "You must miss Ethan," I said.

"You see other kids, and it doesn't matter if they want you to or not, you pick them up."

In fact, Jimmy started crying and Cris took him off Robert's hands.

"Listen," Robert said, "at some point, it doesn't have to be now, I want to talk to you."

"Well, here we are."

"Not now."

"What's this about?"

"Let's have a couple of drinks and celebrate. This is a conversation that can wait."

Walter and Dan Korobkin were in the kitchen. Beatrice was there, too, so was David, the posh English guy, her new boyfriend and agent. So were Bill Russo and Clay Greene. I could hear my name through the open door.

"People are talking about me again," I said and went over to the sink to fill my glass from the tap. "Are you guys out in the open now? Do people know?"

"What does he mean?" David said. He was tall and soft-looking; the skin on his face seemed very lightly stippled. He had big hands.

"That you guys are an item."

"Oh, everybody knows," Walter said. "We're making fun of her book."

"What's wrong with her book?"

"Everybody's in it, everybody we know."

"That's just not true." Beatrice was acting the pretty girl, maybe because of David. She had her hand on his arm. It turns out that she's one of these girls who touches her boyfriend a lot. But then, she always used to put her hands on everybody, she flirted with everybody.

"Has she finished it?"

"I sold it," David said.

"That's terrific. That's terrific news. How come everyone knows except me? Did this just happen?"

"A couple of days ago. There was a lot of action at the London Book Fair."

"That's wonderful news." Cris came round with another bottle of champagne, and I took it off her hands and filled everyone up. "I want to toast something that isn't a guy getting locked up," I said. "So let's toast you."

"Marny," Beatrice said.

"So let me in on the joke. Who's in it?"

"Calm down, it's okay. Anyway, that's not how it works," Beatrice said. "It's not one person or another, you make things up. You put different people together."

"You're in it," Walter said.

"Have you read it?" I asked him.

"The parts I could recognize."

"How come everyone's read this book except me?"

"We figured you had other things on your mind."

Tony came in, but the doorbell rang. He put his hand around my neck and gripped it on his way out. I couldn't tell yet what I felt about him.

"So how do you know it's me?" I said. "What do I look like?"

"Harry Potter," Bill Russo said.

"But that's my line, Beatrice. I told you that story, you can't use that."

"That's not what you should get worked up about," Walter said.

Then the sun came out, through a wet sky, and Tony tried to persuade people out onto his new deck.

"We just had it put in," he said. "It's a three-thousand-dollar deck."

Cris didn't like him smoking in the house and he wanted to hand out cigars. Some of the men went out, Beatrice, too, but I stayed inside to talk to Cris. But then Jimmy needed changing and Michael followed her out. For a minute I had the kitchen to myself. I ran the tap and wet my hands and ran them through my hair. Then Beatrice came back in.

"It's too cold out there. This is Detroit spring, which is like LA winter. People are crazy."

"Was it me," I said.

"Was what you?"

"What happened. Do I have a history of miscommunicating?"

"You were the only one talking to both sides."

"I didn't reconcile these different parts of my life. Do you think it's possible, if I said something different to Nolan, or something different to Tony, that Nolan takes me to his house, and we pick up the kid and drive home, and none of this happens?"

"I thought you told me it could have been much worse."

"That's what I thought. But I don't know anymore. Maybe that kind of thinking was part of the problem." She let that go and I said, "Gloria's not answering my calls."

"Marny, I want to have this conversation with you. But I came in because I needed the bathroom. Give her time."

I went outside and Tony said, "Where's your drink?"

"I don't much feel like celebrating."

"We're not celebrating," he said. "We're getting drunk, we're letting our hair down, there's a difference."

"Well, I feel pretty drunk already."

Walter was sitting by himself on one of the benches, smoking a cigar. "My dad gave me one of these to take back to Yale, the summer before senior year," he said. "I sat in my window and blew smoke out into the courtyard, and somebody called the fire brigade."

"Well, here we are, twenty years down the line. It's a reunion."
He didn't say anything and I said, "How are you doing?"

"Susie and I got married last week."

"That's wonderful, Walter. Does everyone know about that, too?"

"Just you. It's not a big deal, it's something we did for the sake of the adoption."

"Are you guys going through with that?"

"We've got a kid lined up, Shawntell. Guess how she spells it."

"No."

"Like the boy's name plus tell."

"Can you change it if you want? I don't know the rules."

"We can but we won't. We're picking her up tomorrow, as soon as they let her out of the hospital. She's got a little jaundice, nothing serious."

"How old is she?"

"Twelve hours. The whole time you were in court, Susie was texting me. These days they let you take her home even before the legal side goes through."

"Have you met the mother?"

"The mother picked us. She had a one-night stand with a guy on leave from Afghanistan. She was seventeen then, she's eighteen now. The guy got killed six months ago. His name was Shawn, he was a friend of her brother. She didn't have any particular feelings for him, and none of the grandparents is financially or emotionally prepared to deal with this. But she's a smart girl, she wants to go to college. I'm helping her out with that, too."

After a minute, I said, "Are you ready for her?"

"That's all we've been doing, for eighteen months, looking after kids."

"I know what you mean. You get sick of grown-ups after a while."

"Well, you've had a tough few months."

"It's not just that. I'm through. Everything people do, everything they say, is just some clumsy form of self-defense."

"Children in my experience are monsters of selfishness."

"But I've seen people with their kids, there's no separation. They're all on the inside of something."

"That's only true for the first few years. But listen, Marny, I don't know if I should tell you or not. But Beatrice's book. There's a guy who shoots a black guy who breaks into his house."

"You're kidding me. And I'm the guy?"

He nodded.

"Did you say something to her about it?"

"She said it doesn't mean anything. She said it's just the kind of stupid thing you think of."

After a while I went inside to get another drink. The kids were still up, in front of the TV in the TV room, and I wandered in with a bottle in one hand and a glass in the other, and sat down on the floor at the foot of the couch. Cris sat behind me, with a kid on each side. They were watching *Sesame Street*.

"Do you want a drink?" I said.

"My glass is just over there."

So I scooched across and reached it and came back.

"This is a good show," I said. "You look comfortable."

"Sometimes I just want to take these two in the car and drive somewhere, some cabin in the woods, and live like that, like we don't need anybody else."

"Is Tony allowed to come?"

"That depends on my mood. You think I'm one of those mothers."

"I don't think it's just that. You've been retreating in this direction for years."

"Maybe that's right."

When the show was over, I lay on my back and said, "Who wants to fly?"

"Don't whiz them up, Marny, it's getting-ready-for-bed time. You can help them clear up while I run the bath."

So that's what I did. We ended up on the carpet playing some stupid game with a toy telephone, all three of us. It wasn't a toy exactly, but one of those old 1940s phones, an Olivetti rotary, which I bought with Walter at the 7 Day Swap out by Chalmers and Mack. This was in the days when I still cared about my apartment as a personality showcase. But it didn't work and I gave it to Michael. If you hung up hard enough you could make it ping, which is what Jimmy kept doing. Since it got a reaction, he started hitting other things, and when I tried to take the phone away he hit me in the face. The earpiece caught my cheekbone under the eye. It was like somebody unplugged the nerves. I couldn't feel anything, even my lip, or half of it, went numb.

"Jesus," I said, standing up, and spilled the bottle of wine.

I went in the kitchen to get a kitchen towel.

"What happened to you?" Beatrice said.

"Is it bleeding?"

"Is what bleeding? You look like a sheet of paper."

"I'm fine, I just need a drink."

But maybe a half hour later I was talking to Robert in the living room, and my hands started feeling sticky. I touched my forehead but couldn't tell if it was burning or freezing.

"Thanks," Robert said.

"For what?"

He thought for a minute. When he couldn't think of the right word or phrase he usually waited until it came to him. "For holding the line."

"I didn't know there was a line."

"Okay."

We stood there awkwardly; my head felt floaty, not quite right. "I've been meaning to ask you," I said. "What's in this for you?"

"What do you mean?"

"The whole thing. All of this. Two years of your life."

"You know, in my circle right now, when we get together, a lot of us talk about real estate. The people I hang out with buy real estate. They complain about the prices, they brag about their deals, they act like it's the only topic of conversation. And I sometimes think what they don't realize is that it really is the only topic of conversation. I still rent our apartment in New York. None of this means to me what it means to other people. But I travel a lot, I see what it means. I was in Rio two weeks ago, and the people who invited me took me on one of these favela tours. You know, meet the natives. And I asked some guy, do you rent or own? And he kind of looked at me, and he said, when I needed a house, I built a house. When my father built his house, there was still land to build on, but now there isn't any land, so I built on top of his. But you should see these houses. Two rooms. There are no gardens. The only private space for someone with a family is on the roof. So people take showers on the roof, they snack, they sit around. You can see it all from the funicular. It goes right overhead."

"I don't understand why you're telling me this."

"In some of these places I travel, there isn't a woman over the age of twenty that you or I would consider sexually attractive. I'm serious about this, Marny. People talk a lot about Brazilian women, but in poor countries the only women we would consider attractive are young women. It costs money to stay attractive. I'm not even talking about cosmetic surgery. But diet, gym, free time, clothes, all of it costs money. In New York I see a lot of very attractive forty-five-year-old women. But not one in the favelas. And it occurred to me that what's really going on here is an inside-outside thing. A woman needs privacy to look good. She has to say to herself, I'm going out to face the world, and that means having somewhere to prepare herself. It's a question of real estate."

"The reason New York women look good is because they go to the gym, and the reason they go to the gym is they live in shit holes."

"That's not why. You don't know these women—they live alone. This is a very recent thing. We have this whole idea of presenting ourselves that comes from having a room of our own. In poor countries, everybody eats together, everybody sleeps together, everybody lives in the street. But we build houses to go inside, which is fine, but then we have to deal with going out again."

"Where do you get this shit, Robert? Nathan Zwecker? You think it's only rich people who get neuroses? Everything you read about poverty tells you that it's basically symbiotic with mental illness. They go hand in hand."

"That's what I mean. If you solve the real estate problem, you solve everything else."

"You're not making sense, but that's not what I asked you anyway."

I felt a fever coming on and wanted this conversation to stop. My head seemed to be the only thing staying still. There were bright spotlights in Tony's living room, which made the ceiling swell and shift in its plane. The ground wasn't too steady either. Robert thought I was waiting for him to say something.

"When I was at Yale," he said, "all I wanted to do is make money. And then when I was twenty-eight years old, I made a lot of money. I never wanted to spend it, though, that's not how I was brought up. I wanted to win. *That's* how I was brought up. But then you're twenty-eight years old, and you think, what do I do now? It took me a long time to recover."

"So what happens next?"

"That's partly what I want to talk to you about. I think it's a good idea you take a break for while. Maybe go back home."

"What do you mean?"

"I mean back to Baton Rouge."

"Are you kicking me out? Did people vote on this?"

"Marny, I just think it's a good idea. I'm worried. I don't know what happens next. I don't want you caught up in it."

"Something's not right. I don't feel right. I can't feel anything."

"Maybe you should sit down. It's been a long week."

"No, I can't feel anything," I said. "I can't feel my face."

Cris came down from putting the kids to bed and took my temperature. It was raised, but not especially high—maybe 101. But she made Tony take me to the hospital.

"I don't want to go," I said. "People will recognize me there."

"What are you talking about?"

"I'm in the news."

"Just hold an ice pack to your face. No one will look at you."

And eventually I let them put me in the car. My health insurance was only valid for the DMC, so Tony had to drive me into Detroit—against the rush hour mostly, but it still took an hour. He was drunk; he didn't want to get pulled over. There was a three-car pileup on I-94, and we didn't make it to the exit in time. Vehicles with sirens kept pushing past us on the hard shoulder. But we got off at last and he dropped me outside the emergency unit and went to park. There was a big green space opposite, with people drinking outside, under the trees. The weather was changing. The cold air had a spring smell instead of a winter smell. You could see stars and clouds, the street lamps were lit.

I wandered through the automatic doors. There was a reception desk, but it wasn't the right one, and eventually I found the right one. The woman behind the desk had a tear tattooed on her cheek and chunky rings on her fingers. She could type very quickly, clicking the whole time, and told me to take a seat. About fifteen minutes later Tony found me, and then we sat there waiting maybe another hour. It was a busy night.

The chairs were these plastic chairs, but you couldn't move them, and they were spaced to make it difficult to lie down. So people kept fidgeting—all kinds of people. Big floor-to-ceiling windows at one end looked onto a hospital corridor with kids' pictures on the wall—you could tell they were kids' pictures from the bright colors. At one point I stood up to take a closer look. Art from the leukemia unit. The waiting room itself was a kind of public/private space. People talked on their cell phones. They bought snacks from the snack machine and spread out the food like a picnic. There was a kiddie corner with plastic toys, including several of those sit-down cars you have to push along, but the kids kept pushing them outside the gated area, which was a problem, because many people waiting had canes or crutches or some kind of motion aid, including wheelchairs.

People went out to smoke and came back in. Some of the time you could tell what they were waiting for, but not always. I saw a lot of preexisting conditions: guys with splints or stitches or substantial bandaging. Pregnant women. Crying kids, black eyes, bloody noses. Burn victims. I had the usual thoughts you get in a hospital, like, would you have sex with this species? The answer is generally no. From time to time the receptionist read out a name, or a couple of names, and people shuffled up to the desk. Then a nurse came to take them away.

I felt hot and shivery, and sometimes the ice pack helped and sometimes it didn't. The room itself was probably too hot. There was a young man with his shirt off, a good-looking white guy, well built, maybe college age or a little older, pacing back and forth and talking. He was either high on something or coming down from it. "You need to hook us up," he said, loudly but not at the top of his voice. He wasn't shouting. "You have to medicate the people." But he kept repeating himself.

In one corner of the room, opposite reception, there was a TV fixed to the ceiling, not much bigger than the kind of TV you get in a motel. I couldn't hear it but I could see it. They were showing the local news. A reporter stood in front of a camera van in front of a burning house. The house looked more or less like the houses on Johanna Street, and I picked my way through people's legs and bags and kids to get a closer look. At the bottom of the screen a news ticker ran through the day's stories, but there were also captions for the hearing impaired. You could see the reporter moving his mouth, and you could see the words appear on the screen below, not always perfectly spelled but clear enough. This is how I found out about the riots.

39

They lasted three days. Most of the damage was confined to New Jamestown, but there were shops on the periphery, on East Jefferson, on Gratiot, where a few big chains had moved in, that also took a hit. They started a little after six o'clock, when WDIV reported the verdict in Nolan's case. But the truth is, preparations must have been made beforehand; there was an organized element.

Houses and cars were burned, and in some cases the fire spread across entire blocks. That first night was clear, cool and windy, the second day was overcast and slightly warmer, and it finally rained around four in the morning and continued raining for the rest of the third day. But on that first night the fires just jumped around.

Mrs. Smith's house was one of the ones that burned. I don't think she was hurt, though I haven't seen her since the trial; I'm not sure. The fire took out the inside and the second floor fell in, though the walls and the roof survived. From the outside it almost looks livable, except the window frames are charred holes. There's no glass. But the roof on my house went up in smoke. My bed was soaked with rain, and my clothes and books and shoes lay over the open stairs—that's how I found them later. For some reason the living room in Walter's apartment came out okay, but the flames reached such a high temperature in his kitchen that some of the plastic toys in the garden melted on one side.

There were more than a hundred arrests. Seven people died, one of them shot by the police, which came in for a lot of criticism afterwards. Some of my neighbors said it was basically a looting situation, nobody wanted to hurt anyone. It was kids, teenagers, young men; girls and women, too. They just wanted to burn stuff and steal stuff. But it depends who you talked to, I also heard arguments on the other side.

Steve Zipp got hit by a stolen car. The driver was a kid named Kwame Richardson, who tried to help him. He drove him to the emergency room at Henry Ford, and police outside the hospital arrested the boy. Later the charges were dropped. Steve turned out to be okay—two broken ribs and a deep tissue bruise, just above the knee, that made him limp for a month.

While this went on I waited in another hospital to see a doctor. Tony had a hangover already. We talked about his book. He was halfway through the fatherhood memoir, but this Beatrice deal had thrown him. Maybe he was on the wrong track. For years he'd been trying to write a novel about Detroit.

When the doctor, one of these good-looking, rich-looking old white guys, a very competent person, saw me, he said, "You picked a bad night to have an accident."

"My one-year-old hit him with a telephone," Tony said.

Then the doctor sent me off for an X-ray, which meant another half-hour wait. Tony stayed with me the whole time and even stuck around for the X-ray itself. A technician guy sat me down in a kind of dentist's chair, covered my chest with a heavy gray vest and turned on the invisible forces, which made a quick buzzing sound.

After that we waited some more for the results—Tony kept stocking up on chocolate and potato chips from one of the vending machines. It was ten o'clock by this point, but I didn't eat anything. I still had a fever, I kept drinking cans of Sprite.

Then the doctor came back.

"You've got a fracture, there," he said, pointing at a spot on the transparency. The bones and shape of my face were clearly visible; there was a white glowing scar under one of my eyes. And beneath the skull, with that grin you can't help, my brains, my thoughts, like jam in a jar.

"So what do we do?"

"You've got two options. You can do something, or you can do nothing."

"What happens if I do nothing?"

"I don't know yet. The fracture hit the nerve—he got you right on the money. But what we can't tell from this is if it's still exerting pressure. I also can't tell how badly the nerve is damaged. Sometimes you just get a pinch. We could operate and try to relieve the pressure, but it's a very delicate little bone, we might make things worse. There'll be a scar, we do what we can to minimize it, we come up from under the line of your jaw like this. But even if everything goes beautifully it might do no good. How bad is the loss of feeling?"

"About the size of my hand. Half my lip. Even drinking this soda feels like pouring something into a container."

"Well, it's your choice. If you want, I can book you in."

"If everything's fine when will the feeling come back?"

"That's hard to say, too."

But I let it go—I let Tony take me home, back to his place. Another two hours in the car. I-94 was closed, Gratiot was closed, we had to go north on 75. There was a slow river of cars. I fell asleep on the way. Tony did all the driving, perfectly sober by now. When I opened my eyes I saw his forearm on the wheel. I felt like a kid, my temperature must have been close to 103. The Tylenol they gave me at the hospital was wearing off. But I slept anyway. Then around one in the morning he woke me up. We were in his driveway, it was a cool night, I walked inside. Cris had made up the sofa bed.

ABOUT A WEEK AFTER THE riots, Walter and I walked around the neighborhood and looked at the house, to see if there was anything we could salvage. He and Susie were staying at Bill Russo's place on Lake St. Clair. They had a little baby—all of that went through. We drove over in Walter's car and managed to fill up the trunk with clothes and toys and books, but I didn't care about any of this stuff, I was just going along. We saw a few people trawling through the rubble, not all of them familiar faces.

About half the houses on Johanna had burned down, the rest had broken windows, some of them were boarded up. I said to Walter, "Well, this is more or less what it looked like when I got here."

Robert's neighborhood didn't look much better—we walked around there, too. On the night of the riots, he drove home from Tony's and saw what was going on and didn't get out of his car. He drove straight through the night, heading south and east, through Michigan and Ohio and Pennsylvania and New Jersey and the Lincoln Tunnel. He ended up in Manhattan around breakfast time, parked in the street and bought croissants and cups of coffee from one of the delis around there to surprise Peggy with. We talked on the phone the next day, I heard the whole story.

For the first two months I couldn't feel my face, and for the next two months I couldn't tell if I could feel anything, and after that there was a kind of tingling that eventually turned into feeling.

Most of the time I don't think about it now. When I pull at my beard, there's a very slight sensitivity on one side, like a mild sunburn.

Walter and Susie couldn't stay at Bill's place forever. Anyway, they felt isolated out there with the kid. So they moved into Robert's old house, which was more or less intact, and eventually I moved in with them. It's pretty intense, having a baby around. She's present everywhere. You can hear her crying, her toys are on the floor, there are mush stains on the kitchen table. Sometimes I take the night shift, to give them a break. Shawntell sleeps on top of me in bed, and I lie there and try not to move. In the dark like that, my thoughts seem to expand—into the room, into the night. It's strange to think she won't remember any of this.

There are a lot of hands on deck; it's a full house. "You're going to have a happy childhood," Susie says to her. "Everybody loves you." But I don't know how sustainable it is. Steve Zipp lived with us for a while, then went back to Ohio. The Wendelmans are here now. Bert's son, though, has gone to live with his ex-wife in Grand Rapids. It's not really a place for school-age kids. If a room is free, people hear about it, they knock on the door, and we usually let them in.

Franklin's farm survived the riots, though Franklin himself moved to Boston, which is where he studied law. A lot of us pick over his land for things to eat, asparagus, corn, zucchini, beets, tomatoes, not to mention apples, pears, plums and blackberries, and pumpkins later in the year. I used to make a little cash by going through some of the burned-out houses and looking for things other people overlook. The electronic equipment was all gone, whatever could be melted down was gone, door handles, pipe work, etc. But sometimes I found old books in decent condition. Pictures or picture frames, toys can be worth money, flowerpots, even plants.

It's a different place these days. Nobody has anything to show off. Guys help each other out, but there's also a lot of petty theft—there are very thin boundaries.

My brother came and tried to take me away. He gave me two days of his time; I let him buy me dinner. When he couldn't talk me into leaving, he flew home. As soon as he left (I watched his rented car drive off), the old confused feelings returned. I don't know how anyone reconciles childhood and adulthood, it can't be done. He said, "I'm going to leave you alone, but you have to call your mother once in a while." I can't call, our house doesn't have a phone, and anyway, I don't want to hear her voice. But sometimes I go to the public library and send her an email.

The fact is, I keep expecting my mother to turn up. I walk around like a runaway, looking over my shoulder. But either she can't face me or Brad has talked her out of it.

I haven't got a job, though I do some day labor, fruit picking, furniture removal, leafleting, yard work. As little as I can get away with. I still see people, Tony and Cris, for example. Walter and I joke that our fifteen-year reunion is coming up. Maybe we'll go. I sold my car, I don't know how I'd get there unless he drives me. Basically I'm treading water, but what you don't expect from this kind of life is how many shifts of feeling it involves. My point of view is undergoing an alteration, and when your point of view changes you see things you couldn't see before, different aspects of reality become available.

When Beatrice knocked on the door I didn't recognize her. This was sometime in August, a hot gray day, in the nineties, sweaty and overcast. Robert's house has a big front yard; in the summer it gets completely overgrown. The grass was seeding, mallow had run wild and flowered, bamboo was invading the lawn. My synapses had to adjust themselves to make sense of her face. I felt this almost physically. Her cheeks and her eyes, her forehead, realigned themselves until they fit again somewhere in my brain.

"I found you," she said.

She was wearing a summer dress and sandals. I could see the beginning of her thighs, and her bony knees, and her ankles. She had the calves of a woman who jogs and a redhead's pale tough skin. She looked successful and attractive and almost forty.

"I haven't been hiding. Do you want to come in?"

"I want to get you out," she said. "What are you doing to yourself? Is this some kind of penance?"

"Where are you staying?"

"Not with you." This was a joke—she smiled a little too hard to prove it. "At Bill's place, on the lake. He's there, too. You're welcome to join us, he says. I've rented a car."

"For how long?"

"We'll think of something. Is this some kind of penance?" she said again. "Has it worked?"

"I don't know. How are you doing?"

"All right. There's been a lot going on in my life, some of it good. I keep talking to you, Marny, in my head. I'm really very happy to see you. Come for the weekend. You can see Bill. And if you want afterwards you can come back here. I'll drive you myself."

"So I eat his food and sleep in his clean sheets. This isn't what I need, I need my own private life."

"Nobody will ask you anything you don't want to talk about."

"That's not what I mean." We stood like that for a minute, staring at each other. "I feel like I'm starting to get a grip on some important questions, but this may be just another stage of delusion."

"Look," she said, "I'm not going to leave you like this."

"Like what?" I said and saw myself suddenly through her eyes. But I wouldn't go with her; she eventually left in tears.

But that was months ago and it's getting cold again. Everybody talks about the weather but nobody does anything about it. That always struck me as a very funny line. Maybe my brother is right, you need to build fences. You need a wife, you need kids, you need private school. Okay, so you worry about money. Worrying about money is what you pay for. It stops you from worrying about everything else.

I keep thinking about Beatrice. If she can make six figures by writing some novel about me, what should I get for writing this? I could start over. I could move to New York. Robert James is still there. Beatrice told me she was buying an apartment, a studio on the Upper West Side. So she's living alone, I thought. With time on your hands you get all these ideas; you imagine things. But if I stay in Detroit I might run into Gloria, too. This is something else I think about—what to say. If I say the right thing, who knows.

A few of the guys kick a ball around at Butzel Park on Wednesday afternoons. Soccer is one of those recession games, it's cheap, you only need a ball. Even in the cold, so long as it isn't raining, they head out. A couple of hours before dusk, but sometimes they play into the dark, too. Most of us don't have anything else to do. I haven't played soccer since my mom was a soccer mom and used to drive Brad and me every Saturday morning to the Southside YMCA. But maybe once a month I go over to see if there's a game. All kinds of memories come back to me, nothing is lost. Orange wedges and Capri Suns in the ice chest. Grass in your cleats. God knows what the parents are talking about. Their kids. You keep starting over. Somebody kicks the ball away from your feet. And for a few seconds you watch them passing it up the field. While your breath comes back, you just stand there, hands on hips. Fuck this, you think, but then you put your head down anyway, and when it's probably too late to catch them, start running.

ff

Faber & Faber – a home for writers

Faber & Faber is one of the great independent publishing houses in London. We were established in 1929 by Geoffrey Faber and our first editor was T. S. Eliot. We are proud to publish prize-winning fiction and non-fiction, as well as an unrivalled list of modern poets and playwrights. Among our list of writers we have five Booker Prize winners and eleven Nobel Laureates, and we continue to seek out the most exciting and innovative writers at work today.

www.faber.co.uk – a home for readers

The Faber website is the place where you can find all the latest news on our writers and events, and browse and buy in the Faber shop. You can also join the free Faber Members programme for discounts, exclusive access to events and our range of hand-bound Collectors' Editions.